FLAMENCO BABY

Cherry Radford

IndePenPress

With the exception of Paco Peña (with his kind permission), all the characters in this book are fictitious, and any resemblance to actual persons, living or dead, is purely coincidental.

First published in Great Britain by IndePenPress

All paper used in the printing of this book has been made from wood grown in managed, sustainable forests.

ISBN: 978-1-78003-526-0

Printed and bound in the UK

Indepenpress Publishing Limited
25 Eastern Place
Brighton
BN2 1GJ

A catalogue record of this book is available from the British Library

Cover design by Jacqueline Abromeit
Cover photo by Jeremy Woodhouse

Cherry Radford has been a piano teacher at the Royal Ballet Junior School, a keyboard player in a band, and a research optometrist at Moorfields Eye Hospital in London. She lives near Brighton, England.

Flamenco Baby is her second novel; her first, *Men Dancing*, was published in 2011.

For more information, please visit **www.cherryradford.co.uk**

She [Penélope Cruz] is absolutely in my imagination,
and when I'm writing, I'm thinking about her.

- Pedro Almodóvar

1.

consuelo *m* consolation, comfort.

Somehow, it was always his fault.

'I've finished with David.'

He leaned back in his chair; I was looking at the interview photo of him, the one they used for the literary festivals – all benevolent scrutiny and perfect jawline. 'Oh dear. But you know you don't get anything for a dumping. No consolation prizes for send-offs. Heavens, Yol, I know it's a first, but they're in your control – you could bankrupt me.'

Why was he being like this? But then he didn't know what had actually happened. I looked away, fixed on a watery image of a red bus hissing through the slush outside...

He squeezed my arm. 'Okay, let's hear it. D'you want to go across the road? I take it you haven't eaten.'

I shook my head.

'Probably should go to yours anyway. The poor sod might ring.'

He got the lasagne out of the fridge and motioned with his head for me to open the door. We went out into the hall, closed his and stood in front of mine.

'Uh, didn't...'

'Well use my keys, silly.'

I considered putting my hand in his jeans pocket, imagined the warmth in there, but he passed me the dish and pulled them out himself.

There was a wince at the dirty mugs and pistachio shells, the balled-up tissues on the sofa; for someone whose flat was tidied and cleaned for him, he was unfairly disapproving of other people's chaos. 'So what's been—?' The phone blurted. 'Told you.'

David.

'Listen to me, *please*... Yolande?'

'Yes... I'm here.' My throat tightened.

'Don't do this. It was really *nothing*.'

That painful ice through my veins again. 'I can't...' I focussed on the kitchen calendar, willed myself to imagine how much better I was going to feel the next week, the next month. Come spring.

'No, this is no good on the phone – let me come round,' he said.

Yes. I could ask Jeremy to stay here as some kind of referee; let him see David for what he was. But what he'd see was handsome remorse: *I'd* be the monster. And then there was the risk I'd be talked round and waste another precious year.

'Please. We need to talk about it, I need to explain,' he was saying.

'We already have.' Well, *he'd* talked; I'd screamed and sobbed. 'You need to cancel Seville. And there's Saturday...' A *wedding*: just what I needed. 'You go, he's *your* friend.'

'But what about the Trio?'

'Annie can cover for me.'

'But it's rather short notice. And you can't expect her to cope with some of the new pieces in the set without a proper rehearsal, like the...'

Of course – music always came first. Just talking about it was relaxing him – or perhaps he thought it would relax *me*, like discussing football with a chap about to jump off the top of a building. I watched Jeremy clear up, put the oven on, check my face; I was ready to jump.

'Well I need to keep away from you... and right now that's more important than the odd wrong note in the Allegro. I'm going now, David.'

I was pleased with my resolve, even if I'd only managed it because Jeremy was there to catch me. David started pleading; I heard the word *love*, but it was rather late for that.

Jeremy took me over to the sofa. 'I don't get it. There's been a few weeks of you finding him slightly irritating, but...'

Irritations: yes, I needed to remember them. His insistence on *Yolande*. His over-reaction to my inadequate wardrobe. His under-reaction to the inadequate behaviour of the hooray friends I was supposed to impress. The prickly perfection of his white-and-chrome flat. And things I hadn't mentioned, like the way he always jumped up to have a shower straight after lovemaking.

'Can't help feeling a bit sorry for him,' Jeremy was muttering.

He'd always liked David; I'd never had the heart to tell him it wasn't mutual.

'Well if you're considering offering him comfort, I can tell you he's been getting plenty of that elsewhere.'

'What? Oh no.' He put his arm round me. 'Can't believe it... Why didn't you say?'

'Well it just gets so boring, doesn't it? Every bloody time...'

'But what—?'

'A college pupil... brilliant clarinettist, apparently. Says it was just a sudden physical thing, but it went on for *months*.'

'So it's over?'

'That's what he *says*. But he's still teaching her of course. And I couldn't tell, from...'

'From looking at his texts.'

'Don't look at me like that, I had to... I know it's awful... but I was right, wasn't I? Cheating on me, just like all the others—'

'Not *all* the others. Tom was faithful to you.'

'He dropped me after a dinner and who knows what with his ex-wife.'

'And Colin? Oh... no, he was the one who...'

'Exactly. I'm just never... enough.' I yanked a clump of tissues out of the box.

'You're *more* than enough,' Jeremy said, pulling me closer. 'But I think you've tried to rush things again. Sounds like David took up with this girl not long after Venice and... isn't that when you asked about marriage?'

'I didn't! Well, not *exactly*... Anyway, couldn't he have just said no rather than... and what am I supposed to do? I'm thirty-eight, I can't keep hanging around guessing.'

'But he's been married before, had a hell of a time. You seemed so good together, are you sure you can't—?'

'No! How could I ever trust him again? It's over.' Although I still had all the self-torturing to get through: images of us laughing when we improvised duets, making love in that red-walled Venetian hotel and imagining what our children would look like...

'Come here you,' Jeremy said, lifting my legs over his and pulling me onto his lap.

And once again I sank into him, pressed myself against his neat, firm body. Ran my fingers through the soft waves of sandy hair, even though that was probably a bit weird. Not for the first time I thought, *if only Jeremy could be mine* – not completely of course, but there to snuggle with most nights, a calm friendly presence in my flat, my ever-amusing but sensible companion, perhaps keeping his place just for his writing, an escape from my pupils' piercing squeaks, somewhere to be on his own when he needed to be – I could give up on other men altogether. The daydream rumbled on to its inevitable finale: the occupant of the tiny second bedroom – preferably a result of new adventures into heterosexuality, but clinic-assisted if that was how it had to be.

Lasagne had been filling the air and was bleeping for attention. 'Lunch. Up you get.'

I followed him over to the oven and put my arms round him, hanging on like some baby monkey.

'Careful, you'll get burnt.'

I flopped back into my chair.

'Mm – you remembered to put broad beans in,' he said. He put two spoonfuls on my plate, ignoring my stop-sign hand. 'Yes. You're going to need the energy. We're going for a walk this afternoon – you're coming with me to the pet shop, I need to get Pavlova a new collar. Fresh air'll do you good. And you never know, you might get inspiration there.'

'Is that where you got the inspiration for Pavlova? Can't remember.'

'No – she was your idea. You said my consolation prize had to be something to do with ballet, but flicked

9

through the *About the House* magazine and saw a picture of one of the ballerinas holding a white cat.'

'Oh yes, and later Bradley called and objected when you told him about her, saying he was allergic to cats so it would be a problem when he visited. Just assumed he'd still be staying over whenever he performed at Sadler's Wells.'

Jeremy raised his eyebrows. 'Dancers. When will I learn. Your fault – if I hadn't treated us to becoming patrons following Colin's shenanigans I'd never have met him.'

'Or Sergei.'

'God. Colin should be taken to task for setting off such a catalogue of misery. But look, what about consolation from Sadler's for you? You're missing out on Seville so... how about tickets for *all* of the flamenco festival?'

'Well I hate to be ungrateful, but weren't we going to do that anyway? I'm sure last year we promised ourselves—'

'Yes you're quite right, we did. I must get on and book it. Okay. So, let's think...'

'No – you've done far too much for me already. Let's give the consolation prize thing a miss this time. Just some films and chocolate on your sofa, that'll do me fine.'

'Of course. As long as you finish your lunch.' He took another mouthful and closed his eyes in bliss. 'You know, when I first took you on you were a downright bloody awful cook. I just liked the way you left everything exactly as you found it after cleaning, wanted to help you out. But now you're getting to be *almost* good.'

'Just as well, looks like you've got me for keeps.'

'Oh come on, you'll get snapped up again in no time. You should go next Saturday – you've got a phenomenal record of picking up admirers at weddings.'

It was true. Playing in a girl flute trio probably had a better hit rate than speed dating. But I didn't want a hit. Being blonde isn't all it's cracked up to be – constantly being picked up, considered and put down again like some glittery paperweight in a gift shop. I wanted to jump straight to having a man whose happiness with me was more important than games-playing with an ex-wife, a threesome with twins or adventurous sex with a twenty-year old; a man who didn't have to get his pilot licence, buy his own dental practice, move up to being first clarinet in the orchestra, finish alterations to an already stylish docklands flat, tour South America (alone) and do heaven knows what else before he could tell whether or not he wanted to have a family with me.

'What's the *point*? In six months' time, a year, I'll be in the same state. And so on and so on, until either I'm too old for anyone to bother or there are simply no more fish in the pond. That's it – they're all just slippery fish. Fucking *jelly*fish. I don't think London can produce a male with an honest backbone.'

'Hm. I think we're entering the anger phase, so it's definitely time for that fresh air.' He stood up and took the plates to the kitchen. I followed him again, clamping onto him as he tried to stack the dishwasher.

He put his arms round me, stroked the back of my head. I closed my eyes, let them weep; I'd soaked Jeremy's shoulder enough before, he wouldn't mind. I found his spine.

'*You've* got one.'

'One what?'

'A backbone.' You couldn't fault Jeremy's decisiveness. Trouble was, he'd decided many years ago that he'd search as long as it took for a sensitive, intelligent, preferably dark and handsome man.

He twitched: I'd found a susceptible spot, one that had almost certainly been found by one of the sensitive but in other ways deficient men. 'Of course, and if there's one of us there must be more,' he said. 'Let's go then. Look – the sun's come out for you.'

We draped each other in scarves and took the detour through the gardens and along the canal. The sun on the snow made my eyes smart, made me remember walking there with David in the Summer, before the college term and Lucy began, on our way to a pub lunch feeling dazed after...

Jeremy yanked me to his side. 'God... *every* time: watch out for the bikes, Yol! One of these days you'll be flattened.'

As if encouraged by my thoughts, David rang.

'Please don't keep calling.'

'Where are you? I'm outside your flat.'

'On the Regent's canal, by the red and yellow boat.' That we once imagined owning.

'Oh... are you okay? Wait, I'll–'

'Not throwing myself in, if that's what you mean. I'm with Jeremy. Don't wait, I–'

'Of course you are. And what's he giving you this time? A Spanish villa? A dance company? What am I *worth* Yolande? And when's he going to figure out that what you really want is just *him?*'

'Uh, I'm not listening to–'

'No, no – don't go. Sorry. Look, when will you be back? I could have a coffee at the croissant place and wait for you.'

'Tell me now.'

'Sorry?'

'Tell me what you've got to say now. What you wanted to explain.'

'Well I... just don't want to stop seeing you. Lucy was just a... fantasy, I suppose I was just really flattered... but it's over. I was so *stupid*. I'd never do anything like that again, you have to believe me.' There was a pause. 'And really, all this has made me realise how much... I love you.'

I'd waited so long for this but it didn't mean anything now, however many times he said it. He wanted to see me. As before. Living separately, never discussing the future. As before. Presumably until the next time he was flattered.

'Yolande?'

'And that's it.'

'What d'you mean? Look come here now and I'll take you to my place, we'll have—'

'No... Look, I'll call you in a few months' time and we'll go to a film, okay?' I switched off the phone and put it back in my pocket.

Jeremy took my arm. 'He's waiting outside the flat? Better go back—'

'No. He was probably just passing anyway. And Pav needs that new flea collar...'

'Why don't you let me get *you* a Pavlova? Hey – we could get a boy one. I could put off getting her spayed and have kittens.'

'I don't want a kitten, I want a child.' I stopped dead; where had that come from?

'Well... you could think of it as preparation for that. Go on, it would be fun.' He looked at his watch. 'I think it closes at five – we're not going to make it at this rate.'

'That's it exactly – I'm not going to make it at this rate.'

'What? Oh stop it, of course you will. And meanwhile how can you turn down–?'

'I'd love to have a kitten with you. But why don't we just go straight to having a...'

Then *he* stopped dead. Looked down at the frozen puddle in front of us. It had been there all along, of course: the question I was always going to ask. And even though his mouth was open in shock I still felt confident as ever of the answer.

'Come on, don't be daft. You're going to meet a wonderful guy at this gig or another, and one day you'll make me a useless godfather–'

'No I'm not. And I've already met the wonderful guy, I want *your* child.' His hand was going to his face. 'No listen, we could go to a clinic... and I wouldn't expect you to help at all, I know you–'

He took hold of my shoulders. 'Yol... stop. Please. Don't ask me for the one thing I can't give you.'

'What... Why?'

'Because... I haven't given up hope of finding my soul mate.'

'Aren't *we* soul mates?'

'Of course we are... but you know what I mean.'

'I wouldn't stop you... I don't see why–'

'Too... complicated. What about the child? This would be a *person*, growing up and asking questions. And one I'd be letting down from the moment they were born.'

'No you wouldn't, you'd be a fantastic–'

'I'm sure he or she would be wonderful but...' His eyes were glinting with tears. 'Come here.' He held me tightly. Then pressed his lips firmly upon mine, for the first time in ten years. We looked at each other for a moment with shocked watery smiles.

'I'm sorry,' I whispered.

'No, *I'm* sorry.'

We left the canal and took the steps up to the road. Perhaps it had just taken him by surprise. It had taken *me* by surprise.

He looked at his watch again. 'Ten to. We better step on it.' So we started walking faster, soon doing a comical walking race, laughter spreading through us like medicine.

We arrived and quickly picked out a collar and a bag of toy balls.

'Want some fish?' asked Jeremy with a grin.

'Oh go on then, just one of the little bastards.'

'So what d'you fancy watching? One of my new Almodóvars? Ooh – no, I know what.' He produced it with a flourish: *Strictly Ballroom.*

'Oh yes! Haven't seen that in ages. Perfect.'

He went to put it in the machine and then turned round. 'Actually, how about that as your prize – more dancing lessons? Whatever you like – ballet, salsa, tango... How about flamenco, you've never tried that.'

'Wow. Why *haven't* I? There's a school round here, I think.'

'Yes. But how about an intensive week in... Seville. No, it's got to be Granada. And it's compact, you're less likely to keep getting lost.'

'Oh. My. God.'

'The perfect escape from the jellyfish of London – all that self-assertive stamping. Who knows, perhaps you'll meet a black-eyed *bailaor* with a strong but supple backbone.'

'*Bailaor?*'

'Dancer.'

'If I do I promise I'll bring him back for you. You're really spoiling me, I should refuse but—'

He silenced me with another kiss then pressed the controller to start. 'Ready to lap up Paul Mercurio and his *paso doble?*'

We had a whole weekend of flamenco films: the Carlos Saura trilogy, *Gitano* starring Joaquín Cortés as a *granadino* gypsy... The visceral discord and melancholy of the music – those songs of the outcast – resonating with my dejection. We sighed and laughed; Jeremy told me I was doing well.

But back in my flat at one in the morning I was Googling *fertility clinic + single woman* and *sperm donors*. Finding websites supporting single-mothers-by-choice, reading articles about women who'd taken matters into their own hands and were now pictured with a smiling baby on their lap.

I think that's how it happened. It was such a strange juxtaposition. I didn't plan it; I wouldn't even call it an idea. But it was there: the pre-decision, the pre-existence, the pre-conception... of a flamenco baby.

2.
quizás *adv* perhaps, maybe

I didn't even *like* kissing. Boyfriends' reactions had lain along the spectrum from amusement to exasperation; one had even suggested I needed counselling. With Jeremy it was different: childlike, but at the same time...

'Yol?' He looked over from his desk. '*Please...*'

'Okay, nearly finished this one and then I'll stop.' I held the blind away from the window so it didn't clank as I wiped it. He was frowning at the screen. 'Stuck?'

'No – just don't want this bit to happen.'

'Give them a break.'

'They've got to earn it with some suffering first. And how are *you* doing today?'

'Oh...' Tears in my Weetabix. The tacky but innocent gondola mug had been viciously binned, along with a flutey birthday card I'd kept in my bedside table drawer. 'Definitely earning my happy ending. He hasn't called.'

'Did you want him to?'

'No. But you'd think... I dunno. And Helen says nobody can cover for me at the wedding, but I don't believe her for a minute.'

'Well it's a swanky gig – she'll want it to look right.' Jeremy had an unflattering theory that my hair had secured my place in the Trio, my harmonising so well – visually if not always temperamentally – with darkly Irish Helen and auburn-haired Kirsty. 'But hey, you need to check these dates.' He pushed a notepad towards me. 'You can't go at half-term – that's when the flamenco festival is. And Easter's all booked up. So I've got a hold on the 1st March, when you'll be all fired up after the festival. What d'you think?'

'I suppose the school won't mind as long as my pupils get their ten lessons... Heavens,' I said, looking at a white-walled interior with a hazy pink Alhambra visible through a barred window. Another page listed my daily classes: *Flamenco Choreography (Beginner)*, *Flamenco Technique (Beginner)*, Spanish...

'Bloody hell, Jeremy!'

'You've got to do an online test for Spanish so they know what group to put you in.'

'Oh God. And what's this compass thing?'

'*Compás*. Rhythm. Teaches you how to do the *palmas* – flamenco clapping. You'll be good at that.'

'But... look, this is too much,' I said, as he quickly put his hand over some figures, 'at least let me pay for their "charming apartment".'

'Absolutely not. Don't worry, you can send me here for intensive guitar next time *my* heart's broken.'

'Okay,' I said, wondering how I'd ever afford it. 'But you've got to stop spoiling me... You've changed the standing order for the rent again, haven't you.'

'I've given you a rise, you idiot. Like I do every year.'

'This housekeeping thing's crazy – sooner or later you'll be paying me more than I'm paying you. You're daft – you could get a fortune for my place.'

'Who else would put broad beans in my lasagnes? Grow banana trees in my builders' rubble?' He pushed back his chair and pulled me down onto his lap. I leant on his shoulder, enjoyed the citrus after-shave, the warmth and gentle rise and fall of his chest under my hand. Whispered *thank you* into his ear. I could happily have spent the rest of the day there.

'I'm afraid I've got to see Andrew for lunch.'

Of course. The scent, the super-soft shirt. 'Oh.'

'He's got a contract he wants me to sign and some other stuff...'

Other stuff indeed; Andrew was a literary agent who provided a *very* comprehensive service. I looked down at the bulge in Jeremy's cargos and once again wondered what exactly they *did*. I'd tentatively asked a couple of times over the years, but hadn't learnt anything other than that he preferred to call it making love rather than having sex. But surely it was making *like* in Andrew's case; the man was just there to fill in between relationships, stoke Jeremy's passionate fires to keep the writing on the boil.

'Right.'

'Why don't you have a nap before your pupils come?'

'Yeah, I might.'

'I won't be late. How about the Greek place later?'

'Can't – Helen's gone and moved the rehearsal to tonight and then we're supposed to be taking Kirsty to an Indian for her birthday. Can't face any of it.'

'Yes you can.' He hugged me and then did up his jacket. 'I'll see you later. Now get some kip and hang on in there.'

I let him go and suddenly felt exhausted. Took off some clothes and got into bed, set the alarm for the three o'clock piece of toast that would do for lunch before the first of the pupils arrived. Put my arms round one of the pillows and imagined having Jeremy in my bed – it was his fault, starting this kissing on the lips thing. What was he *doing*? But then, what would be wrong with him sleeping in my bed anyway? Or me sleeping in his? It would just be friendly. But warmth was spreading down my body...

I got up and took a couple of hopefully sleep-inducing Nurofens. I stared at the calendar – not this time at the procession of heart-healing weeks, but at the glistening swarthy musculature of the air-borne male ballet dancer, the ecstatic arching of his feet, the sensual elegance of his hands. And reminded myself that Jeremy would see him in the same way as I did. In fact it had become clear, over the years, that we had a laughably similar taste in men.

Including David, of course. Greyhound-sleek on nervous and artistic energy. All half-Jewish curly dark hair – everywhere. An injured, honest guy – or so we'd believed. I suddenly felt heavy with misery and went back to bed. I congratulated myself on having kept almost all of the lovemaking at David's flat; at least I didn't have to be haunted by memories of us naked together here. But the images started to arrive anyway... Oh God: sex. On past form the likelihood was that I'd be going without it for heaven knows how long – unless I got a hell of a lot less fussy. I got up and put my clothes back on.

Love and sex. Or rather love, sex and *trust*: was there any hope of finding one man who could offer all three? On the evidence so far, no.

But I'll be seeing Jeremy later, I told myself, I'll fake a migraine and get out of the Indian restaurant. And he might still change his mind... I busied myself tidying up the living room, practised a tricky accompaniment.

Then they came, and I was glad to be distracted by Olivia's grinning chubby face as she played The Entertainer; Romilly's wilfully wacky take on the Grade One piano pieces; chatty Alison, who used to come in a tartan school pinafore dress but was now my height and considerably better made-up. Then there was Michael – already producing a beautiful tone on the flute, an intelligent boy with a dry sense of humour. Sensitive. The sort of child we could have if...

Love, sex, trust and... children: an even taller order. In fact, I didn't know anybody who seemed to have achieved all of these – or not with anybody I considered worth having them with. That was the problem; nobody was ever going to match up to Jeremy. He'd spoilt me, set a standard, queered my pitch – ha-ha – literally. Perhaps why I allowed him to console me so generously; the heartbreaks always seemed somehow partly his fault.

Perhaps I'd have to separate the factors. Love and trust with Jeremy, intermittently sharing him with a man; sex with whoever was healthy, attractive and available for it; and a baby with... well, whoever was healthy, attractive and available for it. Possibly the same man, initially. What did they call it on that website? *Natural* insemination by the donor.

I should have been getting ready to go to Helen's, but I was back in the second bedroom, the computer helping to conjure the father of the room's future occupant. I clicked on the sperm donor website I'd saved in my favourites – under a discreet 'sd', as if keeping it a secret even from myself. But up came a message: *The traffic limit for the site you are attempting to access is exceeded.* There were obviously bloody thousands of us; you'd think there'd recently been a war, there was such a dearth of Mr Rights.

But there were other websites. Including that of an ex-nurse who'd wasted a fortune in money, time and emotions making trips to clinics, and eventually to the donor-insemination Mecca, the States – and didn't want the rest of us to have to suffer like she had. She smiled reassuringly at me, baby Barney on her lap; maybe I could go and talk to her – as if by fate, her office was just a couple of roads away. I started the long questionnaire for registration, wondering if I was going to press *Send* at the end.

Meanwhile, Helen was leaving a message on my answerphone. 'Where *are* you? It's tonight, remember?'

I looked at my watch: damn, it had to be the tube. Even then I was going to be heinously late, but they were lucky I was coming at all, in my state. Oh God, the wedding. I'd said I needed to go to Jersey for my nephews' birthday; couldn't I have come up with something better than that? Helen probably hadn't even rung Annie to see if she could do it. I should have told the truth; it was going to be obvious soon enough anyway. But Helen and David were old college friends; they sometimes had lunch when she took Rupert up to his Saturday Junior's lessons at the Academy. I wasn't ready for her defence of him. Let the bastard explain himself, I thought, with that now familiar punched-in stomach feeling.

I stomped out to change lines, a blast of metallic air increasing my tears. It was time Kirsty and I questioned why we always had to slog over from our North London homes to Helen's Kensington for the rehearsals. There'd been a few meetings at Kirsty's, since baby Lily's arrival, but I couldn't remember the last time they'd come to my place. The unspoken rationale was that the more children you had, the less you could be expected to leave your house – even if you had full-time live-in help, no day job and a choice of cars.

Sophie opened the door, beckoning me into the kitchen with a podgy finger.

'Are *you* in trouble! Want some?' She was breaking off two pillows of Aero.

'Ooh yes, if you don't mind. Thought you...' *I thought you weren't allowed chocolate*, I was going to say – part of Helen's weight-losing plan for her, that also involved after-school sports activities from which Sophie returned looking flushed and miserable.

'Top cupboard. She won't notice, it's a multipack.'

I moved the chair away from the cupboard and put it under the table. 'She will if you leave the evidence.'

'Oh yes. Thanks.'

Bridget sailed in, swept Sophie's bracelet-making into a box and barked 'Bath!'

I went through. Rupert could be heard practising his oboe upstairs, and Imogen, poring over her school books in the dining room, looked up at me with disapproval – Helen's more dazzling but less appealing offspring, in whose shadow little Sophie dawdled. Three kids suddenly struck me as insensitive genetic greed; Sophie should have been mine.

I opened the door to the vast room they called the Snug.

'*Finally*,' Helen said. 'I'd make you a drink but we've really got to get on. We need to learn this Handel for Saturday, they've specially requested it.'

'Right.' I started putting my flute together. 'Good birthday yesterday?' I asked Kirsty, who was breastfeeding Lily and stroking her silvery-soft head.

'Well she was a bit under the weather so we couldn't face the restaurant. But Rob gave me a beautiful scarf. Thanks for the lovely card.'

'So what about tonight, will she be—?'

'Lily will be fine with Bridget, she's brilliant with babies,' put in Helen.

Kirsty didn't look too happy about handing over her most precious possession. Only the previous year she'd been in my position, but along came sweaty but sweet Robert, whose conversation seemed to be limited to his IT work and the frustrations of the Northern Line, and Bob's-your-uncle – or rather husband and sire; unexpectedly – or expediently – the man of her dreams.

'Ready?' Helen was positioning my music stand.

We were off. My part was easy, Annie could have sight-read it. In fact she was a sickeningly good sight-reader and could probably whip through all the second flute parts...

'Yolly! Here, put a ring round the repeat signs,' Helen said, handing me a pencil. 'From the top.'

Next time I play this, I thought, David will be standing there on the groom's side, watching the bride walk down the aisle. Perhaps wondering whether one would ever again walk down an aisle for him. Or feeling damned relieved to have got shot of a woman so intent on doing so...

'You're lagging behind,' Helen said to me.

Lily started to grizzle.

'Come on girls, let's get it right – we've still got to go over a few of the other pieces.'

Wedding marches: staggering there was one we didn't know. And, call me a bitter old bag, but this was up there with the most hideously pompous; a triumphant I've-bagged-a-stockbroker of a tune, as bad as the comedy Mendelssohn that *wills* a trip on the altar steps...

'Oh for God's *sake!*' Helen said, glaring at me. 'Look, if we can't get this right tonight we're going to have to fix another rehearsal. And with Rupert's music scholarship exam coming up, I really am up against it... You seem to be in some kind of *dream*.'

'I'm not, I can assure you.'

'Well what's the matter then? You're all over the place.'

The nephews' birthday story just wasn't going to cut it. Maybe I needed to elaborate – my sister wasn't well (with what?), she needed me there to help her with the party...

'Yolly?' Gentle now, and that was my undoing.

'David and I have broken up. I can't face Saturday, he'll be there and...'

'Oh *no*,' Kirsty said.

Helen put down her flute, a hand going to her mouth.

I was delving in my bag for a tissue, but I saw it: the worried look between them. The hesitation, waiting for me to explain. Explain *what they already knew*.

'You knew, didn't you.'

Helen had her mouth open; Kirsty needlessly picked up Lily.

'You knew about Lucy.'

Helen shifted in her seat. 'Okay, I'd heard something, but I thought it was just—'

'Then why the fuck didn't you tell me!'

Lily broke into a wail.

'I wasn't sure... somebody said something at the Academy but... I couldn't believe it,' Helen mumbled.

'I *don't* believe it,' Kirsty said, her eyes wide.

'Well you can get it from the horse's mouth on Saturday, can't you?' I pulled my flute apart and packed up.

'Look... *please*... sit down, Yolly. Come on, I'll get you a drink.' Helen started to step round the music stands towards me but she wasn't quick enough; I was off.

'They knew about Lucy and didn't tell me,' I said, pointing to the Greek salad on the menu.

'Is that all? Sorry, I meant food-wise. They're just cowards, and probably weren't sure... come on.'

He, of course, was no coward; later he'd make me call them. But for now he distracted me by suggesting we book one-to-one flamenco classes before the Granada course.

The waitress came to take our order. I let Jeremy do the talking, while I looked at the pale shine on his hair, the way the candlelight emphasised his cheekbones. Wondered if the person who invented the term sight-for-sore-eyes was a heartbroken girl enjoying the soothing beauty of her gay best friend.

'So... was it nice, dear?' I said in my best Margot Fonteyn voice. We'd read that she'd asked this of Nureyev after he'd been with a boy.

'Of course. With men is very quick. Big pleasure,' he replied in his hilarious Nureyev accent. But he started to look thoughtful, twiddled his wine glass. 'I'm sorry, I know it's awful timing, but I'm going to have to go out to Spain for longer than I thought. I'd completely forgotten that I said I'd go to the Sitges carnival with Vicente.'

His Spanish lawyer: another gay professional attending to Jeremy's needs. But unlike Andrew, very *simpático* – all bovine eyes and gentle humour. 'Oh.'

'Worst of it is, I'll have to miss the first two nights of the flamenco festival.'

'Oh *no...*'

'Stick out an olive branch and take Helen one night and Kirsty the other—'

'No way.'

'Have to be Emma then.'

'I'll ask. You'll definitely be back for the rest of it, won't you?'

'Yes. But I'm going to have to start spending more time there, I'm afraid, the novel's going to need a lot more research.' He leaned forward, took my hand. 'And you see... that's another reason why I couldn't say yes to...'

I'd assumed I'd be the one to bring it up again, after giving him time to think it over. It seemed that he already had. I searched his face for the slightest doubt.

'You know I'll help you as much as I can, of course... Anyone else you could ask?'

'No.'

'What about that line-dancing guy you went out with, had to relocate up North...?'

'Steve.'

'You said you were still in touch, emailed each other occasionally.'

'A couple of lines each Christmas.'

'Is he available these days?'

'Doubt it. Anyway, he's stuck in Manchester for good – he's got a small role in Coronation Street.'

'Really? Okay, but maybe he wouldn't mind... donating.'

'Oh I don't know. Could be a bit complicated.'

'Well, have you thought of going along to one of those clinics and—?'

My phone buzzed. 'It'll be Helen again.'

'Well reply then.'

I pulled it from my pocket. 'No, it's David. Helen must have called him. *I won't go on Saturday, if that helps. But I'd love to see you. Lunch soon? Please call.* Four kisses.'

'That's kind of him. Perhaps you should.'

'Should what?' I snapped the phone shut. 'Although, actually... it's not a bad idea. I'm off the pill now...'

Our food arrived. Jeremy waited until the waitress had moved away. 'What? That would be horrendously deceitful, I can't believe you—'

'*He's* been horrendously deceitful—'

'My God, you can't really be thinking of becoming a *sperm bandit*.'

'A what?'

'Sperm bandit. That's what they call women who trick men into fatherhood.'

'Really?' I grinned, seeing an image of myself pulling at David's clothes with a scarf over my mouth. 'I'm joking, you idiot!'

'Hm. Look – you're upset. You need time. Just leave this baby thing for a few months and concentrate on getting healthy, learning flamenco, feeling good about yourself. Then you'll be able to think straight and make some decisions. Okay?' He removed all the hated olives. 'There you go.'

I read out my reply to David. '*Thank you. Will call and have lunch in...*' How long is it going to take me to get my head together, d'you think?'

'Working full-time at it? Well let's see... three months? April. Spring. A fully-fledged flamenco *bailora* by then, *dando la verdad,* as they say. Giving the truth. Sounds about right, doesn't it?'

It did. I reassured him. I reassured myself. But it was too late: the seed had already, somehow, been planted.

3.
flamenco *adj* (Mús) flamenco

Ángel. As in Angel Gabriel, but instead of just delivering the news, providing the very wherewithal for the Immaculate Conception. Or perhaps not so immaculate, because his selected Method of Insemination was 'Flexible', and according to his brief email, to be discussed. Or more likely, *considered*, because presumably there'd be women that he would be physically unable to oblige. And my profile didn't include a photo.

But his did. Hair shorter than I liked, but deliciously dark. Face and shoulders suggesting he could have done with losing a stone, but then slim chefs are probably a rarity. A wide smile and large kind eyes. *Far apart* eyes – isn't that meant to be a sign of honesty? Or was it generosity? He certainly had that: hobbies included working at a summer camp for disabled children and playing guitar for his mother's Sunday school. And seeing his sister's distress at being unable to conceive, he'd wanted to help women in a similar situation.

According to one of the American books I'd ordered – there simply weren't any British ones on the subject – most women want a donor who resembles themselves. To cut down the amount of questions about the father, they said, but it sounded like cloning to me. I felt my pale, vulnerable genes needed to be thoroughly contrasted. Anyway, I was strangely attracted to this man, and that seemed as good a basis for choice as any. He might not have good grammar and a university degree but surely these *simpático* Hispanic genes should be passed on. But I had to wait: he was helping another lady at the moment, he wrote with endearing fidelity, and might not be available until April or May. Spring. When, according to Jeremy, I'd be complete again and ready to make decisions.

Jeremy. So pleased with my progress, but unaware of how it was being achieved – the opioid Ángel-daydreams blocking out painful thoughts of David and the misery-making boyfriends of the past. And possibly the future, because if I had a child I'd no longer have to worry about where relationships were leading; the insistent body clock would be muted or even silenced for good. It was agonizing keeping my plans from Jeremy, but he was so irksomely protective; he would see my Ángel as a servant of the devil. I could just hear him: 'Chef? Probably works for McDonalds. Sunday school? He's going to want his child brought up a Catholic. Healthy? Let's have a copy of the test results then. *Natural* insemination? That's *completely* irresponsible...'

Meanwhile, Ángel and his baby inspired me: I started jogging again to get fitter before pregnancy; worked on a new teach-yourself Spanish book so that I could show Ángel that his child's Hispanic blood would be respected.

Then there was the flamenco.

I'd booked a one-to-one lesson. I went along to what looked like a disused warehouse and followed signs until

31

posters on the walls suggested I'd arrived. They showed Alicia where she'd probably rather be: on a stage – albeit in London rather than Granada or Seville – hoisting up a waterfall of white flounces, twisting and triumphant in spotted pink, scarily intense in sculpted red. Rasping guitar strums vibrated through the door, shortly joined by a complex stamping and clickety-clack of feet; I stifled a nervous giggle at the visceral passion of it – feeling too English, too blonde.

She took me in with a flash of black eyes, indicating the changing room door leading off from the side of the studio. Changing room? All I had to do was switch my shoes. Red: flashy for a beginner, but the only ones the shop had had in my size. If I couldn't get the shoes before the first lesson, Alicia had said on the phone in her disappointingly perfect English, I should just wear something with a heel. I didn't have such a thing, I'd had to confess to shocked silence the other end. I put them on and teetered into the room.

'So Yolande, this is your first flamenco lesson?'

'Yes. Although I've watched it a lot... for years... in Spain and...'

She'd moved in, pulling at my shoulders. 'We need to work at *la postura*. *Abre el pecho*, open the chest...'

'And I speak Spanish – well, a bit.'

'Ah, *bien!*' she said with her first real smile. She looked up and down my body again. '*Pompi* – in,' she said, pointing to my bottom. I pulled in my tummy, tilted my hips. '*Mejor* – but now again *abre el pecho*.' She kept correcting each part of my collapsing body. '*Eso es!* That's it! Look in the mirror! *Ay, que guapa!* How beautiful you look! Remember this all the time, practise wherever you are, not just in the lesson. And now we'll start with some *marcaje* – marking steps. Bend the knees all the time... but *la postura, la postura!*'

'I feel like a puppet with too many strings,' I said, wondering how many lessons I could fit in before what could be a humiliating rather than self-affirming week in Granada.

She laughed. 'It's the same for everybody, don't worry.'

Then she showed me another *marcaje*, one that had a step-in-front, step-behind pattern similar to something I'd learnt in jazz, but with a strange rhythm to the changeover before you came back in the opposite direction. She put on some ponderous guitar music.

'*Y un dos TRES cuatro cinco SEIS siete OCHO nueve DIEZ un dos, un dos TRES... Eso es! Pero la postura!*'

She went to switch off the CD and I waited for another lecture on my deportment.

'Well done, Yoli! You have the *compás* – this is the most important element of flamenco – the rhythm. Are you a musician?'

I told her I was a flautist and she looked pleased; from that moment the round-shouldered English woman became a pupil slightly worth bothering with. She showed me how to rotate my wrists and work my fingers like the opening and closing of a flower; how to raise my arms like the wings of an eagle taking flight; how to use my toes, heels and feet to make rhythms and patterns on the floor, always *a tierra*, 'into the earth'.

And there was a moment when, returning to the *marcaje* to put arms with it, something inside me took over and I had a sense of inner strength and release – understanding a tiny fraction of what generations of persecuted *gitanas* might have felt.

'*Eso es*, Yoli!' exclaimed Alicia afterwards, but in my shock-sudden emotional state I just bent down and picked up my water bottle and fussed with the sports lid.

Returning from the changing room, flat-heeled and English but trying to maintain my posture at least until I left, I booked three more lessons before Granada. But I knew it wouldn't stop there.

'So you didn't find anyone for *either* night?' Jeremy asked.

'No. Emma was busy and the others... well, people don't seem to want to go to flamenco unless they're on holiday. Are you having a nice time there?'

'How couldn't I? Vicente sends you kisses and says David's an idiot. And he's sorry he's dragged me away from you. But the usual crowd will be there – it's not like you've got nobody to chat to all evening.' He obviously hadn't noticed that when we went to the patrons' receptions it was he that did most of the talking – all that appraisal of the choreography and comparisons between dancers and productions. 'You could try out your toddler Spanish on some of the performers.'

'I am second book now, much work!' I said in indignant Spanish. He was laughing. '*No ríes.*'

'It's *no te rías*. If you're going to tell people not to do things you have to use the subjunctive tense. I'll call you tomorrow. Enjoy it for both of us, okay?'

'Yolande! No Jeremy?' Sarah the balletomane banker, coming over to the theatre entrance as if she'd been waiting for us.

'Had to go to Spain.'

'Come on up then, what are you doing down here with *les autres?*' People like me who couldn't possibly afford to be a patron without an over-generous friend.

'Well I've got to see the box office about something... I'll see you later.' I got into the queue until she'd floated upstairs and then took a seat round the corner. I wasn't ready for the patron people. Frankly I was in a bit of a mood: Ángel had sent a brief email telling me I would have to wait until at least June or July; he was going to be away for a month visiting relatives in Argentina. Did that mean he was Argentinian? It didn't matter really, but it would have been nice to know. It would have been nice to know a lot of things, but it seemed like he couldn't interact with more than one potential recipient at a time.

I studied the programme: the impossibly handsome Molino and Morales – all seventies-style shaggy hair and tight black trousers – with ten or so other dancers and a group of musicians. Their show, they explained in a dual interview, drew on their contemporary dance as well as flamenco backgrounds... and would explore the nature of love and caress in movement. Christ. But then weren't most dance performances about that? I was sure Jeremy would have agreed.

Meanwhile, the reception area was filling up: the usual mixture of old and young, the fashionable and the jeans-clad, with the odd dancer or celebrity. I spotted the very tall guy from Strictly Come Dancing. But there were also a lot of dark-haired Spaniards. Well, Hispanics. Shame I couldn't have invited Ángel along.

Jeremy had booked the front row as usual; last year, a *bailaora* had blown him a kiss during the applause. The lights dimmed – late, as we were clearly on Spanish time

– and the rough but intricately modulated tones of a *cantaor* singer filled the auditorium.

A flamenco man in a pool of light: the M with the adorable boy-band face. Now transformed into the very image of concentrated despair, his feet stroking the floor with the cries of the singer, then giving in to a shudder of impetuous footwork.

Another pool of light: the other M. More typically flamenco, with his black hair, Roman nose, and wide-set frightening eyes. Similar anguish, but somehow a release rather than a transformation. The spot-lit dancing alternated between them as the rest of the band was heard, until they danced their thundering *taconeo* in perfect unison – as if the pain of loneliness were universal, the same for all.

But the show was about love – including much of the flamenco type with all its jealousy and tragedy – and dancers in various combinations shared every aspect of it. They seldom touched – a hand following the air-drawn contour of a *bailaora*'s dress, a woman reaching to a man's cheek – but the glances between them, with the sensuality of their rhythms and movements, were *more* than caresses. Most beautiful of all was the inclusion of the musicians: a bewitched *bailaora* weaving around a passionate violinist and nuzzling her head to his chest beneath his bowing arm; the dark M so expressive in his dancing as he responded to a heartrending but untranslatable song from a *cantaora*.

A rousing finale with a few touches of humour brought the show to an end, and then the entire company was in a line at the front of the stage, grinning and commenting to each other as they bowed to the clamorous applause.

I sat in my seat, stunned. Let everyone inch past me. I needed Jeremy: his inevitably outrageous prurient speculation about Molino and Morales – whose attractions he would describe as *torturously unfair* – followed by a hilarious whispered invented backstory for each that would have me giggling all the way up the stairs. I eventually climbed them alone; after all, it would be letting Jeremy down not to go and have a look at them at the reception.

'Yolande! Thought you'd gone,' Sarah said. 'Let's ask her,' she said to her ex-dancer friend Miranda. 'The lads, what d'you think?' She jerked her wine glass towards the other side of the room. There they were, now in tight jeans and jumpers and looking even more like time-travellers from the seventies, laughing and nudging each other.

'Amazing. And such contrasting—'

'Yes, yes, but are they... you know, an *item*?'

'Course not. The Spanish are very tactile, and they're old friends...'

'The Brad Pitt one's got a slight lisp, and the dark one's eyes are just *too* pretty...' Miranda was saying.

They seemed to have forgotten all about the dancing – it obviously didn't reach them in the way ballet did. I also felt indignant on the dancers' behalf; under Jeremy's tutoring I'd developed a sensitive gay-dar, and it was registering a strong double zero.

'Probably just didn't get all his stage make-up off. Who cares? Thing is, why's nobody talking to them?'

'They are. But not for long – probably a language problem. Shame Jeremy's not here to translate.'

He'd like the dark, intense one. Broad-shouldered but lithe and slim: a photographic negative of himself.

Perhaps that's why the guy seemed strangely familiar while at the same time a scary, exotic bird of a man.

Sarah leaned over. 'Go over and talk to him, he won't bite.'

I blushed, realising that she'd been watching me stare at him. But then the *cantaora* with the hauntingly sad song walked past.

'Excuse me,' I said in Spanish. 'I want to say... I like the song a lot. It makes me cry. Many thanks.' She gave me a smile, a rapid burst of Spanish and a pat on my shoulder before she moved on.

'You see?' I said to them. 'Tactile and friendly.'

'Not having any stroganoff?' Sarah asked.

'Don't fancy it. Think I'll polish off all the orange juice instead.'

I went off to a waiter with a tray of drinks, and chatted with a disgruntled patron of the Royal Ballet asking *what was all that about*, and the shy greasy-haired guy that Jeremy and I called Stu-the-Stalker who seemed to be in an Oedipal trance over the mature flamenco dancer with the long *bata de cola* dress.

I wanted to sneak another look at the dark dancer, but the two men seemed to have disappeared. I suddenly felt hungry after all, so I made my way through to the dessert table.

'Just one left,' the waiter said, picking up a bowl of profiteroles. I put my hand out to take it, but it was being passed behind me to someone else.

'*Ay, perdón.*' A very low, gentle voice. A faint smell of musky shower gel.

I turned and met his eyes: black, beautiful. Yes, possibly some residual eyeliner. A little frightening. But then he broke into a lopsided grin.

'Sorry.' I thought he was being gentlemanly and offering it to me.

'No, take it, you danced,' I said in a rather breathless Spanish.

'*Claro*,' he said; he'd obviously already considered that, and was digging his spoon in. I watched him put it in his mouth, close his eyes. Then he suddenly waved his spoon at the waiter to get attention, pointed it at the bowl and then at me. The waiter said something in Spanish and disappeared.

'Is good. You must take. He go to find, for you.'

'Oh... thanks.' My heart fluttered.

'Mm.' He looked up and fixed me with his eyes, swallowed. 'Is what I like, after the show.'

Pudding? A blonde English girl? I could feel my cheeks burn, a giddiness.

'*Cho-co-la-te*.'

How delicious the word sounded in Spanish. 'Not *before* the show?'

'Yes, of course, also. And for now the best is... *chocolate caliente*. You know, to drink. But have to be... *calidad*.'

He had a point there. The delicatessen's in Chapel Market but not the one in the coffee place near the pet shop. 'I know what you mean. It varies.'

He took a glass of wine from the tray of drinks offered by a coy waitress. 'So tell me, how much pay the people to eat, talk with the dancers... or only look.'

'Er... I can't remember.' I didn't like him thinking I was there to *only look*. 'But it helps fund everything, and we can go to rehearsals, get ticket discounts...' And he mustn't think I'm a spoilt, fantasising rich girl. 'My friend bought us patron memberships for a year as a present...'

'Is man very *generoso*.'

39

'Well... I was upset about something,' I said.

'Up... *No entiendo.*'

'Very sad.'

'Oh.' He looked down for a moment then glanced up again, his black eyes serious. 'He is bad to you?'

'No! He's my best friend.'

'Best friend not is good boyfriend?'

I blushed again. 'Well he would but... he's gay. Prefers men.'

He looked up from his glass, startled. I cursed myself for mentioning it; he might well have inherited homophobia along with his family's machismo flamenco heritage.

'He is with you?'

'No. In Spain, actually. But he'll be back soon for the rest of the festival.'

'You come to show of Eva Yerbabuena?'

'Hers and all the others.'

'*Excelente!*'

The waiter had returned with a heaped bowl for me. 'Heavens.'

'You have more.'

'Too much. Would you like some of this?'

'Ah, *sí.*' He moved closer to put his bowl next to mine, our heads bowed together, almost touching. My heart started to pound, my coordination uncertain. I concentrated on spooning the profiteroles onto his bowl without dropping any, waiting for him to stop me.

'*Sueca?*'

'Sorry?'

'You are so... *pálida...* You are from *Suecia?*'

'Sweden? No, just English.' He didn't have to know about my French-Dutch father; I didn't know much myself. 'And where are you from?'

'*Sevilla.*'

'Oh!'

'You visit?'

'No, but I was... I'd like to, one day. But I'm going to Granada in two weeks' time.'

'Ah, to see more flamenco?'

'Well to *do* it actually. But I'm just a beginner... a *principiante.*'

'*Ahora sí*, but after of some years maybe you come to my school in Sevilla, *no?*'

'You teach?'

'Of course. When I can.'

Then one of the organisers was saying she'd love to introduce him to somebody, and he was led away – saying something to me in blurred Spanish that I couldn't understand.

On my own again, I noticed that the room was thinning out. But I wasn't ready for the evening to be in the past; I wanted to look into those black eyes again, hear more of that resonant, caressing voice.

I went to the cloakroom and bumped into Sarah.

'Well aren't you the dark horse! Sharing your pudding – we couldn't believe it!'

'What did you learn?' Miranda asked.

'He likes chocolate. Sorry, desperate for the loo.'

I went in to one of the toilets and waited until I couldn't hear them laughing anymore, then came out and put my coat on, wondering whether I could say *buenas noches* to him as I walked past.

Then there was a gentle hand on my arm. '*Perdón...* I need speak.' I turned and saw the *cantaora*. 'Nando want take *chocolate* with you.'

My ears started ringing.

'*Entiendes mi inglés?*' she asked with a laugh.

'Er... yes, but... where?'

'He say you know, where is good. You say and I say to him.'

'But it's late, the places are closed. Unless...' *Oh God.* 'I have some, at my flat, just in the next street, but...' I laughed nervously.

'*Perfecto.* You write the... *dirección?*' she asked, miming writing movements.

I hoped she couldn't see that my hands were shaky as I pulled a biro and a credit card receipt from my bag. I wrote my address and a picture showing the streets and their names.

'He going soon.' Perhaps I looked worried; I could hear Jeremy's protective voice in my head. '*No te preocupes.* Is good man,' she added with a smile.

I dashed home: I wanted to tidy up, have a word with myself about what the hell I thought I was doing. Because, after a passionate performance in a cold, damp foreign city, how could a man with a fine sense of finale possibly be turning up at my flat for just a hot chocolate? It was going to take more than the correct use of the subjunctive tense to say no to anything more. But then he was so beautiful... A shiver of fear and excitement ran through my body. I glanced at the calendar: I'd had period pain... when? This is stupid, I thought, if I'm going to become a sperm bandit I really need to start being aware of the terrain.

Bandit. Well not really...I wouldn't ask for money or anything... just somehow let him know, let him visit if he wanted to... I could tell the child that his father was an exquisite performer, a *good man.* We had fallen in love one evening, but his touring had made any further relationship

42

impossible. I took a deep breath and breathed out slowly, dazed with nerves. Told myself I wouldn't lie: if he asked, I'd admit I had no contraception. And it couldn't happen immediately: we needed to talk, I needed to get to know him a bit...

The chocolate. Piping hot and delaying things. I opened the cupboard: yes, there it was, but... I shook the tin and prised the lid off. Shit. Barely enough for one. But I'd recently put it on the shopping list. Where the hell was it? I started sliding jars of coffee, tea boxes and Nurofen packets around the shelf. Fuck. I grabbed my keys and dashed across to Jeremy's.

Once in his flat, Jeremy's whispering disapproval in the back of my head became a shout: his desk insisted on the safe sex he included in his novels; the sofa begged me to remember my repeated promise, murmured there in a cuddle, that I wouldn't do anything rash in the next few months. Yes Jeremy, but you're not here, your refusal leaves me no choice, and spring has come unexpectedly early.

I ran to his kitchen, almost tripping over Pavlova who'd leapt into leg-winding action. I shook some more food into her bowl to get her off me and opened the cupboard. Yes: a Bourneville and an unopened Green and Black – we even had a choice. Then my intercom buzzed – faint from there but enough to make my heart stop. Oh God. Did I have time to take the tins to my flat? Yes. But... keys? I scanned the kitchen surfaces, thrust my hand in my skirt pocket. My eyes darted around the room. The sofa: I'd put them on the arm, and yes, they'd slid down the side when Pav had run along it. I dashed out of his flat and to the front door.

He was wearing a leather jacket now; he could have come straight off the set of Starsky and Hutch. And the womanising Latin I was planning to succumb to wasn't there: he was barely able to smile, shivering in the cold rainy wind like an animal out of its habitat.

'Come in, you're soaked.'

He followed me into the living room. '*Lo siento*, I come here but I not remember your name.'

'I don't think I said... And I can't remember which...'

'Is very good here, *tranquilo*, warm,' he said, looking round the room. He took off his jacket, sat down on the sofa.

'*Siéntate*,' he said, patting the sofa beside him. '*Dime, cómo te llamas?*'

'Yolande.' I sat down next to him with my hands on my knees, having difficulty looking at those eyes. Thinking, *I absolutely can't do this.*

'Is Spanish name.'

'With an *e* I think it's French... or from Holland.'

He smiled. 'Yoli. Is good name for you. And please, I am Nando, no Toni. He has wife, Pilar – you have meeting with her.'

'The *cantaora?*'

'Yes.' He leaned back and rested his arm on the back of the sofa. 'And now, Yoli, we find if we like the same...' *Oh God.* 'You make *chocolate* for me now?'

'Right,' I said, smiling with relief. 'But I left it in Jeremy's flat... I'll just go and get them.'

'*Kher-e-mi?*'

'My friend.'

His eyes widened, that frightening look again. 'Is far?'

'About a metre.' I opened my door and unlocked Jeremy's.

'Ah!' He jumped up in one movement and followed me.

I went to the cupboard and got out the tins, turned to explain the difference between them. But he was examining the photos on the bookshelf: Jeremy and I with his mother before she started looking ill, pictures of us with our sand creations on the beach in Cádiz or in various stages of progress with the garden.

'He love you.'

'And I love him.' But right then I resented his intrusion. I went towards the door, but he was running his finger along the books, the DVDs. I had to stop myself saying 'come on now' like I do to my pupils if they start fiddling with things in the room before getting their music out.

'And he love Spain also.'

'We both do. But Jeremy's an expert – he used to be a travel writer.'

'And now?'

'He's working on his third novel.'

He turned to me in surprise, as if wanting to know more. But I held up the two tins. 'We have to decide which.'

He smiled and followed me back to my flat. I set myself to heating up the milk, while he wandered around the room asking questions about my music stand, my flute playing and teaching, photos of Charlotte and my nephews and niece.

'And why *you* are not married?'

I wondered if the Spanish had a word for nosey parker. I got out the mugs, opened the cutlery drawer. 'I don't know.'

'But *en serio*, you *are* married, to Jeremy.'

And I thought, damn Jeremy's photos, damn the way the shopping always ends up in his kitchen, and damn myself for mentioning him in the first place. 'Of course I'm not. Come and see which you prefer.' We sat down on the sofa again and I started to feel buzzily sick.

'*Flamencas!*' I'd used the red spotted mugs I'd bought at Jerez airport.

'Yes.'

'But you know, you not say if you like the show.'

'Didn't I? Well of course I did. Particularly Pilar's song and the way you danced to it. I couldn't understand the Spanish but...Where do you... find that feeling, in the words or...'

'Yes,' he said quietly. 'And more. From my life. There is no other way to dance flamenco.'

Such sadness, anger. Did he have these in his life?

'You miss your family, in Seville?'

'Always. My parents, sisters... But of course I also have my other family – Toni and Pilar, the others.'

I held my mug, wondering if he also had a girlfriend he missed.

'What is this?' He pointed to my Spanish book.

I leaned forward and picked it up. 'I'm trying, but—'

'*Ay, cuidado!*' he said with a laugh. He reached forward to take a bit of my hair that had dipped into my chocolate.

'Oh dear.'

'Permit me help.' Then he moved closer and put the ends of my hair in his mouth.

I laughed nervously. 'Thanks.'

But he wasn't letting go. He stroked the ends of my hair on his upper lip, apparently deep in thought, then his hand was at my forehead, pushing back my hair and running his fingers down it. 'You know, while the chocolate is too hot, we can have... *concierto*. You play for me?'

I was feeling so breathless I didn't know if I could.

'Please?' He touched my shoulder. I suddenly wanted him to put both arms round me and squeeze; perhaps if I played beautifully he would. So I smiled, got up and put my flute together; I was going to sing for my supper, sing for my squeeze... but what? Something dark and dramatic to match his own performance? Or romantic? Maybe both: *Syrinx*.

'What you like, what is you,' he said.

Was I Syrinx? A nymph pursued by the lecherous god Pan, with tragic consequences... I knew it by heart but put the music on the stand, needing somewhere to look.

The haunting calling sentences of the opening filled the flat. A pause. The faster, flamboyantly rippling melodies of the chase, followed by quiet chromatic searching and then, confident of success, a lyrical, excited ascent... Only to end in a long, vibrating note of anguish, heartbreakingly vulnerable falling phrases, and a disappearance into silence.

'Better not play anymore, neighbours don't like it this late,' I said.

He got up and came towards me... but he just stood next to me, looking at the music. 'Beautiful. Very beautiful. Thank you,' he said, nodding his head and smiling to himself.

No squeeze. No *abrazo*. And it suddenly occurred to me that I'd got this all wrong: he really was here for chat-and-a-chocolate, with a bonus concert. An aching sadness spread through me, followed by a wave of irritation. 'Chocolate will be getting cold.'

'No, no. It will be perfect,' he said, back on the sofa.

I sat down again, weary and hurt but more relaxed, tucking my feet up beside me. He tried each mug, and had a preference but I couldn't remember which was which. He asked me whether I thought cocoa being organic affected the flavour and I said I had no idea.

'Yoli? *Qué pasa?*'

'Nothing's the matter.'

'Come, there is something.'

I smiled and picked up my near-empty mug, but he took it from me and put it back on the table, turned my face towards him. '*Qué pasa?*' Almost whispering, those black eyes searching so deeply that they'd see the flicker of lie.

'I want a cuddle.' A puzzled look. '*Quiero un abrazo.*'

'Ah.' He laughed and nodded. 'Is no problem.' A firm warm arm came round my back and pulled me over, and I rested my head on his shoulder. He kissed my hair, my neck. But I needed to believe this was happening, needed to see his face...

'Ay...!' he said, smiling and clutching his chin where I'd bumped it with my head.

'Ooh, sorry.' I cupped his stubbly face in my hand, but he took it and kissed it. Then he pulled me over again and gently kissed me on the lips. Like Jeremy, I realised, and quickly banished the thought. Then he *was* squeezing me, so hard I could hardly breathe, and he was kissing me again, his tongue in my mouth...

And I thought, *this is going to hurt*. But then, didn't it always? It would just be a much accelerated version of the usual pattern: instead of the months before having sex there'd be just hours; all in one night there'd be the excitement and heavenly discovery of each other, followed by comfort, a level of misplaced trust, and then the polite but brutal abandonment. But until then this beautiful man is all mine, I thought, running my hands through his long soft hair. And maybe, just *maybe*... I needed to see his face again, see what he was feeling. *If* he was feeling. It was important, not just for me... I pulled back.

Concerned, his eyes darker than ever but gentle, no longer frightening me. 'Yoli... you not want...?'

Sweet, sweet man. *A good man.* But before anything else happened I wanted to feel the simple comfort of his arms and chest. Without the shirt. Surely not much to ask. I started undoing his buttons, saying something daft like 'better *abrazo*', and he watched for a moment with a bemused grin before taking it off. He started to try and undo mine but I was making it difficult, snuggling into him and exploring his smooth olive skin and fine black hairs, the lean, hard muscles of his chest. And hesitantly, his taut tummy and the arrow of black hairs pointing downwards in to his jeans. He laughed softly as if I was tickling him, and then on impulse I kissed him there, affectionate really, almost joking, but he suddenly tensed, breathed out heavily and groaned, deftly unbuttoning his jeans and starting to push me down... But inside my head I was screaming *no, not this... it's too...*

The phone. I sat up, heard my daft cheery message. I was saved, but also somehow *caught*. Because I knew who I was about to hear.

'Switch your mobile back on, you idiot. Where *are* you? Bit late, Yol. What are you doing? You haven't dragged señor Molino or Morales back to the flat to give you an intensive lesson in Spanish, flamenco or strong, Latin s—'

I'd reached the phone and punched the button to switch off the speaker. 'You woke me up,' I said into the receiver, sounding far from sleepy.

'Oh sorry. Good show?'

'Yes, fantastic. But I'm really tired... speak to you tomorrow, okay?'

'Alright. Night-night then.'

I stood there looking at the phone, couldn't face turning round. But I didn't have to: Nando was putting his arms round me, and kissed my cheek. His shirt was back on, his jacket over his arm.

'He's joking, I don't... I've never—'

'Is okay, I know this. I'm sorry, Yoli, I not understand. And is late now, I go, have to sleep.' He released me and put on his jacket.

I took him in as if for the last time: the black eyes that stood no lies, the full mouth that I'd kissed... I ached for him, hated myself for my failed courage, resented Jeremy for ending the evening. Even if it was all inevitable.

I followed him into the hall; he opened the door, seeming hurtfully keen to escape. But once on the doorstep he turned back to me.

'Come and see me tomorrow, after show. At stage door.'

A rush of speechless pleasure.

'*Si?*'

'*Si.*'

Then he strode down the road, a dark figure quickly blending into the night, as if he'd been a figment of my imagination all along.

Back in the living room I put the mugs on the kitchen work surface, put my flute away. Picked up a cushion that had fallen off the sofa – and saw something flutter to the floor. I picked it up: the credit card slip. I turned it over to see if the trembling of my hand had shown. My heart thudded. An arrow to my house had been added, along with '*aquí vive tu esposa!*' Here lives your wife. Wife: probably what Pilar calls all his chocolate-making infatuated women. A stupid, cruel joke. No, not cruel – I wasn't meant to see it. I threw it into the waste paper basket.

I got undressed and under the covers, shaky with sadness and arousal. Then I remembered his face: dark, mysterious but... concerned. I got out of bed and picked the slip out of the basket, folded it carefully and put it in my bedside table drawer.

4.
esposa *f* wife

It seemed to grow overnight, this seed of an idea, this irresistible word: *esposa*. I woke up imagining myself learning to play flamenco flute and joining the group, making love in a series of hotel beds, and then, when the baby came, living in the house in Sevilla with his family until we found a home of our own, periodically popping down for some beach time with Jeremy in Cádiz...

I padded into the other room and sat down at the computer. *Fernando Morales*: a Puerto Rican volleyball player, a Manchester City striker, a Chilean university professor. Eventually a Spanish article praising Nando's teaching at a Flamenco workshop in Madrid, complete with blurred action picture. On his own, he didn't seem to be cutting much of a profile. *Antonio Molino and Fernando Morales*. Aha. Pages and pages of notices of performances. Reviews by breathlessly infatuated critics, the odd carp from flamenco purists. Some interviews about their shows, in which 'FM' had fewer words but somehow more to say than 'AM.' YouTube clips: dizzying camerawork jumping from sweating, pained faces to the thundering feet and back to spinning arms and wet black hair. A couple of incomprehensible interviews on Spanish TV in which they sat on a sofa, initially serious but then making each other laugh like I'd seen at the reception. But apart from their flamenco heritage, Molino and Morales had managed to conceal every detail of their private lives. Even *Antonio Molino + esposa* failed to reveal his marriage to Pilar.

Their website. Eerie strings behind a full-screen picture of them, sinuously expressive in black silk. A resonant, rhythmic vocalising: *takata con-con, takata con-con, takata con... Ta... Ta...* Unmistakably Nando's voice and speaking directly to my limbic system as other images faded in – moodily sexy or smiling at applause. I clicked on *Biografía*: he was only *thirty-three*. His training, prizes, tours, solo guest appearances. Molino's was an almost identical read. *Calendario*: Madrid, Seville, a frantic criss-crossing of Europe then South America in September; there was no *time* for private lives. *Esposa*: I was beginning to see the joke.

I switched off the computer and switched on the day; I was going to have a good one if it killed me. Breakfast with Pavlova, some Spanish, more on a flute and piano piece I was trying to compose. Tidying the flat to salsa, a turquoise bath. Then out for lunch.

A sunny Sunday lunchtime *and* Valentine's Day: not the easiest of times for a determinedly not-sorry-for-herself single to be strolling by the canal. Even the mad-cap bikes had to defer to the crowds of stuck-together couples dawdling along with wan morning-of-sex faces. Perhaps I could have been one of them, if I'd just... It wasn't that I didn't like... Well, no, it *was* that... I *had* in the past, sort of... *But not the first night, for God's sake.*

Dark, wearing what could be the same jacket, leaning back on the bench with his arm around a girl... No: too bland a face. Asian. But a similar body, his girlfriend's hand on his tummy. That was it: I'd given him the wrong idea. I'd reached the age of thirty-eight, a total of five lovers, and still didn't really understand the language of sex. Like my Spanish, stuck at some lower intermediate level by some unidentified limiting factor.

My phone trilled in my pocket.

'How's my valentine?'

'Fine thanks, how's *mine*?'

'In need of some female company. This festival... mass gayness just isn't my thing. So what're you up to then?'

'I'm on my way to the Narrow Boat with *Mao's Last Dancer*. Bit sad, I know – it'll be chocker with couples.'

'Ha – you won't even notice them with Li Cunxin for company. So tell me, how was the reception? Did you use your Spanish?'

'I did!' I told him about the *cantaora*.

'Oh well done. Anyone else?'

'Well... yes. Guess who I shared profiteroles with?'

'Molino?'

'Nope.'

'Morales?'

I left a dramatic pause. 'Yes! But his English was better than my Spanish so I sort of gave up.'

'Yo! Nice guy? Did he flirt with you?'

'No, of course not!'

'Listen to you. You're gorgeous, when are you going to start believing it?' I heard a Spanish voice in the background. 'Oh... Vicente agrees but says he's starving. You'll have to tell me more tomorrow – we could have a late lunch together, yes?'

I'd arrived and made my way to a cramped table in the corner spurned by the couples.

'No boyfriend today?' asked our usual waitress.

'No. Had to go to Spain for a few days.'

'So you thought you'd celebrate anyway.'

'Something like that, yes.' Bloody hell. It was impossible for Jeremy and me to go anywhere without being thought of as a couple. There were even a few restaurants where we avoided taking partners, not wanting to spoil the illusion.

I tried to re-immerse myself in the Chinese peasant boy's life, periodically turning to the photos of him dancing and leaping later on, but it was difficult now: half two - only an hour and a half before the performance. Afterwards, maybe we'd go for a drink. Or a meal. And then?

Back home, Emma was leaving a message. I picked up the phone.

'Ah there you are! Look, Cassie isn't coming, her ex turned up with an armful of apologetic roses... Wondered if you'd like to come and help me eat this lunch I've made, and then perhaps I could join you for the *flamenco* after all...'

'Couldn't he have done that earlier? I've just had a sad-single lunch at the pub. Oh, hang on, someone at the door...' I looked out of the bay window and could just see the green arm of my neighbour Duncan's hoodie. I went to let him in.

'Sorry, forgot the key,' he said as he went past.

I came back to the living room, thinking hard. If Emma came with me I'd have to explain about Nando. Widowed when Cassie and Lawrie were small, she'd had a colourful romantic life since they'd left home; surely she'd understand? But then she was a bit like Jeremy: happy to throw herself into all sorts of trouble, but irritatingly concerned about me.

'Sorry, daft neighbour with key-ring issues. Shame about the show – Jeremy returned the tickets. But if he can't make any of the others I'll let you know.'

I sat down to a further tinkering with my composition, but it was a bit melancholy. I put on Alicia's flamenco practice DVD, but I was *fuera de compás*. Out of time.

I could only look at *him*: the way the tumultuous *taconeo* sent tremors through his thighs and the perfect curve of his buttocks; the strength of those defining arms; the glistening of his finely haired chest; the way his hair became wavier with sweat, forming a tender curl at the base of his neck... But when Pilar sang her song it was mine: all sadness, yearning and determination.

I took deep breaths to try and stop my heart pounding. Pretended to study the giant boards advertising the flamenco festival, until sultrily stared out by a larger-than-life-size picture of Molino and Morales in which one could study the tiny scar on Nando's stubbled chin in greater detail than in real life. I forced myself round the corner.

Toni was on the pavement smoking with one of the guitarists and the *cajón* player, chatting with some animated young Spaniards. Pilar and the *bata de cola* dancer were smiling at awkward compliments from a middle-aged English couple. Then photo flashes and peals of laughter drew my eyes to inside the entrance; three leggy girls were being kissed by Nando and photographing each other under his arm, while two elegant *señoritas* waited their turn.

I came out with a feeble '*muchas gracias*' for the *cajón* player, who surprised me with a hug and an enthusiastic kiss on each cheek that I rather hoped Nando might have seen. But he was deep in tactile conversation with one of the Spanish ladies, the other having complicitly moved away. He hadn't noticed me. Or he had, and he'd decided to give me some useful perspective; I'd been a pleasant but unfulfilling companion, and second chances were dependent on the rare lack of other options.

But I too had options, and humiliation was not one of them. Not anymore. So I walked on, quickening my pace as I turned the corner into my road. I slammed the door behind me, kicked off my boots and lay on the bed. Heaving with stupid, stupid tears. Then decided I'd tell Jeremy – albeit just up to the flute playing and then jumping to the scene at the stage door. Heavens, he'd fallen for enough dancers himself, he'd understand. There'd be a lecture about being alone at night with an unknown man. I'd counter by reminding him that if I hadn't gone off with an unknown man one evening, after cutting my finger when losing patience with a faulty lock in the Sadler's Wells self-service cloakroom, we wouldn't be sitting together having the conversation. Then perhaps I'd tell him about Ángel.

Ángel. I felt like I'd betrayed him. I'd email and tell him I really needed to meet him soon. I made a hot chocolate, grinning bitterly and saying *look what you're missing* aloud to myself. Then went through to the computer and opened up the SD website.

The doorbell rang and I could hear Duncan's Scottish tones and chuckle outside. It sounded like he'd brought his new girlfriend back for Valentine's night and forgotten his outdoor key yet again. I went to the hall and opened the door. 'When are you going to put it on your key-ring you idiot, what if I'd...? Oh.'

He and Nando were standing there with matching relieved smiles. My heart thudded.

'Thanks, Yol. Have a nice evening, you two,' Duncan said with a big wink as he walked past.

Nando watched him bound up the stairs and then turned to me, his smile fading. 'Why you not come? I not understand.'

'I did.'

'But you go. *Why?* Do you want I go now?'

'No, of course not.'

'Then... we can enter...?'

'Oh – yes.' He followed me into the flat, took off his jacket. He was wearing a pale blue denim shirt with his jeans – a Red Indian in cowboy clothes. The same scent of shower gel, perhaps with a hint of musky aftershave.

'So you were content not see me again?'

He was obviously unaccustomed to being passed over. But just as I was enjoying his earnest expression he caught my arm and wiped his thumb under each of my eyes. '*Not* content...'

I looked away, trying to come up with an alternative explanation for my smudged mascara.

He smiled and shook his head. 'Yoli... Look, always there are girls. We know this. But I ask you to dinner and you not come.'

'No, you didn't say—'

'Of course I say. Or if not, you know this, is evening, you think I ask you come say only hello and goodbye?'

I smiled weakly, shrugged. I needed to sit down. Some chocolate.

'But first, *chocolate*, no?' He saw the cup I'd put on the table on my way to the door. 'Ah – *aquí está*,' he said, feeling the mug and then taking a sip. '*Perfecto*. Sorry. I give couple for it?' he asked with a lopsided smile.

'What?'

'Couple. As you like. *Abrazo*.'

'Ah... you mean *cuddle*,' I said, laughing nervously.

'That,' he said, and I watched him drink, my chest aching with anticipation. 'But come, to do milk for more.'

I filled the pan, put the ring on. Then turned to him and had to stop myself from sighing as he pulled me into his arms, stroked and kissed my hair. I wanted it to go on forever, but a little pat reminded me about the pan.

I poured the milk into my mug and stirred in the Green and Black, tried to relax; we had the whole evening together.

'Hey, I forgot something last night.' I opened a drawer and took out some mini marshmallows. 'I can't remember, d'you have these in—?'

'*Sí, malvaviscos*,' he said, grabbing the bag. 'In America I have. But I prefer not with these – I am *purista*.'

'In chocolate drinking if not in flamenco,' I said, immediately regretting letting on that I'd read his reviews.

He looked serious again. 'This is what you think?'

'No! Well, I wouldn't know... but I suppose I do prefer the solos to the group dances... more like what I've seen in Cádiz.'

'Ah! *Purista*. You have to come to Sevilla, see me dance at a *peña*.'

I smiled and pushed down a resurgence of *esposa* hopes; it was just chat.

He put the *malvaviscos* on top of my chocolate, tipped a few into his mouth. Then he touched my shoulder. 'Oh – I have for you...' He pulled a bit of hotel writing paper out of his pocket and handed it to me. 'From Pilar. We ask Toni write song in English for you.'

At night I go out onto the field, To cry for our love... Some of it hard to understand but basically a woman coming to terms with the impossibility of her relationship, willing nature to heal, time to pass... and leave her with a treasured memory. Perhaps the presence of the male dancer meant that he felt the same.

'Oh... it's beautiful. Thank you. Except now it'll make me cry even more.'

'You come again tomorrow?'

'Yes, with Jeremy.'

'I meet him?'

'Of course.'

We went to sit down on the sofa and he put his arm round me.

'I'm sorry for last night. But *de verdad*, Yoli, I not know what you want. It can be that *you* are not sure.'

'What d'you mean?'

He laughed, shook his head, took his arm away to pick up his drink and finish it. A wave of anxiety: perhaps he was fed up with my mixed messages and about to leave. But he picked up the Spanish book and flicked through. 'So, Yoli, *dime*, what you do today?'

'Yes, a bit of that, some music, reading... just a quiet day really.'

I saw his black eyes look round the room, as if trying to verify what I'd said. And stare at the empty box for

Alicia's flamenco practice DVD. He got up to have a look at it, then picked up the remote control.

'What are you–?'

'I want to see what she teach you.' Then he spotted my shoes on the shelf under the TV; why the hell had I left them there? 'And what you learn,' he added, picking them up.

'Oh no, I'm absolutely not going to–'

'*Ven*, put this.'

'Anyway, if we're eating out we need to go, it'll be busy, being–'

'We have place for nine. Spanish *restaurante* at top of street that Toni and Pilar find.'

Of course. Where else? I'd let Nando sit me back on the sofa and found myself staring at the blue-black shine of his hair as he bent to put on my shoes, his hands warm on my feet.

'Look, I'm really not...'

He picked up the remote again, and with that inborn knowledge that every male except Jeremy had, instantly had it under his control. Alicia filled the screen.

'*Española?*'

'Yes, but born in London.'

He watched, his face suddenly solemn; even these rudimentary steps for foreigners seemed to demand reverence. He fast forwarded to the *marcaje* and pulled me up to my feet.

'Oh not that – I can't follow it, her skirt's too long!'

'You not know, from class?'

I felt like I was being tested; perhaps he was only interested in women with a certain level of flamenco sensitivity. On went the music and I gave it my best shot until I collided with the waste bin and got the giggles. He pressed stop.

'Bravo! *Qué compás para una principiante!* How many classes?'

'Er... four.'

'Is very good. But you have to start to believe...' He put a finger under my chin, pulled at my shoulders like Alicia did. 'I like that you not know you are *guapa*, but is not good for flamenco. And...' He demonstrated the step, his arms strong and precise. 'Always you must say something. Again.'

And I don't know what my body said but I thought of the words to Pilar's song and it must have helped because he started saying '*eso es!*' and doing the *palmas*, as if I was the real thing, and then put his arm round my shoulder and squeezed me. But when he reached for the remote I shook my head.

'Your turn now.' I pointed to the piano.

'*Ay Dios mio!*' he said, but sat down on the stool. I put myself next to him, thrown for a moment by his warm thigh against mine. I showed him the hand position, how to transfer weight from one finger to another. Carefully adjusted his elegant, dark-haired fingers. Then I played a warm chord sequence and explained that he could improvise a melody over it.

It was something that even my least musical pupils felt happy to do, but he was hesitant, making me play my part twice before he would join in.

'It's okay, you can do anything—'

'I know it. We start now?' And then he played, faultlessly rhythmical and naturally coming home to the key note at the final cadence.

'That's lovely—'

'Again!' he demanded, sounding like Romilly, that dark, delightfully wilful child I thought of as Romilly-the-Romany. The sort of child we...

His improvising was becoming more elaborate, more daring: a perfectly executed counter-rhythm, some harmonising left-hand notes, the melody extending into the higher octaves and then down among my fingers until we were going for the same notes and started laughing and nudging each other out of the way. He grabbed my hands and put them to his mouth, saying something in Spanish that I didn't catch, then pulled me over and started kissing me.

Suddenly the evening seemed to be about to develop rather faster than I'd thought; I'd imagined a late-night, wine-blurred submission. But I leant into him and wondered how it would feel to be wrapped together on my bed...

'Is first time?' he asked quietly.

'No.' God, was I that awkward?

'But first time with man that is not boyfriend.'

I gave a little nod.

He held me close, his hand slipping under my top and sending shivers through my body. Spanish in my ear. I listened carefully and my heart started to pound: *follar*, to bother. Or to help a fire. But not in this context; I'd seen enough Almodóvar films to know that. The directness was unnerving, even cloaked in the most beautiful language in the world. He was waiting for a reply: a meek '*sí*'? But I was done with meekness.

'*Antes y después de cenar?*' I said, immediately wondering if I'd gone too far: he'd just done a performance; perhaps he didn't have the energy for it before *and* after dinner.

But he laughed and gave some encouragement that I didn't catch. Then whispered something about *más confortable* and stood up, took my arm and led me to the spare bedroom – where bouncing blocks were kindly hiding the SD website.

'*No, aquí,*' I said, pointing to my bedroom door.

He picked up my stuffed lemur from the bed. 'De Khe-re-mi.' I nodded. He sat Lem on my bedside table, legs dangling over the edge; David had just swept him off with the duvet. Then he was making a suggestion about Jeremy and pointing to the phone.

'Ah, *sí,*' I said, taking it off the stand.

He was starting to unbutton his shirt. I had a moment of panic – the thought of exposing my February-white imperfect body to a man accustomed to passionate, sinuous *señoritas*. Before I hardly knew him.

'What's *your* bedroom like?' A last attempt to learn more about him, sounding like a girl on Blind Date.

He went over to the window and looked out into the gloom. Taking off his shirt, he described a balcony a little larger than mine, a vase that was valuable but always filled with flowers; a painting of horses.

I started to witter on about how Jeremy and I had once gone to the *Feria del Caballo* in Jerez, but he whispered '*Y hay una cama blanca como la tuya*', gently pushing me back onto the bed, white like his own. We were in each other's arms, kissing again... and he was pushing against me, his leg coming between mine...

'*Estás segura?*' he whispered, his black eyes so near to mine now.

Was I sure. I must have nodded. He helped me take off my clothes in between removing his, pulled me under the duvet with him, said something about me being precious,

64

pushed stray hair out of my eyes, stroked my cheek. *Not boyfriend*. But that's not how it felt. He was moving down my body with his kissing, as I ran my fingers through his hair, along his muscular back...

Then he came back to me and quietly asked about using something. Did I *want* to. At least that's what I think he said. Not *necesita*: I would have recognised that word. But there are other words for need. It was madness; I was allowing our futures to depend on his exact choice of words and my unreliable translation of them.

'*No*,' I said, a further wave of excitement and warmth passing through my body. And a little fear, as he seemed about to ask me something else, but he just smiled and started kissing me again... Then there was an urgency, a frenetic need that conjured images of his dancing. Primitive. Except also somehow... spiritual, as if there was no other way to do it.

5.

precioso *adj* precious, lovely, beautiful

'Delicious.'

'Oh good. Haven't done curry for ages, couldn't remember—'

'Lunch too, of course, but...'

Jeremy had found the programme and was running his finger down Nando's profile. 'God, you must have been the envy of Islington.' He closed it and looked at me. 'Just wish you hadn't gone to *our* restaurant.'

'I didn't have any choice, they were all going there.' I'd sat there wishing I'd worked harder at my Spanish, but enjoying his translations in my ear, his hand on my thigh...

'Weren't you worried he'd expect to come back here and shag you? Especially after a few drinks.'

'No!' I got up and put the plates in the dishwasher. 'He didn't drink much... I'd sort of made it clear that... Anyway, he was tired, wanted to get back to his hotel.'

'Surely he walked you back here?'

'Yes.' Arm in arm, his feet rhythmical on the pavement and so fast I had trouble keeping up. 'I gave him a hot chocolate and then he left. Perfect gentleman.'

'Bloody hell, what's wrong with the man? He's a *flamenco bailaor*, and according to this, with *gitano* blood for God's sake. By rights he should have been up for brandy, *Ducados*, a line of coke and some fast sex.'

I opened the freezer. 'Ice-cream or sorbet with the mango?'

Jeremy was shaking his head. '...but he opted for a friendly dinner and a nightcap with the most difficult lay in London.'

I shrugged, took my time selecting bowls from the cupboard. Wished I could find some way to tell him the truth without him seeing me as a deluded little groupie or a shameless trickster.

'Hey – no chance he's gay is there?'

'Sorry, no,' I said, rather too quickly. 'Well... from what I could make out his friends were saying.... Anyway, you'll see for yourself tonight, they're all going there again and he said we should both come along.'

He stopped eating and looked at me. '*We?* Now this really *doesn't* make sense.'

I shrugged again, got up to switch the kettle on. 'That's what he—'

He grabbed my hand. 'Okay, just sit down will you? Look, I know the state you're in at the moment...'

He was going to ask me outright. Of course he was.

'Hasn't it occurred to you that he might actually be... *taken* with you?'

I almost sighed with relief; it obviously hadn't even crossed his mind that I'd... He had such faith in me – such *misplaced* faith... I tried to hide my watery eyes with my hand.

'Oh Yol... You've fallen for him, haven't you? Look, I won't come tonight—'

'No, I want you to meet him.' So that maybe one day he would understand... 'And what if I have? He's touring all over the place, it's impossible.'

He got up and put his arms round me. 'Not *completely* impossible. Admittedly not a very good idea... But I don't want to spoil your last evening—'

'You won't. It'll be good having you there, when he's gone you can help me remember him.'

'As long as you promise you'll get shot of me if you change your mind. Come on now, no more tears.'

Not a boyfriend, but being given the usual treatment. Where he lived and why. How he'd become what he was, his hopes for the future. All in rapid Spanish but the pattern so familiar that I had little difficulty following. And I knew Jeremy would be moving on, almost imperceptibly, to the testing, red-rag *pases*. In the past having demonstrated knowledge and devil's advocate views on a range of subjects including NHS dentistry and Arts Council funding. Sure enough, he went on to discuss the sacrifices needed to perform flamenco in a large theatre, even though I knew he'd loved the show. But surely he'd realise he couldn't go in for the kill with Nando: the questioning on how we'd met – which he'd want described as a life-changing event – and whether the guy realised how lucky he was.

Nando had the earnest stance I'd seen in other victims. But not for long. Jeremy had met his match; Nando was comfortable with their place in the popular flamenco scene and countered enthusiastically. Then turned the tables and prised out Jeremy's theatrical parentage and stage school childhood, even the pivotal teenage relationship with a Spanish dancer at an international summer school that made him come out as gay, fall in love with Andalucía, give up his dance aspirations, study English and Spanish at university and feel inspired to write. He even had the nerve to ask Jeremy if he thought he 'gave difficulties to my *relaciones*'. Jeremy frowned and looked over at me for an answer.

'Of course he doesn't,' I said, putting my hand over Jeremy's.

Then I felt Nando's over mine. '*Lo siento.* You are beautiful friends. Who wants to break this is not good man for Yoli, *así que no es importante.*'

'*Exactamente,*' Jeremy and I said.

'Now we go to your house for *chocolate*, no?'

Back at the flat I didn't mind that I was getting too tired to concentrate properly on their Spanish – jumping as it did between the rest of the shows in the flamenco festival and Jeremy's novels, the contrasting attractions of Sevilla and Cádiz. I just enjoyed seeing Nando getting on so well with Jeremy, as none of my boyfriends had.

'Thank you for... keeping our secret,' I said as soon as Jeremy had bid us *hasta luego* and gone. 'I know it must seem strange, but...'

'Is okay, Yoli, I not understand, but I do this for you. I like to meet him, is special man – but also it is good to miss him,' he said, drawing me closer.

'I think you mean *lose* him. It was certainly kind of him to dis—'

But his lips were on mine. He pulled me up and led me to the bedroom.

We were taking off each other's clothes, smiling and caressing. But I couldn't forget that time was running out.

I shivered. 'I need to turn the heating up.'

'No, come here,' he said pulling me down next to him and putting the covers over us. 'Is okay, Yoli... I see you again, I know this.'

We wrapped around each other and I took his warmth, felt my body melt under his touch again. Not thinking of a baby, just enraptured – as nature intends, perhaps. But afterwards I looked into his eyes and ached to ask *when*.

'No goodbye, Yoli, I *will* see you again. Next year. Maybe before. If you are not married then! But you not wait for me, *entiendes?*'

I tried to understand.

'*Entiendes?*'

I nodded. He held me tightly, stroked my hair, whispered the Spanish about me being precious again, very quietly, over and over... until I must have fallen asleep.

6.

perder *vt* to lose

He'd gone. But that was okay, he'd said he would. As he had the previous night. Sleep was important, he'd said, and there was something about it being easier for me. But I imagined waking and stroking his sleepy body, watching those eyes open, making him breakfast; this, I would never know. *Not boyfriend.* Hot tears ran down my cheek until I fell back to sleep.

A few seconds of blissful confusion and then the pain was back. This time, too weary for tears – just lifeless, empty. But I needed to get up; I didn't want Jeremy to see me in this state. I wandered round the flat, hoping Nando had left a note. A sweater, a hotel key, his mobile. Anything. It was always like this – once he'd gone, his presence here seemed unreal. *His mobile.* Did he *have* one? Maybe it was broken. He could have asked for *my* mobile number. But he'd made it clear, he didn't want contact. *Don't wait for me.*

I showered and got dressed. Collected the post – there was a tiny chance he'd put a note in the letterbox – but there was just a Next catalogue. I used it to distract myself enough to eat a Weetabix.

I'd been planning to surprise Jeremy with some new socks in his drawer and ringed my choices. I looked at the male models: none – not even our favourite, the one with the sexy-soft Caribbean smile – were nearly as beautiful as Nando. I closed the book. Then opened it again. I could order my nephews something for their birthday. There they were, all these gorgeous boys of every age and hue in their coordinated outfits. Every hue, it seemed, other than Hispanic. But then with our opposite colouring, presumably ours would be somewhere in the middle of the spectrum... I found a boy with light brown hair and serious dark eyes. I pulled him closer, imagined holding him, reading him tractor books, taking him to toddlers' music classes and seeing him show early signs of a fine sense of *compás*...

Helen rang; I let her leave a message about a change of rehearsal evening to accommodate something to do with Imogen the following week. It could be a *daughter*. I flicked on and eventually found her. Maybe she was half Indian: black hair but light eyes. An athletic girl in school PE kit, then lithe and laughing in a denim mini skirt. On another page, her hair up and wearing a tulip party dress in which she was much less assured – as her mother would have been...

Rat-a-tat-TAT. Jeremy. I closed the book and opened the door.

'You okay?' he asked, studying my face.

'Yeah,' I said, forcing a smile.

'How did it go?'

'He was lovely. Gave me a big hug.'

'And...?'

'And said he'd see me next year.'

'Well, well. Who'd have thought? Divine fellow – you really should be flattered, Yol.'

'I am.'

'Now look, half term, so leave me to look after myself – go round and see Emma or something. Don't sit around here daydreaming about him... I've got to push on, but come round sixish and I'll make us an omelette before we go to the show, okay?'

I've got to push on meant he had some ideas he had to get down, and I knew better than to come between him and his characters when they were desperate to move forward.

I too needed to move forward; unusually for me, I was off for some retail therapy. The shops on the Green were out; I needed anonymity. I caught a seventy-three to Oxford Street.

First, John Lewis. Cots, white or wooden. High chairs, cute or subtle. A herd of prams and buggies, someone demonstrating the complex folding, unfolding and optional features to a monstrously pregnant woman and her proud mum. I would try them out with Emma or an embarrassed Jeremy, but hopefully somehow being watched from above; Mum had reared Charlotte and me on her own since we were nine and six, but I remembered her as laughing, smiling and serene. Surely she would understand?

I ran my hand along the velour babygrows, the teddy bear dungarees with matching button-necked tops, the ludicrous pink miniskirts for age three to six months... Then started to suffer from some kind of overload and had to hang on to a Sale rail of tiny polar bear coats.

'Are you alright, dear?' A solid, motherly woman with a John Lewis badge.

'Yes... probably didn't have enough breakfast.'

'Oh no, you need little and often. Why don't you sit down for a bit?' She showed me some chairs next to the bottles and nipple protectors. 'I could get you some water. Or the coffee shop's just...'

'Ooh yes, I'll go there. Thanks.'

The thought of a buttered sandwich was turning my stomach. As, oddly, was a cup of tea. But tomato soup and a roll was suddenly essential to my continued existence. Could this be the beginning of morning sickness *already*?

Revived, I turned my attention to more immediate concerns and walked along to Boots. Pregnacare had too fate-tempting a name, so I opted for a simple packet of folic acid tablets. Then it was over to the boxes: pink or blue, as if we should be following our gut instinct about the type of baby possibly inside us. I took a multipack of each.

I needed to get home, examine my cache and find somewhere safe to hide it; I couldn't have it tumbling out of my wardrobe next time Jeremy helped me choose something to wear. Meanwhile I could use the bus ride to ponder when the hell my last period was.

I leant my head against the window and closed my eyes.

I was on Beauport Beach, sitting on a rock and wishing Mum and Charlotte would ignore me so I could get on with my mermaid daydream. *It was risky, coming out of the sea in the height of summer, even in this bay that those four-wheeled things couldn't reach, but it was nice getting some sun on my scales...*

Charlotte had said something, her words carried off on the sea wind, not interesting enough to cut into my world. Then she looked up from her *Jackie*, smirking and raising her eyes to the heavens. Mum was sitting up on her towel and looking at me as if waiting for an answer. Although actually she was waiting for a question, because apparently that's what you do, you wait for the child to ask. But I wasn't asking, even sitting there with a sister in shorts rather than her usual crimson bikini.

'She's nine and three-quarters, Mummy, she really needs to be *told*.'

Mum glared at her.

'Told what?' I expected to hear another story warning me of the danger of the fast Jersey tides. Or wandering off on my own over the head-cracking rocks. But Mum was looking down in concentration, as if choosing her words. Like last time.

'It's okay, I know about the baby thing, what a man has to do with his tweeny... you told me, *everyone*'s told me.' And uh – how I wish they wouldn't. I stretched out on the rock. *I need to enjoy the sun on my half-lady half-fish body before the people come, specially the men with their nasty hairy legs and baggy shorts...*

Charlotte couldn't stand it anymore. Maybe for Mum's sake. Her description of what would happen to me every month, painfully and inevitably, came out like a torrent. A shocking torrent of blood.

I sat up, my hand to my stomach, staring between my legs at the little crease in my swimsuit from where this shameful sludge would gush. 'No! That's disgusting! Dis*gust*ing! I can't live with that!'

I stomped off down the beach towards the rocks. It wasn't going to happen to *me*; I could have an operation, like the one Grandpa had had to stop him weeing all the time. Mum was calling out my name. Then she was lumbering after me pathetically – she'd not been well. So I veered off towards the sea instead and walked in, aching with the sudden chill of the water. Thinking *mermaids don't have legs, so nothing can come out from between them.*

The day became one of those family memories, softened by understanding and humour. But it was hard not to feel that I'd had some kind of premonition of the misery periods would cause me; my first one all over the sleeping bag on a guide camp, followed by years of pressing my aching tummy against school radiators. And now, of course, the monthly reminder that time was running out.

Monthly? Sometimes six weeks apart, but more often three. Or even two. *You're always on,* David would complain. Stress, illness, excitement – the slightest thing would bring it forward. I'd been blighted nearly every important day of my life: Mum's funeral, my final exams... even the evening I met Jeremy. Staggering that I hadn't had one on meeting Nando; it was difficult not to see that as a benevolent sign.

Back home it was time to get scientific. I sat on the bed and opened the two kits. *Can be used up to four days before your period is due.* The other could trump that with up to *six* days. But reading on, they *could* detect it then but might well not; you had to keep repeating the test. What a con, they knew we were all bloody desperate to *know*.

I opened my filo. The date of my last period was either the Saturday of the funeral gig in Kensington or the one with the christening gig in Highgate; I recalled asking

Kirsty for a tampon, but at which I had no idea. I'd been miserable at both, so nothing to differentiate them there. I thought charting the previous period would help, so I waded back through the quagmire misery of post-David January. The break-up weekend on the ninth: surely I'd had one then, making the 31st January more likely if I usually had a three-week cycle. But did I? I flicked back into the previous year with its intermittent frogspawn circles. A flurry of activity in early autumn (flu?), a further spell of two-week cycles in November (tummy bug?), followed by a marathon seven-week gap and an angry circling of December 25th…

On balance it looked like the end of the month was the time to do the test. I'd just have to keep busy: there were more flamenco shows, the usual half-term trip to Jersey, a week of teaching, a final flamenco lesson. Then I'd do the test the day I was to fly out to Granada, feeling weary and nauseous with either pregnancy or disappointment.

'Come here you… it's been far too long.' We squeezed each other hard and then she held my shoulders to examine me. She was still golden after her New Year holiday in Cuba.

'You look a bit peaky, little sis. Not air sick again like the old days, surely?'

'Naa… just a bit tired. So where's the welcome party?' The kids: hearty hugs then running all over the place asking for sweets from the airport shop while we dealt with the car park ticket machine.

'Later. They're at the zoo with Marie-Clare. Thought we'd have a bit of time to ourselves first. Crab Shack okay?'

'Ooh yes. Starving.'

We drove off, Charlotte crawling along because she was in trouble with Simon about yet another scrape to her car. I slumped in the seat; it was the usual Jersey lurgy thing – something to do with the enveloping narrow lanes, the sea level, the return to the place of teenage dopey diffidence.

'So how're you doing? Have you got over David now?'

'Yeah. I can see now that we weren't quite... I had to try too hard.'

'Anybody new on the horizon?'

'Not really.'

'It must be difficult for you to meet guys when you spend so much time with—'

'That's not it, I've told you.' An awkward silence. We'd been through this before, it was pointless telling her how much I loved Jeremy, that the right guy would understand, *does* understand... 'Simon okay?' I asked, as if he ever wasn't.

'Yes, he's fine, busier than ever...'

The top end of the Jersey property market is probably fascinating, but as usual my mind was off... What would Nando think of Simon? He couldn't be faulted as a brother-in-law, but I couldn't forgive him for curtailing Eddie's dance classes. Thought it would turn him gay or something. At *seven*. Signed him up for Saturday tag rugby with George instead. It wouldn't be easy bringing up a half-flamenco boy in the narrow-minded non-dancing UK...

'Here we are.'

I got out of the car and we laughed as my skirt flew up round my waist.

'Bloody hell! I'm fed up of this weather – being frozen, drenched and blown around.'

'Well, you should have come with us, got some mid-season warmth – makes such a difference.' Antigua, Barbados, Cuba. Presumably somewhere beginning with D next winter. But by then I could have a one-month old baby. I grinned and shrugged.

'Same as usual?' she asked.

Fish and chips: heavens no. 'Er... spinach salad for me, I think.'

'Thought you were starving.'

'Leaving room for pudding.'

'Ah.'

Charlotte ordered and then rested her face in her hands, fixed me with Mum's hazel eyes. 'Couple of things I need to talk to you about.'

Here we go. A *lovely* friend is newly single.

'The... er... not so good one first. Father. He's been calling me.'

Every few years he would. Asking how we were doing but mainly bragging about his latest business venture, his current lady. Leaving an address that neither of us would write to.

'He *keeps* calling. Says he really wants to see us. After all this time... it's ridiculous.'

'What did you say?'

'What d'you think? There's no point, we could never forgive him for what he did to Mummy.' And what he did to *her*, although we hadn't spoken about that since the night before she left to go to uni. 'Even if we did agree to meet him, you can be sure something better would come up and he just wouldn't show. You were too young, don't remember.'

He must be about seventy now, I thought, his womanising and other excesses tailing off. Perhaps feeling his age at last. Looking back at his life and wondering what he'd missed, what could be repaired – a different kind of ticking clock.

'What did he sound like?'

'Cocky as ever. Living with some woman in Kensington – probably loaded, because he says he's pretty much retired and I can't imagine he ever sorted out a pension. Thing is, he got quite stroppy about me not giving him your number. Said he was going to track you down. Are you ex-directory?'

'Er... yes, I'm sure I am.'

'But he sounded so determined... Maybe there's some other way he can find you.'

'Would it be that bad? Perhaps I should just get it over with, give him a call and—'

'What? No Yolly. You don't want him in your life, don't even *think* of it.' She sat back in her chair and smiled. 'If you were ever thinking of moving, now would be a good time. Which sort of brings me to the next thing I wanted to talk about.'

Ah yes. My move to Jersey. Getting me away from Jeremy.

'A job's come up at the school for a flute and piano teacher. For September – hasn't even been advertised yet. Eddie's violin teacher says it's the best school she's ever worked for, and top rates of pay... She even knows a company that puts together groups for weddings and stuff... Say you'll go and talk to the head of music – I told her you were going to be over and she said she'd be happy to meet you, even though it's half-term—'

'Charlotte! What are you doing? You know I couldn't live here.'

'Well, that's the other thing, it's brilliant timing, because the lodger in the little house in Gorey moves out at the end of June... It needs completely re-decorating, of course—'

'But—'

'Simon says he wouldn't want any rent, he'd just be happy if you prettied it up and paid the bills.'

'Yes but—'

'Yolly, *think* about it. Speak to them. I could take you to see the house this afternoon, the lodger says he'll be at work. Just don't be too quick to say no.'

I looked out of the window: that huge expanse of beach, with earlier versions of Charlotte and Yolande playing, arguing, and supporting each other. Overlooked by the church where Charlotte and Simon got married, and where we'd wept together at Mum's funeral. Such a small family should stay together, she was saying. If I were to have my *own* tiny family, that closeness and support would be... But I already had closeness and support.

'Jeremy could visit, you could go over for your dance shows now and then... Please say you'll at least *look*.'

Feeling sick, but also nervous; how was I supposed to tell the difference? I sat up in bed and rested my chin on Lem's soft head, picked up the print-out of Early Symptoms. Definites: nausea, fatigue, frequent urination. Breast tenderness... well, sort of, but that could be due to frequent pummelling of them to check. Possibles: bloating (pistachios?), elevated body temperature (central heating level?) and increased sensitivity to odours (but who didn't have that in a plane?). No 'spotting' (unless I'd missed it) or 'cramping' (whatever that was). And of course no missed period – yet.

I flopped through to the bathroom. On the other hand, I could be coming down with something; George had been recovering from a tummy bug, Phoebe had run a fever. But I needed distraction to help the days flip over more quickly, and anyway some of my pupils had exams coming up. Pupils I might soon be abandoning. Another wave of nausea-nervousness: my whole life seemed to be teetering, waiting for a line on a stick to show me which way to fall.

'Stick your jacket and gloves on, we're off to the sixth form bench,' Emma said, putting on hers.

'What?'

'You've got a free. That Polish girl's in Upper Four, right? They've all gone off to the Science Museum.'

'Uh. She's got her grade five—'

'Come in on Friday and you can take her out of my double English. Come on, let's go. You did bring the Sadler's Wells brochure?'

'Er... no, sorry.'

'Yolly! Oh well, we'll just have to discuss the possibilities of the new drama teacher instead.'

'What?'

'You mean you didn't *notice*? The guy in the staff room talking about the Globe Theatre trip – which will also be whisking your little musicians away this week, I'm afraid.'

Good-looking in a neat, unexciting kind of way. A luxurious speaking voice that should have made me realise who he was. Apparently he'd been in a couple of West End show ensembles, and Emma was intrigued because that meant he *danced*.

'So how's the flamenco going?'

Not well. Tears in my lesson when Alicia said 'You're here to dance, not just learn steps. *Say* something!' Tears through Eva Yerbabuena's show – a 'tribute to melancholy', for God's sake. Flamenco had become synonymous with passion and loss. 'Fine.'

I let her tell me about the Alhambra in Granada, even though I'd already been there with Jeremy. A friend of hers had lost her virginity to an Alhambra tour guide. The same friend whose teenage son had drowned on Brighton beach after some hi-jinks, and who'd then discovered she was pregnant.

Perhaps it was the word, because that's when I felt it – the cramping. This extra symptom seemed to tip the balance of probability, and for a moment I was so excited that I wanted to tell her. But the bell would ring soon; there wasn't time to explain. I'd leave it until I was sure.

But suddenly I *was* sure. Sure I *wasn't*. Because as we stood up to walk around, I was aware of what the cramping – and the other symptoms – had been trying to tell me. It was all over the place; I'd been caught out like a thirteen-year-old. Emma gave me a hug and put me in a cab.

I dashed in to the flat as quickly and quietly as I could; I didn't want Jeremy coming out and asking why I'd come home early. I ran a bath, took off my clothes and lay in it. So much blood; maybe it wasn't just a period but a miscarriage. I lay in the bath. Tears, pain and blood: on and on, there was no way of stopping them.

A phone call. Another. A knock on the living room door, too faint to be real or relevant. I closed my eyes, let the water cool around me, drifted. Until I was back in the sea at Beauport, floating on my back like Mum had shown me how to do. If you can do that, she'd said, you

83

won't drown. And I was saying to the boy who'd jumped in beside me, just lie like this, then you don't have to drown and break your mother's heart...

'Yol?' A loud knocking on the door. 'Answer me, *please*.' He sounded angry, as he should. I'd stolen and lost his baby. 'Speak to me or I'm opening this door!' Now he was Jeremy, not Nando. I opened my eyes, cold and confused. Then he burst in and our eyes met.

'Get out!'

He shut the door. 'You look like a ghost – come out of there.'

I steadied myself against the wall and waited for the stars and blackness to subside, put on my dressing gown.

'Yol?'

'Yes, I'm coming.'

He was pressed to the door waiting for me. 'God, you're *freezing* – what the hell were you doing?' He studied my face. 'Didn't you...? You had me really...'

'Just girl problems...' I leant into him, the pain bending me over.

'I know, Emma rang, but she thought there was also something else...'

'Well, you know... one thing and another... I'm still waiting for spring, aren't I?' I tried to smile.

'Yes, and it *will* come, Yol.' He pulled back my duvet. 'Get into bed for a bit – where's your hot water bottle?' I pointed to my bedside table and before I could change my mind he'd got it out, the Boots bag falling out after it. But he pushed the bag back in and went off to the kitchen. 'And *chocolate caliente?*'

7.

calmarse *vpr* to calm down

Raining, and by the look of it had been for some while; there were torrents of muddy water gushing through every little crease in the hills above Malaga. Why hadn't we considered the weather when choosing my course? I could have been sitting in a sunny *plaza* with a freshly squeezed orange juice in Seville. But oh God no, imagine walking around and seeing posters for Nando's show everywhere.

Anyway, it had to be Granada. *Enjoy it*, Ángel had said in his email, *I know it well, my grandparents live in Monachil, not far*. He was Spanish after all. Half *granadino* in fact; something we could talk about when we met up. It was back to the original plan – the only heart-safe, responsible way for me to have a flamenco baby.

I crossed the Plaza Nueva and followed the cobbled road beside a roaring river Darro, taking in the aroma of burnt charcoal, leather and incense. I was drawn into one of the gift shops by the Moorish lamps and silky clothes, coming out with a couple of exercise books with an Alhambra tile design on the front. Then there were the terraces of the Paseo de Los Tristes, where I considered buying a *café con leche* and sitting looking over at the Alhambra for a little while. The truth was, I didn't feel up to dancing; I'd had six days of trying to rid myself of energy-sapping thoughts, six days of Jeremy stuffing food down me and making me go jogging, but my body wasn't convinced.

But I had less than half an hour to get to the school, so I forced myself up the hill towards the Albayzín area. I showed my photocopied hand-drawn map to a man with a guitar on his back, who pointed towards a steep narrow alley. I stomped up it, trying not to slip on the large cobbles, jollying myself along by imagining Joaquín Cortés and his leather-jacketed gun-carrying *Gitano* gang loping down the alley towards me. Eventually I stood panting in front of the huge brown doors of *Escuela Carlota*.

I pushed open the door into a small courtyard of plants and noticeboards, then went through a low-lit reception area to a white cave room – where everybody else was already sitting down listening to Carlota introduce her school in Spanish and perfectly enunciated English. As I expected, my fellow students were mostly very young and very female, with just two boys – English, but long-haired and tight-jeaned like the flamenco guitarists they hoped to be. Then we were asked to help clear away the chairs because we were in the dance studio for the beginners' technique class, and I had just a few minutes to get my shoes on.

Braceo: I was already struggling, wincing in the mirror at my flailing arms compared to the floating sea anemones of my four fellow students. Then *taconeo*: I'd done these feet with Alicia, albeit slower for accuracy – but the track-suited *bailaora* wanted them in *double-time*. I cheated and kept them in singles, which had me ending with the wrong foot. This was followed by arms *with* the footwork – but not for me. Then she wanted us to do the steps from one end of the narrow room to the other, *one by one*. I felt a rise of tearful petulance: this was *not* a beginners' class. I stopped and said I was tired.

I sorted out my pink nose and eyes in the ladies' and then went winding up and down all the little staircases and roof terraces trying to find my Spanish class.

'Sorry I'm late – had a dance class and then couldn't find—'

The teacher smiled but held up her hands to stop me. '*En español!*' she exclaimed, and said she and my two fellow students were happy to hear all about my *problemas* as long as I spoke in Spanish. We had to interview each other and report what we had learnt to the rest of the class. We rambled and laughed, but by the end of the lesson we had covered two forms of past tense; Japanese weddings; scarcity of work for non-Spaniards living in Granada and a clutch of expressions for *skint*; and friendships with gay men and so-called beginners' flamenco classes. According to the fumbled *entrevistas*, teacher Juana was thirty-nine and unmarried, but she looked happy with her lot; perhaps she had a gorgeous *granadino* with whom she had plans for the future.

Liz, about my age and living in Granada with her English partner, invited me back to her low-ceilinged town house for sandwiches in their hidden courtyard garden.

Then it was time for the Flamenco 'choreography' class. In the changing room I learnt that the Finnish girls had been learning for two years. Amparo had taken lessons 'on and off' for some while, and it was generally agreed that her Spanish blood gave her a head start. The frosty Scottish woman claimed to be a beginner, but Amparo pointed to her legs and feet and made her confess that she'd been teaching ballet and tap for twenty years. They all went off to practise before the lesson, but I decided to save myself, walk around barefoot enjoying the cold stone floor on my already aching feet. Then I hobbled out to the drinks machine.

Two guitarists sat near the heater in the reception area: one with a bushy pony-tail and a hooked nose, the other haughtily handsome with long black hair. A third man stood in front of the heater wearing a shabby black coat, rubbing his hands. The ungainly clattering of my shoes as I came out of the changing room had the guitarists looking over briefly before carrying on with their conversation.

The drinks machine had a number of red lights by the sugared tea or coffee options; it was going to have to be hot chocolate. I put my money in and pressed the button. Chocolate spurted into a hole. I put a cup in the machine and tried again. A pale green soup. *Bloody thing.* My last coins, an alternative Chocolate button. Nothing. I gave the machine a thump.

'Ay, *ay, ay*... what you are doing to my poor machine?' The man in the Oxfam overcoat. He pressed the chocolate button. 'You see? You upset her. She will not do anything for you now. *Momento.*' He took a key from a nail above the doorway and opened the machine, started tinkering around inside. I wished he'd hurry up. He had baby-fine mousey hair falling onto his shoulders, what the Spaniards call blonde; if it weren't for the sorrowful dark eyes you'd think he was English. Carlota went past and was saying something about a problem with the printer in the office; he said he'd come in a minute.

He closed the machine and handed me a chocolate. The drink coursed through me – not just the sugar and caffeine but the memories – and I strode into the class with as much determination as I could find.

Manuela looked more like a barrister than a dancer: mature, glasses, a frightening intensity. It looked like the teacher from the morning class had filled her in on my feebleness, because she stood in front of me and fixed me with her eyes after each demonstration; I was going to have to come up with something more dramatic than tiredness to get out of finishing this class. But something about her inspired me. Most of the arms had to go, but I tried to get the rhythm if not the steps, the feel if not the look. Like Alicia, she was a stickler for *compás*; for one of the trickier rhythms she made each of us do the steps on our own, to her clapping of the pulse. '*Fuera*' she said to three of the others. Out. Out of time. A so-so flutter of her hand to Amparo. Then she tilted her chin up in my direction to indicate it was my turn. I gave it my graceless but rhythmical all. A slight nod with raised eyebrows; I was thrilled.

Then she said something I didn't catch and left the room. One Finnish girl adjusted her strappy top and pulled at her skirt, the other released a bob of platinum hair. Amparo put a hand to her mouth and explained that a guitarist was going to accompany us. The chair was next to us, so we persuaded the other girls to swap places. Then tried not to giggle when they slumped with disappointment as the unhandsome guitarist came in. But his playing was an incisive burst of passion in the corner of the room, letting us make believe for a moment that we were *bailaoras*.

Back in the changing room I took off my shoes, the soles of my feet tingling and swollen, my calf muscles tight.

'*Compás* class now,' said one of the Finns. She picked up her timetable. 'Jav-ier Benites. '

'It's pronounced *Hav*-yair,' the Scottish woman informed us.

'Look – he plays tonight, with singer, dancers too – at the Boogaclub,' said the other Finn, looking at the week's list of recommended performances stuck to the wall. 'I think he is other guitar man... Oh, why I not sign for this!'

The others laughed, and we all agreed to meet outside the school at half past eight to go and see him at the club. We left the changing room and went over to *El Rincón*, the corner – a tiny cave room, with five little stools and a box to sit on. One of the guitar boys was telling a Czech girl from the Intermediate class about his brilliant first lesson with Javier.

The technician who'd sorted out the drinks machine came in, sitting down and checking our names against a list. He gave the guitarist some photocopies then said he was going to introduce us to the most important element of flamenco – and he was Javi, by the way. Technician, guitar teacher, taker of the *Compás* class: a versatile, indispensable member of staff. Even if far from exotic – for the romantically inclined women from cooler climes – with his paleness, bally navy jumper and worn-out jeans.

He was showing us the different kinds of *palmas*: open for a louder sound, closed for when the *cantaor* was singing. I remembered Nando clapping and tapping his foot when I showed him my *marcaje*, like he did on stage when not dancing. Sometimes preceded by that brief shudder of his shoulders that was somehow so erotic...

Bang.

I jumped and had to hold on to Amparo's arm to stop myself falling off my stool. Everyone laughed.

'Yolanda! But we call you Yoli, no?' Javi asked.

'Yes.'

'Next time—'

'It was the *cajón* – he's sitting on an instrument, look,' the Czech girl said. I knew what a *cajón* was.

'Next time,' Javi continued, 'if you are in a dream in my class, I will ask you to tell us the story. Then we can all decide which *palo* is right for it.' He was pointing to the handout showing little lines, circles and letters for the flamenco rhythms, the different styles and moods of the songs.

'Oh. Er... *lo siento.*'

'*De nada.* Is okay. Now first, very easy, I show you *palmas* for the tangos...' In four time, three different versions. We clapped while he tapped, knocked and fluttered his fingers on the *cajón*. Easy enough, except I kept forgetting the foot that had to go with it.

'*Muy bien.* Very good everybody. But now we try *Soleá.* Is very slow, profound. You know, songs about death, woman going with other man, these kind of things. We count in twelve but with *once-doce* as *un-dos.* Look at first one, see the accents: *un dos TRES cuatro cinco seis SIETE OCHO nueve DIEZ un DOS un dos TRES...* Yoli, you can count in English.'

As could the other three non-Spaniards; I'd obviously been spotted as a struggler. But it was similar to the one I'd learnt with Alicia, so I managed.

'You are all so good I can go on and show you *remate*. It is when there is a sudden *crescendo* in the rhythm, and it is a signal for the *palmas* to stop. But it has to be in the right place, all at the same time – for *tangos* on the third beat, but for *soleá* on count ten. We try.'

I knew what a *crescendo* was, but I was so intrigued by the opening and curling of Javi's fingers, the complexity and variety of his counter-rhythms, the way he could be so in time without apparently giving a thought to what he was doing, that I was always caught out.

'Yoli, you are dreaming again?'

'No!'

'*Tienes que concentrarte*, you must concentrate. Try it on your own.'

He went through several bars at a slow tempo, then teased me with little bursts of *crescendo* but carried on; the others started to giggle. Eventually there was a growing thunder of excitement from the *cajón* that seemed to reach me through the floor as well as my ears; I was swept along, clapping louder and louder, but managed to stop on count ten with him.

'*Eso es, Yoli!*' he exclaimed, to laughter and applause.

The others were sharing apartments down the hill; my 'charming' *apartamento con encanto* was in the other direction, mercifully also downhill but to the other side, into the *Gitano* alley area. I plodded along on weary legs, the cobbles hurting the sore soles of my feet through my boots. Three breed-less dogs took a worrying interest. Then I took the left fork into an even narrower alley, this one colonised by a number of multicoloured cats, eating dried food thrown out for them by the doorsteps – no bothering with paw-print design earthenware bowls here.

I stopped and looked at the map again, wondering about the second left turn I was supposed to take.

A loud bark right by my hand.

For the second time that afternoon, I jumped and nearly fell over.

'*No te inquietes. Solo juega.*'

The dog had a nasty snarl; he didn't look like he ever only played.

'Are you okay? You not find your house?' I recognised the black shoes, the slim black jeans. Looked up at him. He'd tied back the long black hair, emphasising his high cheekbones.

'Oh... you teach at the school,' I said in Spanish.

'Yes, guitar,' he said, somewhat unnecessarily given there was one on his back.

He'd taken my map and was pointing a long finger with a perfectly manicured nail at it. 'You go too far. Is back over there,' he said, then bounded off down the uneven cobbled steps as easily as a mountain goat.

I stood there for a moment gazing at the map, irritated by the fluttering in my chest; I wasn't there to break my heart over another dark mysterious *flamenco*. I suddenly felt exhausted and needed to get to this place, unpack my suitcase – which was supposed to have been picked up from the previous night's hotel and brought there – and put my feet up with a cup of tea.

I'd missed a tiny path. It took me up the side of a hill, and despite the crazy numbering I eventually found the big wooden gate mentioned on the map.

I put the key in. I needed to get this right quickly; I was desperate for a pee. Round and round one way. Round and round the other. I leant against the gate and tried again. Took it out and reinserted it, but then it wouldn't budge at all. It looked like I was going to have to run all the way down and up the cobbled steps, through the leg-winding cats and scarily nosey dogs, to the school toilet.

'Oh for fuck's sake!' I heard my ugly English ring out towards the Alhambra across the valley.

'Yoli, Yoli, I have told you before, *cálmate*, concentrate, or nothing work for you.'

Javi. These flamenco guitarists seemed to have a way of appearing out of nowhere.

'This key doesn't work.'

'Yes it works.' He motioned to me to stand back. '*Mira*, pull the door and...' He turned the key.

The door opened on to a courtyard with a plastic table and chairs on a roughly paved heap of earth at one side. Ahead was a rail-free break-neck flight of steps to a door.

'*Muchas gracias*,' I said, putting my hand out for the keys; I needed him to leave so I could hare up the steps and find that toilet.

'This one *is* a *cabrón*, if they have not fix it. Come, I will show you.'

I followed him and watched, trying not to wish it was the Joaquín-like guitarist helping me. I wondered how Javi knew about the apartment; surely he hadn't had an affair with one of the students renting it? No way, he almost certainly had a slightly chubby sweetie of an *esposa* to wash his jumpers for him.

The door opened and let out an overpowering smell of cold damp walls, but I could worry about that later.

'Thanks so much. Sorry, need to...' I dashed past him in to a little bedroom – hell – and then out again and in to a narrow bathroom. Relief. The door hadn't closed properly – perhaps couldn't – and swung open. No matter, I'd heard the front door close; I was alone. I looked around. A tiny basin: I'd have to wash my hair in the bath. Where *was* the bath? I pulled back a curtain and found a small trough. Ah. Perhaps I wouldn't mind if it wasn't so damn cold.

Check out the heating, put the kettle on, look at the bed and possibly get into it to warm up. Grotty place really, but exciting to be living like a...

He was still there. Bending over in his black coat and plugging in the heater.

'Have these at eight all the time – not ten or it stops. Very cold in here, I think nobody here since me. And Yoli, you must lock this door when you are here, not say oh-for-fuck's-sake and leave it. Somebody could get in the garden. Okay?'

I blushed. 'Yes.'

'You want that I show you again?'

'No, it's fine.'

'Oh, and one thing more. The *hervidor* is terrible, use a *cacerola* for coffee.' He put the kettle under the sink, then opened a cupboard and pulled out a saucepan, putting it on a cooker ring.

'Right.'

'Cold, but the bed is good and...' He opened the shutters on a postcard view of the faded pink walls of the Alhambra and its hillside of dark green cypress trees, all set against the distant snowy mountains.

'Oh!'

'You can see this from the garden too. The sun *will* come, maybe tomorrow or the next day.'

'That would be nice, haven't seen much of it recently. Thanks for your help.'

'No problem.'

'Better get on with my homework.'

'Oh yes. For *Compás* too, don't forget.'

'Of course. *Hasta mañana.*'

'*Hasta mañana.*'

The place to myself. I filled the *cacerola*. Then thought, how awful, he probably wanted a coffee. A jar of it, packets of tea and sugar and a box of biscuits were sitting there on the work surface; milk and all the other promised welcome pack stuff in the fridge. He'd put the saucepan on the ring, for God's sake. Oh well.

I got out my Spanish homework and school folder. Made my coffee, sat by the heater. But I wasn't thawing out; I was going to have to get into bed and do my homework there.

I went through to the bedroom: a surprisingly soft wooden double bed, a cupboard set in to the wall, a tiny desk with the same view. He'd kindly put the heater on in here too.

I got under the covers and started writing my story-showing-good-use-of-past-tenses in one of the Alhambra-tile exercise books. The past: what did I want to say about that? Most of it I didn't even want to think about. Other than Jeremy.

Jeremy. Better at least send him a text. '*Exhausted, crap at everything except maybe Spanish.*' No, that sounded very ungrateful. '*Exhausted, but having a fascinating time in Gitano land. How's the word count?*'

'*29,998! Will have a break now as Ginny is here for a few days. I want a dance demo when you get back. Have fun but take care Yol xx*'

Ginny. I'd met her once, a few years ago, but since then she'd had an uncanny knack of turning up when I wasn't there. They were probably going to the Bath Festival together. Like a couple. Having slept together.

Okay, in separate bedrooms, but I'd only ever slept in his flat twice in ten years. She'd been an aspiring novelist for one heck of a time; when was she going to give up? Like others he'd taken under his wing, she blatantly had a massive author-awe crush on him, but what made her different is that he seemed to get a lot out of seeing her too.

My phone buzzed again. *'Stop sulking you silly girl, I love you xxxx.'*

I wrote about how we first met. Started to warm up, get sleepy. Dozed for a while. Then woke up and had to turn the lights on. I needed to check a verb in the handout, but out fell the *Recomendaciones Culturales* sheet.

Shit: I'd completely forgotten about the concert. It was already gone eight, I hadn't eaten and there was all the dodgy unlocking and locking of doors to do, cobbles to go down and up, cats and dogs to trip over; I'd never make it to the school in time to meet the others.

Javi. Just because he was pale and a bit pudgy I'd not thanked him at the drinks machine, daydreamed in his class, not apologised for saying fuck on his hillside, peed without shutting the door, failed to give him a coffee for his introduction to my temperamental *apartamento* and not bothered to go to his concert. I got out his handout, swung my aching legs onto the floor. Practised the rhythms until both hands and foot were perfect. Had a go at the *Bulerías* and *Seguiriyas* to give myself a head start on the next lesson. Somehow I'd make it up to him.

8.

reparar *vt* to mend

'How was dance today?' Liz asked as we came out of Spanish. She shook her short-haired head and folded her arms as if she'd just been asked to join in. 'I don't how you can stand it.'

'Awful. And it didn't help that I had to run to it. My shower's *possessed* – squirted all over the place and then fell off the wall, just missed my head.'

'Gord! Look, here's the office – I'm sure they'll sort it out.'

The women behind the desk were discussing something with serious faces; I caught *it couldn't be much longer until she… poor Javi.* It sounded like he was losing a parent; I imagined him looking after a widowed mother, popping in to see her every day, fixing her heating and locks, and now she was dying.

'Can I help you?'

I told her about the shower. She turned to her friend behind her and then came back to me with a broad smile. 'Someone can do this for you this afternoon.'

I thanked her and went off to find the shop Liz had told me about. I trudged painfully down the dog alley, the cat alley and then straight on down to the road. It was a little cave place, giving off a pungent smell of *jamón* and old vegetables. I didn't have long – and it didn't look like I'd *need* long – but where the hell was the bread? I was about to look down the second aisle when I saw Javi there, looking at his mobile, his face almost unrecognizable with concern. I didn't want him to see me and feel he had to say hello, so I quietly picked up a dusty packet of Ryvita.

'*Señora, qué quiere?*' The deep, guttural voice of the shopkeeper, looking my way.

'*Er... estoy buscando el pan.*'

A chuckle from the other side of the aisle. Javi came round the corner, his face back to normal. 'You don't *look* for bread, you *ask* for it. *Integral?*'

'If that's brown, yes please.'

The shopkeeper disappeared and returned with a warm baguette. I thanked them and went off to my apartment, imagining Javi sitting in a similar one with his bread and *jamón*, hopefully being comforted by his *esposa*.

I was still underestimating the time it took to get back to the school. No clacking flamenco shoes and wafts of perfume in the reception area; they'd all gone in. I put my shoes on then remembered I hadn't closed the door to the courtyard. Pushing it, I saw Javi out there – this time with his mobile pressed to his ear, his face angry at what he was hearing. Or perhaps just unbelieving. Poor chap, they should let him have the afternoon off.

But later, there he was in *Compás* class. Teasing Amparo about the way she bit her lip to concentrate. Tolerating some mobile-filming of him playing the *cajón*. Then getting out his guitar and letting us do some *palmas* while he filled the tiny room with exotic chords and intricate twanging melodies. I couldn't tell him I was sorry about his mother or whoever was ill, so I thanked him profusely and told him I loved his class.

Afterwards I hung around the drinks machine comparing foot discomforts with Amparo, she in English and me in Spanish, with lots of *cómo-se-dices* and how-you-says. I liked her gentle humour, soft brown eyes and luscious mahogany ponytail; as I'd said to Jeremy, I could be gay from the neck up. I was also waiting for Javi to leave before me; I'd been a bit too gushy with my thanks after the lesson, and thought it might look a bit too keen if I walked home with him too. But the Czech girl had him trapped against the wall with her rapid Spanish and limited sense of personal space; we heard him call out to the dark guitarist as if in desperation and started giggling. Then Amparo was off to put her feet up at her aunt's, and I was going to do the same in my hopefully now warming up and drying out flat.

But it wasn't doing either; partly because I'd ignored Javi's advice and put the kitchen heater on ten, causing it to shut off altogether just like he'd said it would. The floor of the freezing bathroom was still flooded, the broken shower attachment lying like a dead snake on the floor. I kicked it to one side and flung a couple of towels into the puddle.

The heater forgave me and started working again. I took off my boots, put pink bed socks over my black tights and arranged myself on the tiny sofa, feet up in the air, a blanket over me. Bliss. I opened my Spanish book. We had to continue the story into the future. Liz had begged to be able to use the subjunctive and conditional tenses, but we hadn't gone over them yet so Juana had told us to forget contingencies, play God and get on with it.

Playing God, I thought, I'd have Nando come swooping back and marrying me, a baby arriving nine months later. But then I'd have to live in Seville – and share this fantasy with my bewildered classmates. Anyway, would occasional visits from Jeremy be enough? It was easier if I had *him* marrying me and giving me a kid. So let's see...

A knock on the door? No, just that shutter banging in the wind again. *Tendré un niño...* no, *una niña...* may as well have a girl while I'm at it.

A loud buzz. Must be the plumber. I put the top on my pen, took the books off my tummy and heaved one stiff leg off the sofa.

The door opened: Javi, carrying a plastic bag and a toolbox, guitar on his back.

'Ay, *perdón* Yoli. But why you don't open the door?'

I struggled to get my other leg down, hoping that somehow he hadn't seen up my skirt; I seemed destined to look forever graceless and stupid in front of this man.

'Sorry, couldn't get up...'

'I have to mend the shower. The man who does these things has problems. I can help, but after a time I think we all have problems, maybe sometimes he remember this...'

Oh no. He was here to sort out my shower when perhaps he should be visiting his mother in hospital. 'I'm really sorry. If you're... Look, it can wait, I...'

'No, no. *I'm* sorry. Is not your fault.' He went through to the bathroom.

'Coffee?' I called after him.

'No thank you. You do your homework.'

So perhaps he *was* a bit miffed about not being offered coffee last time. But I couldn't just treat him like an odd

101

job man, even if that was what the school was doing. I pulled on my boots and trailed after him.

He tutted at the puddle and mess of towels and I wished I'd cleared them up. Then he looked over his shoulder. 'You have to use...? I can wait.'

'No, no... I wanted to help.'

He opened the plastic bag with a knife from the toolbox, stepped into the bath. I folded my arms to try and keep warm, waiting to see if there was anything I could do.

He seemed to be ignoring me, but then he looked over and smiled. 'And your head, I need to fix it too?'

'It *nearly* fell on my head.'

'Ah. Lucky.'

Then he pointed to something in the toolbox. 'Pass me... oh...' I put my finger on one tool after another. '*Sí, eso es.*'

I handed it to him and watched him working. He'd taken off the hideous coat and rolled up his sleeves. He shook back his baby hair, his lips parted in concentration. I found myself wondering how many times a week he made love to his *esposa* and whether they had any pale, slightly chubby *niños* for their efforts. Because even though he wasn't wearing a ring he would definitely be married; he seemed about my age and they get hitched younger over here.

He looked over at me again. 'Don't worry, I *can* do this.'

'No. I mean yes, I'm sure you can.'

I started picking up the sodden towels and using a third to mop up the puddle. Then a writhing hose-snake appeared in the corner of my vision.

'Ugh!' I jumped back from it and heard him laugh.

'He wants to know you,' he said, wiggling the hose around in a way that made me laugh but I still somehow wasn't happy about. 'Needs to make friends. He sees what you did to the other.'

'He was wicked and half dead already, I promise,' I said, putting the broken hose in the bin.

'Nearly finished. It is very cold in here. Maybe I will have coffee now, if it's okay. Oh... unless you have to prepare to go out...'

'No, I'm staying in.'

I went through to the kitchen and filled the saucepan, glad that I might learn a little more about this unassuming *flamenco*.

He came through, pulling down his sleeves. 'Finished. But be gentle with it.'

'Thank you *so* much. They shouldn't ask you—'

'So you are not going with your friends to *Le Chien Andalou* tonight?'

'No, I'm feeling all flamenco'd out.' He looked puzzled; it probably didn't translate, and was a pretty daft thing to say to someone whose whole life was flamenco. 'I'm tired, my legs are killing me... I'll go tomorrow night.'

'Good. Tomorrow I have a friend playing there, and you will like the dancer. So how goes *your* dancing?'

'It's difficult. Nobody else is really a beginner, so I look an idiot. I have to keep choosing between arms and feet.'

He nodded vigorously. 'Ah... it was like this for me too, for some time.'

'You dance *as well?*'

'No, no... Well, sometimes at the end of the night.'

'You just picked it up or...?'

'A little. But I have done classes – in another school, in the evening, or everybody laughs.' He looked serious for a moment. 'But no time, at the moment.'

Of course. I got on with the coffees, put some biscuits on a plate. He sat down at the table.

'You will have a baby?'

'No! It's just something I have to write for Spanish.' I blushed, took my time getting the milk out of the fridge.

'It says here you are going to have a girl, with Khe-re-mi.'

'We had to make something up in the future tense – crazy really.'

'But what thinks your boyfriend if he read this?'

'He won't. And anyway, he's not a boyfriend. He's gay.'

I took the biscuits over and sat down. I dunked one in my coffee and we chuckled as half of it plopped in.

'Is wrong type of biscuit for that. Like Je-re-mi is wrong type for this,' he said, pointing to the word *niña*. 'If you want a baby, you need to find the right type, and soon.'

That was a bit much; I was there for healing, distraction, to make spring come sooner – and I didn't like the emphasis on *soon*. 'It's just an exercise... How about you, have you got children?'

'No, I haven't.'

An awkward silence. 'So where are you from? Are you a *granadino* or...?'

'Yoli... you were dreaming in my lesson again. I have said this, when I talked about the *Taranta*. It comes from Almería, like me.'

'Oh. So the flamenco here dragged you away from all that warmth and sunshine?'

'I wanted to learn with the best teachers.'

'In the *conservatorio*?' I'd read that there was a music college in Granada.

'No. My parents wanted me to go there but I was always *flamenco tocaor*, not *guitarrista*.'

'I missed your concert – it was so stupid, I fell asleep doing my homework.'

'Good, it was not the best. Come on Saturday, I will play for the first time with Emilio Heredia, excellent singer.'

'Yes, I'll ask Amparo.' He looked at his watch. 'D'you need to go?'

'No, I have time for another. The rehearsal is at eight.'

I got up and refilled the saucepan. So he wasn't visiting his mother tonight. Perhaps she still lived in Almería, or somebody else was ill.

'So tell me about you. No, I want to guess. You are...' He pointed to my doodles on the Spanish handout. 'An artist.'

'No. That's one, I'll give you ten.'

'*Vale*. Actress.'

'Good God no.'

'I know, *escritora*... writer?'

'No. That's what Jeremy is though. Why are you so sure I'm in the arts?'

'Always dreaming. Am I wrong?'

'Er... no.'

'Maybe something with books, it is how you have met Jeremy...'

'Four. No.'

'You don't work in an office, *administración* of arts.'

'Five.'

'Mm. Is it possible to guess?'

'Very possible. Actually, rather worrying that you haven't been able to already.'

His eyes opened even wider than usual.

'No... musician! Yoli! Why you have not told me this in class?'

'Why would I? I'm the worst in the group.'

'Only when you not concentrate,' he said, touching my arm. 'So what do you play?'

I told him about my teaching, the flute trio. He was beaming, nodding. 'You have it here, your flute?'

'No.' I was glad I hadn't; it would have reminded me of playing for Nando.

'*Qué lástima.* I could show you a little flamenco flute.'

Then I wished I had. 'You play?'

'No, but I could give you the idea of what they do. You should come to the *Teatro Municipal* next week, there is very good—'

'I fly back on Sunday.'

'Oh. Only one week? It is not enough time.'

'I'm beginning to realise that.'

He looked at his watch again. 'I should go. It will be a long evening.'

'Well... would you like something to eat before your rehearsal?'

'No, my home is only two minutes, is okay.'

'Sure? I've got eggs, cheese, tomatoes, tinned peas, pasta... and *pan integral,* of course.'

He looked uncertain. I remembered the sweet chubby *esposa.*

'Sorry, you've probably got to—'

'I'm very hungry, any of these things please. I will help.'

'Okay, you can hand me the tools.'

He did, anticipating each with hilarious timing.

Except for when I reached for the wooden spoon without looking – and put my hand on his.

'Oh... sorry.'

He let go of the spoon. But he'd gone rather still, and I found I had to stare into the bubbling pasta.

'It's okay, you don't have to become pink, Yoli.'

'I'm not.'

'You are. Come on, let's eat.'

He squeezed my hand, his fingers briefly in between mine. Those fingers that rapped out those impossible rhythms, plucked and caressed the guitar. And fixed things.

9.
mano *f* hand

Those hands. Tickling the *cajón* into life, dancing in the air when he was explaining the difference between a *soleá* and *bulerías*, pushing back his curtain of silk hair, scratching his jeaned thigh...

I'd told Amparo about him mending my shower and our coffee together, for some reason deciding to end the story there. *He squeezed my hand*: how silly would that have sounded? But she'd asked me if I wanted him, which probably meant fancied him, and I'd said he was sweet, but no. She was surprised; hadn't I noticed that he was an *oso*? Eventually translated as bear. As in teddy bear. Or bear hug. I looked at those arms and wondered...

A nudge from Amparo. Everyone was waiting, the Czech girl sniggered.

'Is all okay?' Amparo whispered.

'Are you okay with everything, Yoli, can I go on?' asked Javi.

My cheeks burned. 'Yes.'

'And Amparo?'

'Can you go over the *soleá* rhythms one more time?' she asked in Spanish, and then, when he was answering somebody else, muttered behind her hand, 'and show me your hose?'

I coughed to cover up a guffaw and saw Amparo's shoulders shaking with silent laughter.

'What is the problem with these two?' Javi asked the others.

'Make them stay back after class,' said the guitarist.

'Yes maybe, because I don't think they are in correct mood for *soleá*.'

I pretended to study my handout; the puzzled look on his face was going to set me off again. I concentrated for the rest of the lesson, but the more I tried to show him how musical I was, the more mistakes I made. Amparo and I stayed behind to go over the *soleá* rhythms.

When we came out the others were still around, waiting to catch a glimpse of a guest dance teacher for the Advanced class.

'Will we see you at Le Chien?' Amparo asked Javi.

'Yes, but I have students, I will come at about nine. You can save a place for me, no?'

A striking figure came out of one of the studios – tall for a Spaniard, and plenty of machismo and curly black hair – followed by his sweating but graceful students.

'*Muy guapo, sí?*' Javi said with a grin. 'Very handsome, and good dancer. But every time he comes he... plays with the girls and there is trouble in the office. Is not that I am jealous, of course.'

Amparo laughed and asked him something I didn't catch.

'Yes. Carlota tells him this every time, but he is big star for the school, he does what he likes. Ay, look at him now...' The Czech girl was edging her way forward

109

through the crowd. 'Poor Zuzana, I think she will be *víctima*, but what can we do.'

A cave much the same width as our studio, with a bar at the end that took ages to serve you – probably because each drink had to be served with a plate of *tapas*. It looked like nearly the whole school was there, and students from other flamenco schools too, but there were also locals and some exotic creatures in hippy clothes.

Javi took his seat, drink in hand, minutes before the young blonde *cantaora*'s voice silenced the room. There was a balding but longhaired *tocaor* and a buxom, mature *bailaora*. An odd grouping, I thought, until I saw the wordless connection between the three of them.

In the break the other girls were chatting with Javi about the *palmas*, and then he was explaining something to the guitar boys, who'd both bought him a drink. He wanted to help everyone get the most out of their flamenco course, not just the dippy blonde flute woman with the broken shower. I went off to have another go at getting drinks but there now seemed to be a policy of serving the locals first so I queued for the tiny toilet instead.

I got back just in time for the next set. The *cantaora* sang a song that so sounded like she was making it up from her own life that I could feel the start of ridiculous tears; and there was a powerful performance by the *bailaora*, her hammering feet and spinning flounces so near to us that Amparo and I exchanged wide eyes and moved our stools back.

Then another break, and another round of drinks that Amparo and I didn't get involved in. Javi had gone off to chat with the *tocaor*. I started to feel weary, probably dehydrated. I decided to walk home, said goodbye to Amparo and left.

The restaurant terraces were busy, and couples were sitting on the wall looking at the Darro or the lit-up Alhambra above them. There would still be plenty of people about on the way home; it was a good idea not to have stayed any later, I'd already had a great night.

Or had I? That blue mantle was descending. Most people call it a black dog, but mine's a shawl. I can know it's coming, I don't *have to* wear it, so why can't I just shove the damn thing off my shoulders? The trick was to put something else on before it could get there. Quickly. Amparo and I having a giggle and a relaxing soak in the Baños Árabes on Saturday, followed by Javi's concert in the evening. Liz saying she wanted to keep in touch, how I'd be welcome to their sofa for a long weekend.

I turned the corner and started up the hill. Maybe I could somehow coincide the long weekend with another of Javi's concerts...

And there he was. How could he possibly be ten yards in front of me when I'd left before him? If he'd overtaken me – quite possible really, with my blue-shawled pace – wouldn't he have said something? Perhaps there was a short-cut. But now I was going to catch up, because he was leaning against the wall, his hand to his neck. There was a group of laughing youths further up the hill; I was afraid he'd been attacked.

'Javi?'

He turned to look at me. 'Ah, Yoli... you no' enjoy...?' Eyes glazed. It took me a moment to realise he was basically just *borracho*.

'Yes, but I'm tired.' I wanted to ask him if he was alright, but thought perhaps he hoped I couldn't see that he wasn't.

'*Yo también. Pero... dolor de cabeza... migraña... sabes?*'

I knew all about migraine. 'Yes, d'you have something for it?'

He mumbled about getting home.

We carried on up the hill side by side. He didn't seem to want to talk. I started to wonder if the headache was just a cover-up for his drunkenness, but then he winced and leant against another wall, pressed his fingers in to his temple just like I always do.

'Big breaths,' I said, and took his jumpered arm. We were in the little alleys now, stumbling over the cobbled steps, finally reaching my gate.

'Where's your house?'

Slurred Spanish.

'Look, I've got some special pills for *migraña*, half an hour and there'll be no pain. Would you like one?'

He clutched his head. '*Por favor.*'

'Come on then,' I said, guiding him through the gate and up the perilous steps, surprised to hear him managing a *muy bien* as I managed each lock.

I sat him down on a kitchen chair while I went off to the bedroom to find the Naramig. Then I heard rapid heavy footsteps and the unmistakable bark of vomiting. I went through to the bathroom, covering my nose at the stench. He washed his face and gave a muffled '*lo siento*' into a towel.

'It's okay. Come with me.'

'*Lo siento,*' he said again, shielding his eyes as he followed me into the kitchen.

'Just as well, you're probably not meant to take these with alcohol.'

He swallowed the pill with a glass of water, then slumped back onto the chair, his elbow on the table, head in hand. I turned off one of the lights.

I wondered what to do with him next. It was a miracle I'd got him up the steps; I imagined trying to get him down them again and both of us falling down the lot, cracking our heads open and being found dead together in the morning. Besides, I'd given him a prescription medicine; for all I knew he might be on other drugs and have a reaction.

'Lie on my bed, I'm fine on the sofa,' I said, taking his arm and steering him through to the bedroom. He mumbled some resistance, but once he saw the bed he got onto it and closed his eyes. I took off his shoes. It looked like he'd left his hideous coat somewhere but maybe that was for the best, I thought with a grin. I put a couple of blankets over him and hoped he wouldn't throw up on the bed.

But when I went back to sort out the bathroom that didn't seem very likely; there couldn't possibly be any more to come. I got to work, mouth-breathing like Charlotte had taught me to do when changing nappies. Then crept back into the bedroom to check on my sleeping patient and extract the tracksuit that I'd been using for pyjamas.

The sofa was impossible: whichever way I lay on it gave me a stiff back or neck – not an ideal preparation for three hours' dancing the next day. I opened the door to the little bedroom; on Javi's advice I'd shut it off to conserve heat. It was like walking into a fridge, and some droppings suggested that the room had already been taken.

So then I thought, for goodness sake, what could happen? He's flat out and will be until morning. He couldn't try anything, and probably wouldn't want to anyway. So I got in next to him, bedding between us. Listened to him softly breathing.

I was nearly asleep when his warm arm came round me. I moved onto my side, fitting my body into the contour of his. Sending the blue shawl sliding to the floor.

10.
compás *m* (Mús) time, rhythm

He'd gone. That was okay, he was probably embarrassed and had left a note in loopy Spanish writing. But no: a drawer closing, the tinkle of cutlery.

He knocked on the door. 'Yoli?'

'*Buenos días.*'

'*A ti también.* Come, have breakfast now, or you have pain in the stomach when you dance.'

He'd been out: eggs, toast and some tomato paste stuff. Peach juice and coffee. And sugary sticks of *churros* with a polystyrene cup of thick chocolate.

'Wow! Thanks. How are you feeling?' I made a start on the *churros*.

'Better than I deserve.' He had a sip of juice then turned to me. 'I'm very sorry Yoli. I know alcohol can give me *migraña*, I was idiot... and then... You are on holiday, it was bad to make you care for me—'

'Well you've been looking after *me*, haven't you?'

'No, no... I want to do something. Maybe... I can make dinner for you tonight? If you have no plans...'

'Oh... Yes, that would be lovely.' A date, with this sweet *oso* of a man. Just as a friend of course, because he probably didn't know he'd put his arm round me and that I'd snuggled into him. Maybe he'd been dreaming of a past girlfriend. Or a present one. He was saying something about beans.

'Sorry?'

'Green beans.'

'Yes... I love all vegetables.' I wasn't going to put him off the idea by admitting to being ninety per cent vegetarian.

'I have some friends who will come to my home to collect some things, but I am sure they will go before eight – you can come then.'

He tore off a piece of paper from my pad and drew a map – complete with a tree and his neighbour's bird-cage in the window – and wrote down his mobile number in case I got lost. Even though he was just off the alley round the corner.

'Come on, eat.' He pointed to my box of Shreddies. 'It's okay, you can have *guiri* breakfast if you prefer.'

'No way. Maybe that's where I've been going wrong – I need a Spanish breakfast for my Spanish dancing.'

He smiled and patted my arm. '*Eso es.*'

Incredible: my feet just *did* it. Double time and *a compás*. The trick was to not think about it, just let it happen.

In Spanish, Juana said I must have had extra coffee that morning, and it suited me.

The cobbles didn't hurt anymore, I talked to the dogs and cats, smiled at the Alhambra, reached my gate and admired its ancient dark wood. Looked up and saw turquoise breaking up the heavy sky.

Bread and honey lunch. Juice and yet more coffee. Then I pressed Jeremy's number on my phone; I could remind him about his memory stick and the other things he always forgot to pack for festivals, thank him properly for this wonderful experience.

A woman's voice.

'Oh... who's this?'

'Sorry, it's Ginny. Is that you, Yol?'

'Yes.' But only Jeremy calls me that. Sometimes Emma.

'He's at his dance class. I can't believe he's gone back to the same one he used to do when we were... you know...' *What?* 'When we were at uni.'

'You were at uni together. I didn't... I'd forgotten that. So you must be off soon then?'

'Well, before the rush hour, yes. So how's it going? It sounds *fascinating* – I'd *love* to do something like that.'

So they're driving down together, in Jeremy's Noddy car.

'Yol?'

Yol*ande*. 'Yes it's great. But a week's just not long enough.'

'I'll get him to call you, he'll be back any minute.'

'Well I'm going out, I'll be...'

'He'll text you then.' I heard the *bing* of Jeremy's oven. 'Oh. Gotta go.'

'Yes me too, bye.'

'Bye.'

I put down the phone and stared at it. Okay, I thought they'd met at the Winchester festival but they'd met at uni; perhaps I'd misheard and Jeremy had said they'd *re-*met at the festival. She'd known him about twice as long as I had, but then she really only saw him a few times a year, so... so what. But there was something else, a little clutch of words that were tripping a switch, clamping my hands to the table: *when we were you know.*

No, I didn't bloody know. He came out at eighteen. For the sake of his writing, he was glad he'd experienced heterosexuality as a youth; I'd imagined fifteen-year-old fumblings, first sex in an older girl's car. But by the time he went to university he was gay – or so I'd been led to believe. I tried to remember what she looked like: thick brown hair with some grey strands, glasses, a slight squint that gave her gaze an intensity. Rather overweight but with an enviably colourful and bohemian dress sense. Twenty years ago she... But what the hell? He's absolutely gay now, I practically live with him, I *know*, so it's not as if...

I grabbed my bag and opened the door. Javi was right, the sun had arrived. I took off my jacket and went down to a plastic chair on the roughly paved mound, turned my face up to the surprising heat. Told myself to stop this jealousy thing about Jeremy, especially when I was going to be having dinner with a sweet-natured *tocaor*. My legs started to feel strong and ready to dance again.

As, amazingly, did my arms. At the *same time*. Even the dark *tocaor*'s sonorous strumming and unashamed leering at us wasn't going to put me off.

'*Mejor*,' said Manuela, fixing me with her eyes for a moment. Better. She still didn't remember my name, but I was thrilled.

The girls were planning to meet at the club again, and asked me if I was coming.

'No, I'm meeting up with a friend.'

'Oh?' said Amparo, looking up at me as she bent down to change her shoes. We made our way to the *rincón* room. 'Meeting up...?'

'He's making me some friendly beans, that's all.'

'Mm.'

'I want to sit somewhere different, not opposite him all the time.'

'Next to him?'

'No! Here,' I said, pulling her down next to me.

She laughed. 'Yoli, I think you have problem but you not know it.'

The others came in. Followed by Javi, slightly late and making apologies. Floppy hair shiny as ever. A checked shirt over a white top – a bit lumberjack, but a vast improvement. I willed myself to concentrate on the different kinds of fandangos. In three hours' time... no, listen. In five hours' time... no, that's *ridiculous*. Then he got out his guitar, cradled it in his arms and filled the room with its sensual resonance.

Eight. Time to leave, to arrive slightly and hispanically late. I'd showered and dried my hair in front of the heater. Decided against the black floral skirt that had looked *flamenco* in Islington but now looked *guiri* – and somewhat overdoing things, considering my host's wardrobe – and had put on the denim one. I'd done my homework, and shoved the stupid Ginny-Jeremy thoughts firmly to the back of my skull. I was ready.

But he wasn't. There was a heavily built man waiting arms-folded next to some old suitcases and a cardboard box; a scary woman with heavy earrings spitting out rapid, impassioned Spanish. To Javi, I then noticed, standing there in the doorway. Then a stone crunched under my foot and all the dark eyes fixed on me.

The woman was saying something about me being the answer and added something under her breath; the man looked me up and down and smirked.

Javi came forward and took my arm. 'Don't worry Yoli, they don't mean it. I will explain.'

He spoke to the woman in a fast impenetrable Spanish but then more gently, something about how could she ask this when she had seen... when she knew... The next moment they were hugging each other and the man patted Javi's shoulder. Fingers dug into my arm as I followed Javi into the apartment, but I turned and saw the woman was half-smiling and whispering 'sor-ry'.

'Come in, I will have to tell you about it, but then we can have our nice evening.'

The door led straight in to a living room with a kitchen – rather like mine but a lot warmer. And more cluttered: guitar cases, a couple of *cajóns*, a music stand and stacked boxes. We sat down with a couple of brandies on a rug-covered sofa.

He took a deep breath. 'They are the brother and sister of my wife. It is finished between us, some years, but now I left the apartment that we had and came here, I am making new start, and I asked them take her things. They are unhappy because they say I am throwing her out, and this is big shame for the family. But really they know that it has to be the end.'

'She... lives a long way—'

'She is *bailaora*, always on tour. Or in Madrid.'

A female version of Nando. 'Oh. That must have been...'

'She is proud, she would prefer that I keep our home. She was here in Granada but has not take her things...'

'She's gone?' I didn't want to be there if she hadn't. I thought of those phone calls on Tuesday; they must have been with her.

'Yesterday.'

But I'd picked out a few words of the argument with his sister-in-law. There was something he wasn't telling me. I took another sip of the sweet brandy.

'But... she said something about children.'

He winced. 'Your Spanish is better than I knew! Yes, children we did not have... Is why she give everything to dancing.'

'Oh. I'm sorry.'

There was an awkward silence.

'It was me, I have... low number. There, now you know everything.' He finished his brandy. 'But Yoli, I am okay you know. I have my new home, and it is a good time for me, maybe I will join with this excellent *cantaor* who is interested in my playing... And you are here to have dinner and fun, okay?'

We smiled at each other.

'The dancing was much better today?'

'Yes, it was.'

'*Maravillosa*. Manuela told me.'

'What?'

'After your class. She asked me what I have done.'

I put a hand to my face.

He chuckled. 'How I help you in my class. Don't worry, I have not told her of the breakfast.'

He got up and took a large saucepan out of a cupboard. Some chopped onion, tomato paste. 'Are you going to sit and become pink, or do you want to help?'

'It's just that it's warm in here compared to what I'm used to.' I stood up.

121

'Well, take off something,' he said, indicating my top with a down and up finger.

A further rush of burning to my cheeks. I started pulling arms out of my cardigan.

He put down a chopping board and came over to me, his warm hands on my shoulders. 'Look Yoli, we are here as friends, okay? Please relax.'

'Of course. I am.'

'*Vale.*'

He tore open a paper bag of long green beans and started cutting them into squares. 'You cut like this, okay?'

I nodded, pleased to be occupied.

He started on some thin pieces of ham. Of course: *jamón* with everything here, even the vegetarian dishes. He must have seen my concern.

'You don't like the *grasa*? I cut it off.'

'Thanks.'

'So you will come back to the school?' He was pouring boiling water into the pan, looking unconcerned one way or the other.

'I'd like to, yes.'

'Next year or...?'

'Yes. Maybe earlier.'

He looked at me for a moment then bent down to get out another pan.

'Perhaps with warmer weather next time,' I said. 'Can I do anything else?'

'The History and Style of Flamenco – this is a good course.'

'I meant for dinner.'

'Put these on the table,' he said, handing me some cutlery. 'Of course you would be in *Compás Intermedio*.'

'You sure about that?'

'Maybe just take one class of dance each day, more time for Spanish.'

'Yes. Well, that's the timetable sorted out. Just a question of when.'

He was frying the ham. I was surprised to find the salty smell rather appealing. I was surprised to find his t-shirted broad shoulders rather appealing. He's an appealing friend, I told myself, but I'm used to that.

'Yoli, you have to take out these from the beans, look.'

'Oh. Okay.' I started pulling off the strings.

Perhaps I could come in the summer half-term, if I could afford it. I wondered whether it was more important to splash out on a last holiday for myself or to be saving for Ángel's baby. I should have come here years ago, I thought sadly.

'*Qué pasa?*'

'Nothing. Why?'

He pushed the beans into the boiling water and winced as water splashed up.

'*Ay*... every time I hurt myself.'

'Me too.'

He tidied up the work surface. 'What about the weeks where your school is closed, after *Semana Santa?*' he asked, without looking up. *He wanted me to come back in just over a month's time.* 'Then you remember what you have learned.'

'Maybe.' We grinned at each other. *Friends.* 'What shall I do now?'

'Put on some music.' He pointed to a bulging box of CDs.

I knelt down to have a look. Paco de Lucia. Tomatito. That famous *cantaor* who died early. Other flamenco artists I hadn't heard of. One with Arabic on the front. Spanish equivalents of Easy Listening Classics. Ketama. And the entire collection of...

'Chambao! I *love* them.'

'They are popular in England?'

'I don't know. They didn't fill the Brighton theatre when we saw them, but God knows why, they were amazing.'

I put it on, their flamenco-chill and the singer's sweet voice sounding perfect in the cosy Granada apartment.

He put the dish of steaming *judias verdes* on the table, with a plate of brown and white bread and a bottle of sparkling water.

'Sorry, no wine.'

'That reminds me.' I pulled out the packet of Naramig from my bag. 'Have these and get a doctor to prescribe them for you.'

He thanked me, put his hand on my arm again. Tactile, the Spanish. But it doesn't have to mean anything; Nando had been touchy and caressing, but left without so much as a note and had probably touched and caressed any number of women since.

I took another mouthful. '*Delicioso.*'

'After, we have *arroz con leche*. My neighbour has made it, we just make it warm.'

'Sounds perfect.'

And over the Spanish rice pudding I learnt that his father was a builder and his mother and sister taught Spanish in a language school. That he liked most but not all of the Almodóvar films. That he sometimes played football on Sundays and thought Spain would win the World Cup.

Over coffee, he asked why I'd decided to take up flamenco dancing, and I told him about the break-up with David, and how the week was a consolation present from Jeremy.

'Poor Yoli, and what a generous friend.' He took another sip of coffee. 'You know, if it is difficult, you could save money... I have another bedroom, you could stay here.'

My heart thudded. 'Oh... that would be—'

'Come, have a look. It's very small, but...'

There was a single bed, with a pile of clothes and the hideous black coat that hadn't been lost after all. More boxes.

'I will have everything in a place by then.' He opened the door to a tiny balcony overlooking roof terraces and lights the other side of the valley.

'This is lovely.'

'Look,' he said coming out with me and pointing to a balcony further along. 'We could talk from our balconies.'

Like I do with Jeremy. 'And from this side you can just see the—'

'No! Not safe!' he said, his arm quickly coming round my waist.

I looked down. 'It looks fine.'

'There is a crack there, may be it is dangerous. I need to fix it, to be sure.'

His grip around my waist was loosening. But I didn't want it to. I put my forearm over his - just a friendly gesture for keeping me safe. Then he put his other arm round me and put his chin on my shoulder, his chest warm against my back. It was like being on my bed again; I wanted to push myself back into his body. I settled for putting my flushed cheek against his, but he turned me to face him, his hand lifting my face...

'Um... this is very... sudden,' I said, gently pulling back.

'I'm sorry, of course,' he said letting go. 'Don't worry, we will... practise.'

What? He took me through to the living room. Friends. But friends who... No, this couldn't happen.

'You are not walking well?' he asked.

'I keep getting cramp in my leg.'

'Cramp?'

'Pain.'

'Ah. I can help with this.'

We sat back down on the sofa.

'Put your legs here,' he said, patting his lap.

I was trying to work out how to do that without my skirt riding up. But he bent down and grabbed both legs, took off my boots. He dug his thumbs into my calf muscles.

'Ow!' But he carried on working his way down my leg, and then started squeezing and rubbing my feet. Like he must have done for his *bailaora* wife.

'You should do this every day.'

'Right. Oh...'

'Good, *no*?'

Then he pulled me further onto his lap and I was in his arms, a warmth spreading through my body. He started kissing me again, tentatively, his hand coming up under my top and stroking my back, and I realised I was going to be lulled in to believing this was all okay. Until

I was back in England, crying and alone after giving yet more of myself away.

'I should really go now, I need my sleep for all this dancing...'

A weary smile, perhaps a little sigh. 'I'll walk with you.' I put on my boots, he found my cardigan. 'Ah. I have an idea.' He went off to the little bedroom and came back with a small fan heater. 'I should lend you this before.'

We walked down the alley arm in arm. Somewhere below us one of the flamenco clubs opened its doors for a moment and released guitar and clattering footwork into the cool night air. We reached my gate and stood there looking at it.

'I come in and do this for you?'

I was quite capable of plugging in a fan heater but nodded anyway. I started fussing with the key.

'Let me, or we will be here all the night.'

'I was fine when you were—'

'I know.'

We got inside and he went through to the bedroom with the heater. After a few minutes I heard its gentle whir.

He came back. 'Tonight you don't have to sleep in your trousers.'

'Thanks, that's great. A peach juice before you go?'

'Yes please.'

He pointed to my filo. 'Do you want to look? We see when you can come.'

We sat down on the sofa and put it on my knee for us to look at together.

'What means 'TR'... oh, this is the trio?'

'Yes.' Gigs spattered over Easter and the odd Saturday afterwards. 'But with notice someone can cover for me... take my place.'

'But you lose money. Listen... let me buy your ticket for the plane.'

'What? No! You can't—'

'I insist. It's okay, I still have some money from my grandmother. She would like it, always saying forget the *bailaoras*, take a musician for girlfriend.'

Girlfriend.

'Tomorrow I will go to the Plaza and get the ticket, and you can book the classes with the office. This week here with only one TR and one rehearsal. Yes?'

'Yes...' I said, my mind whirling. 'And then it won't be so hard to leave...'

We smiled at each other. He put his arms round me and started kissing me again.

I pulled back. 'Why did you say we were just having dinner as friends?'

'I wanted to see the *reacción*.'

'And what was it? I can't remember.'

He pulled a sulky face.

'No! I didn't do that.'

He pulled me back over to him, but I needed some daylight on this, I couldn't just... Somehow we needed to end up in our own apartments. But all I'd managed so far was to get from his sofa to mine, and I was hardly giving out the right message by letting him lay me back and kiss my tummy on it.

Then he said he wanted to sleep on my bed again.

Well I think it was *on*, but it could have been *in*. Anyway, it didn't feel like there was much chance that one wouldn't lead to the other. What? It usually took *months* to get to this with a guy – but somehow it had only taken two evenings. My heart pounded. *Say something.* But I'd gone into a stupor, my brain taken over by a primal need to be as entwined with him as possible on a large soft surface; it was just a question of how to get there.

'Don't worry,' he said. 'You get ready for bed and I will make tidy here, okay?'

I went off to the bathroom and had a nervous pee, did my teeth. Took off my boots and padded through to the kitchen, put my arms round him as he washed up our glasses, then went off to the bedroom and started taking off my clothes. I considered the Tesco's pink pyjamas with a large flower-holding bear, for women who'd never grown up or weren't expecting company. I settled for the teddy top and my knickers and got under the covers.

He'd done much the same, coming into the bedroom in his t-shirt and boxers, revealing surprisingly footballery legs. He got in beside me and cuddled up.

'Don't look so worried,' he said.

'I'm not.'

'You are. What is it?'

I'm not good at this, too inhibited; I've been told enough times. And sex has become synonymous with betrayal and rejection. 'Um...'

'Is not an *espectáculo*, Yoli. Come here, just leave it to me, I don't mind...'

I started to believe him. How could I not, with his body so tangled up with mine, his hands seeming to know me better than I did myself.

'I think now we are warm enough to take away the bear,' he said pulling off my top and then his own.

And then off came our underwear too, but I was past caring, calmed by those hands and starting to run mine over him. Then he reached for something on the dressing table.

'I hate those things,' I said, wanting him back.

He looked over at me. 'Well... we don't have to, I mean...' He shrugged.

'I'm... not taking anything.'

'It's okay, nothing will happen,' he said, a sadness in his smile that made me pull him into my arms.

Then his kisses were straying over my body, on and on... so that when he was inside me it was almost instantly over. But he wasn't letting that happen, not that soon... An image of him teasing me with crescendos in that first *Compás* class came to me...

'*Rem-at-e*, now,' I finally begged and he grinned and obliged, arriving at the last beat in perfect unison.

He was still here, I hadn't dreamt it. I pushed back into him like I had before, but this time into his warm bare body. I reached behind me, but he was silent, perhaps still half asleep. So I turned over and started to run my hand down him.

But he took it and put it to his mouth. 'Wait,' he said, opening his eyes.

With a cold thud in my chest I turned and lay on my back. *No. Please. Just go, I don't want to hear it.*

He turned me towards him. 'Listen... you have to listen Yoli, because maybe you want to go to the *farmacia* and get that new pill this morning... I was wrong to say nothing can happen. It is not probable, but it can – my wife was pregnant for two months. I'm sorry, I have lie to you.'

I put my hand to his face and smiled. In fact, tried not to laugh; I'd been beaten at my own game. Egg-bandited.

'What would you *like* me to do?'

'Do you understand what I am telling you?'

'Yes. If you want me to take it I will. But... if it's very unlikely—'

'It has to be nearly a *milagro*...'

'Well... if there *is* going to be a miracle, I wouldn't want to stop it.'

His face broke into a smile. He kissed me firmly, then more gently, moving on top of me.

'We can't be long, I've got—'

'I know, it's okay, just a quick *tango* this time.'

11.
escoger *vt* to choose

'Yes... yes definitely in time for Frankfurt... Mm... Thursday? Yes that looks...'

I plonked down the iron and hung up the new orange shirt. God, he'd been getting through a few – must have been out a hell of a lot. Somehow all his other clothes were here too; you'd think I'd been away a month.

Now he was writing in his filo, grinning and talking softly so I couldn't hear. As he'd been doing earlier with poor old Vicente. If he didn't spend so much time on the bloody phone maybe he'd have time to do a bit of his own ironing.

Another one done, the standard already declining. I slammed down the iron – fucking heavy annoying thing.

He put down the phone and looked over. 'Okay. I'm sorry. If you think this married, spermless, penniless *tocaor* is the answer to—'

'There you go again! So why say you're sorry?'

'Oh Yol, come on—'

'And by the way, he's not *penniless*.'

'Euroless then.'

'Uh. He's a music teacher and in a group – just like me. Sometimes...' Earning extra on the side with mundane chores, also like me, but he didn't need to know that.

'Sometimes helping himself to one of the flushed *flamencas* clapping along to his beat.'

'Just *shut up.*'

'Look, it's great you're going out for another week, but just try to keep some perspective.'

'Oh right. And is that what you tell Andrew, Vicente and everyone else clapping along to *your* beat?' His face puckered with gratifying confusion. 'Yeah, how d'you like them apples?'

His mouth opened to protest but closed again, the corners twitching. 'Them apples are different.'

'No they're not. They're all hoping that one day you'll... *pick* them.'

Ginny: not specifically mentioned but certainly sitting there in the basket. A can of worms that I'd decided to leave unopened for now. Or perhaps I'd just make a small hole and pull a few through. Which reminded me. I held up some thick brown tights between my thumb and forefinger.

'What's that?'

'Ginny's tights. Washed and dried. What shall I do with them?'

'I suppose we could post them. But then Oxford's only a couple of weeks.'

'Oh yes. That'll be nice for you, meeting up in your old stomping ground.'

'What?'

'Where you were at uni together.'

He shrugged. If he was worried about my discovery of his lie-by-omission, he was hiding it very well. 'Hardly a reunion, I'll be working my arse off.'

Another shirt done. Come to think of it, couldn't she have mucked in and got out the ironing board while she was here? He'd turned back to his emails. The writing might no longer be on a roll, but by God his social life was. Housekeeper to an author is one thing, to a playboy is another; I've better things to do, I thought, looking at the back of his self-satisfied head. Misjudging the board and clonking the iron down on the metal edge.

'Can you stop banging that thing around?'

'*Sí señor*. I come back later. You tell me when, Mr Jeremy.'

He spun his chair round and studied my face.

'Okay. Ginny – is that what all this is really about?'

'No! And Christ, when did you get so bloody full of yourself?'

'Your fault,' he said with a smile. 'All your loving care of me. Come here,' he said, patting his lap.

'No, get on with your work.'

'Oh dear, don't tell me our little *granadino* has banned cuddling.'

'Course not. Although he asked if we did.'

'Shit, he really *is* bad news.'

'No he's not. He's the best news I've had in a long, long while.'

He watched me hang up another shirt. Folded his arms. The sentence hung in the air, undisputed.

'Feed me,' he said quietly, the Audrey Two plant from Little Shop of Horrors.

'No, you've had enough of my blood already, you monster,' I said in my Rick Moranis voice.

'Feed me!' he said, a bit louder.

I went over and we mimed the pricking of my finger, his gulping of my blood. And then he grabbed me and pulled me onto his lap.

'I *am* sorry Yol. Really. I'm just worried about you. And... for me too, I have to admit, even though it's monstrously selfish of me.'

'But we'd spend some time here as well.'

'No way, there's nothing for him here. Anyway, it wouldn't work once you had a kid... He could probably get treatment, you know.'

'Yes...' I sighed, sinking into him. Then I tapped his chest. 'Hey... maybe... you wondered about getting a tiny apartment in Granada once...'

He smiled, nodded. 'D'you know, I think I might be able to push on now. Why don't you leave all this and go and push on with that new piece before your pupils come.'

'Yes, I think I will. Come to me at half eight for some pasta?'

'*Perfecto.*'

'And no more...'

'I promise. Perhaps it would help if I met him.'

'No, he's busy with this new singer – I can't expect him to come over here.'

'Surely at some point...?'

'Well... I don't know.'

You see, I could tell he was thinking as he smiled and shrugged, *this is what I mean.*

12.
música *f* music

'So how goes your *composición*?'

'Well actually...' I moved the phone to the other hand and clicked on the file. 'It's sort of finished.'

'*Vale*. I want to hear it.'

'It'll sound much better live... being played.'

'Yes, of course.'

'And remember I'm writing it for students, so it's very simple—'

'Yes I know this. Like when I make *falsetas* for mine. Come on, put it on.'

'And it's just the *flavour* of flamenco... you know, as experienced by a *guiri*. You're going to find it really—'

'*Ay por Dios!* Start now or I don't tell you the surprise.'

'Surprise? Oh... Well here goes.'

I pressed Enter, watched the cursor bounce over the beats, heard the flawless flutes pipe up; I was still both amazed and horrified at the technology. But how wonderful to hear flutes play my piece rather than try to imagine them as I plodded about on the piano, to press Print for the music rather than pore over a smudged and

Tippexed manuscript. And the piece: it seemed such appalling vanity, but I just couldn't stop wanting to hear it. *Granada*, it was called, although I hadn't told him that. It's constant switching between major and minor – rather like flamenco – seemed to capture the cold and the warmth, the happiness and the pain of having to leave.

Silence.

'That was... beautiful. Yoli, why you don't do more of these? It is not important that the trio don't want them... Your students, they will love this. Make two more and try for *publicación*. And... maybe you can try with guitar too, very easy of course. The guitar could be played or left.'

'I don't know how to write for guitar.'

'Well...'

'But *you* could...'

'And this is what I want to tell you... *Semana Santa* the school is closed and Emilio is away... I was going to Almería all week but my family will understand...'

'You're... coming here?'

'Yes, maybe the Sunday to the Wednesday, when anyway you have rehearsal—'

'Oh yes, yes!'

'But look, it is Wednesday today, you need to go to rehearsal now, *no*? Hurry, you will be late. And I have rehearsal too. *Vámonos. Besos*, Yoli.'

'*Muchos besos.*'

I put down the phone. Just eighteen days and he'd be here. In my English life. Walking by the canal, in my flat, in my bed. I felt both elated and a little nervous. I rushed to the bus stop; being late would put me on the back foot before I even started bringing up the things I intended to say to Helen.

'Got your filo, I hope – you wouldn't believe how many bookings I've taken,' Helen said. I followed her into the kitchen. 'Great you're early for once, we can catch up a bit.'

Early? I looked at my watch. Javi must have thought the rehearsal started at seven and I'd just done as I was told and dashed here. 'Well yes, that's what I thought.'

'Kirsty's going to be late – something about waiting for Rob.'

'He's getting back later, with his new job. Perhaps sometimes we could rehearse at Kirsty's... or my place.'

Her face hardened. 'Seems a shame when there's so much more room here, and the acoustics... but maybe.'

I grinned to myself, pleased to be ticking off point number one so soon. Pudgy little arms came round my waist.

'Hi Sophes.' But she was looking at the floor, eyelids pink. 'Hey, what's up?'

'She's given up Multisports. Or rather they gave *her* up.'

'Oh. Well what else is on offer... swimming?'

Sophie shook her head vehemently and hugged her ample self.

'Dance?'

'Ballet, yes.' Sophie pulled a face and Helen mouthed *can you imagine*.

'Well what about... You know that dance show on telly with those sparkly dresses you liked? You could do Strictly Come Dancing type dancing.'

'They don't do that,' said Helen.

'Somewhere will.'

'Yes, like the American Smooth,' asked Sophie, trying to waltz round the kitchen.

138

'Not very aerobic,' said Helen.

'You kidding? All the celebs are dying to go on it to lose... er... to get themselves feeling good.'

Helen said she'd look for a class and we left Sophie getting her colours out to design a dress.

'So how was the flamenco?'

'Really hard at first, but incredible. And...'

'You found someone?' As if I'd been flicking through people like a pack of cards.

'I've now got a boyfriend, yes.'

'Great! Where does he live and can he do a sexy *paso doble*?'

'Er... Granada. And I don't know, but he could probably do one on the guitar.'

'Granada? Is he coming back to England or...'

'He's Spanish. He'll come over when he can, but he's in a group, two now actually... so sometimes I'll go there.'

'But you're also in a group, Yolly.'

'Well obviously I'll try to avoid missing the gigs. But I wanted to talk to you about this... I mean, especially now we're getting so booked up, I think we should make sure we've got proper cover. You know how often one of us has had to play with a streaming flu... Maybe we should recruit a couple of part-time members who we can call on occasionally.'

She finished her coffee, opened her filo. 'So come on, when are you going and for how long? Presumably that's what you're working up to telling me.'

'No, I've thought this for a long time. And it's not just me – Kirsty's finding it increasingly difficult... I wouldn't be surprised if she quits once she's off maternity leave.'

'No, she *wouldn't*.'

'She might. And what about you? You're forever talking about winter holidays with the family but they seldom actually get booked, do they?'

She nodded slowly, agreed there was no harm in asking around.

I flicked over another page in her filo. Two more gigs had landed in the week I was going to Granada.

'*All* that week?' she asked.

'Yes. Sorry, but...'

'Well, we've got a bit of time. I'll see what I can do.'

A weary Kirsty arrived, perking up when we told her about our plan. Then we got our diaries out to write down the dates of the new bookings.

'It's ever since we got the new website,' said Helen. 'A stream of emails, calls and letters. Ooh – which reminds me. Yolly, you've got some fan mail.'

'What? Oh, not that funeral director guy again, *please.*'

'He's sweet, it'll be different when you see him in a pair of jeans,' Kirsty said.

'Ah, but she's spoken for now, haven't you heard?'

Helen filled her in and I watched Kirsty's enthusiasm wane, probably anticipating that I would soon be going through yet another bout of gig-missing heartbreak.

'Well at least answer him this time,' she said, as Helen pulled out an envelope from her new TRIO folder. She put her finger on the postmark. 'Oh. Can't be him, it's from round here. Come on, Miss Yolande Martin, let's find out who your new admirer is.'

She handed it over. Or rather *them*. Two letters addressed in the same slightly wobbly ink.

'Bit of a cheek, just assuming I'm a Miss.'

Helen and Kirsty started discussing the likelihood of someone noticing my ringless finger while I was playing, or from the website photographs. But their voices had become a background hum blending with the ringing in my ears.

It was Father.

13.
librería *f* bookshop

I could change buses and go and have a look at his place in Kensington. But what was the point? It wouldn't be *his*, nowhere ever was; Father was a chameleon, assuming the style of his environment. My feelings were equally changeable: deciding not to write back, composing a letter in my head, then wondering what I wanted a father for anyway.

Mother's Day. I should have been thinking about *her*, not him. Jeremy and I usually spent it together, celebrating our Mums with things they'd liked. Fawlty Towers. Shepherd's pie. Cream tea. Chrysanths. Elvis Presley. Nineteen fifties' Monopoly with metal figures and a yellow-sellotaped board. But he was helping with another mother's day; a friend's wife had gone into labour early with their second child and he'd been drafted in as an emergency and presumably last-resort babysitter. He'd texted me about it during the previous night's gig, and I was still a bit miffed that he'd declined my offer to come over and join him when I finished. What the hell did he know about looking after a three-year-old?

Helen had said, never mind, go and have one of your Sundays at Foyles tomorrow – we could do with getting hold of the Scottish stuff before Monday's rehearsal, and you can see what else we might add to our repertoire. Good idea, I'd replied, immediately thinking how I could also look for flute-guitar duets to play with Javi, a new Spanish course, some novels I wanted to check out. And perhaps something on male infertility.

I was dressed for the mission: hair in plaits, tracky bottoms for sitting on the carpet, thin floppy top for the Foyles climate, rucksack for stowing purchases from each floor before moving on free-handed to the next. I looked up and smiled to myself: five fantastic floors of fun. I took the lift to the top.

The volume of twee but essential Scottish traditional music, a promising new book of movie themes, and – oh my God – an arrangement of excerpts from Carmen. I moved on to the Guitar Plus drawer. A collection of famous classics, with a cover showing a flute leaning wistfully against a guitar. And *Salut d'Amour*, with a shaggy-haired guitarist and a long-haired flautist girl on the front...

'Love's greeting, eh?' The dark curls, the Sunday morning stubble, the darting blue eyes behind the glasses: so familiar but now so alarming.

'Oh... hello!'

'How are you doing? What a lovely surprise.' He put his phone away, kissed each of my cheeks. 'So what d'you say, buy these now and go for a coffee, or spend a bit longer here and make it lunch?'

'David, I'm sorry but I've really got quite a lot to do, so...' I forced a smile.

'There's that Italian round the corner—'

'No, I'll... er... get these and take a break.'

'Come on then.'

We queued to pay. He tapped the guitarist on the front cover. 'For you and your chap?'

'Helen told you.'

'Are you sure he can actually read music?'

'Of course he can, he *teaches*.'

'I thought these flamenco guys just made it up as they went along.'

'There's a lot more to it than that, I can assure you.' I moved the pile of music to under my arm.

'Really. You're an expert now I suppose, having done the course... not to mention the concurrent private instruction.'

I put my card into the machine. He was looking me up and down, probably appalled at my backpacker appearance. I should have been countering with questions about the musical ability of *his* new lover – some kind of doctor, Helen had said. Apart from an inexplicable relief that he hadn't taken up again with luscious Lucy, I didn't really care. But we were going to have coffee and no doubt I'd hear about it whether I did or not.

'Sorry, don't mean to make fun,' he said, looking at me over his glasses. The cute penitent look.

'I wouldn't worry, everybody else does.'

'Here for one of your Foyles buy-ups?'

'Yup.' We took the lift to Floor One, walked through the Cookery section where we'd once chosen a book for his sister.

'I came with you one time, remember? Caved in after a couple of hours.'

'No, you stayed – just spent the last bit in the cafe.'

'Yes. Sat here actually,' he said, taking me to the corner table. 'Chai latte with soya?'

I smiled and nodded, then glanced at my watch under the table; I still had nearly four hours, but in the time-shrinking medium of the place that was nothing.

He sat down and asked after Jeremy, Charlotte and the kids, where I thought the Trio was going. I learnt he'd been covering for the Principal Clarinet and hoped to take over when the guy retired, how he'd cut down on his teaching to give himself more free time.

Silence.

'That's good, gives you more time for...'

'Vanessa.'

'How did you meet an audiologist?'

'An *ophthalmologist*. She's the mother of one of my juniors.'

'Oh. Divorced?'

'Yes. Two kids, a full-time job and a great musician. A busy lady. And what with all the orchestra dates, it's not easy.'

Probably just the way he liked it. 'But you're happy.'

'Yes. I suppose I am.'

We sipped our drinks. There didn't seem to be much more to say. But then he put down his mug and patted my arm, smiling. 'Yolande. So good to see you – really didn't believe you'd be here. What happened to the Mother's Day ritual with Jeremy?'

'Postponed. He had to...' He *didn't believe*...? Helen. I looked up from my drink.

His hand went to his mouth. 'Okay, she told me you'd be here – and we all know that means the entire day.'

'You could have just rung.'

'There's never an answer.'

145

'Yes there is.'

'Only to texts.'

'No, I spoke to you—'

'When you were teaching, said you'd call me back later.'

'Oh. Yes, sorry about that.' Several weeks ago, when I was preoccupied with my fantasy pregnancy.

'You've never really given me the chance to—'

'Oh, you don't have to—'

'Yes I do.' He leaned forward and lowered his voice. 'I've never cheated on anyone before, and I'm so sorry - really staggered - that it was on you. I still can't believe it happened.'

'It's okay, we—'

'It's *not* okay.'

I began to wonder where this was going; he'd apologised, we were both happy with other people.

He put his hands together as if in prayer. 'Yolande... Can you ever forgive me?'

'I do. Really.' I briefly put my hand on his. *We all make mistakes*, I wanted to add, thinking of Nando.

'I couldn't give you what you wanted... and I suppose when you're scared... But Lucy - what *was* I thinking?' He sat back again. 'And are you sure you're not doing the same with your guitarist? You can't honestly think there's a chance you'll go off to Granada, leaving the Trio.'

Aha, Helen's little messenger; they went back a long way, he would do anything for her. And, of course, the God of Music.

'I don't know. It's too soon to tell.'

'And let's not forget Sadler's Wells, Covent Garden, this place. And Jeremy - could you actually survive without him?'

I folded my arms and considered walking out. Up just one floor to Languages, where I could stand in front of all the red-and-yellow Spanish courses, just the sight of them conjuring the reassuring warmth of his hug.

'I'm sorry. Out of order again. I think what I'm trying to say is... don't do anything rash. And... I don't want you to go. I want to be able to see you.'

I smiled, wanting to ask how Vanessa would feel about that when they already had limited time together. I quickly assumed it wouldn't happen.

'Priscilla Queen of the Desert's on at the corner,' he said.

'I know.'

'Seen it yet?'

'No, I keep trying to pin Jeremy down.'

'Well why don't we go instead? A friend of mine's in the orchestra and can get us good seats with a few days' notice.'

'You *hate* musicals.'

'Vanessa's been educating me – getting me to relax about the indifferent singing and just go with the schmaltzy flow and spectacle of it all. Apparently this one's amazing.'

'Wouldn't she—?'

'She'll understand. She's off to a conference at the end of April, how about we go then? A treat to mark the beginning of... well, being friends.'

I wondered how good a friend I could make of a guy who had cheated on me, however sorry he was, but he'd given up his Sunday to ask me this and was biting his lip waiting for a response.

'Is that a yes?'

'Okay.'

'Great. And are you ready for lunch yet?'

I probably was, but the shock of our meeting had taken its toll on my energies; I'd had enough of him for one day. I said I needed to press on, but he wanted to look for some music so we went back to the top floor together.

The Guitar Plus drawer was out where I'd left it, but I didn't want any more comments so I got started on the list of music for my pupils.

I took off my rucksack. 'Why's it so bloody hot in this place?'

'It's fine over here. Bit cold actually,' he said from behind a wall of drawers.

'What?'

'No really, come here.'

I went round to where he was. He was looking through piano music, for some reason.

'Here,' he said, pointing in front of him.

I stepped forward into an isolated polar blast of air con. 'Bloody hell, it's like standing in a waterfall!'

'Ssh! Our secret,' he said. Arms came round me, his hug bony and tense compared to Javi's. 'Sorry, just had to,' he said into my neck. Then he put his hand to my face...

'No,' I said, pulling back.

'Sorry. Well, that's the ground rules laid – hugs but no kisses.'

'That's right, and you're going to have to let me get on now.'

'Okay. I'll be in touch. Take care.'

He picked up his music – probably a duet for him and Vanessa, I then realised – and went off to pay.

Unless I counted Christmas messages from Steve in Manchester, I'd never stayed friends with a boyfriend; the hurt had always been too great, along with the mortifying realisation that the person I'd fallen for was actually a right bastard. But David had gone out of his way to apologise and explain himself; he really was the sensitive guy I'd thought him to be, so perhaps I was at last showing some discernment. Our friendship would be awkward, but I couldn't help feeling it was rather grown up to be trying. Perhaps we should have just been friends all along; we were so different.

Take music for an example, I thought, picking up a volume of Tchaikovsky themes that would have made him gag. He was a devoted apostle of classical and contemporary music, his playing flawlessly respectful; I was a user, needing music to enhance or soothe, provide a backdrop to my condition or a narrative distraction away from it. *What does this make you think of?* I would ask my pupils. *Never mind the boring title, hear it as a wordless song, a film score.* My playing disobediently departed from the dots, my tempos reliable but frequently mine. Then there was the physicality: I was addicted to the feel of the silky silver keys under my fingertips, the way the phrase-end use of my diaphragm-pressed lung felt like the depth of a sob, the last heave of a laugh. Musically, I was a hedonist. I pictured Javi cradling his guitar, plucking and stroking those strings; he was the same.

Javi. I went down to his section and pulled out the shiny next level of my course and a Spanish crossword book. Heaved a huge dictionary onto the floor, looked up some of the swear words Javi had taught me and put it in the pile.

Then it was back down to the cafe for a panini lunch on a wobbly wooden table. Not David's kind of thing at all. I looked around the room at my fellow book buyers and found it was like everywhere else – people in pairs. Why would anybody want to come here in tandem? *I'll meet you in Gardening/Travel/the cafe in half an hour*: how bloody annoying. Strange I'd never come here with Jeremy, though.

Jeremy. Down another floor to Fiction. Although *I* knew that much of *Cádiz* and *After Lorca* wasn't. He was always on the bottom shelf, where I could crouch down to run my finger along until I reached Webster. As his mum used to, she'd told me once. Yes, both there. I pulled out *After Lorca* – I'd lent it to David and didn't like to be without a copy – and turned to the last page. *Thanks to Yol Martin...* How many times had I bought one of his books? Enough to stop telling the cashier he was my best friend, but not enough to stop grinning throughout the entire purchase.

Stairs were the only way to descend to the Minus One floor. Inevitably. Reverentially. Mind, Body and Spirit, but particularly body: the medical floor. It even *smelt* medical, slight damp fusing with new-book acidity to produce a hospital aroma. The most important floor – life and death, and holding up all the others – but denied the relative luxury of the backless seating above; a middle-aged academic squatted to decide between two hefty tomes, two women were camping out on the floor by Alternative Medicine.

Childcare and Pregnancy. Not for me this time the excruciating beauty of the developing foetus, the glimpses of the welcome problems of late pregnancy, wakeful babies and toddler tantrums.

My phone buzzed. *'Remind me again why you want one of these?'*

'Put him in front of a DVD. How's mum and baby?' I texted back.

'Tried that. It was gruesome but they're fine now. It's a girl thank God, they don't need another of this type. Should have agreed to your offer.'

'Yes,' I replied, adding a smiley face.

I took off my backpack, snapped off some of the emergency chocolate and scanned the shelves. *The Complete Guide to IVF.* A book by the TV Winston guy. A very pink *Female Infertility.*

I moved along to a much narrower section dealing with the other half of the procreative experience, with titles like *Night of the Living Dad, The Modern Dad's Dilemma, The Bloke's Top Tips for Surviving Pregnancy* and *Making Sense of Fatherhood;* I appeared to be correct in my impression that most men were unwilling and befuddled participants.

This, of course, is the ultimate narrative: how a woman gets a man to give her a child. So the life energy can push forward, on and on. And how sometimes it doesn't – even, so unfairly, for the men who want and deserve to be fathers.

I went back to the female section; I must have missed something. Or maybe I was in the wrong place altogether, like looking for a book on malnutrition in the Cookery section. But wedged between two fat copies of *What to Expect When You're Expecting,* there it was: *Infertility.* A slim, blue pictureless cover. *Very* slim, as if there wasn't much to say. Inside, a black and white picture of three smiling but sensible lady consultant authors. They *did* have plenty to say, just in rather small print. I sat down on the carpet for a desperate skim read... and smiled to myself; it looked like Javi still had a chance of featuring – starring – in a story of fatherhood. And I might one day have to decide whether Mitch should miss out on being a grandfather as well as a father.

14.
papá *m* daddy

Father. Daddy. As in *when Daddy comes you could show him that*. But Daddy often missed the show, Charlotte and I waiting around in our party dresses while Mummy tidied the house and prepared something yucky for dinner that he'd seldom stay for. If he did turn up he'd call himself Papa. As in *Papa's missed you, ma chérie*.

Father, Daddy, Papa: he wasn't really any of these. Charlotte said he might not have even had a part in her creation anyway, with her dark hair and fine features. I said Mummy wouldn't have *done* that; she said, no, but she wished she had.

I leant against the plane window examining the ends of a lank bunch of hair before pushing it behind my ear; no such let out for me. I often wondered how Mummy could have loved me so much, my blurred features and pale hair a constant reminder; my inattentive music-filled head a frequent and familiar concern. Only once, when I'd asked to take up the saxophone to join a friend's band, had she looked at me in horror and said *no*. I could borrow Uncle Tim's, I'd said, reminding her that she wouldn't have to ask Grandpa for help with the expense, and that not all band players ended up... well, like *him*.

What *was* he like? All I had were a few scenes, but I could still hear his voice – clipped and hesitant, as if he was forever trying to find the right word. As well he might have been; he was trilingual – English, Dutch and French – and, according to Charlotte, not fluent in any of them. Nor in music either, it would appear: a singer-songwriter, drummer, lead and bass guitarist – but switching between them, and between bands, and, apart from a brief entry into the bottom of the Top 40, never achieving any real success. Anybody else would have given up – would have had to – but apparently Jean-Michel 'Mitch' Martin always had a sponsor. A wealthy, female one, willing to take him on in return for enjoyment of his irresistible butter-blonde appeal. Until, presumably, they discovered their enjoyment was not exclusive, or was marred by the drink and other excesses, and he had to move on.

But that was later. Mummy never asked him to move on; he just left. His visits became increasingly infrequent and unreliable, until Charlotte, off to university, said we were old enough to decide not to bother with him anymore.

The Corbière lighthouse and the wide yellow beach of St Ouen's came into view; perhaps Father had looked down and remembered family outings there when we were little, wondering if Mummy would allow him to take us there. Now it was Charlotte vetoing his plans.

I pulled the letters out of my bag.

My Dear Yolande,

How wonderful to see you after all these years, beautiful, looking so happy holding your flute. How I would love to hear you play.

Yolette, I don't want to waste any more time, we have to put the mistakes of the past behind us and try again, before it's too late.

Call me or write, please.

Affectueusement, Papa.

The mistakes. Shouldn't that be *his* mistakes? But perhaps... I took out the other one, written just four days later; never a patient man.

My Dear Yolette,

Don't listen to Charlie, make your own decision this time.

Come for dinner. Judy is looking forward to meeting you almost as much as I am. If it is easier for you, bring a friend.

But call soon, because on 6ᵗʰ April we are away until 10th June. Please, ma chérie.

Charlie and Yolette: I'd forgotten about them. I folded the letters and put them deep inside the side pocket of my bag; perhaps I wouldn't show them to her after all. I'd tell her he'd written, but reading them to her would make her think I was contemplating a reply.

'It's like summer,' I said, stretching out on the woolly rug.

Charlotte finished sorting out a sandcastle power struggle. 'Auntie Yolly will help you with the finishing touches, just let me have some time with her first okay?' she yelled to the kids.

Eddie and Phoebe looked over and smiled; George took the opportunity to grab the larger spade. If it had happened, Javi and I would have had a gentle child like Eddie. Or Sophie. Phoebe was cute but self-centred – arguing about the chocolate duck I'd given her not being as big as the boys' chocolate bunnies, for heaven's sake – and a bit of *une princesse* with all that swishing back of the

155

hair. But that could be Simon's fault, having a limited but over-indulgent input. Javi would be a more hands-on *papá*, changing nappies without a twitch of the nose, winning over a stroppy toddler with a joke and some physical play...

'Yolly?'

I opened an eye.

'Thought you'd nodded off. So come on, how it's going? When's he coming over?'

I turned my head, shielded my eyes from the sun. She was smiling down at me.

'D'you know, I can't tell you how nice it is to hear some enthusiasm – everyone else is so damn cynical or anxious for me.'

'Well Jeremy's bound to be worried – how would he manage without you? Don't get me wrong, I'm not chuffed about the possibility of you ending up in Granada either, but you haven't seemed this happy in ages. So is he coming over or...?'

'Both. In fact he'll get in to Gatwick just after I do on Sunday, so we'll go home together. Then I'm going over on the eleventh for a week.'

She nodded and grinned. 'So... I know I shouldn't ask, but... how quickly could he get divorced from his wife, having been separated for so long?'

'Oh, I dunno.'

'Haven't you Googled Spanish divorce laws?'

'No.' Why hadn't I? All I'd done was look up Violeta and regretted allowing her beautiful arch-backed image to make an imprint on my brain. 'It's not important yet.'

'Well...'

'Look, just for once I'm not thinking about it too hard. Probably where I went wrong with all the others. He just makes me feel good, and that's enough for now.'

She patted my arm. 'Quite right, I'll shut up.' Then she lay down next to me, propping herself up on her elbow so that she could still see the kids. She leaned over to me.

'Makes you feel good, eh?'

'Yes.'

'So... he's good, is he?'

'Oh for God's sake,' I said without opening my eyes.

'No Yolly, I think... it's another thing that might not have been right with the others.'

'How do *you* know?'

'Sisterly intuition.' She nudged me. 'Well? Am I right?'

I put a hand to my face. 'Okay, yes he is. But end of discussion.'

'God I shouldn't have had that,' I said, hauling myself out of the car.

'Sorry – beach and pizza's become a bit of an Auntie Yolly tradition.'

'Hey you lot, take some of the stuff,' I shouted after the kids, who were running off without carrying anything in. They ignored me, just like they did their mother; she really needed to make them help more. But then maybe it's easier to get that sort of thing right when you've only got one, which is probably all Javi and I would have.

'I'll make amends and give you a salad for dinner. Got to have you looking good for your *señor*. What does *he* look like by the way, you haven't said.'

'Big brown eyes, quite tall, fair...'

'*Fair?*'

'Apparently there might have been a Dutch great-grandfather.'

'Oh.'

'I know, bit of a coincidence, eh.'

'And it didn't put you off.'

'What? We can't write off the whole Dutch race.'

'Suppose not. Anyway, it was probably the French side that was to blame; apparently *grand-père* Martin was a right sod.'

'Oh?'

'Left him and his mother when he was about the age we were when he left us.'

She handed me a mug of tea and I followed her out to the patio, sat down and admired the daffodils and forsythia, the cows looking over at us from the next-door field.

'So he hasn't tracked you down yet then.'

'Well... he's written to me through the Trio website, Helen's address.'

She shook her head. 'And did you reply?'

'No.'

'What did he say, exactly?'

'Oh... the usual stuff, do let's talk bla-bla.'

'Perhaps he thinks you might come in with him on his latest stupid business venture... something to do with the Trio, maybe.'

I'd Googled and discovered a recording studio and rehearsal room in a Fulham mews; perhaps she had a point. 'I thought you said he was shacked up with some wealthy woman.'

'Maybe he wants to impress her, needs to act out the caring father. Believe me, there'll be an ulterior motive.'

I started to feel rather weary, and dug fingers into my pelvis in the usual futile effort to stop the ache.

'Can I have a couple of those co-thingumies? My tum's completely clenched.'

She went inside and came back with a fizzing glass.

'Shouldn't be this bad if you're on the pill. You *are* on the pill, aren't you?'

'Of course.' Well, since yesterday.

'Then you should see someone. Can't be right, Yolly, every time you're here you're bent double. I've got a friend who was like you, same age, and she went—'

The boys charged past us, waving foam swords.

'Get Javi some treatment and have one of those,' she said. 'That'll sort you out.'

'Hang on, I've only just met him, remember.'

'Yes, but I can tell there's something serious here... The only thing that worries me is you're on such a high you'll go and do something stupid like agreeing to see Father. He might start pestering Helen, coming to her house... you'll end up giving in.'

I swallowed the medicine, pulled a face.

'Remember, if it wasn't for him, Mummy would probably still be with us. Think of that,' she said.

'You can't *give* someone multiple sclerosis.'

'Autoimmune diseases can be caused by stress.'

'But she got it years after he'd left.'

'Probably started long before she was actually diagnosed.'

'Well we don't know that, do we?'

Charlotte folded her arms, her mouth hard. The real reason she couldn't forgive him hung in the air, a door we didn't open.

She got up. 'It's getting cold out here, I'm going in.'

'Can I come in too?'

She looked back, then came over and put her hand out, pulled me up from the chair.

'I'm sorry,' she said. 'Don't let's argue about this. It's up to you, I know that. Just be very, very careful.'

'I will.' I gave her a squeeze. 'I'll just take my bag upstairs.'

She apologised about some extra furniture, something to do with having Marie-Claire's room decorated while she was away. *Just be very, very careful.* She'd said this before, many years ago. One of the random phrases from my childhood. I climbed the stairs, looked out of the window at the boys laughing on their climbing frame...

I was going to the play park with Daddy. Papa. Charlotte was staying at home with a friend, considering herself too old for it. Papa and I drove to the place with the really scary tall slides, and the roundabout thing that could be lovely if there wasn't always some boy spinning it dangerously too fast; I was going to be very careful.

But when we got there Papa wouldn't let me go in; he didn't like the look of some of the big lads on the swings, *you could get hurt*, he said. So we went for a walk by the reservoir instead, and he helped me climb a knobbly tree, finally shoving me up by my bottom to the thick Jungle Book branch, where I sat dangling my legs. A girl Mowgli fighting off the snake; Tarzan's little sister, escaping the panther trying to catch my feet with his paws...

Later, she asked me if he'd touched me. You know, *down there*. I thought, well yes, I suppose he did. He pushed me there to get me up to the branch. Then it had come to me that perhaps it wasn't right. And much worse, perhaps it wasn't right that I hadn't minded...

I flung my bag onto the bed. I had to stop thinking about Papa. Father. It was all so long ago now, how could it possibly matter? Unpack, get downstairs. Play with the kids, help Charlotte with the garden. I unzipped the bag and lifted out a clump of clothes, turned to put them in the usual chest of drawers. But it wasn't there. It had been moved into the corner to make space for some hulking mahogany pieces I hadn't seen for a while: a dressing table, Mum's old bureau, a wardrobe. *The* wardrobe.

Smaller than I remembered, and the keyhole had been replaced by a near-matching knob. I opened it: the same mournful squeak and dark-woody smell. I half expected to see Charlotte's blue school pinafore and blazer, but now it just held a few ball dresses and a witch's costume. I closed it...

I could hear our cousins running around the landing choosing somewhere to hide, Papa's voice downstairs counting backwards – thirteen, ten... he'd had a lot of wine at lunch.

'Quick, lock me in,' Charlotte said, crouching there under the skirts and dresses.

'Why?'

'He mustn't find me, not when he's like this.'

She pulled its door closed. I wiggled the little key from side to side. I wanted to ask her how to do it but I was suddenly alone. Then I jumped as she banged on the inside of the wardrobe door and shouted something about the bedroom door key too.

'Why?'

'Because I don't want him locking it anymore.'

'Why does he—?'

'Come *on* Yolly, hurry.'

Then I got that thing that happened at school: I was listening but the words would jumble, I'd separate the words but lose the order. I looked at the key in my fingers, and over towards the bigger one in the bedroom door. I turned the little one round in one direction, then round in the other. Just as I was wondering how I'd know if it was right, it came out in my hand. That's it, I thought, I had to take it out, that's what she'd said. Now I just had to do a lock with the big key. I went over and held the door in one hand and twisted the key with the other until it made a click. Then I dashed out onto the landing after a beckoning cousin, the door making a rebounding bang behind me.

Later she must have found the wardrobe key, slipped from my sweaty fingers, and replaced it. Taken out the bedroom door key and got rid of it herself. *Much* later. After the game, after Papa had found her and... And after she'd grabbed my arm and asked me *why can't you just listen, Yolly, why didn't you lock it, you're such an idiot.*

'Oh no... Why didn't you say you wanted a lie down?' She was unpacking the rest of my things, lifting the bag off the bed and sitting next to me.

'No, I'll come down, the pills are going to kick in soon.'

'We'll put you on the sofa with a hottie. I can watch the kids from there and show you the DVD of the school play – but you'll have to hold on to your tummy, it's hilarious.'

We went downstairs, sighed and laughed at Eddie's heartfelt Mayor of the Munchkins, George's hyperactive monkey, Phoebe vainly swishing her green skirt but forgetting to sing. I sank into the squishy sofa, lightheaded and wondering if they did the Wizard of Oz in Granada schools.

'Oh... is that your phone?' Charlotte asked. I looked at my watch to see if it could be Javi. 'Kitchen? Stay there, I'll get it.'

She came back with it to her ear. 'Yes, that's what *I* said... well, she's perking up now.' She handed me the phone. 'Guess who.'

'I've been trying all day, Yol. Are you alright?' Jeremy.

'Course I am. How's the festival?'

'It's great but... I'm ready to come home now.' He asked me again if I thought my periods were normal, was I sure I didn't need to see a doctor. I gave him a string of yeses.

'Haven't you got to give a Masterclass in a minute?'

'At three, yes.'

'Well stop fussing about me and go and get yourself ready.'

'Okay. But Yolly, you've forgotten about Romeo and Juliet on Tuesday, haven't you.'

'Oh *no*...'

'Don't worry, I'll give my ticket to Javi if you think he'd like to go. Presumably he's never been to a ballet.'

'Are you sure?'

'Well I can hardly take you off to it and leave him on his own, can I? Call it making amends... I'll see you Sunday night then – oh no, better leave you two to er...'

'We'll come and see you some time on Monday.'

'Okay. Look after yourself.'

'You too. Bye now.'

Charlotte shook her head. 'Tell Mitch you don't need a father in your life – you've already got one.'

15.
problema *m* problem

Three nights, four days. Exactly what we'd had in Granada. Javi had planned a tit-for-tat length of stay, as if we were a couple of teenage exchange students... *What's the matter with me? I'm lucky he's coming at all.* Must be these hours of jitters and cold. I squinted up at the board: still delayed. *Atrasada.* No, *atrasado*, a plane is a boy.

'Another?' The café guy pointed at my soup-bowl mug.

'Go on then. Might as well.'

And it'll give him something to do, I thought; everybody else seems to have winged off, arrived, or got who they were getting. Hm, story of my life. But hopefully that was to change. Four days. Counting the hand-squeeze shower-fixing evening, perhaps you could call it five. But still very few. I'd been so busy pondering the future with Charlotte or defending our relationship with everyone else that I'd rather lost sight of that.

A reassuring buzz in my pocket. But it was Jeremy.

'*Are you alright? Did he miss the flight?*' Obviously listening out for us.

'Plane delayed. Spanish always late,' I texted back, although rather unfairly – Javi was a superb time-keeper. In many ways.

'Go to sofa place near Arrivals.'

'Have. On third latte.'

'Careful, not good idea before exercise. Or is he happy to do all the work?'

'Shut up.'

Another buzz. *'Estoy aquí!'*

I dashed off, wanting to be there before he came out and cursing Jeremy's stupid texts for distracting me from the board.

He was wearing a brown leather jacket and dark jeans; it looked like he'd been shopping. He was all at once flamenco hunk and sweet, vulnerable displaced person; I needed to get my arms round him and take him home immediately.

'Javi!'

He looked over, his face breaking into a big smile. Then we were in each other's arms and squeezing away the nerves and doubts, all that sea and mountain between our homes.

'Yoli! No llores!'

'I can't help it,' I said, wiping under each eye, 'and I thought you'd never get here.'

'I know, the aeroplane had problems. But come now, we take the metro.'

'No, the train.'

'But the metro is faster?'

'If there was one, maybe.' He looked puzzled. 'Didn't you look out of the window? You're in the countryside, *el campo.*'

'Then why it is called *London* Gatwick?'

165

'Good question. But it's just half an hour on the train and—'

'So we go here,' he said, turning us towards the monorail.

'No, that's a... train to the other half of the airport.'

'*Dios mío.*'

I got in the ticket office queue but he went over to a machine and took some notes out of a plastic envelope.

'Which station?' he asked.

'Well... we need travelcards for zone—'

'*Qué?*'

We'd just have to get bus tickets later. 'London Bridge.'

'*Vale.*'

He tapped away; I half expected him to make it produce a hot chocolate. He pulled out the tickets with a triumphant grin and we went down to the platform.

'*Ay qué frio!*' He shivered.

'What's it like in Granada?'

'We have some warm days now,' he said, and under the harsh lighting I could see a sprinkle of un-Spanish freckles over his nose.

We cuddled up in the train. I told him about the tour bus but he wasn't interested; he was here to see me, he said, not London, although he liked the idea of walking along the canal. Perhaps he thought it would be like the Darro and make him feel at home.

We stood in front of the house, looking up at the facade.

'Beautiful. Very old building?'

'Yes, but the flats inside are modern.'

'Is a shame.'

'Yes. But we can't blame Jeremy, they were like this before he bought the house.'

I quickly searched my bag for the keys; I didn't want Jeremy – probably hearing every word of this – breaking his word and accidentally-on-purpose coming out into the hall to give him a full explanation.

'Very nice, Yoli,' he said, as I opened the door. 'And warm too. You leave heat on while you are away?' He took off his jacket.

'No, Jeremy must have put it on for us earlier.'

'Ah, kind.' He went over to the mantelpiece and looked at my photos. I'd put the two of Jeremy and me in a drawer, but the little sod must have noticed and put them back – including the one of us riding an airbed in the sea, my arms around his bronzed chest.

'David?'

'No! Why would I have one of *him*? Jeremy.'

'*Qué quapo*. Tell me again that he *is* completely gay.'

'He is completely gay.'

'But he likes to hug you.'

'Sometimes.'

'And kiss you.' He pointed to the bookshelf. A new photo: the one Emma had taken of us down by the canal. What the hell was Jeremy doing?

'Just friendly, that's all. Come on, we've been through this.' I opened the fridge: paper-thin ham, Spanish omelette and tomato salad from the deli. A bottle of wine – I hadn't told Jeremy about Javi's problem with it – and some juice. 'Want a drink? Something to eat?'

'No, just you,' he said, and I giggled as his arms came round me and he nibbled my neck. 'Ah. You have six messages – look.'

The phone's red light was flashing.

'It'll just be Helen telling me what we're wearing on Wednesday.'

'Six times?'

'I wouldn't put it past her.'

'What?'

'She doesn't give up easily,' I explained.

He was fixing me with those big eyes. I looked at the phone. I looked back at him. I didn't want to stand there listening to a gushy *have-a-great-time-together* from Charlotte, a burst of crudity from Emma. But I also didn't want to look like I had something to hide.

My alto flute was repaired and ready for collection.

Helen wanted us in our burgundy dresses.

Helen wanted my hair *up* please, not just in a plait. Javi laughed and started winding my hair up into a mad bun, while clicking noises suggested that she had indeed not given up easily, but decided she needed to speak to me rather than leave any more messages.

And then David wanted me to know how much he'd loved seeing me, did I like the photo, and was the first of May okay for the show.

The crazy hairdo landed back on my shoulders. I stared at the phone in disbelief; it felt like a prank.

'Maybe he has sent in e-mail,' Javi said quietly.

'I don't know what he means.'

He folded his arms and looked at the floor. 'But you have much more idea than *me*,' he said. If I were him, I thought, I'd want to know what the hell was going on and be saying so with both volume and tears. But he just stood there, waiting patiently. But then not so patiently. 'Are you going to tell me about this?' He picked a glass off the drainer and filled it with tap water, downed the lot.

'I bumped into him in Foy... where I buy music. A few weeks ago. We went to the coffee shop and he said sorry for... what he did. We talked about you, his new girlfriend...'

'But he wants to take *you* to a show.'

'Yes. I thought he'd forget about that.'

'But he can't forget. Perhaps he—'

'No! It's not like that.' I breathed out heavily. 'Look, he just wants to be friends. Probably coz he feels bad. And the photo – I don't know what he's on about.'

'Maybe he made one on his mobile, when you were in the shop.'

'Then it'll just be me gazing at something. Oh – I think I know...'

I grabbed his arm and took him through to the computer. Yes, me gazing lovingly at the Javi and Yoli on the front cover of *Salut d'Amour*. He'd taken it without me noticing.

He smiled. 'You buy this?'

'Yes, and a couple of others too. You don't have to play it, I just—'

But he'd pulled me up from the chair and started kissing me. Then led me into the bedroom without bothering with the light, and started to undo his jeans. No first clearing up and getting ready for bed tonight then, I thought, a flutter of excitement shooting through me. But when he pushed me down onto the bed before I could take my top off I realised there wasn't going to be much else first either. Then he yanked down my jeans and knickers and was on top of me, pushing in hard then just lying there, silent, his face in darkness.

'Javi?' I put my arms round him, stroked his t-shirted back and waited for the Javi I knew to come back. I could hardly breathe. I wriggled underneath him.

He put a hand to my cheek. 'Is where I want to be. *Te quiero tanto.*' He wanted or loved me so much. Perhaps both. '*Es problema.*'

'*No es problema.*'

A shard of light. A burst of conversation. *Spanish* conversation. What? I opened my eyes. Javi was on the balcony discussing – as far as I could tell – the winter wrapping of the banana plants. I imagined Jeremy out on his balcony the minute he'd heard the door of mine open. Something was planned for half an hour's time. I heard my name followed by laughter.

Javi came back into the room and sat on the bed, combing my hair with his fingers. I tried to pull him in next to me.

'No,' he said with a grin, getting up and picking up the breakfast tray. 'Greedy girl. And you would sleep again. We are going to take coffee with Jeremy. *Ven.* Bath.'

I waited until Javi was in the kitchen and then grabbed my phone.

'*No inquisition please,*' I texted.

'*The Spanish like inquisitions.*'

'*Don't or you in big trouble.*'

It had been his idea for me to do the *Compás* class (Javi thanked him); did he know *La Encima* in Almería's *Plaza Vieja*, one of Jeremy's all-time favourite restaurants? (he didn't); why had Javi chosen Granada instead of Sevilla or Madrid (a discussion that ended rather flatly in geographical convenience). All this even before the coffee was ready.

We sat down on the sofa, Jeremy opposite us like an earnest interviewer. Pavlova scrutinized each of us and decided that the lap of least tension was Javi's.

Then Jeremy moved on to Granada and they lost me, but judging from the awkwardness of the exchanges he was discussing his difficulties there when researching for *After Lorca*. Then Javi watched Jeremy's hand patting my thigh as he described how I'd gone with him once and kept dragging him off to the Tetería Kasbah for exotic tea and crepes.

'Yes! She has taken me there too,' Javi replied in English. 'And the book, the English are interested in Lorca?'

'Well, the novel's as much about the researcher and what he learns about himself while he's there.'

'So... it's about you?'

Jeremy hesitated. 'Partly. As for any writer.'

'He's got a copy in Spanish, if you'd like to read it,' I said.

'Oh yes, thank you.' Jeremy pulled one from the shelf. 'And thank you for the tickets for the ballet show tomorrow also. Can I—?'

'Oh no. My treat,' Jeremy said. 'If you've only ever seen a touring company's Swan Lake, you're in for a surprise. And the Royal Opera House is a beautiful place. But we don't go there very often, being patrons of Sadler's Wells – the dance theatre round the corner.'

'*Patrones?*' I wondered if *patrones* was the right word in Spanish. How it was translating into his financially modest *granadino* life. 'So... you have paid to help...?'

'Each year. We get priority tickets, rehearsals. And first night parties where we can talk to choreographers and dancers.'

'Jeremy does. I just eat up all the puddings...' I sipped my coffee. 'Haven't you got any biscuits, Jeremy?'

Jeremy seemed to be ignoring my glares. 'It's a great theatre – they put on all kinds of different dance. Including an annual flamenco festival.'

'Ah yes, Yoli has told me of this.'

Jeremy pulled the festival programme out of the shelf and handed it to Javi.

I watched him flick through. 'Oh – María Pagés... you met her at theatre party?'

'No, I was in Spain. Yol went.'

I shrugged as if there was no way I was going to recognise or talk to anybody there, gave Javi back his arm and got up. 'I'm sure I got you some Ginger Thins.'

I went to the cupboard, but even from there I could see that Javi had turned over to Nando and Toni's double spread, the two of them moodily standing there on opposite pages.

'*Molino y Morales*. Of course,' he said.

'You've seen them?' asked Jeremy.

'No. Is not my kind of *flamenco*. But sometimes they are interviewed on television – very nice men, and funny.'

'Would you agree with that, Yol?'

I was moving jars and packets around in the cupboard, including the Green and Black for Nando's chocolate, for God's sake. I pretended I hadn't heard, hoping the conversation would somehow go away. Wondered if *I* could go away, suggest looking in my kitchen...

'Yol? What do you think – are Molino and Morales nice, funny men?' He turned to Javi. 'It's true, she mostly just eats the puddings there, but on this occasion she shared one with Fernando Morales. Then went for dinner with him the next evening! Very intelligent, agreeable chap, I liked him. Where are you going, Yol? We don't need biscuits, sit down.'

'Where did he take you?' Javi asked, smiling but with wide, serious eyes.

'The Spanish place on the corner,' I said, sinking down next to him and resting my hand on a tense shoulder. 'It was no big deal, they were all going there.'

Jeremy said something in Spanish about me not realising something about myself, leaning forward and stroking my knee.

Javi pushed Pavolva off his lap, thanked Jeremy for the coffee and said we better let him get on with his writing, perhaps we'd see him later.

Back in my flat he clapped Jeremy's novel down on the table.

'So this is why you take flamenco.'

'What?'

'You meet Fernando Morales then you decide to come to Granada for flamenco. Or for flamencos.'

'No! I told you, I booked my course and started flamenco lessons in January.'

'Why you didn't tell me that you met him? You told me of the festival, so why not this? I don't understand.'

'I suppose I thought you might get the wrong idea,' I said. He was scowling. 'And it looks like I was right,' I added, trying to smile.

He picked up his jacket from the chair and put it on.

'Where are we going?'

'I forget the cream for shaving.'

'Oh don't bother – Jeremy can give you some.'

'Already I have enough from Jeremy,' he said. 'And also I need to go out.' I went to unhook my fleece. '*Solo*.'

Before I could think what to say he was out of the flat and through the front door. I grabbed my keys and stood in the hallway, wondering whether I should dash out after him. But that could have meant having a scene right in front of Jeremy's window.

Jeremy. I unlocked his door and barged in.

'What the *fuck* are you doing? He's gone off! Happy?'

He turned round from his computer, leaned back in his chair. 'Well go after him then, what are you doing here?'

'I'm *here* because *you're* the problem! It's got to *stop*!'

An irritating sigh. 'What *are* you on about? This is your life Yol, if he can't cope with it, *that's* the problem.'

'No it's *you* – the photos on the mantelpiece–'

'What–?'

'And then you have to bring up Nando. How the hell d'you think that looks?'

'I thought you would have told him. You said you had no secrets, were sublimely *confortable* together.'

'We were, until you messed it up!'

'Now look, calm down.' He stood up and came towards me. 'Come on, it'll be fine, he'll be back soon – as long as he doesn't get lost out there...'

I considered falling into his arms, but it was suddenly more gratifying to give that pitying and impenitent face a hard slap.

'Ow!' He put a hand to his cheek. 'What's that for? I'm on your side, you stupid girl!' He examined his fingers. 'And next time trim your claws, you've drawn blood.'

'Good!' I slammed the door behind me, just getting to my bed in time for the tears.

He had it coming, served him bloody well right. And yes, Javi would be back soon, it would be okay. But I'd never again be quite so much his sweet, trustworthy Yoli. Nor the fellow money-strapped music teacher, now Jeremy had painted us as a couple of spoilt, wealthy benefactors. Hell! Why hadn't I told Jeremy off about that too? But then talking about Sadler's was just stupid, compared to the deliberately inciting bit about Nando.

Nando. Suddenly it all came back to me: lying here crying the morning after... Oh why did I have to go and let him... So wrong. Desperate. Just be grateful nobody will ever know. Including Jeremy: proud of his good-girl Yol being asked out to dinner by such a talented and beautiful man. Oh God, perhaps I'd been a bit unfair: *he didn't know.*

A faint doorbell: Jeremy's. Spanish. Javi must have pressed Jeremy's by mistake. Then Jeremy was letting him into the flat.

'Where are you?' Javi was saying. He came through to the bedroom.

'Oh no,' he said, sitting me back on the bed with his arm round me. 'I'm sorry. But you have to understand – David, Jeremy, Fernando Morales...'

'You've got absolutely *nothing* to worry about. Surely you can see that.'

He put his finger under my chin and searched my eyes. Then smiled. 'Okay. But living so far, we need to have much *confianza* in each other. I always tell you the truth, even from before we were *novios*, and you must do the same. *Dame la verdad*, like they say in flamenco.'

'Yes, I promise.'

He pushed me back onto the bed and cuddled me. 'I'm sorry I went out like that. It was... *everything* too much. But I found your river... your canal. Let's have lunch there.'

I smiled and nodded: lunch at the Darro-substitute. He stroked my cheek and I fought down guilty feelings about Jeremy's.

'After we are completely mend...'

'*That's beautiful. Can I come and listen?*' Jeremy texted.

'*Tomorrow, when ready.*'

'*When concert is ready, or you are ready to forgive me?*'

'*Both.*'

A few minutes passed.

'*LU,*' I read.

'*LU2 and sorry.*'

'Helen?' Javi asked.

'Jeremy. He wants a concert. I said tomorrow, when we've got a full programme for him.'

'Yes, because still we need more flamenco.'

'What d'you mean, we've already got—'

'Of course, but also together.'

'Oh no, I really can't, come on.'

'Maybe if we take something you know, some flamenco fusion... Ah yes, like the instrumental *por tangos*, you know, on your Ketama CD. You could play the part for the violin on the flute.'

We listened to the track. The melody was easy enough, but even though I'd heard it many times the form still seemed to obey an ancient code; as usual, flamenco bewitched me but kept its secrets out of my reach.

'Okay, but you'll have to give me a nod whenever I have to come in.'

'*Vale.*'

176

Javi could play the whole thing by ear, and with his help I was thrilled to put in the little bursts of passionate gypsy melody.

'Bravo, Yoli!'

'Only problem is, I can't play and grin at the same time!'

'We need one more. What is your favourite? *Problema?*'

'Oh yes! I can just play the tune.'

'No, no, I'll sing that. You know what the words mean?'

I picked out the CD booklet. 'Er... *tell me if today I'm that problem, Tell me if I'm worth the trouble.* And oh God: *better leave it as yesterday.* I've gone right off this song.'

'You do the piano and the girl singing.'

'I don't sing.'

'Of course you sing.'

He started, adding rhythm to the chords with taps on the wood. His voice gentle but resonant. I joined in, loving the way my part overlapped and then moved in close harmony with his, as warm as hand-on-hand.

'*Ahora eres cantaora! Ven aquí.*'

Not exactly much of a singer, but I went over and draped my arms over him, put my cheek against his. Making me think again of that other cheek.

As I kept doing the rest of the day. Every time I put my hand to my face, even when Javi was kissing me after making love again.

Then Javi wanted to put the finishing touches to *Granada*'s guitar part, having mastered the programme – even in a foreign language – in half the time I had.

'Leave me to think, you go and do something. Not the dinner, I want to do that together, like always, but maybe call Helen or some other thing you have to do...'

'Okay. Would you mind if I looked in on Jeremy? I shouted at him when you went off for that walk and I—'

'Why you have done that? Go to say sorry. Have a drink – when you come back I am finished and you can bring him for concert.'

I squeezed him and went off to Jeremy's, giving the door the usual rat-a-tat TAT. Javi had pointed out that the rhythm was one of the *palmas* patterns for the tango.

The door opened slowly. 'Ah,' he said, touching his cheek as if it were still hurting, even hours later. 'What can I do for you?'

'You can...' Quit meddling with my love life, accept the fact that you may well have to manage without me, and... put a bag over your beautiful and suddenly vulnerable features. 'Come here.' I put my hands either side of his face and examined his cheek, feeling his arms come round me. 'Where's the...'

'Just under my eye.'

There was a tiny dark line. 'Is that it? I've spent all afternoon imagining some huge scarring gash.'

'I'm sorry to disappoint. But don't worry, it's the thin end of the wedge – you should check out the impact on my pride and well-being. Not to mention my productivity.'

'What's that then?' I asked, pointing to a new pile of printed papers on his desk.

'Handouts for the York workshops. All I felt up to doing.'

I picked up a sheet. 'Hm. This stuff about the *gradual* dripping in of backstory. Shame you can't grasp the importance of that in real life.'

'Okay, I've got the message,' he said, placing it back on the pile. 'But everything's alright now, isn't it?'

'Yes. *More* than alright. So are you going to give me some tea or what?'

'I don't know. You can't go around slapping people, Yol. And really there's only one way to make you remember that.'

He suddenly pulled me under his arm and thwacked my bottom hard.

'Ow!'

'God you've got a hard little arse!' he said, laughing and shaking his hand in pain.

'Uh, give me sugared tea, I'm in shock here,' I said, rubbing my backside.

'No more slapping?'

'Promise.'

I followed him to the kitchen. But he was wearing those cargos... I couldn't resist it.

A satisfying yelp.

'Hurts, doesn't it,' I said.

'Okay you've asked for it,' he said. He dragged me under his arm again, but I wriggled free and dashed behind the sofa, squealing like a six-year-old. The next thing I knew he'd rugby-tackled me onto it, there was a further stinging blow and we were in a wrestling match. Then he was on top of me.

'I'm sorry if you are,' he said.

'Deal.'

'Tea?'

'I think so, yes.'

He got up, but I stayed there waiting for my heart to slow down. The kettle whined.

'Don't you need to get back? I don't want to cause any more—'

'No, he's doing something on the piece, wanted me to stop hovering over him.'

'Not a general complaint, I hope.'

'Course not.'

'So has he said anything?'

I sat up and tidied the cushions. 'Lots of lovely things.'

'And?'

'And what?'

'Has he said what he *wants*... what could happen?'

'Not exactly. But if we're happy and enjoying each other, it will fall into place.'

'Is that what *he* said?'

'No, just what I feel.'

'I hope you're right.'

I didn't for a minute believe he did, but at least he seemed to be trying to.

We sat down on the sofa, Pavlova watching us uncertainly from the window sill.

'We're nearly ready to give you the concert, if you like.'

'Now? Perfect. Tell you what, let's make Javi a coffee and see if he's finished.'

Javi was sitting cradling his guitar. 'Ah, coffee – *perfecto*.'

'So where's the programme then?' Jeremy asked. Javi laughed. But I produced a handwritten list from the top of the piano.

'Yoli! I want to see.' Javi took it from me and stroked my head. 'We have to keep this. Look, even it has the date and place.' He passed it to Jeremy, who murmured approval and sank back into the sofa with his tea.

'I'm probably going to make a mess of all this,' I said, prompting groans from them both. Then Jeremy clapped as if we'd just come onto the stage and we had to start.

Air on a G String: a Trio standard that my flute could have played by itself but I'd told Javi how Jeremy – along with the rest of the world – loved it. Followed by *Chanson d'Amour*, the yearning melody passing between us, almost indecently romantic.

'Lovely,' Jeremy said, then studied the programme. 'And now flamenco all the way?'

'Well, Spanish anyway,' I said.

Javi's contribution: one of the Granados *Danzas Espanolas – Andaluza*, indeed – a haunting, fickle melody for me over his dependable accompaniment. Earlier I'd said it made me feel like a spoilt little *bailaora*, forgetting for a moment that he'd been married to one.

Jeremy loved it. 'Delicious! I need that on my iPod.' I grinned at him: as a musical audience he was always an adorable pushover.

Next up was my cunningly blagged and abridged version of one of the Zgaja *Virtuoso Flamenco Studies* I'd studied at college, drawing undeserved compliments.

In an inspired bit of programming we followed this frantic piece with the sad and simple magic of Javi's *Falseta*, which prompted a burst of appreciative Spanish from Jeremy.

Then came the Trio piece, with a backing CD that left out the guitar and first flute parts so we could play along with it; a bit cheesy after the real thing but earning me two hugs.

It was time for the song. I sat at the piano ready to come in on the second verse.

'*Dime si soy para ti ese problema,*' Javi sang. Jeremy's eyes widened, surprised as I had been at the gentle beauty of his voice, perhaps – or wondering about the significance of the words. I joined in, exhilarated by the musical intimacy.

This time he didn't clap, just smiled and looked taken aback. Javi pushed on with the final number, in which my drunken gypsy flautist made a couple of hilarious wrong entries.

'Encore! *Bis! Otra!*' Jeremy demanded.

'Which? You choose,' Javi said.

'Everything. But starting with *Problema*. Love the way you've done that. D'you understand the lyrics, Yol?'

'All except the last bit. *Hay de ti, si llevo la razón. Hay de ti?* There is of you?'

'No,' said Javi, putting down his guitar and pulling me onto his lap. '*Ay de ti. Ay* like in *ay pobrecita.*'

'Oh. So it means... 'poor you if I'm right?'' I asked.

Jeremy nodded his head slowly.

16.
primavera *f* spring

Eleven o'clock, in his dressing gown. One of those days when he'd woken with an idea and got writing without so much as a tea. No – the computer was off, his research box on the sofa under a pile of albums and loose photos.

'You alright?'

'Yeah? Why?' He went to the sofa and swept the pictures into an envelope. 'Research.'

'Cádiz? Wouldn't have thought you'd–'

'Can't explain.' Or rather wouldn't, but I was used to this.

'Hot cross bun and tea?'

'Mm, yes please.'

I put the cleaning wipes and a plastic bag down on the sofa.

'Oh, don't bother–'

'Just a quick go round before I assemble your Easter clutter.'

It needed more than that. An avalanche of unopened letters, a congealed mug, crumbs, a banana skin, earth on the floor from a Pavlova-ravaged pot plant; for Jeremy, this was nothing less than a domestic tantrum. And I had a feeling I knew the cause.

'So he got off okay,' he said.

'Course. He does know how to use an airport, Jeremy.'

'But maybe not a large international one.' I raised my eyebrows. 'Sorry. Great he loved the ballet. We'll have to take him round the corner next time.'

'I was telling him about Matthew Bourne – he wants to come over for the next show.'

'That'll be Christmas...' By which time, Jeremy might be getting us both over from Spain to see it. Maybe that's what he was thinking, because he'd forgotten about the buns, picked up Pavlova and gone over to the window. 'We'll have to get Duncan to look after Pav again – I'll be in Seville when you go to Javi's.'

'Oh?'

'Gabi and Nico keep asking me and I need to go for some research. Shame you can't come with me.'

'Gabi and...?'

'You know, you met them on the beach last year, got fed up with Gabi complaining about the heat and bought her a hat.'

'Oh yes. Good for you. Ooh – and talking of heat, apparently it's going to get up to twenty degrees today. Spring has definitely arrived.'

As had my new start. I'd even emailed Ángel and told him that I no longer needed his services, getting a reply saying that he was relieved because his donations were not going down well with his new girlfriend.

'Great. I'll get the chairs out in the garden,' he said, but went on gazing out in to the street, his chin on Pav's head.

'So how's the book going?'

'I'm... stepping back a bit.'

'Having a mull.'

'Yes.' He turned and smiled at me. 'So do composers do that? Mull?'

'I wouldn't know – I can hardly call myself one. But yes, I do.'

He put Pav on the sofa and sat down next to me. 'You *are* a composer. You just need to stop fretting about what Helen thinks and try and get published instead.'

'Uh – it's about as likely as winning the lottery.'

'Maybe, but you haven't even tried.'

'I know, that's what Javi says.'

He got up and put the photo albums and the envelope back in the cupboard.

I stared at the box file on the table. 'Can't you tell me *something* about the novel?'

'You know I can't.'

'Not the plot, just the *sort* of novel it is. I mean, is it a love story?'

'Of course it is. As all novels should be, in one way or another.'

'Well that's not saying much, is it? Come on, just age, gender and occupation for the two main characters and I'll shut up.'

His face fell. 'Yol, you haven't been... peeking?'

'No! I'd never do that!' Indignation earned through many triumphs over temptation.

'Okay, okay,' he said, patting my thigh. 'Because remember, just as I trust you about that, I want honest feedback on the first draft when it's ready.'

'When will that be?'

'Not sure. But you'll be the first to know.'

'The first?'

'Yes, like last time.'

My mouth fell open. 'Was I the first to read it? I thought—'

'I made out you weren't but...'

'Oh Christ.' I turned to him. 'That's really quite an honour.'

He pushed the mail back into a neat pile. 'Haven't you heard how many authors say they have someone they always write *to*, almost as if the whole thing is a big letter... someone they want to make laugh, cry, understand...? Stephen King talks about his Ideal Reader.' He pulled me over to him. 'Think it's time you knew that... well, you're mine.'

I was stunned. English 'A' level with a Grade C, a keen but not very discerning booklover. 'Why me?'

'I don't know. It must be one of those instinctive things, like choosing homes. All I know is, it works.'

My eyes stung. 'I can't believe this,' I said, shaking my head.

'Certainly not difficult to make you cry anyway,' he said with a grin, seeing me reach for a tissue. 'How does it feel to be a muse?'

'Bit scary. But also quite... I mean, when the book eventually comes out, it'll be sort of like we've had a kid, won't it?'

'Absolutely. Now come on, put all those chicks and stuff on my mantelpiece and we'll get outside. What time's poor old Emma coming round?'

'Not till about three. She's very wobbly, she'll need lots of choc and hugs.'

'Is the drama teacher *worth* all this heartbreak?'

'Probably not. And he's said it's the age difference, the bastard.'

'Ouch. Okay, major salvage operation required. But I don't get it – surely he was aware of that in the first place.'

'I know. And it's not like either of them wants children, she's got hers and he's much too interested in himself.'

'Bit harsh – how d'you know? He might be planning them for later – by which time she'll be too old to have them, if she isn't already.'

An awkward pause in which I imagined him recalling The Question.

'I'll get ready while you do whatever you must here,' he said, getting up.

'Yes, and then I'll get the garden nice for her. You can help or mull, whatever.'

'Sounds good,' he said, heading for the bathroom, which probably meant he would be issuing praise and amusing suggestions from the sun lounger. Then he turned back. 'Oh – I think Helen's sent you something more from your father. Sorry – I picked it up by mistake among all the one-to-one subs for York. Here.' He handed me an envelope with her rushed scrawl on the front. 'I thought he was going away.'

'He is. Tuesday,' I said, opening it. 'Hell, how am I going to cope with this?'

'Do I answer that? I don't want my head bitten off again.'

I opened the smaller envelope inside and read it out.

'*Yolette, ma chérie,*

How happy your little letter makes me! And Judy too! Now we can enjoy our cruise – you will inspire the holiday. We look forward to receiving your call when we get back.

Look after yourself. We are thinking of you.

Affectueusement, Papa.'

'That's lovely. What did you say?'

'Pretty much as you suggested, and not giving my address. Sneaked out and posted it in Jersey without showing Charlotte. Now I've just got to hope the ship hits an iceberg.'

'Oh come on, I'll be with you, remember? Anyway, you've now got plenty of time to get used to the idea.'

'Suppose so.'

He looked inside the bag and pulled out the large Lindt chocolate rabbit. 'Aha. Thanks. Think I'll have some in the bath.'

'No you won't, it's for sharing,' I said, grabbing it back from him. 'Along with those buns. Come on, let's get cracking.'

He went off to the bathroom. I filled the dishwasher, wiped the mantelpiece and arranged the animals, fake daffodils and painted eggs. Spring. New starts. *Inspiring* new starts. How can I *inspire* their holiday, I thought, what a daft thing to say. But... nice. Ideal Reader and Inspiring Daughter; I could get quite a big head, the way the day was going.

I needed to clean the table. I picked up the box file to put it on his desk but it was heavy and not pressed closed; a print-out fell onto the floor. This sort of thing had happened before, of course; I never told him, making him worry unnecessarily, and I knew what to do. I picked it up, my eyes fixed to one side of it. The reader was not a peeper. But a corner of it, I reckoned – and thought I could feel – must have fallen into the pot plant earth. No problem: I swept it off with my fingers, eyes still averted. But what if he wondered about a brown dust mark? I allowed myself a lightning-glance check of the edge.

And there it was. Opposite the sharp staple under my thumb, so in the top right hand corner. Where the title goes. Two tiny words that surely I shouldn't have been able to make out at that speed, in that gloom under the table, after years of keeping my promise: The Reader.

17.
todo *pron* all, everything

'This is *delicioso*. How come, after all that Spanish conversation practice, I never found out you two were vegetarian?'

'*Soy vegetariana*. Much too easy compared to discussing things like what one can learn from gay best friends and brothers...' Liz said.

'Good grief,' said her partner Ian, looking up for a moment from the ads section in the Olive Press. 'That poor little Japanese girl, what did she make of you two?'

'She was alright – sat there correcting our grammar,' Liz said. 'But Yolly, I'm afraid it's rather different in the new class. Núria is no Juana. Excellent teacher but it's all a bit more... directed. And... I better warn you, rumour has it that—'

'I know. Javi took her out a few times, some while ago.'

'Well yes, maybe that's all it was. People exaggerate.'

I'd suddenly had enough to eat. 'Why, what did you hear?'

Ian mumbled his excuses and took his paper indoors.

'Oh, you know, they were an item for a while, not long before you came along.'

People might exaggerate, but there was no obvious reason for them to be wrong about the timing.

'Anyway, she's very professional, she's not going to say anything. It'll be fine.'

It wasn't. Right from the first piercing look over her designer glasses and the 'you must be Yoli – sorry, Yolan-der'.

Good-looking in an absence-of-bad-features kind of way. Agreeable – well, with everybody else, but her smiles seemed to stop halfway, as if she needed to go somewhere very warm for a while and be thawed. Perhaps Javi had managed this, I thought, because in her present state I couldn't imagine him even shaking hands with her, let alone anything else.

She kept saying I wasn't listening and that she was surprised I wasn't getting more *practice*.

The bell. Liz and I were going to go have lunch by the Darro and discuss the best way of handling her, but Carlota was waiting for me at the bottom of the stairs.

'Ah, Yoli. Can I have a chat with you? Please, go to my office and I will join you in a minute with coffee for us.'

A formidable dancer in her time, and now a formidable businesswoman – but fair and kind with it, according to Javi. I opened the door marked *Directora* and sat down, gazing at the flamenco posters all over the walls. I spotted one with Javi hunched over his guitar in the background and got up to have a better look.

'A talented *tocaor*,' said Carlota behind me. Raised eyebrows and a quick nod told me to sit down opposite her. 'And a wonderful teacher, very *simpático*.'

'Yes.'

'If you make him happy, I am pleased. But you must understand, we are many people in a small space, and students pay much to be here. It is easy for them to be... offended.'

'Offended?'

'Perhaps it is not the correct word. But Yoli, I am trying to tell you that you must be discreet. It is important.'

'Of course.'

'Teachers should not have relations with students. They know this. But it happens, so all I can ask is, I prefer that the other students do not know. You understand?'

'Yes. Alright.'

'It is easier this way, we have had troubles before.'

I sipped my coffee. There'd been the German girl who, at the end of her visit, had admitted to being married. He hadn't told me of any others. Perhaps she meant that love-himself star dancer guy.

'I have given him the same warning. I'm sure it will be okay now we have spoken.'

'Perhaps you could talk to Núria. *She's* not being discreet. I can't imagine anybody in my Spanish class being in any doubt that she was... *offended* by me before I even walked in.'

'Núria.' She shook her head. 'Javi tried to mend her... I will talk to her. I'm sorry. Tell me if there are more problems. Now go and have lunch before your next class.'

Liz was waiting for me in the courtyard. 'I've got Pepe to save us a table – don't worry, locals get served more quickly.' I followed her into the alley. 'Something you might find out, of course.'

'Don't. And in fact careful what you say, because I've basically been gagged about Javi and me. Annoying really, I mean what about that Belgian girl and the Cultural Programmes guy...?'

'They're *married*, Yolly. And until you two are, she'll just see you as another blonde *guiri* with a romantic flamenco fixation, dubious morals and a stack of euros.'

'Bloody cheek. But at least I told her about Núria and she promised to have a word.'

We'd reached the terrace; a guitarist was coming round with his hat while the next performers for the spot by the fountain – a ponytailed bubble-blower with his cropped-haired girl assistant – were setting up. Pepe led us to a table in front of it and took our orders.

Becoming a local. On the next table, two young Spanish women were laughing over their lunches while the babies gurgled in their prams. I wondered if Liz and I might sit here with a pram one day. That would be only one pram, of course, because when our Spanish conversation practice had covered the mothering issue, Liz had confessed to being vehemently against the idea. She hadn't said why. But then maybe, like my cousin and Emma's sister, there wasn't a reason. It seemed that if you didn't want children, you just didn't want them and that was it. Enviably simple and certain.

'Are you okay, Yolly?'

'Yeah, just starving. So you haven't told me how the business is going.'

'Much the same. But then there was never going to be much of a call for English website design out here. God, you were right about Helen, by the way. At least she was happy with the website in the end. I gather it's almost doubled the bookings – but that's probably not what you want anymore.'

'Oh bloody hell,' I said, dodging a massive bubble wobbling past the table. I watched it burst over an irritating group of Japanese girls practising castanets and exchanged a grin with one of the Spanish women.

'Doesn't make it easy to come out here, no. And Javi's in two groups now, so heaven knows when he'll next be able to come over to me again. Says he can't leave his old group until he's found another guitarist for them.'

'Too nice a guy, eh? So he gets back from Córdoba later, but how many evenings will you have together this week?'

'Er... alone, just tonight and Thursday. But I'll go to the gigs, of course. Have you decided which evenings you want to join me?'

'Just Friday, I'm afraid. Sorry, but you know I can only handle so much flamenco. Think you have to grow up with it. It's different for you, learning it and being a musician.'

'I'm enthralled, yes, but it's still a mystery.'

We watched another bubble sail past, this time with ludicrous quivering purpose towards the restaurant across the road. And that's where I saw her. The unmistakable thick black ponytail, and possibly the same earrings.

'Oh God, I think that's Isabel over there – Javi's ex sister-in-law. Red jacket.' I moved my chair round a bit so as to have my back to the road.

Liz looked over. 'Well what's she going to do? And she did say sorry last time. I'll let you know when she's gone round the corner.'

Our tortillas arrived. I asked her where she thought Javi should take me in the car on Saturday. She started to tell me about a romantic place from where we could look down on the city... But along came another huge bubble, this time apparently created for one of the Spanish babies, now sitting up with rapt admiration. Until she put out a finger and it burst right over her.

There was a gasp from the Japanese. The mother pulled out a pack of tissues. Then the high-pitched screaming started, followed by a rapid burst of complaint from the other Spanish woman and guttural, toothless support from a withered old man at the next table.

All eyes on the terrace were on the bubble-blower, who'd decided to launch his apology and reassurance about the contents of his mixture from beside our table. All eyes except Isabel's.

'Shit, she's spotted me.'

It was suddenly quiet again, the baby having presumably cried out all the soap, and everyone else back minding their own business. Except for Isabel, moving swiftly towards us.

'Okay. Finished? We can go and pay and get out of here...' Liz was saying.

But Isabel was already there, looking down at me, hand on hip. 'How-are-you?'

'*Bien, gracias.*'

'Good? How *is*? You come here but Javier eat tortilla today in Córdoba with his wife,' she said, indicating my plate with a quick tilt of her prominent chin.

'He's working.'

A short laugh. '*Es verdad.* Violeta is work. But not *explica* why you here.'

'She doesn't have to explain anything to you,' Liz said.

Isabel nodded her head, earrings jangling. 'No.' She jabbed a finger at me. 'But he need explain *her*.' She walked off, her boots clicking on the pavement.

The Spanish women were staring, now seeing me as a nasty husband-stealing *guiri*.

'D'you know, I'm beginning to feel somewhat unwelcome round here.'

'Come on, she's probably just making it all up. Javi'll sort her out.'

I struggled with the flamenco class until I was seeing a glittery zigzag line and had to make my excuses and walk home. To Javi's, where the previous night I'd lain alone but happily snuggled up to a jumper he'd left behind on the bed. Now I just lay there, hoping the migraine tablet would block everything out until he got back. Which would only be a couple of hours, he'd texted from the van, adding in Spanish that he couldn't wait to be round me, on me, in me.

My phone buzzed again. Jeremy.

Thinking of my flamenco dancer – time you showed me what you can do. Perhaps next time your tocaor comes over? Meanwhile guess who I'm watching tonight? G and N have booked for us to see M+M! Might say hello to Nando. LU XX

One day I was going to have to tell him what happened, if only to stop him mentioning that bloody name.

I started to float; the medicine was having fun rewiring my brain but hadn't yet reached the pain. A rhythmical throbbing – I could see it written down in musical notation; a hairpin sign to show the *crescendo* increases in intensity, an italicised *accel* to show the speeding up to the climax of... I sat up and grabbed the just-in-case washing up bowl.

Great, I thought. Now Javi will be coming home to a sick-smelling flat. I staggered through to the bathroom to deal with the bowl. Decided to wash my teeth. Looked for toothpaste in the tiny cupboard on the wall.

Shaving cream. That glue stuff he had to use on his long right-hand fingernails. A clatter of nail files. The packet of migraine tablets. Round it, a red hair elastic. I picked it up for a closer look and watched it disappear into the scintillating diamond into which the zigzag had morphed. Held it further away and fixed my eyes slightly to one side of it. Good, at least she hadn't left any black hair in it, her tempestuous DNA burning my fingers. I stomped back to bed and closed my eyes.

I was watching Jim'll Fix It with Papa. Two girls had got to meet ABBA, and now they were singing 'Thank You For The Music' with them in a recording studio. Benny had his arm round the smaller girl, just like Papa had round me. I'd been in a recording studio once, but it had been much smaller and a lot less shiny.

Mummy came in to say something but looked at us and went out again. She was in one of her pink-eyed whiny moods with Papa, but I couldn't see why. Charlotte was also in a paddy, going on about her ballet bun not being neat enough for Miss Hermione and demanding that Mummy did it again. Papa and I exchanged a look; he patted my itchy net ballet skirt and told me that Charlie needed to understand that it was more important to focus on her performance than her hairgrips.

But Charlotte had come downstairs and stamped into the room. 'I *heard* that. What do you care anyway? You can't even be bothered to come and watch us.'

'You're wrong, he's got a *ticket*,' I said, picturing the two pink paper squares by the hall phone.

'Of course he has. But something better has come up. Some*one* better.'

What did she mean? Someone putting on a better ballet show? How could that be – we'd had extra afternoons in the hall to get it right, and Miss Hermione had said it was going to be her *best show ever*. And Papa still had his big arm round me, stroking my hair as I leant back against his warm shirt; he wasn't saying that he wasn't coming. But then, he wasn't saying he *was*, either...

I pushed back against him, waking and confused for a moment. Javi. His arm around me, his warm breath on my neck.

'Ah... hello,' he said, feeling me stir. '*Qué pasa Yoli, migraña?*'

'Yes. Uh... need the loo. *Momento.*'

I swung my legs onto the floor and swayed off to the bathroom. Shielding my eyes from the low sun coming through the window but relieved to be able to see properly again.

I sat on the loo and stared at the red hair band – now on the glass shelf and wrapped round the migraine pills packet again. The red band that I'd worn that first evening I'd come here, holding back some of my hair. The one I used to keep it out of the way when I had a shower. How on earth could I have thought it wasn't mine?

Javi was making drinks in the kitchen.

'Come here.' He wrapped his arms round me. 'At last. I've missed you so much.' We stood there for a while. It felt good, but not as good as it should have done.

'Toast and honey?'

'No. Oh... well yes, I'll try.'

'I will bring it.'

I went back to bed – but sitting up, stuffing pillows behind me and trying to rally my brain. I could have done with the usual post-migraine hyperactivity, but that hadn't arrived and I had a feeling it wasn't going to. As if the pill was only keeping the migraine in a holding pattern; sooner or later I was going to have to land this mother myself. Perhaps more sleep would do it. More water. And of course – or maybe *only* this – talking to Javi about... But no, he would talk to *me*. I just had to be patient.

He came in with a tray and sat on the bed next to me. Asked about the school.

'I've got Núria for Spanish. She doesn't seem too keen on me,' I said, looking over for a reaction.

'Oh no. I have to talk with her. What did she say?'

I gave him some examples and he shook his head.

'Er... can you tell me again about you and her?'

'We are friends. I help her move things when she left her husband last year. She was... very sad, tired... I took her to restaurants some times, we talked. But soon she was going out with friend of her sister.'

'And then?'

A slight hesitation, perhaps wondering whether he could get away with leaving it at that. 'At Christmas she was alone, and I had trouble with Violeta's family, I was very... *deprimido, no?* I think she wanted help me, but...' He breathed out heavily. 'One evening she started to... well, you know, we had too much wine...'

I looked away, trying not to imagine it.

'I'm sorry, Yoli, I don't want to remember and you don't want hear. She was cross but I thought now she accepts we are only friends. I will talk with her—'

'You probably don't have to. Carlota grabbed me for a lecture about how we have to keep our relationship a secret, and I told her about it.'

'Oh Yoli, no – now you put her in trouble.'

'Well maybe she should be,' I said, folding my arms. He stared at me. 'No I'm sorry, I don't mean that. It's just that...' It's just that it's been quite a day, and it would be nice if at least one of these Spanish women could be taken to task for it.

'What?'

'I don't know... I'll try and be really nice to her tomorrow.'

'That's my Yoli.'

He put the tray on the floor and cuddled up next to me.

'Better after that?'

'Yes. And the medicine's starting to work.'

'Those pills are *mágicos* – and of course we have to thank them for putting us together,' he said.

I usually loved to talk about how we became a couple, the funny speculations about whether it would have happened if I hadn't had trouble with the key, if he hadn't got drunk. But I wasn't in the mood for it. Nor was I happy when the hand that may have held Violeta's across the table strayed down between my legs.

'No.' I said, gently pushing him away. 'Not better enough for that.'

A little puzzled, but smiling and pulling me closer. 'Anything more, *mi cariño*? Your camomile tea? We need to make you better as fast as possible, please! What would help?'

You telling me about Violeta, I wanted to say. I shrugged, looking into his eyes and willing him to talk.

But he leapt off the bed muttering something about *deshidratación* and a drink he wanted me to try.

I looked at my phone: a message from Jeremy that I'd missed.

Everything okay? J xxxx

As if he knew it wasn't. I'd answer him when it was; surely that couldn't be long. A fluttering in my stomach. Maybe Javi was sparing me, just as I had kept my encounter with David to myself. Trouble was, I *hadn't* been spared.

'*Aquí está*,' he said, bringing in a brownish milky drink. '*Horchata*. You have tried?'

'No.'

'Is from Valencia. *Chufas* – ah, *no sé como se dice* – and sugar. Very good for health and energy. I make it hot for you, is more *relajante*.'

I took a sip: a sort of marzipan Horlicks.

He sat back down next to me on the bed, with my timetable. 'Belén for *Compás* – but you have missed this today?'

'Yes.'

'You will like her. And ah, this is good – we have hour and quarter for lunch at same time, can eat together. Maybe more...' He grinned.

The fluttering in my tummy was turning to an ache. I put the drink on the bedside table. I could say, *today my lunch was interrupted by your witch of a sister-in-law*. Possibly adding *while you were having lunch and maybe more with Violeta*.

'Don't you like it?'

'I love it,' I said, picking up the mug again and feeling the sugar course through me. 'So... what did you do today then – celebrate with the group?'

'We met with two dancers who may join.'

My heart thumped. 'No.'

He laughed. 'What you mean, *no?*'

'Well, won't two more dancers be too many?'

'They are couple. Emilio is thinking about it.'

'Oh.' But did that mean other dancers auditioned? Was there *anything* I could ask that would make him tell me? I finished the drink, for something to do, and started to feel sick again. I lay down on the bed, facing away from him. He cuddled me, pressing himself against my back. As before. How much longer would I have to wait? Would he tell me over dinner? After dinner? Tomorrow? Or perhaps he felt it was nothing to do with me; they were married still, after all. Married. *He's married.* There was a faint but unmistakable return of the hammering in my head, my tummy wondering what to do with the comfort drink I'd been given instead of the truth...

I pushed his arm away and sat up. 'When the fuck are you going to tell me you had lunch with Violeta today?'

He winced. 'I was waiting until you are better. You are not yourself, you are—'

'Just *tell* me!' I folded my arms, staring at a loose thread in the blanket while my heart raced.

He took my hand. 'Listen, you don't have to be upset. She was at the club, this week she performs at other club there but she had a night free—'

'You knew that?'

'No! She goes everywhere all the time. Last time I didn't know even when she came to Granada. But I talked with her in the break, things are not good for her. Problems with boyfriend, much pain from the shoulder and... I think having too many drugs again. So I ask her have lunch with me today. She talked, I tried to encourage.' He put a hand to my cheek and turned my face toward him. 'Is that a bad thing that I do?'

Too nice a guy. I smiled weakly at him. 'Of course not. And did it help?'

'I don't know, I hope that yes. At the end she ask about you, and liked that you play the flute. She is not like her sister. Isabel told you, yes?'

'When Liz and I were having lunch by the fountain. She hates me.'

'No, no. It is because she thinks of Violeta. When their mother died she look after her, gave up many things. But she is tired of the *responsabilidad* – is why Violeta can have many boyfriends, but still Isabel wants me to be alone and wait for her to come back.'

'She thinks... she will?'

'*Exactamente* – she is crazy! One day she will understand. Maybe already she begins, because it was different with other girls, I could tell her it is not serious. But with you...'

I found myself holding my breath. 'With me..?'

'I... could not say that.'

The first time that he had ever spoken of our future. Having been on the edge of screaming about Violeta, I was now sending a silent thank you to her and the mad sister for making this discussion happen.

'Serious,' I said, hoping he'd say more. But he just carried on stroking my hair. I wanted to press him, ask what I always asked boyfriends sooner or later. Even though I always ended up like the Spanish baby, covered in burst bubble and utterly miserable. *No, leave it*, I told myself firmly. But then opened my mouth anyway. 'What's going to happen with us?'

'Happen?' The classic stall; not a good sign.

'In the future.'

'The future,' he repeated, as if we were in an English lesson.

Damn it, why did I have to do this? He's right, I'm not well. And now I'm about to start crying like a spoilt child. 'Need the loo,' I said, getting up.

He pulled me back. 'No you don't,' he said gently. Then put me on my back and leaned over me. 'The truth is, I don't know. But I know what I *want* to happen.'

He wanted us to always stay friends. How many times had I heard that? Almost as many times as I hadn't. 'What?' I whispered.

'*Todo.*'

'All?'

'And for now I want...' He ran his hand down my body. '*Todo esto.*'

I laughed, my head light and clearing. 'All yours.'

18.
reconciliar *vt* to reconcile

'*Call me.*'

There wasn't long before Spanish, but I had to make sure Jeremy was okay, that Duncan hadn't rung to say Pavlova had had an accident...

'Hi, anything wrong?'

'No, not at all. Just promised Nando I'd say hello to you. And give you an *abrazo* from him next time I see you.'

'Oh.' Did I care about that? After an evening of Javi showing me how he'd bought a keyboard and the software so we could start on our next piece; a hilarious co-cooked *judias verdes*, re-enacting our first date; talk of a weekend in Almería meeting his family? No. Well, a bit. It was good to hear Nando could remember who I was. That perhaps some of that tenderness was real, giving a modicum of meaning to what I'd done.

'Yol?'

'That's nice.'

'He's got tickets for us to go again tonight. But Nico's not sure, wasn't happy about the way Gabi was flirting with him when they shared a lemon mousse.'

'Hang on – you went to dinner?'

'Yes. It was a great evening. You'd never think a dancing *gitano* who left school at fifteen would be so well-read, a follower of not just flamenco but contemporary and ballet... Art too, he's been to most of the best galleries in the world... and you should see him sketch. Behind all that sensual machismo there's a self-educated intellectual. Fascinating.'

Clearly Jeremy was fascinated; he'd probably fallen in love, the first time in a long while. Poor, poor Jeremy; he was so horrendously barking up the wrong tree.

'So will you go?'

'Maybe, I'll see what they... No, what am I saying, course I will. I know what you're thinking, Yol, but... at least he's good research material.'

'I can imagine.' Once again I envied the way he went through life taking on disappointments and sculpting them for his artistic, emotional – and nowadays financial – fulfilment.

'So how's it going there?' he asked.

'Great. But I've got Spanish now. I'll text you later, okay? Actually you could call me tonight – Javi's suggested I stay at home and work on our new piece while he's out playing with his old group.' That's if you haven't gone clubbing with Nando, I nearly added, but it didn't feel right to tease him when he was on such a hopeless quest. '*Abrazos.*'

'*Abrazos a ti también,*' he said. Hugs. I texted some to Javi too and then bounded up the stairs to be nice to miserable hug-free Núria.

But she wasn't miserable; she gave me a smiling welcome – which was just as well as nobody else was there yet. She offered me a mint, asked how I'd got on with my homework and patiently re-explained the imperfect subjunctive; Carlota must have had a word.

The others arrived: Liz with a heavy cold; the two young German girls looking pale after a late night at Le Chien Andalou. All horribly better than me, even with their ailments, as became even more evident when Núria started the class with a listening test. Liz was kneeing me and mouthing *are you alright?*

I was relieved when it was time for our break, knowing that after it we'd be back on the solid earth of grammar and homework corrections. But Núria wanted a word.

She waited until we were alone, then patted the chair next to her and pulled out a thermos. I sat down and watched her hand encircling a cup, trying not to envisage where it might have drunkenly touched Javi...

Carlota came in, her mouth falling open and then turning into a smile. '*No es importante*,' she said, and went out again.

'Ac-tu-ally,' Núria said, 'let's take these outside. I will show you my secret *azotea*.'

I followed her through the door beads out into the sun. At this level, the building was a warren of rooftop sun terraces, outdoor staircases and stone paths leading to the cave-like classrooms dug into the hill. Amparo and I had had fun exploring every corner of it on my first visit. But Núria took me through a metal door marked *Privado* onto a flower-filled and newly whitewashed terrace – the one in the website that we'd laughed about not being able to find. She closed the door behind her and I imagined myself joking with Liz later, saying *I mean, we were three floors up with non-health-and-safety-height walls – thought she was going to throw me from the bloody roof.*

But she got me to sit down on the bench next to her, gave me a low-fat biscuit and started to tell me how my understanding of Spanish was on a markedly lower level compared to my speaking and writing, and that she suspected that I had difficulties with attention. *Trastorno de déficit de atención.*

I'd had pupils with Attention Deficit: a girl at school who never remembered her lesson time and was forever coming out with tangential comments about Dr Who, a boy in a previous school who kept getting off the piano stool to look out of the window. In my schooldays, kids like me who were fidgets or dippy daydreamers were just expected to *behave*; it had been difficult and demoralising. But somehow that didn't make it any easier being diagnosed with special needs at the age of thirty-eight.

'Yolanda?'

'I'm not good with concentration, no,' I said, feeling the first prick of idiotic tears and pretending to shield my eyes from the sun. Then I reminded myself of my flute performances. 'Although I can, for some things.'

'For your music, or something else that you are very interested in.'

'But I'm very interested in Spanish.'

'Perhaps. No, I'm sure you are. But you have no confidence.'

'Maybe I should go back to the easier class.'

'No. But I suggest that next time you come, book one-to-one classes to work on your listening. I do these and would like to help you. Meanwhile, practise listening to any Spanish person who will speak slowly for you. Oh, this is stupid...' She lowered her voice. 'Javi speaks good English, but you must make him talk to you more in Spanish, okay?'

I smiled, nodded. He only really tended to speak Spanish to me when we were in bed, but she didn't need to hear that. 'He does sometimes, when he sees me doing my homework and remembers.' Just like Jeremy, he ended up laughing at my blank face and putting me out of my misery. 'Maybe if I go to the office and ask, I could do some one-to-ones *this* week.'

She had a space in her timetable, and although it clashed with my *Compás* class we agreed that Javi might be better at helping me with that.

After the lesson I went off to the office to arrange it, Liz shaking her head in amazement. Javi had texted that he couldn't get home for lunch, so I invited her back to the flat for a sandwich.

'*Qué bonita!*' she was saying as I unlocked the door.

'Not a word of Spanish, please, I'm about to have another hour of it.'

'Are you sure Javi's going to like this?'

'Well, he said be nice to her. If I'm ever going to live here I need to be able to understand what the hell people are saying. Like you – I don't know how you do it.'

'You'll get there. But... has he said something then?'

'Sort of, yes.'

He opened the door before I could get my key out. I put my arms round him and sank into his chest. 'I'm so completely Spanished out, you'll never believe what—'

'Yes I've heard. This is good, Yoli. But we have a visitor.' The girl Isabel had been chatting to before she came over to me at the restaurant, at this proximity looking about twelve. I glanced around to confirm that Isabel wasn't with her. 'But don't worry, no more Spanish. This is my *sobrina*, and she speaks excellent English, don't you Rosita?'

Rosita smiled broadly, apparently unashamed of her set of protruding and uneven teeth. And presumably unashamed of the behaviour of her... (what the hell was *sobrina*?) the previous day. 'Pleased to meet you,' she said, holding out a bangled hand.

'Rosita works hard and saved money to go to England this summer. Do you know the best place to do a course?' Rosita was dipping *churros* in to a bowl of chocolate and getting quite a mucky mouth; was she old enough to come to England on her own? 'In autumn she will study *turismo* in the university.'

Eighteen? 'Oh! Well, my friend Emma sometimes does summer work at a language school in Brighton...'

'Bry-ton,' Rosita repeated. 'I know it, in the South. She can tell me the name of—'

'Of course.'

She asked me where I lived, what Brighton was like. Then the door buzzer went and she stopped mid-sentence. It suddenly came to me: *sobrina,* niece. She was Isabel's *daughter* – and by the look on her face she was expecting a displeased *mamá* at the door.

'Wait,' I said to Javi, getting up and planning to hide in the loo until Isabel had gone.

But he smiled, put an arm round my waist as if preventing my escape and opened the door. Isabel was there with her usual hand-on-hip, chin-in-the-air stance. There was a moment where incredulous looks were exchanged, then a simultaneous burst of rapid Spanish from the three of them. It began to look like the loudest voice would win the argument; and for pitch and intensity, together with the energy of youth, Rosita had the edge.

Javi suddenly let go of me, opened a bottle of wine and poured a glass for Isabel. Rosita was talking calmly to her mother now, something about friend and kindness.

Isabel turned to me. 'Sorry what I say at *restaurante*. And... thank you help to Rosita.' Then she put her hand out, ran her fingers down some of my hair and made some comment about it.

'She says you have pretty hair but need a little cut. She wants to do this for you, she is *peluquera*.'

'That's very kind, but maybe another time...'

She'd gone. 'She means *now*, Yoli. She goes to find her scissors.'

Gone eleven but it looked like every little house on the hillside still had lights on. Perhaps somewhere out there slept adorable Spanish children who'd learn to play flute or piano with me, musicians who'd speak slowly enough and let me join their trio or quartet.

I leaned over the repaired wall on the side of the balcony for the glimpse of the Alhambra, presiding with such benevolence over the city. What had the guide said? The Moorish rulers hadn't wanted to show off; people would look up at these homely pink blocks, never guessing at the paradise-like interiors they contained.

Above it, a starry sky promised another sunny day tomorrow. That's mostly how it would be from now until October, Javi had said, even if the nights were cool. I went inside and listened again to what would be the first section of *Sevilla*, smiled to myself and closed down the computer. Sorted out the kitchen; in this *bonita* but tiny home there wasn't room to be untidy.

Of course, maybe after a while we could afford – might even *need* – something a bit larger. But meanwhile, where would I put my things? The bed in the second room would have to go so that we could have a piano for my teaching. But most of my stuff would have to be left behind in England. Perhaps Jeremy would give me a section of his basement; I could visit it like a shrine when I went over to see him. I'd go for a week or ten days; that would be okay, wouldn't it? We'd walk along the canal to the Narrow Boat, cuddle up on the sofa with Pavlova and watch films, go to Sadler's in December for the Matthew Bourne show. In the spring I'd sort out the garden. In the summer I'd check he was looking after it, maybe visit him in Cádiz... But winter, spring and summer: how often would Javi be happy for me to go back and stay with Jeremy?

Eleven thirty: Jeremy wasn't going to ring. I started to worry about his evening, imagined him walking home alone, with a depth of depression and anger at self-delusion that only Fernando Morales Montoya could bring about. I decided to call him in the morning.

I washed, put on my pyjamas – even though they'd probably get taken off later – and got under the covers. Then my phone rang, as if he'd been waiting for me to get into bed before he called, to have a bed-to-bed chat like we sometimes had at home.

'Yol! Not too late are we? Haven't woken you up?'

'No, no. I'm waiting for Javi anyway. Good show?'

'Wonderful. Oh... Gabi says hello... hold on.' Chatter in the background; it sounded like they were in a restaurant. '...wants to talk to you.'

What was I going to say to Gabi? I didn't know anything about her, other than that she moaned about the sun and had flirted with Nando in front of her husband. But what a relief to hear Jeremy sounding so chipper...

'Yoli! How-are-you?' Nando. That deep, caressing voice resonating painfully. Even after all this time, even though he didn't matter anymore.

'Oh... fine!' I said, quickly sitting up; I couldn't speak to him lying on my back in bed. I couldn't speak to him anyway; I was trying to form a question about the show, but nothing was coming out.

'Jeremy say you are with boyfriend, *tocaor granadino*. What he is called?'

'Javi.'

'Javier...?'

'Benites.'

'Mm. I not hear of him.'

'He only plays in Granada. Although he recently joined—'

'And he play you well?'

God, how could he know that's what we... 'Er... yes. *Es muy simpatico*.'

'*Si*. But he is married.'

'Separated. For some—'

'*Pues*... why he not have *divorcio*?'

How much had Jeremy told him? We'd be discussing infertility treatments next.

'Yoli?'

'Yes.'

'Ah, still you are there. *Lo siento*, I ask too much.'

I'd said too many yeses already. Was this caring or just bloody nosey? It was hard to tell, but I didn't want to seem too bothered. 'So... are you pleased with your show?'

'We have changed some things, is better. Even the dance to the song of Pilar, remember that?'

'Of course.'

'At the end is now more... *conexión*. I like you see it. Why you not come, can tell me if prefer.'

Because I'm here with Javi, you self-absorbed *hombre*.

'Oh... Jeremy wants his *móvil*. *Adiós Yoli, besos*.'

He'd gone. I lay back in bed and breathed out heavily; it was okay, I'd spoken with him, and now probably wouldn't have to again for...

'Everything okay there?' Jeremy asked.

'Don't do that again.'

'What?'

'Putting Nando on the phone.'

'He asked to talk to you, just like all my friends do,' he said, more quietly.

'Friends as in... Vicente, or Nico?' I asked. 'How's it going?'

'As in the latter. But... good anyway.'

'Oh. You know it's funny, he talked to me like a Spanish Jeremy.'

'Mm.'

'And I never told you... when I first met him I thought he looked like a photo negative of you...'

He sighed; I wasn't helping.

'Oh dear. What are you going to do?'

He answered in a whisper. 'Get over it. Or rather, used to it.'

As I'd had to.

19.
cuidar *vt* to look after

Still asleep, the curtain of baby-soft hair flopping over his heavy features. *Look better on little girl*, he'd said. But I loved it. Anyway, I'd pointed out, it made him easier to pick out in *cuevas* full of curly dark heads. Like the night before, when Liz and I had bought him a beer and a plate of *tapas* during the break. The place was packed, but it was no problem finding him – taller than most, and standing near one of the stage lights, his hair gleamed like a halo. And I liked the way it fell over his face as he concentrated on those plaintive shivers of melody between Emilio's singing lines, or those gut-hitting drum-roll *rasgueados*...

I felt a rush of excitement and butterflies on his behalf about that evening: the group's first appearance at La Chumbera. A huge modern theatre up on the hill, eerily not visible from the road. I was looking forward to hearing the full group; in the *cuevas* Emilio only used his *tocaor*, his brother on the *cajón* and a moody, heavily testosteroned dancer with the longest ponytail I'd seen yet. Now they'd be joined by an accordion player, another percussionist, and a guy Javi had told me about who played flamenco flute and sax but was also a classical musician. Javi would be nervous but was too *flamenco* to admit it; he'd planned a day in the country for me, probably hoping for distraction.

I pushed myself into him and smiled as his arm came over. Then decided to be a good Spanish *mujer* for once and make breakfast for him. *Mujer*. Meaning woman or wife. Like *novia* meant girlfriend or fiancée. And there was no such thing as being a Mrs somebody; Spanish men could keep their commitments under wraps.

I showered, got dressed. Laid the table. His mobile rang from inside his jacket. I didn't want to wake him up, but I didn't want to answer it either – all that rapid Spanish and explanation as to who I was. And of course it could be... It stopped. Everything was ready; I just had to wait until he woke up. I started sorting out my bag, chucking out the handouts with the glee of an end-of-term schoolgirl and putting in my sunglasses and the map.

An aggressive buzz at the door made me jump. I peeped through the half-closed shutters: a big dark man, possibly the moody dancer. I'd have to let him in and converse, but he appeared to be a chap of few words so perhaps it wouldn't be too difficult. But he was wearing football boots, and as he yawned and stretched, the stripy top under his jacket rode up to reveal rather un-dancer-like abdominals. He buzzed again then swung his ape-like arms in irritation. Wondering if I should open the door and ask what he wanted, I assessed his face for the likelihood of criminal tendencies: narrow eyes, a hard mouth, and a pushed out chin above a thick, gold-chained neck. Medium to High. But it also seemed to be the face of the man in front of the house that first evening I'd come here: Isabel and Violeta's brother.

'*Buenos dias.* Javi...?' he asked, with a jerk of his chin towards the bedroom. I launched into a reasonable explanation of how he was asleep and I didn't want to wake him up because he had an important performance that night.

His eyes widened to almost normal size for a moment before mumbling something that may not have even been Spanish.

'Victor,' I heard; Javi was behind me, listening to this consonant-free rumble. He said something to him and then turned to me.

'He wants me to play football this morning. A guy is ill and we have a big match. But it is boring for you and we will lose the morning—'

'What about your hands, supposing you—'

'Oh no, no. I wear good gloves. But listen—'

'Could I watch?'

'Of course, but...'

'Better get eating breakfast then!'

An hour later we were in the car Emilio had lent us, driving to the other side of the city. Javi in a faded but appealing blue-and-white football kit that I assured him, as I stroked his thigh, made the halving of my outing more than worthwhile.

We arrived at a patchy field with a graffiti-covered pavilion but an impressive number of supporters waiting either side of the pitch. Javi left me with Rosita, there to watch a schoolfriend striker as well as her uncles in defence. The whistle blew. The ball was in Javi's half for most of the game, but he and Victor played well together

217

and no goals were scored until the green team lost patience in the second half and caused a penalty.

'Javi is good *defensa, no?*' Rosita said.

A sweaty Javi and Victor came over to us, both grinning, but then Victor asked why Isabel hadn't come. Rosita glanced at me and shrugged. But he persisted, and it began to look like I might be going to witness another family shout-down. She answered him in fast, quiet Spanish and then looked at Javi anxiously.

Javi's face creased in disbelief. Then he looked at me to see if I'd understood.

'Is something wrong?' I asked.

'Don't worry. I tell you in a moment.'

We started walking back.

'What?'

'It's okay, I will tell you in—'

'Then why can't you tell me now?'

He didn't answer. We walked in silence, got into the car.

'Violeta is having an operation for her shoulder. Also she needs break from her boyfriend and for this... she will have operation in Granada. It will be two or three months to *recuperar*... Isabel will look after her.'

'Isabel.'

'And Rosita, of course. And she has friends here...'

And a former husband. *Three months...* I turned my head to look out of the window at the emptying pitch. I opened it, needing some air.

'Yoli, is only that she wants to be with her sister, not a boyfriend who is busy and not very patient.'

'How patient will he be when he realises that she's spending three months just three minutes' walk from her ex-husband? Well, not even *ex*-husband, is it?'

'Oh stop, Yoli. Calm down and—'

'No I won't calm down! How would *you* like it?'

'I would hate it, I *do* hate it, but why you are cross with me, as if I decide this?'

'Because I think you *did*. You suggested this when you saw her, didn't you.'

'Yes, to have operation, she needs for long time, but—'

'Obviously she was going to come here.'

He sighed and massaged the fingers of his right hand. Perhaps remembering the concert and cursing me for no longer providing the pleasant distraction he needed.

He looked over again. 'Is it so bad to suggest the best thing for a friend?'

'Don't you mean *wife*?'

'No, she is not. Or *soon* not... when she is better, I will talk to her about a *divorcio*. There is no difference, I am with *you* now, so please, we stop this and enjoy our time, *no*?'

He pulled me over and kissed me, wiped the tears from my cheeks. We drove off.

Divorcio. 'And what was that about Isabel, am I an enemy again then?'

'No, no. She... went to the station to meet Violeta.'

I went cold all over: she was *here*.

'The operation is next week. Look, I will visit her after the operation, of course, talk sometimes, say hello in the street... but she is not part of my life now. Yoli, *please*.'

We drove home in silence. He had a shower while I packed the picnic things that we'd happily planned the previous day but I now couldn't imagine eating. My phone buzzed: jolly texts from Charlotte and Jeremy that I couldn't face answering. Then we were back in the car again, driving up out of the city, until he parked and led me up a hill towards a fallen tree, put down a rug and pulled me down to sit on it in his arms.

'Yoli... relax, come on.'

He looked at me for a moment then pulled out a little tin from the side pocket of the picnic bag. Inside were some scrawny-looking cigarettes.

'I thought you'd given up.'

'Yes. But this is different.'

I found the thermos and pulled off its two plastic cups.

'Even better than English cup-of-tea,' he said, taking them from me. 'Come here.'

'I don't smoke. I don't even know how.'

But he lit the cigarette and... there was that smell, always reminding me of Father... He drew on it, and then put it to my lips and held my nose, chuckling.

A bitter dryness hit the back of my throat and made me cough. 'God!' I steadied myself with my hand on the tree; I was woozy, needed to eat after all. But he put it to my mouth again and, drawing a breath to protest, I must have taken in a big gulp.

I had to lie down. 'I don't feel right.' He was laughing, helping me get comfortable. 'Though actually...' I closed my eyes. 'I'm not going to roll down the hill am I?' Over and over until something was in the way... the Alhambra perhaps. I giggled.

'I won't let that happen,' he said, kissing my neck, running his hands over me.

'Tickles! Oh...'

I was beginning to worry about the incline again, briefly opening my eyes and taking in a touchable blue sky.

The dizzying drop down to the city below. An unrealistic background of snowy mountains.

But Javi had it covered. Or rather he had *me* covered, his weight on top of me taking care of my lack of gravity. And as a warmth spread through my body, taking care of the need inside me too. Then saying – in my ear in case the breeze took the words away down the hill – that he loved me.

'It's okay, I'm *in* the coach, Jeremy.'

'Just checking. How are you doing? You didn't answer my text yesterday.'

'Sorry. I'm not doing well. It might be six weeks now – half-term – unless one of us can get out of school or some gigs...'

'Oh dear. Look... if you can't afford to hand over a bit more to that new flute girl, I'm sure I can—'

'No.'

'It's alright Yol, I've got plenty you could do to earn it, if you must.'

'Like what?'

'Well let's see. Er... sorting out my accounts stuff?'

'Oh no.'

'It's not hard, it's just a question of being arsed. Or wanting to cancel work to wing off and see a Spanish boyfriend.'

'Mm. Okay, maybe.'

'Good. So what have you two been up to then?'

Doped sex on the side of a mountain – he might not need to hear about that. I described the concert, how Javi's was the best of the 'promising new groups' that evening, how listening to him play against that vast glass wall behind the stage – against the lit-up Alhambra and maybe the very slope on which he'd said he loved me – had filled my heart.

He was quiet for a moment. 'But he hasn't taken you to the Alhambra. We had such a special time there.'

'I know. And how about Seville? Did you get everything you needed?'

'Pretty much. Now I've got to get my head down and make sense of it all.'

'Right.' I wondered whether I should ask about Nando. If he felt lonely now, sitting in the Cádiz flat all on his own.

'So did you *read* my text?'

'Of course... You might see Nando again soon?'

'We. He's just had it confirmed. He'll be standing in for one of Paco Peña's dancers for the Sadler's Wells shows in June.'

'Oh.'

'And after a few days at Paco's he's going to stay with me. Although can you believe it – had to be the week of the Winchester conference, didn't it. I'll see what I can do, obviously, but I told him you'd look after him.'

20.
esperar *vt* to wait for, to hope

'She's not doing it,' I said to Jeremy, scratching Pavlova's fat white cheek. And I wasn't going to purr down the phone either. I said I had a pupil coming and had to go. Made a hot chocolate – of all things – and sat on the sofa with my arms crossed.

I'd told him before: my services were strictly non-transferable. After Andrew had stayed for an interminable fortnight during the extensive re-designing of his unused kitchen. Vicente, however, stranded after losing his passport (maybe deliberately, but forgetting that Jeremy was off to the States), had been an adorable burden, almost blushing when I offered to do his washing. Vicente: now in a *relación exclusiva*, his communications limited to friendly emails. Good for him, he'd got over Jeremy and moved on. As I had with Nando, of course, but that didn't mean I was happy to have him two walls away for more than a week.

Look after him. Bloody hell. I suppose I could just leave food for him and tidy up his mess while he was out. As for a disagreeable cat. Certainly if he thinks I'm going to wash his sweaty stage shirts and black boxers he's got another think coming. I could pointedly leave out the washing machine instruction leaflet; if he's never done laundry before, it's time he learnt. Javi had to and coped well, ironed better than I did. That's the other thing: how was I going to smooth all this out with Javi? He'd wonder how much invitation had gone into the dancer-caring arrangement, possibly seeing it as some kind of tit for tat. But the end of June...

I went through to my flat and flipped over the pages of my filo. It'd be seven... eight weeks after Violeta's shoulder operation, and yes, my school term ended that week; hopefully I wouldn't be here after a few days, having flown out to a Violeta-free Granada. For the summer, returning for the odd wedding gig and to see Jeremy, but otherwise...

My phone buzzed: Javi wanting to know which weekend I could go and meet his family in Almería. I was excited and nervous about it, but it would be less scary than creeping around the alleys in Granada hoping not to encounter Violeta. I texted back the earlier of the two possible dates, only three weeks away.

'Uh, always knackering first day back,' I said, putting down my bag and collapsing onto the sofa.

'Oh come on, how hard can it be, one-to-one tooting away? Try taking on a classroom-full,' said Emma. 'Looks like I'll have to make the drinks.' She went over to the kitchen and filled the kettle.

'So are you up for the Thai place later then?' I asked.

'Course.'

'But it's only five o'clock... scones? There's gooseberry or damson jam.'

'After that treacle sponge at lunchtime? God, look at us: both eating ourselves stupid, one for comfort, one for joy,' she said, but opening the packet.

'So did you see Jason today then?'

'Well of course I did. And we've still got the play rehearsals to get through. Bit late to remember why you don't have flings at work. Didn't you go through this at your last school?'

'My first boyfriend. Head of English. Head of bullshit, more like.'

'First? You mean you went all through Music College without...?'

'I was always waiting for the right guy. Shame I didn't wait a bit longer. Like fifteen years.'

'So let's see, there was the English bullshitter, the line-dancing guy now in Corrie, the salsa-class dentist, the screwed up photographer bloke and Darling David of course. Five. Plus fillers.'

'What? No! That's it.' Once again I marvelled at the way that every time I didn't admit to my shameful episode with Nando it came a little closer to never having actually happened.

'And now it looks like you're going to stick at six. Although... I still can't imagine you actually leaving Jeremy. You're like a married couple.'

But en serio, *you are married, to Jeremy.* 'That's ridiculous. And anyway, I'd still see him quite—'

'No you wouldn't. Once Violeta's fixed and out of the way you'll be busy with IVF and then triplets.' I started to protest. 'Meanwhile he'll get Ginny installed, picking up after him. Maybe developing the touchy-feely thing you've got going with him these days—'

'She lives in Oxford.'

225

'People can *move*, Yol.'

I finished my scone. I tried to recall what ties Ginny had to her home town; surely her job in that little publishing company would act as a thickly anchoring guy rope.

'But coming back to you two... I mean I don't blame you – I loved all his hugs when I came over here in bits – but have you ever wondered...?'

'It's ever since he said no to The Question. Weird, it's somehow made us closer. But not like you're suggesting – gays don't suddenly stop being gay, Emma. In fact he's just fallen in love with a flamenco dancer in Seville.'

'Mutual?'

'We'll have to wait and see.' Wait for the disappointment, and see how much I can comfort him without letting him know how much I understand.

'We can't wait much longer, the vicar's got another Thanksgiving at half past,' said the mother. She pulled the three-year-old off the floor, moaning about grubby trousers, and warned a friend to stop jiggling the baby about or she'd throw up on her white dress.

Helen was nodding her head; after the service she had to speed off to Rupert's school to be sure of getting front row seats in the concert. 'Get your flute out, Yolly – we'll start the minute he gets here.'

'I'll try him again,' I said, pulling out my phone.

'I'm nearly there, five minutes,' Jeremy said.

Lateness, he would often remind me, is a form of arrogance. But with exceptions. And for Jeremy the only exception was romantic necessity. He'd obviously met someone in Cádiz. Why else would he have changed his flight? I should have been pleased for him, but felt strangely disappointed that he'd so quickly abandoned his infatuation with Nando and moved on to someone else. Even though that was exactly what I'd done myself.

He arrived, quickly disarming everyone with his heartfelt apologies and sun-golden appeal, and took his place among the semi-circle of guests.

A nod from Helen and we started. The Vivaldi *Allegro* from *Spring*: the usual smile on the adults' faces followed by frightened yelps from the baby. Calming down to *What a Wonderful World*. Later, the inevitable indulgence of the *Arrival of the Queen of Sheba*.

We made our way over the common to their pink-ballooned house.

'Are you speaking to me?' he asked.

'Maybe.'

'I couldn't help it. You'll understand when I tell you.'

'Everyone was holding me responsible.'

'Well... quite rightly, in a way.'

'What?'

'I'll explain later.'

It was time for pass-the-baby. Friends comparing stories of births and christenings, moist-eyed aunts and enchanted eight-year-old girls.

'Look at your boyfriend – he's a natural,' said a pregnant woman who'd asked Helen for the Trio's card. I turned and saw Jeremy rocking baby Florence in his arms. 'Are you two thinking of...'

'No. Well... not yet.' I put a strawberry meringue and a cherry cupcake on my pink plate.

'Why don't you hold Florrie for a bit?' Jeremy asked.

'Oh no, too small.'

'I'll help you, you just need to support her head. Come on, put that plate down.'

She immediately sensed the tension in my arms; her face puckered.

'Sit down,' he said, stroking her velvety-bald head.

'I thought you didn't like babies,' I whispered.

'Shush – she might hear you,' he said, opening up the spidery fingers of a tiny hand.

What was going on here? Love had made him go completely soft. And it was catching; I'd suddenly lost interest in stuffing myself with sweet pink food. I could hear the faint whistle of her breath, feel her grow heavy as she sank into me and fell back to sleep on my lap. It was crazy but I felt strangely in tune with this friend of a friend's baby who I probably wouldn't see again until she was a spoilt three-year-old Queen of Sheba.

And strangely in tune with myself; I'd seldom ever noticed the twinges of ovulation, but at that moment the little needles of pain surprised me with their insistence. And when I thought about it, with their *existence*; clearly my pill-taking had reached a critical level of haphazard. I pondered how, at this very moment, I could hand Florrie back and become a future mother myself. Except that the intended father was possibly infertile, over a thousand miles away and – judging by his switched-off mobile – visiting his wife in hospital.

Florrie started to grizzle and make pouty mouthing movements. I wondered how it felt to have a baby at one's breast; Charlotte had said it was the next best thing to sex. Then the snorting and mewing started and an aunt swooped down and took Florrie away.

The shawl descended, its grey-blue tones in stark contrast to the rosy happiness around me. I went to find Jeremy.

'Freddy's taken him to meet his rabbit,' said Florrie's father. 'Suddenly spotted him as the guy who looked after him and made up stories about all his plastic animals.'

Spitting rain was keeping all but a couple of teenage smokers indoors. But there was Jeremy by the hutch, impressing Freddy with a running commentary of the rabbit's thoughts and aspirations.

Freddy eyed me with interest. 'Does your wife make stories too?'

'Only in her head, but maybe that's why she's so good at listening to them.' He took my arm. 'Time to go.'

'Yours or mine?' I asked when we got back.

'Yours. I want to see this new pin-board, check I'm sufficiently represented.'

I opened my door. 'There. Picture of us right in the middle. Although maybe I should move things around a bit before Javi next comes over.'

I ran my eyes over Mitch's postcards. The chunks of green-velveted rocks plunging into the sea in Madeira ('*could be Jersey!*'); the sandy beach and pale green sea at St Maarten ('*an island with our name and a French and Dutch side!*'); a St Lucian playing a banjo ('*remember me trying to teach you?*').

So what does your father say on these postcards?'

'The picture always brings back a memory... Helen's given me another today – let's see...' I pulled it out of my bag and opened it. 'Oh...'

'*The Barbados Green Monkey,*' Jeremy read.

I turned it over. '*Do you still like monkeys? Thought of you when we went to the Wildlife Reserve...*'

'When did the monkey thing start then?'

'Jersey zoo, I suppose. He'd take us there when he came back to visit.' Sometimes buying us big cuddly animals; other times struggling to find enough cash for lollies.

We sat down on the sofa with some tea. He received a text that made him smile; I received one telling me what I knew already – that Javi had visited 'V' in hospital, and now had to dash off to Málaga with the group.

'Javi alright?'

'Yeah.'

'And Violeta?'

'He doesn't say. Do we care?'

'Yes we do. You want everything to go well for her so that she gets better quickly. Good karma, remember. Positive for her is positive for you.'

It had only been a week, but I was already positively fed up with being positive about Violeta.

'You're not going to be silly about this, are you? Because if you are you could ruin everything. You do—'

'Yes, yes I know.'

'Just think, you could be living there this summer.'

I looked over at him. Since when was he so keen for me to move to Granada? But he'd had another smile-inducing text and was tapping out a reply.

Then he put his phone on the table and turned to me, pulled me closer. 'Listen, I've been thinking. If it turns out that you and Javi can't have a kid, I'd like to help you out.'

'Oh my God – really? That would be...' I hugged him and he patted my tummy. Then it struck me: he was offering me a *consolation*. What he knew to be the ultimate prize, and probably a final one. He was leaving.

'So... how was Cádiz?'

'It was... perfect.'

'Did you...' *Did you meet someone so perfect that, even after just a week, you knew you'd be leaving me after ten years.*

'He had a couple of days off so he came to see me.'

'Who?'

'Who d'you think?' he said with a chuckle. 'He's got an idea for his next show – he wants it to be entirely narrative and I've been helping him with some ideas.'

'Oh. That's good.' An artistic alliance, probably leading to a lasting friendship.

'And... well, I don't know how to describe it, uh...' He smiled and bit his lip. 'God, this finally happens to me and all I can come up with is clichés.'

'You're in love with him.'

He looked at the floor. 'Completely.'

'But he's not...'

'He's not gay, no.'

'So...'

'But he says he's never found a woman who really... *excited* him.'

I didn't recall him having any problems with excitement.

'And he's weary of all the female attention he gets. Probably explains his gentlemanly behaviour with you – it must have been a relief to spend time with a lovely girl who wasn't throwing herself at him.'

Throwing myself: I hoped Nando didn't think I'd done that. A mutual attraction, and just maybe, at the time, a little more...

'I'm sorry Yol – you don't still have a bit of a crush on him, do you?'

'No, of course not.' I smiled at him. 'I'm just worried for you, that's all.'

'Well don't be, because... he says he feels the same.'

231

Nando. Gay. I started to feel rather nauseous. All that pink food. 'You mean...'

'We're getting so close, I think... he just needs time. And I'm happy to give him all the time he needs.'

He would wait, forever if need be, to have sex with Nando. No doubt wondering when it would be. *How* it would be. Not knowing – thanks to Nando's admirable promise-keeping – that I could tell him. I hugged him and closed my eyes tightly on the memory. But it wouldn't go away. This is how it will be, I could have said. He will hold you firmly, murmuring Spanish in your ear. Then it will be happening. Fluently: that sinuous, sensitive body – his very being – so exquisitely made for sex. Fast: one's own pleasure embarrassingly swiftly assured. And then there'll be the blissful tenderness of his arms – later, even more painful to dwell on than the act itself. Except that, for you, there may not be any pain; it could be just the start of your lives entwining.

'Yol?'

'Yes,' I said into his chest.

'Remember what we said – there'll always be an us, okay? You know I can't be without you. Don't start getting—'

'So we could both... How far is Seville from Granada?' I asked, trying to smile. 'We could be in Andalucía together.'

'About three hours. Not really a day trip. But that's good, it means we'd have to make it a few days at a time. Maybe a week or more if they were both off touring... But no more talking like this, it's making me nervous.'

21.
engañar *vt* to cheat, trick

'So... if you and Nando were a couple, and you helped me have a baby with Javi, what d'you think he'd feel about that?'

'What? Where did that come from! I'm trying to concentrate here.' Jeremy pointed the controller at the television; another house exploded into being. 'Don't worry,' he said.

I wasn't sure whether he was referring to Nando's reaction or my ability to pay the *Monopoly* Mayfair rent. He started developing Leicester Square.

'Uh. Thought you didn't like the West End.'

'I do like some musicals – *Les Misérables*, the ballet boy one...'

'If you'd agreed to see *Priscilla* with me I wouldn't have been tempted to take up David's offer.'

'Oh come on, you'll be fine. Just don't mention it to Javi.'

'Not mentioning is the same as lying.'

'Well mention it in a few days' time then, but not... Oh, look what you've made me do – I've just gone and *sold* three houses instead of buying them.'

'Good,' I said, grabbing his controller and ending his turn before he could put it right.

'Hey! You little cheat!'

I shook my controller to roll the dice. 'So what was it like playing Monopoly with Nando? I just can't imagine... Bet *he* cheats.'

'Why? That's very unfair. And he didn't, actually.'

'Or was just very good at it.'

'A-ha: jail. Serves you right for your slanderous comments.'

'Good, keeps me out of harm's way for a bit.'

'You could show him how to play it on the *Wii* when he's here and I'm at Winchester.'

'There won't be time – I'm teaching all day and he's dancing all night.'

'A nice wind-down after the show. I'm sure he'd love it.'

Sitting here with hot chocolate, trying not to remember how we'd wound down after the show last time; that was *not* going to happen.

'So what about after-the-show tonight? Are you sure David's not going to try anything?' He passed me the controller. 'Right, six or an eight and you're all mine.'

'Uh. Course he's not. Anyway, he won't be invited back – just imagine if Javi called.'

The phone rang. 'Talk of the devil,' Jeremy said.

'The *angel*, if you don't mind.'

I picked it up and he told me how Almería was all arranged, we'd cuddle up in the bus on the Saturday morning and be there for lunch. I wasn't to worry, his mother and sister were used to speaking slow Spanish for their students and were very keen to meet me. It sounded like maybe his father wasn't, but Javi was moving on to how it would be sunny, how we would eat in their courtyard garden then perhaps take a stroll along the beach. The thought of it shone a ray of warmth and comfort over me. One that was probably designed to see me through the next part of the conversation.

I asked how Violeta was doing, prompting a grinning thumbs up from Jeremy, and learnt that it looked like the operation had been a success. As usual, he told me how she'd asked about me. And then he said that she'd loved both our pieces.

There was a silence in which I realised that meant she'd been to his apartment, and he probably realised that he would have preferred not to have let that drop.

'Good,' I said, wrestling with a need to ask where she'd sat to listen to them. In the kitchen with the CD player? Or – please, no – in our music room, where he'd first tried to kiss me, where we had made music and, on one mutually congratulating occasion, love.

Jeremy was making rolling motions with his hand to make me say more; I flapped a wave of reassurance. But meanwhile, Javi was letting me know about an agreeable change in Violeta.

'Oh,' I said.

'It makes her more calm.'

I considered repeating *oh*. I looked at Jeremy and shrugged, watched his face become serious.

'This is why is more easy to talk with her about you,' he explained. 'Is good thing, Yoli. Ah... I have a student. I will call you later, *no?*'

'That would be nice. Oh – but not too much later, I'll be out.' A further crease of concern in Jeremy's face.

'Where?'

'I'm going to a show.' Jeremy shook his head and waved his hand from side to side.

'Jeremy. Or... *not* with David,' Javi said.

'Yes.'

'With who, Yoli?'

'David.' Jeremy put a hand over his face and looked at me through his fingers; I made a shooing motion with my hand. 'But I'll be back before eleven, you could–'

'I don't understand, why a big show, a big... present. You could meet in a cafe as friends.'

'Well it's not that much of a–'

'I know. Because he has much money, it is nothing.'

'No! His friend got us discounted tickets.'

'But not one for Jeremy.'

'Jeremy doesn't like musicals, too many auditions for them as a child.'

'No, is that he wants you alone.'

'Uh... it's not like that. Please, don't let's start this again. I mean, how d'you think I feel about...' A vehement shake of the head from Jeremy; I turned so I couldn't see him.

'Ah... so is why you go.'

'You know it isn't, he asked me ages ago. Look... I'll call you when I get in, okay?'

'No, I don't want you to do this, like making report.'

A burst of music and '*no te preocupes, es la tuya*' from the television. Don't worry, it's yours. Jeremy must have switched the game back on by mistake.

'Who is that?'

'The man in the Monopoly game – we're playing it on the Wii.'

'On what?'

'You know, playing it on the television with controllers.'

'But... is Spanish man.'

'Of course, we always use the Spanish version. I've picked up all sorts of useful phrases, like "*has sacado doble*"!'

'*Muy bien*,' he said with a little chuckle. 'So Jeremy is there.'

'Yes.'

'You are never alone, Yoli.'

'What? Course I am.' Although it was true that Jeremy and I seemed to be spending more time together than ever, perhaps now that it looked like we might be going to be living three hours rather than three seconds apart. 'It doesn't stop me missing you.'

'Good. But is not long to wait this time. I'm sorry I am so... I hope you enjoy the show. I will call tomorrow, yes? *Besos, mi Yolandita*.'

'*Muchos besos*.'

'Well? Can't have been as good as the film.' He took the programme off me and started to flick through. 'Come in and tell me about it.'

I showed him the costumes and described others, but was distracted by Jeremy's attire – or rather lack of it; there was an unspoken rule that we didn't see each other in underwear, but there he was in brazen boxers and singlet.

'Couldn't sleep,' he said, by way of explanation. 'Felt like a parent of a teenager on a dodgy date.'

'Dodgy? Only a few months ago you were suggesting I gave him another chance.'

'Well, I suppose Javi's won me round.'

237

'Now he's part of the Andalucian plan.'

'Don't – we're not allowed to talk like that, remember? Gives me the...'

'Willies?'

He frowned. 'That's very coarse, Yol.' He put down the programme. 'So how was it with David?'

'Fine. Well, so-so – bit intense over coffee afterwards. He's bothered about how Vanessa doesn't have enough time for him.'

'He still wants you back, doesn't he.'

'No, no. And too bad if he did – even if I wasn't with Javi I could never go back to having a relationship where I'd have to try so bloody hard. I'd rather be on my own.'

'Bravo,' he said, pulling me over, his golden-haired thigh touching mine.

'Go and put your dressing gown on, you'll get cold.'

'Oh yes, pardon me.' He went off to the bedroom.

I took out my phone: no missed calls or texts. But then he'd said he wouldn't ring until tomorrow. *If I wasn't with Javi.* A shiver passed through me. One of those *distancia* moments. Or perhaps something else: telepathy, or just a sudden physical need to hear his voice. I called but there was no answer. A last minute decision to support a friend playing at Le Chien or another club; I'd hear about it tomorrow. And tomorrow will be another day less until we're together again. The sooner I go to bed, the sooner it will come.

Jeremy came back. One more drink, one more hug. Much longer than Javi would have liked me to have, but for some reason I couldn't let go.

'Triple pay on a Sunday. In fact you may as well just tell me which flights you want and I'll book them now.'

'No you won't Jeremy, that's too much. Besides, I'm quite enjoying myself.'

'I'll get you another tea,' he said, stepping over my legs and the piles of receipts.

'I mean, look at this. Hire of *bicicletas* in Maria Luisa Park. How the hell is that tax-deductible?'

'Research, isn't it? Needed the experience. And they're not normal bicycles – they're four-wheeled *cyclos*... lovely way of exploring the park and such a laugh. Have to take you one day.'

'Yeah, but where d'you draw the line? You could put absolutely anything down – the cost of the experience of buying loo rolls, the cost of committing a crime and paying bail...'

'Fair wear and tear on my mind and emotional well-being. You're right, my whole life is just one big tax-deductible expense,' he said. I groaned. 'But the *cyclo* receipt shouldn't really be there, I just had to keep it...' He tapped at his Blackberry and held it out in front of me. A little film of him and Nando laughing like schoolboys on a tractor-size bike.

'Oh my God, that's so *sweet*.'

'*Sweet*? D'you mind? This is hopefully the love of my life you're talking about here.' My phone rang. 'And that's probably yours.' He picked up my mug and went over to the kettle, mumble-singing an old Chambao song involving a *bicicleta*.

'*Hola! Qué tal?*' I asked. I was aching from sitting on the floor, stood up and stretched. 'Javi?'

'Your voice...'

'Well who else's did you expect to hear, *hombre*? Hey, forgot to tell you, I've moved my Friday pupils so now I can turn up about the time you get back from the school.'

I thought he said 'good'.

'Can't hear you very well.' A pause. It sounded like we'd been cut off. 'You still there?'

'Listen, Yoli... you know how much I love you...'

A rush of pleasure. 'Yes, and I—'

'Remember this, because... *Dios*...' He seemed out of breath.

'Are you alright?'

He sighed. 'Is difficult but...' I couldn't catch the rest; maybe it was in Spanish. A pause. Then suddenly he was almost shouting at me. '*Entiendes*, Yoli?'

'No, what's the—'

'Is mistake... *no sé cómo*... too much wine...'

'So now you've got a migraine. Have you—'

'No, no! Violeta... *pasó la noche aquí!*' He started sobbing.

Cold ice through the veins. But I wasn't ready to believe it. Not of Javi. She'd spent the night – but surely on the sofa. Now he was going on, saying something about how she'd tricked him, taken him back in time... How sorry he was. How sorry *she* was.

But still I hoped. 'You...'

More crying, more sorrys.

'Did you...?'

Silence.

Then almost a whisper, but a sickening blow that pushed me onto the sofa. The rest was incoherent, or maybe I just couldn't follow it.

I took my mobile from my ear and looked at it. I could snap-close the sobbing, but how could I get rid of the hundreds of texts, the hours of warmth and laughter I'd had with it in my hand?

'No!' The phone shattering on the floor. The sobbing transferring to me. Jeremy asking me something.

He picked up the phone. 'Javi?' He put it down again and grabbed his own.

'Don't!' I said, but he was speaking to him in Spanish, listening, pulling me over.

'He loves you, he made a mistake... come on.' He tried to put the phone to my ear but I pushed it away. 'Yol! He's hurting as much as you are.'

'How *can* he be, the filthy bastard!'

He took my shoulders. 'Well he is. Just listen to him. He's still Javi.'

I grabbed the phone. 'Why? Why did you have to *ruin* everything!'

'I don't want that... Yoli I'm sorry, I'm sorry...never again... Please, nothing changes for me, I still only want you.'

Still Javi.

'Yoli?'

How many times had I been through this? The pointless screaming and unanswerable questions. 'I need some time... I can't talk now.'

'I understand. Tell Jeremy that I say to give you hug for me.'

His hugs.

'Can I call you later?' he asked. 'When do you–'

'No... I'll call you.'

'Today?'

'I don't know.'

'I am home all day.' I imagined him tidying up the apartment, the bedroom... 'I am busy... moving things... to make better for us the music room.'

The music room. On Friday night I could still be there, I thought, still trying to forgive – as I would for who knows how long – but *there*. My throat tightened again. 'Yes.'

'I love you Yoli.'

I put down the phone. Jeremy put his arms round me, started to say how surely I could see this was nothing like what David had done, how having been married all those years it would have been easy to have...

'Gone back in time, yes, that's what he said, but...'

'Specially as he was feeling... vulnerable.'

'What?'

'Well, about you being out with a wealthy ex-boyfriend.'

I sat up. 'So you think this is *my* fault?'

'Of course not, but—'

'No, that's exactly what you're saying. Bloody hell, I don't deserve this! Fuck you both!'

'Yol—'

'I need to be on my *own*,' I said, shaking him off and going into the hall. But I'd left my keys in his flat, and anyway, did I really want to cry on my bed, yet again... I opened the front door and started striding down the street.

But Jeremy dashed out after me and took my arm firmly, his other round my waist. 'You're *not* going for a walk in this state.'

I let him take me back to my flat, make me a hot chocolate. We sat down and talked it through until instead of dwelling on what Javi had done, we were trying to work out why. I told him how I'd looked after a drunken Javi that first night, and about what had happened with Nuria. Jeremy thought he was insecure about me.

'Think, have you ever actually told him that you want to live with him there?'

'Er... perhaps not exactly, but...'

'Maybe he doesn't believe that you'll ever move away from your Trio, the theatres—'

'And you. Yes, I see what you mean. But that's no bloody excuse for—'

'Of course not, but it might make him more susceptible...'

'Well I'm in no mind to give him any reassurance *now*.'

'No, you need some time.' He looked at his watch. 'Can you face some lunch? I booked the window table at the Narrow Boat and we could still make it.'

I shrugged.

'Come on then.'

We crossed the road, walked down the side street towards the canal. He yanked me out of the cycle lane as we heard a *ting-ting* behind us. A bike whizzed past.

'Careful, Yol. The Maria Luisa Park this is not.'

'No. Damn things. Healthy for them but bloody stressful for everyone else.'

We took the steps down to the canal.

'Quiet, isn't it? Suppose everyone's gone off for the long weekend. Shame it's not always like this,' he said. We walked on, past our favourite barge and the fish-shaped seats. 'You'll have to bring Nando down here when it's quiet during the week.'

'I've told you, I'll be working.'

'Not on the Monday. You could have lunch.'

'I've got other things to do than entertain him.' It came out rather too harshly, but... bloody Spanish men. Bloody *flamenco* men: all passion and tenderness, then floating off as easily as the untamed melody over those strangely shifting chords.

Jeremy was looking at me. 'I want you and Nando to be friends, Yol. I thought you *were*. But sometimes you seem a bit—'

'Of course I am... we are. It's just that I don't want to spend too much time... I mean, even after all this – *especially* after this – I don't want to upset Javi.'

'No.' He stopped, looked pensive for a moment.

'Come on, we'll be late,' I said. But we couldn't move on; a couple of bikes were coming down the path, we had to wait before going under the bridge.

'Yol, don't get cross with me but... tell me the truth, did you—'

'Of course I fancied him. Who wouldn't?'

'But it was more than that... you fell for him, didn't you.'

'Well a bit, as I owned up to at the time, but that was before Javi.'

'Yes but... if you're still in love with him—'

'Oh for God's *sake* Jeremy,' I said, turning from him and walking on.

And then... it's blurred. Not that I can't remember what happened. But mostly I live with the sounds: *ting-ting*, shouting, *screaming*, the rip of my blouse as Jeremy grabbed my arm, a monstrous bang and whirring.

And the whack of Jeremy's head hitting the wall.

22.
mente *f* mind

Pavlova, call Emma, things into bag, get back. Maybe
bath. Oh, and speak Duncan. And... something else
– possibly the most important – but what? Thinking
difficult, should have written it down... but not easy
either. I scanned his room for ideas... just as I closed my
eyes on it the phone flashed at me. That's it. Charge the
Blackberry. I went through to the bedroom, connected it
on the bedside table. Next to his pillow. Where his head
goes. *His head.* I put my head where his head... just a few
minutes... because got to get back...

  '*I take it you haven't eaten?*'

  I opened my eyes, almost expecting to see him leaning
against the door frame. Found myself in front of the
fridge. The moussaka we'd been going to have for dinner.
Energy that might push me onwards through this strange
new thick-aired world. But in a heavy thing that Ginny
had bought. No way I'd get it out with one hand. With
one eye, too: the other one had clouded over again. No,
fuck, I can do this. I pulled the dish to the edge of the
shelf, knelt down on my usable knee. But then reminded
myself that it was real, three-dimensional; Jeremy would

hate the mess and the waste. Even though he'd never see it.

I got up, closed the fridge. Tried to remember what I was doing. Needed to sit on the sofa to work it out. Looked at my knee. *A schoolgirl playground knee*, that's what he'd called it when I'd slipped off the low wall at the beach in Cádiz... The flat turned watery. Can't think of that now. Can't think of *anything* now, just what I've got to do. Come *on*. Duncan, phone, food. Duncan? Why. Or maybe to do with the food and the phone. Perhaps he can help. I picked it up and called him. No answer. But then of course not, he was at work. It had been Sunday for a long time, but now it wasn't.

Monday. I should be cleaning, ironing. Jeremy should be writing, telling me to leave the hoovering. I considered picking the receipts and bits of broken phone off the floor. But what was the point? And I needed to get back.

'*You need to eat, Yol.*' Still bossing me about. Hopefully always would.

Back to the fridge. Tomatoes. Strawberries. Too many red things. I closed it again.

Back to the bedroom. The Blackberry gratefully taking on energy.

Back to the kitchen. Got into the Ginger Thins with my teeth.

Back to the Blackberry. How long would it take? Maybe bath while waiting. But even then, would I be able to...? I *had* to. Somebody, anybody, would have to show me how. If there was anything I could do to make a difference, *anything* at all, please God, I had to do it.

Then the phone rang. I'd already ignored it twice: Andrew, the Winchester festival woman. But this time

I made my way purposefully through the thick-air and picked it up.

'Jeremy.' I kissed his forehead, combed the blooded hair with my fingers.

Still. Except for the breathing that he wasn't doing himself. *But he may be able to hear you and feel your hand.*

'That's it, you have a good sleep. You're still beautiful, just two little holes to let out the bruise-blood. The doctor said it all went really well. And the crack will mend. Now you've just got to rest and get better.'

Silence. A brief two-tone bleeping I'd been told not to worry about, the nurse calmly changing a bag.

'And you really need to. I've brought something to remind you why.' I pulled out the Blackberry, tapped at it as the taxi driver had shown me and played the *bicicleta* film quietly in his ear. I put my head by his and could just hear Nando's rapid Spanish, Jeremy's protestations, the excited whooping as they sped away.

A twitch of an eyelid.

'Yes, you twitch away, because guess what, he's *coming to see you.* He'll be here in about five hours' time. But don't worry, you don't have to be awake, he'll be here tomorrow too, and Wednesday morning. He loves you Jeremy, he really does. I can tell.' I took a deep breath. 'Almost as much as I do.'

I stopped. He mustn't hear a whine in my voice. I quietly wiped my nose.

'You should have heard us trying to communicate about broken heads and pipes. But I've got my dictionary with me and when he calls from the airport I'll try and do better.'

The nurse tapped me on the shoulder.

'See you later Jeremy, I'm off to the coffee shop. I'll have one of those gross toffee-chocolate things for you.' I kissed his forehead. Found a cool, smooth hand under the blanket and kissed that too. Walked into the corridor and let the tears stream. Let the angel-like Irish nurse take me into the interview room with its boxes of tissues and tell me how well he was doing.

I went down to the cafe and waited. It wasn't the one that did the toffee-chocolate thing – that was in the other hospital. Where Jeremy had looked like he just had a simple fracture and would soon be home. Until I'd gone to visit him, panicked on finding his bed empty, and been told that he'd had an emergency transfer here.

I started to feel sick again, but the vomiting in sympathy had to stop – another order into my head from Jeremy. I picked up a cereal bar and ordered a drink, sat down on a squishy sofa that threatened to drag me down into sleep. Got out the dictionary and struggled to look up some words...

Eventually the call came. I told him all I knew. He listened, asked questions. Not all of which I could answer. But I told him how Jeremy's eyelid had twitched when I'd played him the sounds of him and Jeremy in the park. He couldn't reply for some time, then said he'd find me in the cafe, I should try to sleep. To do that I needed to stop Jeremy's phone buzzing in my pocket; I spoke to a shocked Andrew and asked him to deal with the Winchester woman, called a tearful Emma and gave her Kirsty's number and those of my pupils. Then sank back into the sofa and was soon dreaming of being on Jeremy's, cuddling up with him and watching Strictly Ballroom...

He'd sat down next to me, and was pushing stray hair and a soap-sticky plait off my face.

'Ay, *pobrecita*, you not say,' he said, looking at my injuries.

'I'm fine, it's a nuisance that's all.'

'I can help you now. And Jeremy, how he is? When we see him?'

I looked at my watch. 'Soon. They said seven o'clock.'

'Okay. We eat something, have to be... strong for him, no?'

I looked over at the sandwich display. It went double. I got out a tissue and removed a jelly slick from my eye.

'They not give...' He made a cover shape with his hand.

'Only for one day. I've got some drops but I can't get the top off.'

'*Dámelas.*'

I got them out of my bag. He made me put my head back on the arm of the sofa, leant over me – like he had done before... but that all seemed so long ago.

'*Abre.*'

'That's as open as it goes.'

He pulled down my lower lid and squeezed in the cold drop. I squealed. Briefly heard myself laugh.

'We do... four every day,' he said, examining the box.

People were looking over, seeing an intimate couple rather than two people who loved the same man.

We ate our sandwiches, I asked about the show. Almost like nothing was wrong, and nothing wrong had ever happened between us.

Then at half six, when we were counting the minutes, the Blackberry rang in my pocket. 'Yolande? It's Deirdre in ICU. D'you want to come now? He's started to come round.'

'Yes!' I said, and closed the phone. 'He's waking up.' We grin-wept at each other and picked up our things, linked arms as we walked towards the lift.

We reached the buzzer and I warned him of a wait, but Deirdre opened it almost immediately.

'We took the tube out – he wasn't tolerating it – and couldn't work out what he was trying to say, over and over, something like "you're...",' she said, beaming. 'And then I suddenly got it, didn't I? I said to him, "Yolande?" and he nodded.'

Nando squeezed my arm. 'Oh no, I've got to stop this,' I said, grabbing a tissue. 'Mustn't see me crying.'

'No. And he's still very drowsy and needs a lot of rest. Just a few minutes – perhaps just you at first and then your friend.'

The antibacterial stuff. The plastic aprons. 'Okay. Do I look alright? Don't look weepy, I mean.'

'You're fine. Go and see him. He'll be asleep but if you talk to him he'll open his eyes. Keep it simple, he's still very confused, and just a few minutes, remember.'

He looked calm, beautiful. The pain gone. But hopefully not too much Jeremy gone, or not forever. I sat down next to him, took the hand without the wires. 'Jeremy?' A whisper, not wanting to alarm his bruised mind.

He opened his eyes. A slightly delayed recognition, or perhaps just unsure as to whether I was real or not. A weak smile. 'Yol.' He squeezed my hand. 'You're-right?'

'Of course. How are you feeling?'

'Mm. But...' He nodded at my bound hand.

'Middle one's broken. But it'll be okay.'

'Come-ere.' I shuffled to the edge of the chair and leaned forward, a bit worried about the wires. 'No, *here.*' I stood up and put my face in front of his. Smiled. Desperately tried not to cry. 'Eye?'

'Just a scratch.'

'Wha' been *doing?*'

Oh God. He obviously didn't remember. I should have asked Deirdre what to say. 'Um... well, you and I had a bit of an accident. But we're all okay.' He looked puzzled for a moment. Then weary, as if trying to remember was a strain. 'You just need to rest and get better.' I kissed his forehead, his cheeks. 'And you've got another visitor. Nando's here.'

'Where...?'

'In the corridor, we were told one at a time.'

He smiled. 'I think you...' He closed his eyes, opened them again. Seemed to have lost track of what he was going to say.

'Shall I get him? If you're too tired he'll understand. He can come tomorrow.'

'No, he...' His smile faded. 'But don'go.'

'You want me with him.' He nodded.

I fetched Nando, coming back to Jeremy together, one each side of the bed.

'*Khe-re-mi?*' Nando asked, his voice low and gentle. Jeremy opened his eyes. They smiled at each other. Nando held his hand and kissed it. Then put his face close to Jeremy's and softly talked with him. I wanted to let Sleeping Beauty enjoy Prince Charming on his own, started to edge away.

'No, toge'her,' Jeremy said suddenly, and held out the wired hand with the clip on his thumb. I took it as well as I could. But he pulled my hand towards the one holding Nando's, and looked at each of us with a faint smile before closing his eyes.

23.

abrazar *vt* to hug, to take charge of

How could I have had nearly twelve hours' sleep and still feel completely lifeless? I picked up the Blackberry and realised I hadn't remembered to switch it back on again after ICU. Which was unfair on quite a few people. Including Javi. I'd replied to a text on Sunday, telling him Jeremy and I had had an accident but were okay. Just before I found out that Jeremy wasn't. And then... I could only think of Jeremy. I'd contacted other people, giving information and asking favours, but I'd had nothing to say to Javi. Then there was Nando, always there. I didn't want to speak to Javi in front of him; Jeremy had said their relationship had to be a secret, and with a brain full of thick-air I couldn't trust myself.

Two more texts from Andrew, and he must have contacted Ginny because there was a long one from her. Emma asking what else she could do, Kirsty telling me that my teaching was sorted out between her and Helen, and one of the new girls was covering me for the Trio. Some other people I didn't recognise. And amongst all these, numerous texts from Javi. How was Jeremy? How was my finger? Had I gone back for my eye check?

Thinking about me. Loving me. Please could I call when I had a moment...

'Yoli! I was thinking of you this minute... How are you and Jeremy?'

'I'm okay but he's had a... bleed between the skull and the brain. He had to have an operation, and they're still trying to get the pressure down. He's awake now but rather confused...'

'*Dios*, but with time...?'

'He should recover completely, but it's likely there'll be difficulties... they just can't say for how long.'

'Oh... poor Jeremy. And for you... Can I look after *you*? I could come Friday night and stay to Sunday, yes?'

'I... can't think that far ahead.'

'But it must be so difficult for you with the hand, and so tired, worrying...'

'I'm okay.'

'Is that... still you can't forgive me?'

'No. We need to talk but... I just need to concentrate on Jeremy.'

'If you change your mind...'

'Of course. Everything okay with the group?'

'Yes. It's certain now about Jerez, so Rafa and Diego will teach for me on Wednesday and Thursday. Oh – but I must be there now. Call again when you can. Take care of yourself too, *no*? *Muchos besos.*'

A knock on the door. Perfect timing, or perhaps he could hear I was on the phone and had been waiting.

'Yoli, you sleep well?' That just-showered smell and wet blue-black hair, the jeans and pale blue shirt. Just a twitch of memory, then thinking how delighted Jeremy would be, having looked forward to seeing him all morning. If he was capable of looking forward.

'Still you are tired.' He helped me get my arm into the dressing gown sleeve, pulled the belt tight. 'You call the hospital?'

'Yes. They said he's had a good night and made some healthy complaints about the choice of cereals. But they're busy with him now and suggested eleven o'clock.'

'Okay. I have prepare *our* breakfast.'

I followed him through to Jeremy's flat. Pavlova was rattling away as she spluttered through a heaped bowl. But ours consisted of cutlery, glasses, juice and ketchup on the table; eggs, saucepan and bread on the work surface.

'But you want me to make it.'

'No, no, you say me how to do it.'

'*Tell* you how to do it.'

'Uff... yes. I am studying English now, you know. Even I have done it this morning, like something I can do for Jeremy.' He disappeared to the bedroom and came back with a book on *gramática inglesa*. 'You not see the difference?'

'Not yet, I'm afraid.'

'You *are going* to see. Any-way, sit down and say... tell me how to make the eggs.'

I did, but it was ridiculous; he had absolutely *ninguna idea*, and stood there with a smirking can't-believe-I'm-doing-this look on his face. Rather like the one I'd been accused of having in Jersey when Simon decided that his single sister-in-law should know a few things about a car, starting with how to check the oil. I told Nando about it while he was stirring the eggs.

'But is not necessary, Jeremy can do the car.'

'Are you joking? When a light comes on we just go to Dan at the garage. But cooking's different – I mean, even Jeremy can make an omelette.'

'He can? I don't know, in Cádiz we went to restaurants for all the meals.'

All the meals: so he'd stayed the night. I imagined them sleeping together – not... well, *doing* anything, just side by side. Then getting up in the morning and doing their dancer stretches together; two beautiful men in harmony with each other, like Nureyev and Bruhn...

'Yoli? What I do now? I put–'

'No, first you have to... What d'you want in it? Cheese? Onion? Sorry, no ham.'

He looked uncertain. 'I think we make it simple, first time.'

Their first time was still to come, and – simple or not – would now be much delayed. Perhaps in the summer... I imagined them entwined on Jeremy's bed. Wondered which one of them would be the 'man', although Jeremy had once told me it wasn't really like that...

He looked over. 'Yoli? You dream, think too far... you not watch.'

I let him serve up, taught him how to slice a tomato.

'So who does the cooking at home?'

'The two Marias. They do the house for us. But also my mother and sisters.'

'So your sisters aren't married?'

'Estrella, yes, but came home. Very difficult time, and my parents...' He tutted and shook his head. 'And Carmelita... she will not marry, is *autista*, you know?'

'Oh, that must be–'

'Very good *tocaora*, but cannot play with others. Can do very little with others, content to be in house. But is beautiful person.'

'Ah... So are they younger or...'

'Forty-two and forty.'

'So quite a gap then. You were a surprise?'

'No. No gap. I had a brother, but he die.'

'Oh. How awful... as a baby, or...'

'He was twenty-two. Problem with drugs. We both, even that already die a cousin and a musician friend.'

'Oh no. I'm sorry. What was his name?'

'Jose Luis. Very good dancer.' He collected up the plates. 'So you take bath now?'

'Yes.' I wondered if I'd asked too many questions.

'But is difficult. How you do the hair?'

'I'm about to work that out.'

'No, call me when you are ready and I do it for you.'

'Oh no, I'm sure I—'

'Yes, Yoli. Is okay, I have done for my sister. Then we do the eye.'

I went back to my flat. There was no arguing with the man; how did this work between him and bossy Jeremy?

Like most things, baths took twice as long with one hand. And then I lay there wondering which of the nurses would wash Jeremy's golden-haired body in his bed. Or perhaps they would get him up and help him in the shower today...

Nando was knocking on the door to the flat. 'Yoli? *Apúrate*.'

Why *should* I hurry up? We still had plenty of time. I got out and dried myself, struggled with my underwear, put on a blouse and a pull-on skirt.

I went to the door and found him pacing around. He chuckled and corrected my mismatched buttons and buttonholes, his hands against my chest and tummy. Then he led me through to the bathroom and unravelled my plait.

'*Ay qué sucia.*' Dirty. I suppose it was.

'Sorry. Just didn't—'

'We make pretty your hair for Jeremy. Put the head...'

I leant over the bath and felt a hot burst of water on my head followed by a large cold dollop of shampoo that was going to take a lot of rinsing. I thought about Javi joking around with the snaky shower attachment and felt a bit guilty as Nando started to rub my head firmly, his body against mine as he bent over me. I closed my eyes, told myself that now he was probably gay I could try and see him as a Spanish Jeremy.

'Yoli? You sleep?'

'It's really nice. And I don't think my hair's ever been this clean.'

He put a towel round my head and got me to stand up.

'Sit on bed.' He used the hairdryer like a professional, but combed my hair rather painfully. 'Now the eye. Down.'

I put my head back.

'Is better if...' He pushed me back onto the pillow and sat next to me. I wasn't too happy about the manhandling but it would have looked silly to make a fuss. The first drop was a hit. 'We are good at this now,' he said.

'Yes.'

He leaned closer. 'I think it is a little better.' Of course, he was examining my eye.

'Shall we go now?' I said, getting up. 'If we're early we can always go to the café.'

Duncan had sorted the post and added a couple of newspaper clippings; I put it all in my bag to look at in the taxi.

There were several cards, including one from Andrew saying that he'd been deluged with get-well wishes from Jeremy's readers since the accident came out in the paper. I found the articles: the *After Lorca* picture and an inaccurate description of what had happened to author Jeremy Webster, 39, followed by one or two anti-cyclist paragraphs.

'That's so unfair,' I said.

'They were fast.'

'But only because they thought we'd stepped out of their way. Which we had until...' My eyes stung. 'I said all this to the police.'

'Yoli, you have to stop this. Is an accident. You step out, they go too fast. Both.'

'I'll send the cyclist another text, I don't want him thinking I've said this stuff to the papers. He's feeling bad enough as it is.'

I got out the Blackberry and typed a message.

'*Your* phone, what happened?'

'Oh... I dropped it.'

'I know, I see the *pedazos*.'

'Bits.'

'But why?'

'Why I dropped it? I dunno – why does one drop anything?'

'Look like drop from very high place. Or... with *mucha fuerza*. Other word: *echar*. Throw, I think.'

I looked out of the window.

'Yoli.'

'What.'

'Is correct word?'

'*Echar* does mean throw, yes.'

'But is correct word for what happen?'

I turned to him. 'Oh alright yes, I threw it.' I gazed out again. 'What's this traffic about...'

'You and Jeremy have... *pelea?*'

'An argument? No!'

He looked relieved. 'Then why you throw the phone?'

I turned to him. 'What's the Spanish for nosey-parker?' I asked, tapping my nose.

He picked something off his jeans. Then looked up again. 'Javi.'

'You don't give up, do you? Yes, I had a row with Javi, and maybe if I... But I really don't want to talk about it, it's okay now, and Jeremy's going to get better...' My eyes were filling up with tears.

'I'm sorry, Yoli.' He pulled a packet of tissues out of his jacket. 'I don't know why I... *Cálmate.* Yoli, no pink nose for Jeremy, come.'

'He's okay now, and his anticonvulsant's been adjusted so hopefully he won't have another...' Deirdre was saying.

'But you said it was less likely he'd have fits now.'

'Yes, but as I say, maybe that'll be the only one. Go and see him, he's been asking for you.'

I sat down on the chair next to the bed and leaned over. 'Jeremy?'

His eyes remained shut; maybe the medication had sent him into a deeper sleep. I kissed his forehead. Then felt a sharp tug of my hair.

'Yol. Called you earlier.'

'Called me?'

'Yes. You said you'd come but you're late. *Always* late.'

He pulled harder, painfully, as if to speed up my reply; I tried to put my hand in his, hoping to release some hair. 'I think you were dreaming. Deirdre said to come at eleven.'

'Deer-dree.'

'Yes... your nurse.'

A pause. 'I know who she is, Yol.'

I wished Nando had come in with me. 'Look, I'd be here day and night with you if I could.'

'In bed with me.'

'Yes.' I stroked his hair.

'You always wanted me to... but I'm gay.'

'I meant cuddle, like we do on the sofa with Pavlova.'

'The sofa, yes.' He closed his eyes, smiling weakly.

'Shall I get—?'

He opened his eyes again, the smile fading. 'Sorry about your boyfriend.'

'It's okay now.'

'You've forgiven me?'

Him? 'You haven't done anything wrong, Jeremy.'

'He's mine now.'

'Wh... He was never... I'm with Javi, and you're with Nando, it's fine.'

'Javi?' Surely he could remember who Javi was. 'Javier. Javier Bardem...'

'Yes, it's a common name in....'

He seemed to have fallen asleep. But then he was pulling my hair again, bringing my face close to his, his eyes fixed on mine as if trying to tell me something. Then he let go and moved his hand to my head.

'Soft.'

I wanted to tell him Nando had washed it, but wasn't sure what he'd make of that now.

'Javi,' he said, slowly nodding his head. A tear trickled down his cheek. 'Take me home, Yol. Can't think in here.'

I smiled at him. 'Don't worry, I will the minute you're ready.'

'Ready now.'

'Not quite. But look, Nando wants to say hello.'

He shook his head. 'No... not like this.'

'He understands, Jeremy.' I wiped away another tear with my finger. 'But if you like we could come back later when you've had a sleep.'

He nodded but held onto me. I stroked his forehead, over and over, until his grip weakened and his breathing slowed. Then I put his hands under the covers and went out to the corridor.

'Doesn't feel he can... see you now,' I said to Nando. 'He's...' Concerned faces, the box of tissues, and no, I didn't want to talk. So Deirdre patted my arm and suggested coming back at about five.

I remembered the first time I'd come to the gallery with Jeremy. He thought Tom's love of abstract expressionism had left me with a kind of art phobia, and wanted to administer the antidote. I'd said I didn't want to float round a whole load of old pictures, furniture and crap; he'd said, you *will*. In the cab on the way back I'd opened up my party bag and found the Wallace Collection book, marquetry-inspired velvet scarf and Laughing Cavalier playing cards that he'd seen me look at in the shop. The first consolation prize.

'Where we pay?'

'It's free. But they like you to donate – and oh look, you get a Laughing Cavalier badge now.'

He picked one up. 'It is here?' He bounded up the stairs two at a time. I caught up with him in the room with all the Venice pictures.

'I thought you said you were always careful with stairs...'

He was standing open-mouthed in front of a view of the Grand Canal.

'Tell me artist Jeremy likes the best, it makes like he is with us.'

'Guess.'

'Guardi more than Canaletto.'

'*Correcto*. And his favourite in the whole place.'

I let the picture draw me in with its busy little boat people, turquoise blues and dream-like shimmer. 'God, I can hear the lapping of the waves.'

He smiled at the painting and nodded. 'You have gone to Venice? Oh yes, with musician boyfriend.'

'Uh, why would Jeremy tell you about that?'

'Five English men: teacher, actor, *dentista*, *fotógrafo* and Da-vid.'

'Blimey, can't you two find anything more interesting to talk about than my miserable past love life?'

'Of course he talks much of you. You are wife, mother, child... and also *inspiración*.'

My eyes started to sting.

He gave me a squeeze. 'Ah – this.' We gazed in silence. 'I love this... the Rialto, *no*? Maybe one day we go in gondola under this and think of today.'

'He'd love that.'

'And you too, Yoli.' On holiday with them; nice thought, but hardly likely.

'Okay. To the *caballero*.' He took my arm and strode forward, reverently slowing his pace when he approached the painting.

'The Laughing Cava-li-er,' he read. 'You and Jeremy—'

'Oh yes, we love it. But we're never quite sure why.'

'Not what he appear. He is confident, looking at us with *desprecio*, but also there is his beautiful jacket, with all the *símbolos* of the pain and pleasure of love...'

We walked on.

'God, looks just like Javi,' I said, looking at a chunky chap in a Van Dyke.

'He plays rugby?'

'No! He's a gentle person. Bit of football, that's all.'

'Mm. The Shepherd Paris. Have to hope he not like him in other way, he make bad choose of woman.'

'*Choice*. Oh.'

The Rubens blonde toddler John the Baptist caught my eye: *you as a baby*, I'd said to Jeremy.

'*Precioso*. But you should look at Spanish children like these,' he said, pointing to the Velazquez serious, brown-eyed boy and an older version of him on a horse.

'Don't, it might never happen.' And if it does the child won't look Spanish anyway.

'So... your favourite?'

I took him through into the oval room. 'Here she is. Madame de Pompadour.'

'Ah yes, *amante* of King Lou-is fifteen.'

'But later platonic friends. She looked after artists, asked for paintings about friendship and loyalty. She loved music and beautiful things. A good and gorgeous person.'

'Look like you.'

'Well, the slight double chin maybe.'

He shook his head and laughed, then went over to admire the next paintings. Pale, voluptuous and immodest Venus in various settings.

'Mars and Venus *surprised* by Vulcan,' I read. 'Her husband's caught them out? Oh dear. But he doesn't look that bothered.'

'No. Look, here they are again. And more... *Dios mío*, why not make Boucher an enormous picture of her *follando* and finish with this?'

I guffawed. 'Why don't I take you to lunch before you get us thrown out of here?'

We went down to the restaurant. The waiter overheard him and started talking to him in Spanish, then recognised him and said how much he had enjoyed his show in Madrid.

'Does that happen a lot?'

'In Madrid, Sevilla... Most are women.'

'That must be... er...'

He leaned forward. 'Listen, I'm not gay, Yoli. But with Jeremy... I am *enamorado*. And *en serio*... for the first time.'

A sharp pain – one that I used to know all too well, but now cruelly taking me by surprise. I'd so wanted him to be in love with me, even just a little, even just briefly. He stroked my cheek, all sympathy; no doubt he'd seen my expression on many a face before. I quickly reminded myself how it didn't matter anymore, this was about Jeremy.

'But how are... Aren't you a bit worried that...?'

'Worried? *Aterrorizado*! But also... sure. He is...I wait for him all this time. But is difficult with the dancing, my family... has to be secret.'

'So you could never... live together?'

'No. And Jeremy understand this.'

Our meals arrived.

He took my hand. 'And Yoli, is important, I not take Jeremy from you, *entiendes*? You will come to Sevilla many times, can be together as three in all the holidays. Like I say, Venice, *no*?'

'That would have to be *four*.'

'Ah, yes.'

'We should come here again, with Jeremy,' I said. A more feasible outing. 'I've heard you're good at painting yourself.'

'I am better at *caricaturas*. Jeremy not show you the one I did of him?'

'He said he left it in Cádiz. Can you do one of yourself? It would be a nice surprise for him when he comes home.'

'Maybe. I wish I could stay more time...'

He finished his lunch and rang the hospital. After a succession of *sís* and a few *say agains* he put the phone down and grinned.

'Much better. He sleeped, had good lunch, sleeped again and then they take... test and find the *presión* is lower. She says he goes to normal ward soon, maybe tomorrow. Oh, and he sit in chair and read maga...?'

'Magazine, *revista*. That's great!' Nothing about his confusion, but surely if he was reading... 'But let's correct some of that English: slept, said, sat...'

The Blackberry buzzed a text.

'Javi.'

Nando said he'd pay and meet me in the shop.

'*Hola!* I'm in an art gallery, waiting to go back and see Jeremy.' I told him how much better he was doing.

'And you? Did you go to the check for your eye?'

'Er... no. But we're... I'm putting the drops in and it's fine.'

'And your finger?'

'Okay with Nurofen. You alright?'

'Of course. But I miss you. Are you sure you don't want me to come this weekend?'

'I don't know. It's just possible that Jeremy might come out of hospital then and I'll have to help him a lot.'

'Already?'

'Well hopefully. Maybe I could get his friend Ginny to come and stay the following weekend so I could come over.'

'Oh yes. Ask her, Yoli. Send my *saludos a* Jeremy.'

Jeremy asked me to come closer. He went for my plait, but just wanted to admire my Madame de Pompadour hair bobble. I let Nando describe our outing, and watched Jeremy remember the paintings, agree that the three of us should go to Venice, and then look delighted with his Guardi pen, Canaletto jigsaw puzzle and Laughing Cavalier mints. The fog of confusion seemed to be lifting.

'*Vale. Me toca a mí.* My turn. English again now.'

'Thank God. Although here we should really be speaking Spanish,' I said, trying to use the Spanish version of the menu.

'We will have *champaña*, no? Celebrate that Jeremy moves from ICU.'

'And has stopped pulling my hair.'

'And calling me Fernando.'

We talked about the exhausting Eastern European tour he was about to go on. He asked me about my compositions with Javi. He also knew I'd seen David, and warned me that Madame de Pompadour was lucky; true *amigos platónicos* were very rare.

We walked back and agreed that relief about Jeremy was almost as exhausting as worrying about him; Duncan passed us in the hall and looked startled to see us wishing each other goodnight at just gone nine.

Then Nando pulled out two mugs he'd bought for me in the shop, suggesting we had some hot chocolate before we went to bed. We sat on the sofa trying to decide between Green and Black in the Laughing Cavalier or Bourneville in Madame de Pompadour.

'Does this remind you of meeting Jeremy that first time?'

'No. It remind me of us. You not like to talk of this, I know. But you don't have to be so... *avergonzada*.'

'I'm not ashamed.' I stared into my mug. 'No, that's exactly what I am. It shouldn't have happened. But we're friends now so it doesn't feel so bad.' He put his arm round me. 'But tell me, did you fall for Jeremy the first time you met him?'

'I ask myself this. Maybe even a little from you talking of him before, I don't know.'

'So that's why you wanted to come back here with me.'

'*No! Qué tontería!* I asked to go for chocolate somewhere, remember? How you say this.' He pulled me closer. 'Repeat: I am not a-shamed.'

'I'm not *completely* ashamed.'

'*No, no*, try again.'

'I'm not *utterly* ashamed.'

'Utter-ly? I like, I will use.'

'Okay. But I'm utterly exhausted, so... breakfast about nine, okay? I'll show you scrambled eggs... untidy eggs, as you would call them. Night-night then.'

We hugged. For some while, perhaps too tired to pull apart. Until he took my face in his hands and kissed me on the lips.

'Night then,' I said again, and started to get up. But he wasn't letting me go. Another kiss, his lips soft, a tension in his arms...

I drew back. 'Um... this isn't...'

His arms tightened around me. I put my head down to stop him kissing me again, leant my forehead on his chest.

'Look, I'm sorry if I've given you the wrong idea but...' *I wouldn't sleep with you again if you were the very last man on earth.* That's what I thought. Then, perhaps too weary to come up with anything else, I said it.

His smile faded. '*Qué?*'

'Well, I don't think I can make it much clearer than that.'

'*No entiendo.* In Spanish.'

I gave him a subjunctive-free rendition. 'It's an expression.'

He laughed. 'Is stupid expression. Woman wants a baby.'

'What?'

'If one man in world. And any-way, why is so bad, if we sleep before...'

'Sleep? That's hardly the word! You just buggered off, scarpered, *desapareciste* in the night. Not a note or a phone number, *nada*.' I started to feel shaky; I couldn't believe I was saying this.

'Yoli, I have explained before, I was trying to make more easy for you.'

'I know, I know, you didn't want to hurt me.' That old chorus.

'But is different now.'

I looked up. 'That's right, it *is* different now. But even if there wasn't Jeremy and Javi—'

'There is no problem for Jeremy.'

'Well of *course* there is - I mean *would* be. How could you *think* of—'

'No, no - I don't hurt Jeremy, never. You don't understand. Javi? Ha. Violeta is back.'

'Back in Granada, yes, just for—'

'Repair of arm, but also of other things... and for this she needs Javi.'

'Well *no*, but obviously he—'

'She needs him, he needs that she need him.'

'Is that what Jeremy told you?'

'No, he not want to believe it.'

'So what the hell d'you know about it then?'

He breathed out heavily. 'I know *her*. Have met a few times. She try for place in the group.' My mouth must have fallen open. 'Don't make face like this, I not fuck with her, even if was possible... Beautiful, talented, but very... *frágil* - is why I not take her in the group, or... Needs *una piedra*, to go home.'

'So you think I should just stand aside and give her rock back to her?' I had another go at standing up but he held me.

'No, I not say this. You are good for Javi, Jeremy says. But Violeta is...' He sighed. 'Javi can make error.'

And already had. 'How can you—'

'I'm sorry Yoli. I don't know what I say, I'm tired. No more of this. You need to have good dreams and sleep well.' He kissed my forehead. '*Sola,* or with me if you like.'

I shook my head.

'Okay. Goodnight, *mi cariño.*'

24.
recordar *vt* to remember

Jemery. Throughout the letter. Surely the spell check would have zig-zagged a red line under them? I nearly phoned the secretary to complain. But that was before I realised that they were indeed discharging a Jemery: a twisted version of the person who went in.

But there was also Jem. Like his mum had called him. Jem was there when he woke from his afternoon nap, slow and sweetly muddled; and in the evening, when tiredness felled Jemery like daylight a vampire. *You just want to squeeze him*, Emma had said, *he's like Jeff Bridges' alien in Starman*. Yes, I'd said, Ginny says it's like seeing the sweetness of his soul, bared. I was trusting Emma to make a gagging face, but she smiled and nodded. But then neither of them really knew about Jemery.

He burst in, another day beginning.

'Where the fuck is it?' In his boxers, hands on his hips.

'Where's what? Calm down, I'll come and—'

'*You've* got it again, haven't you? Get your own, fuck's sake!'

'I just borrowed it for a few seconds yesterday.' To get the cyclist's number – before he found it, didn't understand and deleted it. 'I gave it back to you at the table, remember?'

Of course he didn't. He didn't remember anything – including, it seemed, coming with me to choose a new pink phone. 'Let's go and have a look. Perhaps I put it down somewhere stupid. I was just about to come and make us some breakfast.' Or *more* breakfast in my case; I didn't deal with Jemery on an empty stomach. 'Fancy pancakes?'

'About to come and check I've taken the *drugs*, you mean.'

I didn't answer; that battle was scheduled for later.

I went through to his flat and started rooting around while he stood there, arms folded like a foreman. I went to the bedroom but he didn't follow; he'd picked up a mid-breakfast Pavlova and had possibly already forgotten what he'd got me looking for.

'Ah! Found your phone! Dressing gown pocket. But it needs charging.'

'But I haven't worn the dressing gown.' And didn't I know it. 'Ow!' Pavlova had clawed herself out of his arms; he wouldn't leave her alone, seemed to have lost the ability to read her body language.

'She wants to eat. And so do we – d'you want to do the table?'

'You put it there, didn't you.'

'No I didn't. But it doesn't matter, it's easy to—'

'Because you want me to wear it.'

We looked at each other; I wondered if he was nearly ready to talk.

'Look, if I'm going to do this, you'll have to help. And actually I think I've slept on my hand – can I have some of your ibuprofen?'

'Of course.' He opened a cupboard of cereals and pasta and closed it again. Opened another and pressed out two pills.

'Perhaps get your stuff out while you're at it?'

I braced myself. But he got out the packets without complaint; surely an improvement. *Look for little improvements every day*, the booklet had said. Ensure plenty of rest and quiet. Lots of water to drink. Possibly other things, but Jemery had thrown it away; he didn't want me ticking off the symptoms. Things like memory problems, irritability, changes in...

He was watching me messily breaking the eggs with one hand. Then his gaze wandered uncertainly over to the packets.

'I need to stop the phenytoin.'

'Yes, but the doctor will tell you how, it has to be gradually. Only three days until we see him now.'

He went to the calendar, flipping over the page and putting his finger on *Winchester*.

'That's a long time off, don't worry.' Although I'd had to tell Andrew it was unlikely. 'Can you get the saucepan out?'

He produced it with a Jem-grin. 'Have we got lemons?' We'd bought them the day before, gone to a second shop to get better ones. I wanted to put my arms round him and say *try to remember, think*. 'Yol?'

'We've got everything we need, yes.'

He opened the fridge. 'Why did you put them in here?' Pointless telling him I hadn't. He got them out, picked up one and held it with two hands like a child. I'd be in

274

trouble if I was caught staring, so I poured the mixture into the pan.

'Always better at shop on the Green, for fruit.'

I looked over and must have smiled.

'I do remember some things, I'm not completely gaga.'

I wanted to hug him. 'And I think you also remember we don't tend to eat together in our underwear?'

'Yes.'

'We don't *have* to finish it,' he said, his hand hovering over the puzzle with a blatantly obvious piece of the Dogana.

'We'll have to do it again when Nando comes. It's certainly great for me – I can forget I'm one-handed.'

'Yes, but I need to start pushing on.'

Only the day before we'd had the tantrum with his emails; how could he possibly think he was ready to get back to his novel?

'Why don't you start an article on your experience, how it feels to—'

'Have a bruised brain. Be constantly man-sat. Forced to take pills that make me stupid so that I won't bother you with a fit.'

'Surely *you* don't want another fit either?'

'I want my brain back Yol, and you're stopping that.'

'Fits are *dangerous* Jeremy. Come on, we've—'

'And you call sitting around struggling with jigsaw puzzles being *alive*?'

'We'll tell the doctor that on Monday morning, get you off it as quickly as possible.'

'*We?*'

'*You'll* tell him.'

'Yes. Cause you're not coming, going on about...' He looked down. Perhaps he did remember.

'I shan't say a thing, just keep you company, that's all.'

'I *said*, I don't want you there!' He stood up, banging in to the table and sending the Venetian sky over the edge.

'But I've got my appointment in the afternoon, we were going to help each other, lunch at that Thai place in between, remember?'

'Remember, *remember*! That's fucking all you ever say!' He picked up the car keys.

'I'll drive you somewhere. Change of scene. Where shall we—?'

'*We* aren't going anywhere.'

My heart pounded. 'But you *can't drive* Jeremy, where d'you—?'

'None of your fucking business!'

The door slammed. I grabbed my keys and ran out after him, catching up with him near the theatre.

'Come back in, you're not going anywhere in this state!' I grabbed hold of him with both arms and was about to shout for help, but suddenly there was no resistance.

He turned to me, his face twisted with confusion. 'You're... always saying that.'

'No. You said it to me, rem... When *I* was upset. And I listened to you and went back to the flat, we had a drink and talked.'

'We talked about...?'

'Javi.'

He put his hand to his head; sometimes it looked like thinking *hurt*.

I put my face near his. 'Jeremy, this isn't good for you. You need to relax, rest.'

'I've done that to hell.'

'Well okay, we'll rest but do something useful.' We started walking back to the flat.

'Like what? I can't think with this shit in my head.'

'The first few one-to-one submissions for Winchester have come through. How about I read them and you make some notes?'

He shook his head. 'And tell me what to think. Fuck that.'

'I won't, I promise. We'll just make a start. Come on, it might even be a laugh.'

'I don't know, Andrew. Can you stop asking me? Nobody knows how long it takes. I read some submissions to him yesterday and he can talk about what works, what doesn't. But he can't really *read*... Well it might be his eyes, he says the words keep swinging around... No, I fixed an appointment with an ophthalmologist. Private, we can't wait... No, it's okay...'

'I don't know, Ginny. He's less sleepy but... not himself. But every day there's little improvements. Yes, he'd love to see you... That's fine, and you're welcome to my sofabed... No, best to sleep here, he needs his space at the moment.' And you don't want to be in his space at the *wrong* moment.

'I don't know, Charlotte, I can't think that far ahead... Well for Jeremy it is... Of course I'd love to, would you believe Javi's on tour the whole of half-term... Minorca might be too hot for Jeremy in his present... To be honest

I don't think he'd cope with the kids' noise... Sorry, yes I did. Thanks so much, I'm sure Jeremy will pay you back when he's...'

'I don't know... I *will* ask Ginny... No, Emma's got her hands full at the weekends, what with her mother... No, that wouldn't be fair on you... I'll try and get hold of her in the next few days... Yes *maybe* next weekend... *Muchos besos...*'

'Nando wants to talk to you.' He handed me the phone.
    '*Qué tal?*' I asked.
    'Don't give me how-are-you, why you not call, give me the new number? You are cross with me?'
    'No.'
    'Something happen?'
    'No!' I went over to the windowsill as if to stroke Pavlova. 'Sorry, I...'
    'Is difficult to talk?'
    'Yes.'
    'I can say my number and you remember it? Call me later, say how he is.'
    'Yes.'
    Jeremy's smile had faded. 'Why are you *so* unfriendly,' he was muttering over the number Nando was giving me.
    'Sorry, couldn't hear you,' I said, putting a finger to my lips and smiling at Jeremy. Although it rather looked like Jemery might have taken his place. 'Tell me again?'
    He said the number. Twice. Pavlova was in cahoots and padded along the windowsill to where I'd left the shopping list. I scribbled it down and quickly tore off the corner.

'Right! Well that must have been great!' I improvised, making Nando laugh.

'Tell him all the audience in Minsk were clapping and stamping feet for ten minutes. Is good the doctor is happy with Jeremy, *no*? And how is your finger?'

'Not as achy. But I've got to have the splint for another two hideous weeks.'

'Is important to do it right. Ah Yoli... I think of you and Jeremy all the time. You give one to the other a strong *abrazo* from me, *no*?'

'Yes. I'll pass you back.'

He chatted with Nando a bit longer then put the phone down. Fixed me with his eyes.

Like he'd done on Wednesday.

'Nando said we have to give each other a hug from him.' He didn't say anything, so I sat down and put my arms round him; Jemery wasn't sure but Jem leaned into me.

Then a sudden surge of unexpected energy, his hands taking my shoulders. 'I'm sorry about it, but you have to stop this.'

My heart started racing, remembering...

You have to stop hating him for not falling in love with you, he'd said on Wednesday.

'Stop what?' I asked.

'No, no, yes, yes, yes I'll pass you back. Like a robot.'

'No, it was a nice chat.'

'You have to be friends. *Good* friends. Get over your...'

Get over wanting him for yourself and give in, he'd said.

'Please Jeremy, believe me, it's all fine.'

It was true; Nando and I were friends now. But it wasn't completely fine, and somehow – perhaps injury of one part of the brain enhances another – he could sense that.

It's not just him. I know what you want, I've always known, he'd said.

How could I change the track of his thoughts? Not by doing what I did on Wednesday, telling him he was out of order and stamping back to my flat like a nanny giving time out. Only to receive that call that would drag me straight back again: *Come quickly, I need you now. Now, now NOW!*

'Nando doesn't think I'm unfriendly, does he?'

'He thinks you're adorable. But that's not enough for you, is it.'

'It's more than enough. Please Jeremy, don't start this again, *please...*'

I'd burst in, fearing he was hurting himself. But quite the opposite. He was pleasuring himself, standing there holding his erection. Telling me he knew what I wanted. He loved me, so he could do it. As I could see, he'd said with a chuckle.

'You're crying,' he said. He wouldn't let me go, his eyes widening. He held my face in his hands. 'I need to know. Is it a dream, or did I...?'

'It wasn't *you*, Jeremy. And nobody else is ever going to know.'

'Oh God.' Laughing. Crying. 'But are you ever going to really forgive me?'

'There's nothing to forgive.'

It was time to tell him about Jemery.

25.
visita *f* visit

'Are you coming or what?' Jemery, but at least he was dressed.

'And good morning to you too,' Ginny said, hastily buttoning her purple sundress.

'What happened to knocking first?'

'Assumed you'd be up. I'm starving.'

We followed him through to his flat. Ginny asked how he was.

'Tired. Couldn't sleep, wondering what you two were nattering about.'

'Oh... lots of things,' I said. Including their brief physical relationship, about which little was recalled other than the fact that it had soon fizzled down into a friendship. 'Mostly talking about Andrew, actually.'

He picked up Pavlova and sat down on the sofa with her. Studied the plastic jewels in her collar. It was only twelve hours or so since Ginny had told us how all those years of him putting in a good word for her with Andrew had finally paid off; he was going to take her on and she had some flats to look at on Sunday. He'd been so pleased for her; shouldn't that feeling have left a little dent in his brain? He nodded slowly. No more agitated repeating of words, nowadays he just waited for you to go on, hoping something would set off a spark and make the memory catch fire.

'Great that Andrew's going to employ her, isn't it? And one of the flats she's looking at is just minutes from us.'

'For God's sake Yol, I *know*, you don't have to keep repeating everything. I'm not your kid.'

I looked out of the window and was surprised to see the cafe opposite wobble with a watery blur; he'd said worse things to me. But I had a sudden urge to tell Jemery to fuck off and go and find Jeremy; apart from anything else, he should have been pleased that I'd made such rapid progress with Ginny. I said I had to go and check my phone.

'Okay, time out,' I said to myself back in my flat, flopping onto the sofa and closing my eyes. I wanted to call Javi but there wasn't time before Ginny completed her mound of perfect pancakes. Javi: that's who I needed. If I hadn't spent the whole of Ginny's last visit with a migraine I could have got to know her then, maybe have been able to leave Jeremy with her and be in Granada now.

I could tell they'd been talking about me; Jeremy came over and gave me a hug. We sat down at the table, Ginny at the head with the two of us either side of her.

'I've got an idea,' she said. 'You need some more sleep, Jeremy, so I suggest that you go back to bed while—' He started to protest. 'No, listen. While you're having a kip I'll mow your grass and soak up some rays on it with Yol. If you feel up to it later maybe we could go on a short outing. Regent's Park, perhaps?'

'Go and get your glasses, Jeremy. And your cap – can't be good to get your wound sunburnt.'

'Glasses?' Ginny asked, adjusting hers.

'Yes. He needs them for reading.'

'No I *don't*,' he said. 'It's just temporary – they've got something in them to stop me seeing double.'

'Okay, okay, but just get them so you can have a look at these,' I said, waving the estate agents details at him.

He yawned and disappeared back indoors, came out again some while later and put them on. He tilted his head to one side and looked at the details about the flat in Colebrooke Row. 'Tiny. But a bit of garden and near the canal – lovely.'

There was no longer anything lovely about the canal; it was a dangerous place that had nearly taken him away from me forever. In fact the whole area, with its tinging and whizzing bikes, had lost its appeal. But he couldn't remember anything about the accident, stubbornly asserting that it had happened on the road above the bridge. I lay back and tried not to hear the shout, scream, whirring and...

Ginny patted my shoulder. 'You stay there and gather your energies. Jeremy and I'll clear up a bit and then we're ready to go, yes?'

I smiled and closed my eyes. Jemery seemed to have disappeared for now; I could hear banter in the kitchen. Giggling. Like on one of the school's rooftop terraces in Granada; I was lying over the chairs, Javi performing an operation on my heart like we were a couple of five-year-olds. The heart he'd since ripped out and was trying to put back in again. But warmer... I was on the beach at Beauport... No, St Aubin's, the flap-flap of the sails... The hiss of the waves in Cádiz, Jeremy telling me to put creme on my face or he'd do it, Nando pinging open the bottle and laughing, Spanish in my ear, nearer, insistent... A kiss on the lips.

I woke with a start. He was there. Not Nando, Javi.

'Oh! How did you get—?'

'I couldn't wait any longer.'

He kissed me, examined my bound fingers, then carefully pulled me off the sunlounger so I was in his arms on the towel. Under him on the towel.

'Get off, they'll come out in a—'

'They went to the zoo.' His hand under my bra. 'Come, let's go inside.'

A tingling warmth spread through me, but also a nervous reluctance.

'Did you have lunch?' I asked.

'Yes, so—'

'How about a *cerveza* and a piece of Ginny's organic banana bread thing?'

He closed his eyes and breathed out. 'Oh... *si insistes*.'

I went to the kitchen, thinking perhaps it would be easier once we'd... I needed to just get the first-time-after over with. He came in to help me, took the tray outside to the little table next to the Mexican orange blossom.

'You eat here a lot with Jeremy in the summer?'

'When we can. It gets the late afternoon sun.'

He put down his beer. 'Too much, I will leave it. I'm very good now, with this.'

I nodded; so he damn well should be.

'Really, I have found I like the San Miguel *sin alcohol*. And I put water with wine.'

I nodded again. Looked at his hand and imagined it touching Violeta.

'Is important, I need clear head. Is not very *flamenco*, but is best for me.'

'And for me too.'

He looked down at his plate. 'I'm *so* sorry, Yoli. And she is too.'

'*She's* sorry?'

'She knows very well how you feel... She is a person complicated and *egocéntrica*, but kind. And one day she would like to meet you.'

'Well... I don't think so. But then unless I avoid the Darro for the next... When d'you think she'll go back to Madrid?'

He shrugged. 'I don't know. Still she can't dance.' He took my hand. 'Is why you don't want to come to Granada to see me?'

'No, of course I want to.'

'Then... why you didn't come this weekend? Ginny is looking after Jeremy.'

'Well, I wasn't sure she *could*.'

'If you asked her, like you said—'

'No, I mean I wasn't sure she would be able to *cope* with him. He's unpredictable, you don't know the half of it.'

He leaned back in his chair. 'I know both halfs. One half is you *want* to look after him, the other is you don't want to *share* him with this woman.'

'What? Look, it's been difficult to think straight, about anything, about anybody... Mostly I've just been trying to get through each day, keep my eyes open... You've no idea what it's been like...' I went inside to find a tissue.

He followed, put his arms round me as I blew my nose.

'D'you want to talk about it? What's he—'

285

'Not now. He's having a good day. And... there's you.'
I kissed him, felt him push against me; but the hurt was
still there.

He led me through to my flat, went in to the bathroom
and turned on the taps. 'I have an idea. We have big bath
together, wash away these tears and worries... When
we come out, no more of this, *entiendes*? Enjoy our
weekend.'

'As simple as that?'

'If we want, yes.'

Fluffy arms round my neck.

'Oh! He's beautiful! Like Lem but... what is he?'

'A red-ruffed lemur. Thought they'd go well, one dark,
one fair – like Nando and me.'

Not an uncommon name, and Javi knew Jeremy had
had a few Spanish boyfriends, but perhaps I needed to
somehow remind Jeremy...

'Oh, and something else for you. We went into Sadler's
on the way and managed to pick up tickets for Rambert
on Tuesday.'

'Tuesday?'

'What's the matter?'

'Well perhaps I forgot to tell you... we've got tickets for
Thursday with Emma.'

He studied me for a moment, his face pale again,
features twisted with the effort to recall. 'Did you tell me
or not?'

'Yes. But look, we'll love seeing them twice, and we
deserve it.'

'Quite. That's what I thought. We need to get out,' he
said, smiling at the others. 'In fact, let's all go out this
evening. My treat. Two votes each, mine are Thai and

Greek. What's the name of that new Thai, Yol? I wrote it down somewhere...'

He disappeared inside. I could see through the window that he was opening the cupboard for an ibuprofen.

'He's had enough, we can't do this.'

'It's my fault,' Ginny said. 'We should have left earlier, but he just...'

'Won you round with sweetness one moment, bullying the next?'

Ginny nodded.

Jeremy came out onto the steps. 'The River Thai, that's it. Does everyone like—?'

'We can get take-away, eat here in the garden?' Javi suggested.

'This is England, Javi. In an hour's time we'd have to be eating in our overcoats. I'll give them a ring.'

'Jeremy – another time. You've done enough for—'

He turned back and glared at me. 'For God's sake Yol, it's *my* head, okay? I'm absolutely fine.'

I started picking at the grass.

'I'll get an early table, we'll be back in time for you to tuck me up in bed at half nine, okay? And you two'll still have plenty of evening left for making babies.'

Then Javi was picking at the grass. There was a wrinkling of Jeremy's brows, the look he had when he remembered there was something *to* remember. He went back indoors.

Javi stroked my arm. 'Maybe he calms down with a meal. We will not be late, it will be okay.'

It started with an argument about the wine: we didn't need two bottles when I wasn't drinking, he shouldn't be and Javi would only be having one glass – prompting a further comment about fertility. I gave him a kick; he winced and opened his mouth to protest but then closed it again, looked down at his napkin.

The food came. Javi was right, he seemed to calm down. Ginny said she'd love to hear the concert we'd given Jeremy; I was touched that memory hadn't been obliterated. Javi told them about our new pieces with titles from the sights in Madrid – even though neither of us had ever been there.

'Never been to Madrid?' Jeremy asked.

'Well I hope soon, with the group...'

'Lovely this time of year. I'm going next week.'

Nando was supposed to be waiting for me to tell him when I thought Jeremy was well enough to visit him.

'Not next week, but as soon as you're ready to, when you've got the energy to get the most out of—'

'I'm *going*, Nando's sorted out the flights. He's there for a week and wants me to join him, thought it would do me good.'

'What?'

'Please don't make a fuss, he's made me promise to *siesta* every day, I'll be fine.'

I went to the loo and called Nando. Spanish voicemail; of course, he was stamping his feet and showing his perfect outline to a crowd of Czechs this evening. Bloody man, what the hell was he thinking? Or maybe it was my fault for keeping some of Jeremy's more extreme behaviour to myself. I sent him an angry text and went back to the table.

Ginny wasn't there, she was talking to our waiter the other side of the room, giving me a cheque-writing hand sign and a weary smile. Jeremy and Javi had run out of conversation. Or rather, run *into* a conversation and collided, each painfully holding their head in their hands.

'Why?'

'I don't know, it just didn't come up,' I said, hanging up my jacket. He followed me through to the bedroom.

'Of course it came up. Every time we talked and you said *I* instead of *we*, it came up.'

'He's Jeremy's bo… special friend, Javi. *Jeremy's.*'

'But he *adores* you.'

'That's just Jeremy exaggerating.'

He took my arms gently. 'Maybe you have… *consuelo* together, when you were worried. I only want the truth.'

'Oh for heaven's sake, nothing like that!'

'Then why?'

I shrugged.

'*Vale.*' He went into the bathroom, came out with his wash bag. Pulled his holdall onto the bed.

'What're you doing?'

'I have to go. There is a hotel just—'

'No!'

'Then just tell—'

'Because I thought you'd immediately jump into bed with Violeta again, that's why!'

He looked at me for a moment then carried on packing.

I slumped down onto the bed, curled into myself, let the crying take me over.

He stood there for a moment then sat down next to me. 'There is no trust here now.'

'Well that's not *my* fault.'

'Except the lies.'

I sat up. 'Look, I needed Nando for Jeremy. When anything I could do felt like it might make the difference... How can you think I would... I nearly lost Jeremy, d'you understand? *Jeremy*. If you want to go off on a strop about something so stupid compared to what we've been through – what we're *still* going through – then go.'

He put his head in his hand. 'Okay. The truth is... there's Fernando but... it's Jeremy. Your love for each other, so strong, I see it like the first time. It is stupid, as you say, and very bad of me, but it is difficult not be jealous. I'm sorry Yol. So sorry.'

26.
perdonar *vt* to forgive

'So has he forgiven me?' Jeremy put down the programme and leaned over to read the text I was tapping out.

'Forgiven you what?'

'Everything. The baby-making comments, our kiss goodnight – although he should understand there was a lot of apology going into that. And... I dunno, keeping you from him by having the accident in the first place – although arguably that was partly his fault.'

'So you do remember something about—'

'Perhaps *remember*'s too strong a claim, but I've sort of pieced it together, yes.'

'I don't want us to blame him.'

'Of course we don't. But am I *perdonado* or what?'

'Well, I don't think he would have bothered sending you that email if you weren't.'

'Email.'

'Yesterday. Come on, *think*.' He started reaching into his pocket. 'Without the notebook. I don't think you wrote it down anyway.'

'Uh.' He prodded at his forehead as if pressing a button; I started to giggle. 'How d'you stand being this dippy all the time? It's like being another species.'

'Thanks a lot. Come on, try harder. I'll give you a clue: Lor—'

'Oh yes. Sent me that article on films and books about Lorca. Brilliant. I'm going to add it to my website... once I can recall how the hell to do that.' He looked at his watch and then opened the programme. 'Aha, we're starting with your favourite. *Hush*. Look, the one about the clown family.'

'I know, I can't wait.' I flicked on to the cast pages. 'All the same faces. Must feel like a family themselves.'

'Yes, but can you imagine, stuck together on tour for months... Never mind listing the *shows* each dancer's been in, they should list the other *dancers* they've been in – now that would push up the programme sales.'

'God, you really are disgusting sometimes, Jeremy.'

'But it's what we're all wondering, isn't it?'

I turned the page: more faces, sultry or smiling. 'Yeah, but imagine the upsets when the lists don't tally, people denying or even *forgetting*...'

'True. Perhaps some kind of grid would be more efficient.'

'But this sweet chap, and where's my favourite... Edina. I'm sure they don't just...'

He shook his head. 'Dancers tend to be comfortable with their sexuality, there's nothing wrong with that. And not just dancers, probably most under-thirties these days.'

'So you think I'm just a hung-up old prude.'

He squeezed my arm. 'Nothing wrong with that either. Nando thinks it's sweet.'

'Oh yes, I was going to ask what you were doing listing my lovers for him.'

'He doesn't like *mujeres faciles,* must be the gypsy blood in him. They're supposed to marry virgins, you know.'

'Ah. So a man-slag himself but likes women to—'

'Hang on there! There's been plenty of ladies, yes, but mostly it's been relationships with dancers in the group. Hasn't shagged a fan in ages.'

So a *lying* man-slag.

'Have you forgiven him yet?' he asked.

My heart stopped. 'What?'

'Madrid. Buying the tickets before obtaining a progress report from Matron.'

'We've had words. I explained a few... Doesn't like criticism, does he?'

'Can't have you two falling out... only four weeks until he comes to stay, you know.'

'Er... must be more like—'

'No, he'll stay at Paco's for some of the rehearsal period but he's hoping to move to us during the week before the show. How's Javi going to like that?'

'He's not. But I've sort of told him, it's okay.'

'Sort of?'

'Well... not the bit about you being away for some of it.'

'Yol. Whatever happened to *dame la verdad?*'

'Why don't you just tell him?' Charlotte asked.

'Tell him what?' It wasn't just the sun and the sea; I'd sunk into a stupor out there, too in limbo, too distant – despite being geographically nearer to Javi and probably on the same line of latitude as Nando and Jeremy.

I ran my hand through the sand, enjoying the free if uncertain movement of my middle finger. I should have brought my flute out with me, started getting my technique back; it would have helped tether me to my real life. Whatever that was going to be.

'Yolly? That you want to move to Granada. It might speed things up if he knew how you felt.'

How I felt. How did I feel? I still loved him. But somehow I didn't feel a need to *speed things up*. We needed time together, without Violeta round every street corner, Jeremy next door. Even if he could have joined me here with the family, finding chances to be alone together... I watched the grains of sand flow through my fingers. Almería: shame we missed that. Perhaps he'd rearrange it soon, maybe add a couple of days together at that place he was talking about further along the coast. Before the Granada festival started in a few weeks' time and he'd be playing almost every night until the middle of July.

'How's the tum?'

'Paracetamol's kicking in,' I said.

'Have you thought about going to the doctor? Hate to say it, Yolly, but this could all be a sign you're heading towards an early menopause.'

Helen, fed up of me rifling her bag for painkillers at gigs, had once said the same thing. Told me there was some test you could buy. Great, I could put it in the cupboard next to my pregnancy ones. But I'd had that ovulation feeling at the Thanksgiving...

'I'm not having that.'

'Yes but if you are, wouldn't it be worth knowing?'

I didn't want to think about it, and anyway there was nothing I could do; they were hardly likely to sell the tests in Minorca, holiday-land of the happy young English family.

Simon was issuing instructions; Emma had an appealing theory that dominant males were the most likely to have kick-up teenagers, but for now the boys were at his feet, enthusiastically unwrapping something.

'A dinghy?'

'A little tent. Encourages them to get out of the sun a bit.' It popped up within minutes; nothing like the old days, all those poles, strings and pegs... I lay back and turned over. 'D'you remember how we used to have a tent up nearly all summer when we were little? Mummy used to get fed up about the grass.' I closed my eyes. 'Yolly? Sleepy thing, aren't you.'

Mitch's last postcard. From Ketchi... somewhere in Alaska. Not showing a tent, but a scary-faced totem pole. How cross Mum had been when she found he'd given a five-year-old a sharp knife to help him carve ours. There was possibly a tent in the background. It was the only card without a memory – but perhaps that too was there in the background.

I sat up. 'I'm going in. Coming?'

'Gotta hold the fort, Simon's going off for some ice-creams.'

The waves were just foam and frills, not like the passionate pulling and clapping ones at Cádiz, where Jeremy hoped to be spending time with Nando at the end of July. Where Javi and I were welcome to join them, they'd both said, although that didn't seem very likely...

'Yolly!' She waved a huge ice-cream in the air.

I waded out and was met by Phoebe, grabbing my wet arm with her sandy little hands. 'Come and eat it in the tent, *we* all are.'

'Sorry Feebs, need to get dry and warm up.'

'It's *boiling* in the tent!' she said.

I smiled and went over to my towel. *Boiling in the tent...*

Charlotte was trying to calm a Magnum-dispute between the twins.

'Look, have mine, I'll just have a bite or two of Mum's,' I said.

I lay back down. Turned my head. Turned my thoughts back to Almería, concentrated on trying to remember the name of that village Javi had mentioned. I pictured a cove, perhaps sandy with some pebbles. Rock pools Javi could show me. Looking up from the beach we would just see pine trees, donkeys in a field. Maybe a camper van or two. No tents. Or maybe a few. Boiling tents. Inside, the smell of sweaty grass, the sickly green light on faces...

'Yolette, how many of the papas of your friends can make grass skirts, you think?'

A difficult question. I had just two friends, and I'd only met one of their Daddies – a very white man in stripes who didn't look like he'd ever even *sat* on grass, let alone made anything with it. Secondly, as often with Papa, things were not being what they were called; what he was holding up was too knicker-showing to be a skirt, and wasn't made of grass at all but the long leaves of that sprouty plant that Mummy was going to be angry about.

'It's boiling in here,' I said.

'Are you going to try it on?'

'In my bedroom.'

'But the idea is you come out and give Maman and Charlie a surprise.'

'They've gone in.'

'Have they?' He looked cross or worried, it was hard to tell which. Or why. 'I'll help you. We have to be very careful or it will break.'

He started to lift off my dress.

'No,' I said, pushing it back down.

'You're sweaty in this, Yolette, don't you want to be a cool girl of the jungle?'

He pulled the dress up again. It was round my neck, covering my face, he didn't know about the buttons at the side... I started to feel trapped and flail around.

'Shush, calm down. Let's try again.'

He found the buttons. My dress was going to come off. Just my dress, to put on the leaf-grass not-skirt. But jungle girls don't wear knickers, so maybe not just my dress...

'Don't! I *know*! I know what you do with Charlie! And I'm *telling*, so go away!'

I scrambled to the tent flap... but looked back at him. Why would I do that? There was no point in listening to him denying it, if that was what he was going to do. But perhaps I wanted him to say that he'd stopped. Later, *much* later, I found out he could have said that. But he just looked at me with wide eyes, slowly shaking his head. He never said it. Not then, or when he left that evening with the guitar cases and the big bag. Or when he came to visit us a few weeks later. Or in any of the other visits, stretching further and further apart until he did, completely, go away.

I opened my eyes, my heart beating. 'Charlotte. It's time to see Papa.' I sat up. 'Well, for me anyway. We're going to meet when he comes back from his cruise next month.'

Her mouth was open in shock – an expression oddly similar to Papa's in the tent.

'Lunch at his flat, with his ladyfriend.'

'On your–'

'With Jeremy, of course.'

'Yes.' She put a hand on my arm. 'Just don't expect too much, Yolly. I don't know if *I* ever could... but if you feel you can forgive–'

'Well actually, I'm rather hoping he'll forgive *me*.'

27.

volver *vi* to return, go back

'There,' I said.

'Here? But where did I...?'

I pointed to the wall and tried not to hear those sounds.

'Blimey, they could have cleaned up the blood.' He was tracing the dark smear with his finger and chuckling.

I opened my bag. 'I think I've got some water...'

'No, I rather like it.'

Then he was doing some slow motion re-enactment.

'Oh please. How can you find this *funny*.'

'Easy, when you don't remember a damn thing about it.'

I started up the steps to the road. Up where Jeremy had been carried in a lurching stretcher.

'Yol! Where are you going?'

'Home.'

'No! Back down here, *now*!'

I hesitated, then flopped down the steps with my arms folded.

'Come on, we've come this far... and okay, I'll have to tell you – I booked a table at the Narrowboat. Or rather they booked *us*.'

Ting-ting and a whirring. This time not in my head. Jeremy pulled me over with a nervy excess of force. Especially considering the speed of the bike, which seemed to have slowed down to look at us, a lycra'd leg coming down to stop it. I was about to tell the insect-person on it to piss off.

'I'm sorry, are you Jeremy Webster?'

'Most of the time now, more or less.'

'You're looking so well... I'm a friend of Kev's, he was so cut up about... Would you... We'd love it if you came to dinner with us one evening. Both of you, of course...'

'That's very kind, but no thank you. If I bump into – no let's re-phrase that – *see* him down here, we'll get a coffee at the barge cafe together, but...' He put his arm round me. 'Think we need to move on from this.'

They nodded at each other, and Kev's friend waved us on to go under the bridge.

They'd been looking out for us, patted us as if we'd just run the marathon and led us to a table with a white tablecloth covering the uneven wood. A vase of red roses. A big card with a possibly tactless canal-view picture on the front. Champagne.

'Like a wedding!' One of the waitresses remarked. 'You deserve it.'

Jeremy picked up my hand and kissed it. 'She does.'

'Not really,' I said when we were on our own. 'Look... you do realise it was my fault? I stepped in front of the cyclists and you grabbed me and took the impact.'

He sipped his champagne.

'You didn't know that, did you.'

'Of course I did. You were forever... Oh please, don't start crying, it was an *accident*. Enough of this. Look how much better I'm getting, especially since Madrid. You've been wonderful, but I think I needed a change. Going there did me a world of good.'

'Stimulation. A place where the siestas you need are part of the culture. Or were they stimulating too?'

He put a hand to his face; Jeremy, *blushing*. 'Don't tease me, please.'

'So you're... well, properly together now, lovers.'

'As together as we can be. It has to be a secret. But Toni and Pilar know and were lovely about it...' He leaned forward and took my hand. 'He's so beautiful, Yol, you just can't imagine.'

I could. 'You're both beautiful,' I whispered back, picking up my glass and clinking his. 'I'm really happy for you.'

Our meals arrived, but I looked at my watch and pulled out my phone. 'Sorry, just got to try Javi again. He said he'd check about the weekend. I'm still hoping we might get away to the coast.'

'Nice to have you back... even if you do stop me getting my marking done,' Emma said, sipping her coffee over a third form comprehension. 'Never saw either Helen or Kirsty in the staff room – think they thought it was a bit beneath them.'

'That's definitely Helen. Kirsty's just a bit shy. Can't complain though, they did a great job. But I've got to sort out who's doing what for the concert.'

'You *are* going to do one of your Martin-Benites compositions, aren't you?'

'If they learn the parts in time. How did the play go?'

'Okay. It's getting easier. So any plans for the weekend?' She looked out of the window and jerked her head towards some girls walking past in sodden PE clothes. 'Looks like they abandoned Sports Day practice and you'll be getting a little flautist next lesson.'

'Good. No, no plans. Yesterday I was still hoping to get a last-minute flight, but I couldn't get hold of Javi. Times like this he just seems so far away.'

'Why don't you do what he did? Just go next weekend. If he's busy you could always go and see your friend again.'

'Liz. Yes, I could, and I could take my flute out and practise. Good idea.'

I'd become accustomed to him looking out for me, but he wasn't there. Then I remembered something about Andrew picking him up for a meeting.

I went into my flat, took off my shoes and soaked cardigan. A good time to call Javi, but there was no reply again; perhaps he too had pupils to catch up on. I checked my phone: no missed messages. Checked my calendar: nothing to do with Javi on the June page at all, unless you counted the opening of the Granada festival on the twenty-fourth and the World Cup Spanish matches that Jeremy had scribbled in.

I padded through to the second bedroom. Why did I call it that? It had no bed and was unlikely to ever have an occupant; if and when I had a baby it would be a *Granadino*. The flights website, one at a horrible hour the next Friday morning...

Then the phone rang; I dashed through to the kitchen. But it was Jeremy.

'Are you seeing Helen and Kirsty tonight?'

'No, they moved it to Monday. How are you doing? Come over, you idiot.' A pause.

'Jeremy?'

'Yes.'

I put the kettle on, pulled out the Laughing Cavalier and Madame Pompadour; I'd pushed them to the back of the cupboard when Javi was here and they didn't look too happy about it. Tea bags in. Soya milk. Normal milk. Teaspoon. He was taking a heck of a time.

He arrived, staring at some pieces of paper in his hand. It looked like he'd finished off that article and had printed it off for me to read, but for some reason it was just single spaced like an email. Then I realised it *was* an email.

He looked up briefly. Eyes watering.

'What's the matter?'

He took my arm, sat me next to him on the sofa. Held me tightly against him, the papers in one hand. I waited to hear about Andrew's cutting feedback, how writing was still so difficult. Poor Jeremy. I moved closer.

Then saw it.

'Give it to her, hold her for me. She will hate me but one day will forgive. Love and take care of her for me, as I know you can.'

'NO!' I pulled away from him, my heart racing.

He grabbed me with both arms. 'See what he says Yol, maybe it's—'

I snatched it from him, let the first page fall to the floor.

Yoli,

I don't think I told you how much I love you. I was afraid of pushing you to decide, that I lose you. I should to have said it more. I know we could be very happy together, and started to believe you think this too. But only if there is trust. It is very sad that we not have this. I don't blame you Yoli, I was stupid with my jealousy, when all the time I was the problem.

I was thinking it was going to help, Violeta here, we could talk and end it. But she has changed. She wants to come back to me, a life more simple, to be in the group. She has asked me to give her another chance. I have tried to say no, and except for that one time we have stayed separate, I promise you. But she needs me, and I can't forget the promises when we married. I love her still. I have to give her this chance.

Part of me hopes that we will fail, so I am free to find courage to ask you to come here and live with me. But I can't ask that you will wait, so I have to wish everything the best for you and let you go. Is so difficult thinking of you hurting and can't hug you. For that you will read this with your Jeremy there, who loves you and will look after you. I wish I could do more. Call me if you think it will help to talk.

But Yoli, we have our music, and in this way we can keep together, no? In a few days I will finish the guitar for the new one and send it to you. You will hate it, you will hate me, and not want to listen. Please, give yourself time and try to forgive me. Hear the music as a celebration of us and the beginning of a long musical friendship. I have faith you will keep this little flame between us.

With much love, abrazos, besos, forever
Javi

28.
llorar *vt, vi* to cry, weep

Seconds of before, a hot midday Granada, waiting for him on the music room balcony... Then the blow of awareness, curling me up as the pain seared through. No. Not Javi. It wasn't possible. Not possible that I would never again wake up with him. See his shoulders shaking as he laughed. Make an almost-ponytail with his baby-soft hair. Play together, harmonising intuitively. As we made love. *We would never again make love.*

I opened my eyes. Looked at the phone. The one I'd held on to as if drowning yesterday. He couldn't say what I wanted to hear. I picked up the letter. *How much I love you... should to have said it more.* As I too should have done. And now part of him hopes they will fail, so just *maybe...* But only part of him. And meanwhile he'll wake up with her.

I turned over. But supposing Jeremy had a... I turned back again, pushed back until I felt the warmth of his chest against my back. His arm came over.

'How's my Yol.'

I couldn't say. I was thinking how I wished the bike had gone crashing into me instead of him. I wouldn't have had the strength, so wouldn't now be...

'Ready for some breakfast? We should get going.'

God. Eating, showering, getting dressed. Never mind *packing a bag*. I should have been used to forging on, but this was different: *thin*-air, so little distance between thoughts and actions. Already a bin full of Granada cardigan, uneaten dinner and ripped up photos. An insulted patronising Helen. A frayed Jeremy. Only the promise of the first part of my 'trilogy' consolation prize – his cuddling me to sleep – had had any control.

'Yol?'

'Feel a bit sick.'

He leaned over and peered into my face. 'No chance you could be pregnant, is there? That could change things.'

'Huh? I'm on the pill. Anyway I've got period pains – surprise, surprise.'

'Right. So mustn't forget some Nurofen. That bar of Lindt. Sit up, come on. How about we start with some weak tea?'

He got up and came over to my side of the bed. Folded the letter and put it in the bedside table. For a second it pleased me to think how annoyed Javi would be to know it was inches from the *esposa*-map I'd drawn for Nando's first hot chocolate visit. Until I remembered he wouldn't care about that now, he was moving on. As I was supposed to do. I forced myself to think of Jeremy's little boat; when he was heartbroken, he'd said, he imagined himself setting off in one, every day a little further from that cruel coastline.

'Lovely.' He was opening the curtains on to a garishly sunny day. He put the hotel book next to me and went off to the kitchen. An old Royal Pavilion leaflet made it fall open at the Regency frontage of the hotel with miraculous last-minute availability of a sea-view room. Brighton: he'd had at least two romantic trysts there that had since kept him away, but he'd said he didn't mind about that anymore. Provided I ate and didn't throw things around, I'd hear about the third part of my consolation prize on Monday.

Nice for a couple of bites, but the honey was leaking and the paper cone reminded me of *churros* in Granada. I put the cone on the ironwork railing. Put my elbow on the ironwork railing. Then gently nudged the cone over, watched it fall to the swirling water below. Comically slowly. Or perhaps, thrillingly, it was much further than it seemed. *I* would fall much more quickly, of course, torpedoing into the achingly cold sea, momentarily – if not permanently – relieved from all this. But I was tethered here, by Jeremy, Charlotte, Emma, my flute; there was no escape other than the stacking up of days in the little boat...

'What the hell are you doing?' Jeremy was asking. 'Good mind to make you go down to the beach and pick it up.'

The cone was now edging underneath the pier. 'No point. It's going to get caught up in the pier's leg things.'

'Everything ends up on the beach, Yol.'

Everything reaches an end point. Even this pain, if I could hang on long enough.

He pulled my phone out of my pocket and put it into his. 'If you can't stop throwing things around I better take this. And remember, no third part of your CP until you do.'

His phone rang and made him smile. Obviously Nando.

'Yes, we're here already, on the pier... Er, a walk way that sticks out into the sea, with *atracciones* and fun food...? Yes, this afternoon... Definitely... Really? Oh that's *great*, I'm sure she would... Yes... Okay, here she is...'

He handed me the phone.

'Yoli, I am sad for you, but you know, always this was going to happen. Maybe at the end is the best, *no*? Because...'

It was going to happen because he knew I didn't stand a chance against Violeta. I pushed the phone back at Jeremy, who said something into it about me being *frágil*.

Back came the phone. 'Yoli, *lo siento, mi cariño*. You must feel for *him*, he chooses badly. Listen, you have Jeremy, *no*? And when I will stay I give you many *abrazos* too. Then at end of July you can come to the house near Conil with Jeremy, it will be ready after some work, I hear today, you will have long holiday, can repair.'

'That's very kind, but I wouldn't want to—'

'Tt! I invite to you. Toni and Pilar will be there also, is good that Pilar will have other girl. You *have* to come.'

'Oh... well, we can talk about it when you come over.'

'Yes,' he said. 'And Yoli, still you take classes of flamenco?'

'Not recently, no.'

'Start another time. Is good for pain like this. Help you stand up, tall. *Abrazos y besos*, mi Yolandita.'

'A *ti también*.'

'What d'you think, eh? We're going to have such a wonderful time,' Jeremy said.

'Are you sure? I don't want to be in the way.'

'Course you won't be.' A small boy walked past with a blue octopus. 'Let's go and see if we can win one of them. Then you'll want the log ride...' He took my arm, glowing as he always did after hearing from Nando. People looked on, seeing two people in love, a lucky woman to have nabbed such a handsome man. He guided me through the stressed parents and excited children, the confident loved-up couples. He was keeping up a non-stop distracting chatter – the villa's seaside location and its steps down to a tiny cove; how I'd get on with Pilar and how well Toni spoke English. Then it was *The End of the Affair* and other films that had used the pier... The day was passing, the little boat moving forward; I just had to keep busy. And there was still just a chance I'd return, he'd change his mind...

'So lunch and then... Uh. It's gone again. *Already*. What the hell's it called, big palace thing...'

'The Royal Pavilion.'

We found an outside table at the restaurant.

'Can't remember the last time I had fish and chips,' I said, surprisingly hungry.

'My last time was here. Possibly at this very table.'

'Sergei.'

'Yes. But he was a right spoil-sport, going on and on about the calories.'

'Doesn't Nando fuss about that kind of thing?'

'No way. Loves his food. He keeps an eye on himself, but doesn't bore you with it.'

His phone buzzed a text.

'Not again – seems like every time we talk about him it makes him text you.'

He put a hand in his pocket. Then into the other. 'Yours,' he said. He pulled it out. The smile disappeared.

'Yoli, I am thinking of you. I wish I could take away your pain, stop you hating me. But time and Jeremy will make you better, I know you will find happiness. Un abrazo, Javi x.'

Not changing his mind. Making sure he had made himself clear. Pushing home the knife, gently but deeply.

I bent over the table. 'I'll never see him again! Like he's *dead!*'

Jeremy handed me a napkin, whispered in my ear as I shook and gasped. Told me to hold his hand tightly. Tighter. It's like bereavement, he'd said the day before: agonising waves with peaceful interludes, you don't have to do it all at once. So I closed my eyes, locked away alone with that agony, waiting for it to pass – until the next time.

I sat up and blew my nose, exhausted. The waitress approached, with an embarrassed smile – imagining I'd lost a parent, perhaps. I let go of Jeremy.

'Well that's your hand exercises done for today,' he said, flexing his fingers. He kissed my wet cheek and then squeezed lemon over my plaice. 'Now just stick your nose in this and remind yourself life's got a lot going for it.'

I stared up at a hefty chandelier hanging from the claws of a silvered dragon, imagined it smashing down onto the crystal goblets and plastic food below.

'So what did Sergei make of all this?'

'Felt like he was on stage, had a sudden urge for *grand jeté en tournant* in the Music Room. Come on, let's go and see it.'

This time nine lotus-shaped chandeliers to crush you to death, possibly while dancing or playing an instrument – a good way to go. *Our* music room – what would become of that? Violeta would probably put one of those rail things in there for all her flamenco dresses. He said he wanted to continue with our music. Why? The group was taking more and more of his time, and now Violeta would be too. It had just been a sweet way of ending the letter.

'Yol? Did you hear that?' Jeremy asked, pausing his audio guide.

I hadn't; mine had been speaking to a thin-aired brain and at some point I must have switched it off.

'What.'

He started telling me how the Music Room had survived both damage by fire and a heavy stone ball that had fallen through the plaster cockleshell ceiling. I was just wishing it hadn't when a phone buzzed, the sound punching me in the stomach.

He handed it to me.

'*I finished it. I changed the second flute to give freedom for the guitar to echo the melody, hope you don't mind. How are your school girls with Sevilla? Do you want me to make the guitar more easy? Please answer me Yoli, I need to know you are okay. Javi x.*'

I slumped onto the carpet against the wall. Jeremy asked if I was okay. I nodded my head. *Changed the flute to give freedom to the guitar.* Had he already forgotten how we used to talk about the instruments as if they were us?

Needed to know I was okay. Of course I wasn't fucking okay. I looked back at Jeremy and shook my head.

He came over to me and knelt down. I leant forward, whispered in his ear. 'Please make him go away. Unless he... I don't care what you say, just make it stop.'

'Sounds like he had time on his hands yesterday. D'you think he's leaving a respectful gap between dumping me and...'

'Oh Yol, come *on*. He loves you, but he's made a decision. The rest is irrelevant – and best not pondered. Come on, let's get to the Sea Life Centre before it gets too busy.'

'Turn round then.'

He obeyed. I dropped my towel and rummaged for underwear.

'Course, I can see you in the mirror,' he said.

'What!'

'Only joking. But actually it's not fair, you've seen *me* with nothing on.'

'Well... turn back then,' I said, crossing my hands in front of my most private bit.

'Aren't you *sweet*! But God, if only this did it for me I'd be the luckiest guy on earth, and life would be one hell of a lot simpler.' He laughed at my spotty pants and then got up, put my sundress over my head and pulled it down.

'I need a–'

'Nobody else wears a bra under a sundress, Yol.'

He picked up my nightie and put it on the pillow next to his old tee-shirt.

'I love sleeping with you. Can't we...?'

'Not every night, no. Maybe weekends? Unless either of us have other plans.'

'Well *I* won't have any. Finished. No more CPs. If Nando asks you to move to Seville I might give living with sun and oranges a go too – do a course and teach English there until my Spanish is good enough to have pupils and join a group... If that's alright with you.'

'Alright? I already *asked* you to do that.'

'No you didn't.'

'Yes I... God, don't say my memory's got holes *and* making up stuff.' He squeezed me. 'Of *course* you've got to come. But we're not allowed to talk about it, remember? Makes me nervous, it's early days.'

I opened the door to the little balcony. 'Let's finish our tea out here.' He came out and joined me. We looked out at a calmer grey sea, a white sky. 'Thanks for bringing me here, it's good to be... elsewhere.'

'Wish it could be longer.'

'Mm.' I looked over at him. 'Go on, tell me now. The third part of the CP.' He shook his head. 'Look how good I've been... well, I could have been lot worse. *Please*.'

He sipped his tea. 'Okay. Guess.'

'You said I won't actually *get* it for a few months. It's a holiday, isn't it.'

'It's certainly *not* that. Anyway, you're already going to Nando's, maybe back to Minorca again with Charlotte, Cádiz at some point, how many holidays d'you need, woman?'

'No, no, I didn't *expect* that it would—'

'Try again.'

'Um... a thing or an event? Some other course... Learning the tango.'

'Good God no, coming back from Argentina with some... But you're worrying me, I thought you'd... It's a big thing, you might have to re-consider...'

'*Big* thing? Can I take it to Seville?'

'Don't worry, it's highly transportable... *Jesus* Yol, why are you being so...'

A big intake of breath.

'What else would I give you for the final consolation prize?'

29.
paciencia *f* patience

I leant forward and clicked on Products. 'There you go, *Essential Insemination Kit.*'

He took the mouse. 'Oh look, there's a *choice*. What's this, the *Complete*... and the *Ultimate*, for God's sake! What do they do, stick a dildo in that pack?'

'Don't be disgusting.'

He stared at the display of pots and syringes, a strange pink-rimmed cup-like contraption. 'Good *grief*. We'll just have to light some candles, put some music on...'

A romantic assisted insemination; there was an unspoken understanding that the other kind could lead to hurt and confusion, for me anyway. But even the thought of his baby inside me, however it had got there, sent a warm glow through my body.

'We could go to the office and talk to her, it's just round–'

'No Yol, too soon.'

'Nando. How can you be *sure* he won't mind?'

'Well obviously I need to talk to him – about this and other things. Probably in Spain. Anyway, why ruin your holidays with morning sickness? It's got to be September.

Meanwhile you can get yourself healthy, read up about what you're in for—'

'Come off the pill.'

'I wouldn't do that quite yet. Last time your hormones wreaked havoc for both of us – not what you need at the moment.'

'Let me get you some tea and one of Sophie's green cupcakes,' Helen said.

'Where *is* Sophes?'

'Having supper with one of her new dancing friends. She hasn't lost much weight yet but she's certainly gained a social life.'

'Good for her.'

'Which is what you need to start doing. Anyway, we're certainly going to keep you busy.'

They wanted to go through some of the standards, obviously checking to see if I was back on form. Then they showed me some new repertoire.

'Just have a go so you get the hang of the tempo,' Kirsty said, more patient than Helen with my appalling sight-reading.

But I had a thirst for playing, a heightened concentration.

'Well done, Yolly! Your dinner's definitely now on me.' Helen looked at her watch. 'Table's booked for eight thirty. Ooh, mustn't forget your post.'

A postcard of two New York City ballet dancers in the wedding-like Diamonds costume from Balanchine's Jewels, but with a Southampton postmark.

'None of my business, but isn't it about time you gave your old dad your address?'

Ma chère Yolette,

Do you still like ballet? I took Judy for a last night treat, but didn't expect to enjoy it myself. We are back, a wonderful holiday in so many ways. I've enjoyed sending you the cards, sharing it a little with you. But now I hope you will call, that I will hear you voice soon! Will you come to lunch or dinner with us next week?

A bientôt. Affectueusement, Papa

I'd have to ring tomorrow evening, after a day at school thinking about it too much...

'I'm sorry but... have I got time for a quick call before we go?'

They smiled and nodded, left the room.

I got out my phone. Pressed Contacts. Add New. Name. Father? Papa? No, probably too late for that. It had to be Mitch. But Mitch was still Papa. Doors without keys. Sickly green light in a tent. Suitcases. Waiting for him at the living room window or watching him leave... I pressed Back, Back, Back. Tapped out the number and put the phone to my ear.

Why were mornings the hardest? Hitting the Snooze button again and again, lying staring at the phone – that low, gentle voice only seconds away. But it wasn't his anymore; that Javi had gone.

I got up, stood under the shower. Wondered if I should ban emails too. Because really, how could I ever want to work on a piece with him again? It was bad enough having to rehearse one of the damn things at school. Despite my lack of response he'd patiently sent a version of *Seville* with an easier guitar part, and refinements to the other two. And another email with presumably further changes late the previous night, when surely Violeta would have been waiting for him. I'd left it unopened.

I got dressed, went through to the computer. Clicked on the email and then noticed – with a racing heart – that it didn't have an attachment.

Yoli, still no answer. I have finished all I can do now, I will wait for a new idea from you. Jeremy says you want me to leave you alone. I understand. But I hope we will be friends and make music again soon. Look after yourself. Con mucho cariño, Javi.

So now no emails either. There was nothing more to say. I picked up my bag but hesitated by the calendar. Dinner with Mitch and Judy, a couple of big wedding gigs, Nando and the Paco Peña show, helping get Jeremy ready for Winchester: the month would march on regardless. I would recover, perhaps this time not completely, but enough. I lifted up a few pages, saw the tiny cartoon baby that Jeremy had drawn on the first of September and gave him a watery smile.

30.

sofá *m* couch

'Thought I saw you looking weepy in the courtyard after lunch break,' Emma said, handing me a coffee.

'Just overcome by the way the girls had worked on the pieces, as if they...'

'Don't be daft, they just love the music. Poor old Yol, it's going to take time.' She reached over and patted my arm.

I was on the sun lounger on her roof garden. We called it the couch; many a heartache had been shared there.

'Thought I saw *you* looking tactile with Jason in the staff room. You're not...?'

'No. Well... he misses me.'

'Serves him right.'

'He's asked me to help him adapt a play he's written that he wants to do next term.'

'Oh God. Just don't go jumping in there.'

'Mm.'

I looked over. She raised her eyebrows.

'Emma. *Was* that a good idea.'

'It rather was.'

'Yes, but you're the one who always says that going back doesn't work.'

'That's only if it wasn't working before. Like you and Javi – wouldn't you go back?'

'Don't. That's not going to happen.'

'At least you've got something to show for it. Those pieces – a musical gene fusion.'

Our flamenco babies. Destined, no doubt – like so many *gitanos flamencos* through history – for rejection. In their case by inundated publishers. A flamenco *baby*: what a ridiculous idea. Flamenco: bewitching music born of centuries of gypsy persecution – the tragic result of their refusal to adapt their ways. Songs – even the party *bulerías* – essentially tinged with misery. It was time to disassociate flamenco from my longed-for child, or confine it to the exotic charms of his godfather, stepfather, or whatever Nando turned out to be. Assuming he didn't put a stop to the whole plan in the first place.

'Yolly?'

'Oh, sorry...'

'I said tell me more about you and Jeremy... I mean, how's it going to work? And when will you start—?'

'September, when Nando goes off to South America for months. And it gives me time to get emotionally and physically in top form.'

'Oh yes – how did it go at the VD clinic?'

'*Sexual health* clinic, Emma, *please*.' I shook my head and chuckled. 'Jeremy insisted on the *Premier* Female Screening Package, no less. But it was okay, I just took my iPod and tried to forget it was me, focussed on Jeremy's promise of Thai Elephant dinner that night if I went through with it all. He now admits he was quite worried, what with Violeta and her drugs. And you know how persuasive he can be. He even managed to get Nando to go along to a similar place in Madrid.'

'So they must be going all the way, or however they'd call it,' Emma said. 'How lovely. But oh, what a waste – for us poor women – of two divine male bodies.'

I looked over.

'I Googled Fernando Morales – good *God*, Yol. Just hot *chocolate* with him? But then I suppose – we now realise – that was all that was on offer.'

I shrugged. The couch wasn't going to make me give up *that* secret.

'Anyway, at least one of them's going to reproduce. But Jeremy – nappies, noise. I can't quite—'

'He says he's not having the child plonked in a playpen in his room while he's trying to write. Strictly minimal sole charge. No surprise, really.'

'It sounds like he's entirely doing it for you. Has he never had any paternal urges?'

'His books are his babies.'

'But look at him with Pavlova... Once there's a real little *person* – blonde, arty, completely useless with anything remotely technical...'

A sudden throb of pain in the right side of my head; I covered my eyes. Too much sun. Caffeine. The curdling of adjacent misery and euphoria.

'I'll get you some sunglasses,' Emma said, and disappeared indoors.

My mobile spouted some kind of a tango; Jeremy had been fiddling with it again.

'Where are you? Nando's here after his rehearsal with some flowers for you.'

'Oh... I'm at Emma's – I'll come and see you later.'

He was counting the days – now just two – until Nando could leave Paco's and come and stay. The thudding intensified, jolting my head with each blow. I lay back with my cardigan over my face. Nando. That was it. How could Jeremy be so sure that Nando would be happy for him to be a parent? And how could I be so sure that I would conceive anyway...

Jeremy was looking out for me. 'I hope you don't mind, but I had to tell Nando about your father. We were in your kitchen putting the flowers in a vase when I heard Mitch leaving a message. They can't do tomorrow because Judy's not well, so they want you to come for lunch next week. I'm sorry Yol, could Emma go with you? I can't leave Winchester.'

'She'll be busy with the play... I'll go on my own, it'll be fine.'

'Nando said he'd come with you.'

'Oh no.'

'Why not? You said he was a wonderful support when I was in hospital. He was very interested, very sympathetic. He understands why you've kept away, but has such a strong sense of family – very traditional.'

31.
novia *f* girlfriend, fiancée

It just came to me, when I was putting a cauliflower in the trolley next to the lump of cheese then lifting it out again as I remembered how flamenco legend Camarón de la Isla had apparently complained that English food made him vomit. So maybe I'd been thinking about Nando. But earlier, Javi. Mitch. Who knows? But I stood in the car park wanting to just leave the trolley, dash home and play this tune.

But then Nando arrived, giving me his promised *abrazos*, and Jeremy was thanking me for the chewy chocolate brownies I'd made. I left them alone – after a peep at them kissing and laughing together in the garden – and went to the computer to get the main theme down before it evaporated.

I added the bracketed staves for the piano accomp... No. It wasn't going to have an *accompaniment*. That was the point. The flute was an independent singleton. I could leave it like that, a new *Syrinx* for the twenty-first century – were it ever to get published. But it was more interesting to have this loner playing against an out-of-step partner – just as in flamenco, Javi had told me, the *bailaor* and the *tocaor* are in the same *compás* but with differently accented beats. The piano would comment and challenge, sometimes sympathise, at one point deserting altogether, and then nonchalantly arrive at a final unison.

I'd got it down, with some of the piano ideas sketched in, but needed to play it. Jeremy liked to spend time in the settings of important scenes in his novels, said he had to *be there to know*; I now completely understood what he meant. I needed to feel it in my fingers, breathe out the melody and hear it bounce back to me from the walls. *Consummate* it. But how could I wail this out while Nando and Jeremy were happily enjoying their love in the garden, or even, by now, *consummating* it? I had to wait.

And wait. A day of school. Some after-school pupils. An invitation to join Jeremy and Nando for pizza in front of the Spain-Chile match.

'No, *you* sit in the middle,' I said to Jeremy.

'No, *you*.'

'Actually, Nando should.'

'Me?'

'Because you're the least likely to get up and fetch anything from the kitchen.'

He gave a vaguely indignant shrug and sat down between us.

'Difficult,' Nando said over the pre-match analysis, 'I love the *chilenos*, have friends I will see in September – but of course Spain makes football into a dance and deserve to win. You know, Villa and Iniesta, in Spain people say... *ay, qué dice este hombre?*'

'You can't expect us to translate if you talk over the commentary,' Jeremy said.

'I thought that you would like hear Spanish point-of-view, to give *sabor*... flavour to this experience...'

324

And so the evening went on, lots of teasing and pushing between the three of us, screams and hugs after the goals and Spanish victory.

I was about to say goodnight when Nando put his hand on my shoulder.

'Yoli, I have forgot to ask you, Paco has invited me to dinner tomorrow and asked that I bring my girlfriend. You will be back from the wedding before seven?'

'Sorry?'

'You come as girlfriend, he not know about Jeremy, *claro*, so I was having to say—'

'You were going to stay with your *girl*friend, yes I get it.'

I looked at Jeremy, but he was grinning and nodding as if I'd just won a golden ticket.

'You will like him, very easy to talk – and we will speak English. His wife is from Holland and his daughters are...'

I was shaking my head.

'Why not Yol, you'll easily be back by then,' Jeremy said. 'You'll have a wonderful evening.'

'Sorry, no. I'm no good at lying.'

'But is not lying, not really,' Nando said. I looked at him in alarm. 'We are good friends, I give you many *abrazos* all the time, like a girlfriend, it will not be difficult. Why you will not come, I don't understand.'

Because I'm nobody's girlfriend, won't be one for the foreseeable future and certainly don't want to have an insight into what it would have been like to be yours... Not that that matters now.

'Anyway, I'm busy tomorrow evening. I want to work on my composition.'

'With *Javi*?' Nando asked with disbelief.

'No. On my own. I know it sounds stupid, and it's probably pretentious crap, but I'm desperate to get on with it.' Jeremy swept off to the kitchen with our plates but Nando nodded slowly. I liked the way he seemed to understand. 'But perhaps I'll meet Paco at the Stage Door next week, I could briefly be your decoy girlfriend then.'

'De-coy?'

'I'll let Jeremy explain. Better get to bed, we've got early starts.'

Jeremy was cursing and clattering around in the dishwasher.

'I don't know why you're in such a grump,' I said to him.

'You're so *stubborn*, Yol. A right *donkey*.'

Nando stood behind me and gave me some arm-ears and realistic *burro* braying.

'But come through in the morning and I'll do your mane for you.'

Nando opened the door, showered and wide awake even though he had several hours before his rehearsal.

'You look like... bride.'

I walked past him. 'These white outfits are ridiculous. But Helen decided we'd offer ourselves in a selection of shades, so now we wear whichever the client wants.'

He didn't seem to be listening. Just looked me up and down and then ran his hand along the contour of my dress in a way that was flattering but not quite right.

'Scrubs up well, doesn't she?' Jeremy said to Nando. 'Sit down then, Yol.' I handed him the tin of grips.

He brushed my hair then started winding and twisting it.

'*Por Dios*, how you learned to do this?' Nando asked.

'One of the top London hairdressers,' I said, but noticed a cloud come over Nando's face. 'Ages ago.'

Ginny arrived. 'Look at you!'

'Don't. Jeremy, did you pack your pills? Just in case—'

'Yes.' He patted my shoulder. 'There you go.'

'Glasses?'

'Oh.' He went off to the bedroom.

'I think I saw...' Nando followed him.

'He's so much better, but...'

'Don't worry, I'll look after him,' Ginny whispered. 'You ready? Certainly *look* like you are. He did tell you we're dropping you off at Helen's on the way?'

'Oh! No he didn't, that's great. I'll just get my stuff...'

We heard laughter and some excited Spanish from the bedroom.

'What's he *doing*?' Ginny said. 'But then it can't be easy leaving that gorgeous creature behind.'

At last. Drained from the wedding – but finally alone and free to try it.

It sang. I played it again, refining it. And again. Yes, *me dice*, as they'd say in flamenco, it speaks to me. I allowed myself one more play. I wondered what Nando had said to Paco about his girlfriend's no-show. His *girlfriend*: damn cheek of it. But I couldn't waste time thinking about that, not when I only had a couple of hours before he'd get back, knock on my door, tell me about what I'd missed. What I *hadn't* missed.

I went back to the computer to adjust the flute part. Started on the piano. The beginning was easy: a chasing of the melody, with unexpected harmonies casting a shadow over the flute's folky song. The last section fell in to place as planned. But the middle: nothing worked.

327

Jeremy once told me he plans his plots with mathematical detail, but then the characters turn up and do what the fuck they like with it. I loved the idea of that, but my characters were just folding their arms and staring at each other.

Bowl of cereal, cup of tea. No, still not working. I went back to the kitchen and considered opening a bottle of wine: no, that would just make it even harder to resist the expected. I glared with resentment at the wedding repertoire I'd slung on top of the piano. I couldn't fend off the four-square traditional harmonies, the ingrained dictates of form; they were inching their way in like water finding a level.

I went back to the computer and played what I'd done. Despite the very unflamenco melody and the sound of the piano, that's how it felt: flamenco. Something about the rhythms, the abruptness of feeling. Perhaps that's why I felt there was only one person who could possibly help... I clicked on email, attached the file.

'It's not flamenco, but I think you might understand what I'm trying to do. Don't worry if you don't, I just wondered. Hope the festival's going well. Yoli.'

Send/Receive Complete. Not for me it wasn't. But then he'd probably had a late night show and was sleeping in. Lying there mouth slightly open, floppy hair over his face, his arm coming over... No, no, *no.* Have to forget. Gone. Over. Just need his music, and chances are he'll fail me there too.

A knock on the door. 'Yoli – *que haces? Monos, elefantes, jirafas...* Come on, we go now.' He'd decided to spend his day off taking me to the zoo.

I opened the door. He was wearing a white t-shirt and denim shorts. As I was.

'We look like...'

'*Novios.* You see? I said this.'

'I just need to... make a call. I'll come through in about ten minutes?'

He groaned but smiled and disappeared, pulling his mobile out of his pocket.

Back to the computer, just one more time. Well, for ten minutes.

Receiving message 1 of 1... Oh God.

'*Yoli! What beautiful surprise! And the piece, extraordinario. But you understand it is very busy time for me, I don't know when I can work with it. Besos, Javi.*'

Reply. '*Don't worry if you're too busy.*'

Receiving... '*It is not that I not want to do it.*'

Reply. '*Forget it.*'

'*Is okay I call?*'

Reply. What should I reply? My heart was banging away stupidly; speaking to him wasn't going to make any difference, surely I knew that now. But it might help the piece.

'*Yes.*'

I just had time to fetch the glass of water from my bedside table. The box of tissues, just in case.

'Yoli?'

'Hello.'

'I... we are talking again, this is good.'

My throat constricted painfully.

'I will try this when I can. It is beautiful, very special, tells me many things... But I don't want to work too fast, I need time to think, you know?'

Still Javi, but not Javi. I could hear crockery in the background; Violeta getting breakfast.

'Yoli?'

'Yes, of course. But if you decide—'

'No, I *have* decided. I want to do this, and not just because it lead us to talk.'

I swallowed.

'Now, piano or guitar? *Dime.*'

'Guitar. It goes without saying.'

'Nothing goes without saying. Not now, for us.'

I pulled out a tissue as quietly as I could and wiped my nose.

'Yoli?'

'Are you... okay?'

'Yes. And you? I hear Fernando Morales is dancing for Paco Peña in London, so he is staying with Jeremy?'

'Yes. They're lovely together. But you know not to tell—'

'Of course. Good for Jeremy, he deserves this.'

Nando was knocking on my door again, with a '*Yoli! Vámonos!*'

'I've got to go.'

'Okay Yoli. I will call when I have tried something?'

'No. Email. We can talk if we need to. *Adiós.*'

'*Ay...* too many people.'

'I did warn you. Jeremy usually won't come here unless it's actually raining. Let's leave the reptiles for now, gross things.'

'*Gorilas*, you like these too?'

A grumpy macho silverback looked at me disapprovingly. 'Not as much, no.'

'Ah, here... *Gibones... ay qué preciosos...*'

'Oh great,' I said. In the glassed covered area a pair was swiftly copulating, the female continuing to pick up pieces of fruit from the floor. 'Uh, it's like the art gallery again.'

Nando smirked and watched with interest. 'Is big part of life Yoli, can't escape it.'

Oh yes you can. I took his arm and pulled him away.

'And here the reason,' he said.

'Oh! Isn't he just...' Huge black eyes in a blonde woolly head, faltering little limbs. Then there was a screeching commotion between two males next to him and the mother swooped by and whisked the baby into her arms.

'Uh, fathers in nature... This one probably doesn't even know that's his kid he almost flattened.'

'Of course he know. He just has different part to play.'

'Hm.'

He patted my arm. 'You and Jeremy have bad view of fathers, I know. Is very sad his *papá* never accepted... and he tells me of yours... You are brave to meet and try to forgive. You know, I can come with you. Would be good, because after we can talk about it.'

But I'd have to explain who he was. It occurred to me that there wasn't a sufficient term for our relationship. Perhaps *brother-in-law*, although... 'Yoli? Think about it, *no?*'

'That's very kind of you, but I'm sure I'll be fine.'

We bought some lollies and sat down next to a small boy and his teenage brother.

'Must be hard for you to understand, coming from such a close family,' I said.

'Every family has their problems, I think. We are close, we live together, but I was having difficulties with my father also, for a long time.'

'But wasn't he a dancer? Surely—'

'Yes, and with much success. He worked hard, and in a time very difficult for *gitanos* in Sevilla. But he is very *tradicional* dancer, cannot understand that I want something different. For years he not want to see me dance or talk of it, better now but...'

I shook my head. 'What a shame, when he should be so proud.'

'Ah, but I am not the only son, remember. He never forgets José Luis.'

'What about your mother?'

'She tries to understand. But he is *machista*, does not listen to her opinion.'

The little boy suddenly spotted the baby gibbon and pulled at his brother's arm, sending the brother's half-eaten Magnum splatting to the ground.

'Fuckin' idiot!' The teenager grabbed the boy's ninety-nine, threw it into the bush behind us and sloped off. The little chap started to sob, his nose a glutinous bubbling mess.

I pulled a couple of tissues out of my bag and offered them to him, then tentatively sorted out his nose on his behalf. 'Where's your Mummy?'

He scanned the area resentfully but eventually stuck out a pointing arm. A wobbling red-faced woman bore down on us and yanked him away.

'The English – everywhere I see it, they hate children. But not you, I hear you with your students the Thursday. What are you going to do about that?'

I'm going to have one with your boyfriend. 'Well, I haven't completely given up hope.'

We went off to see the Diana monkeys and mangabeys, all with babies; it wasn't turning out to be the best place to take my mind off reproduction. But I was enjoying the constant touching, glances at his dark-haired muscular calves and perfect denimed *trasero*... in a Jeremy kind of way, of course. Confident, now they were in a physical relationship, that I didn't have to worry about him repeating his offer. It had probably just been a last attempt to deny his homosexual urges.

'It's stupid, could go to the zoo in Madrid but never have time when I'm there. You would like it, has the monkeys like on your bed, and of course the *osos panda*.'

'Pandas? Oh—'

'I think they try to have a baby, but they have to do *inseminación artificial*. Maybe the pandas don't have wish *follar*, I don't know...'

'Maybe the boy one's gay.' It was a tactless thing to say, but the insemination word had set me on tilt. 'I thought Seville had a zoo.'

'No, you think of Barcelona. But don't worry, we have everything else.'

I was amusing myself staring out a tiger, but I looked round to see Nando looking pensive.

'Why Jeremy has not taken you to Sevilla? You have gone to Jerez, Cádiz, Granada, Córdoba...'

'I don't know, it's just the way it's... and actually I *haven't* been to Cor—'

'He prefers the other cities?'

'No, he *loves* Seville.' *He wants to come and live there, if you'd only ask him.* 'It was his idea that I went there for a long weekend with David, but we had to cancel it.'

'Because he went with another girl. Like all the boyfriends. *Pobrecita*.' He stroked my arm.

'Not *all* of them, there was...'

'Steve. Went back to old girlfriend when returned to the North, but have to ask if was with her the weekends before...'

'That's what Jeremy thinks?'

He put a hand to his mouth.

'I can't believe I never thought of that.' So I'd probably been one hundred per cent cheated on. Well sod the lot of them, hopefully I was going to have a baby with the only man I truly loved and trusted. But that was in *this* man's hands; I wanted to back-track to the panda conversation and tell him about what Jeremy and I were planning to do.

Nando was replying to a text. 'Toni, wishing luck for the performance. But is not good, because I was trying to forget.'

'You're nervous about it?'

'No. I don't get nervous, only... excited. If I was nervous before dancing all the time I...' He made a spinning motion with his finger by his head. 'You will see Toni and Pilar at the villa, they will stay for a few days. Pilar speaks very little English, you must start your Spanish again, *no?*'

'Oh – alpacas!'

He took me over to them. 'And you can start now!' I laughed as Nando addressed them in soothing Spanish and a caramel one seemed to come over to us in response. 'I know it makes you think of Javi. But with Jeremy, Spain will always be part of your life, you have to continue with it.' He looked at me and smiled. I bit my lip and nodded.

Offered the baby some grass. Asked a large chestnut one, in Spanish, to come over and let me kiss him.

'*Eso es!*' Nando said, kissing my cheek.

Austere flamenco came through the walls; was he still irritated about me missing his first night? I hadn't *chosen* to have a migraine, any more than I'd chosen to have that fraught call from Charlotte trying to persuade me to cancel my lunch with Mitch. He softened a bit when I told him about that.

But after the show, and his exhilarated responses as to how it went, he started up again.

'How you order Chinese meal if you are ill?' he said, pointing to a bag of containers by the kitchen bin.

'I didn't. David dropped by to pick up some music – well *my* music, actually – and got himself some from across the road while I was printing it out.'

He frowned. 'But how he can visit when you are ill?'

'Well, as I say, he was just passing.'

A little jerk of the chin suggested he thought I was an idiot to believe that.

'He's got a friend at college who wants to try some of them with his pupils. He thinks I should try and get them published.'

'Is Spanish music, should try Spanish publisher.'

'Oh...' I was intensely flattered; I'd feared that, despite his kind remarks when Jeremy played him the CD, he'd thought it was *guiri* pastiche.

'What is there for David from this?' He got out the Laughing Cavalier and Madame Pompadour while I put the milk on.

'Nothing. Even if it ever got published, there'd be practically nothing for anyone.'

'Is not what I mean.'

'Oh... No, he's got a lady, and anyway, I wouldn't start up again with him if—'

'If he is last man in the world, yes.'

I poured the drinks, tried not to blush.

'There *is* a last man? Somebody interest you?'

'Give us a chance, I've only just broken up with Javi.'

'And want to go back, *no*? If he change his mind, you would go to him.'

'It depends how... but yes, probably.'

He sat down on the sofa. 'But it would be error, because, how you forget what happen? You would find a scar that changes everything... Any-way, you need a man that can give you *monitos*.'

Baby monkeys. A faint return of the banging in my head; I really didn't need this. I sat down on the other end of the sofa, now unsure about the chocolate. 'How are you doing, Yoli?' I said. 'Any better? Would a Spanish inquisition help?'

He laughed and moved over to me, pulled me to him and kissed the side of my head that I'd been pressing with my fingers.

'*Lo siento*. Sleep now, or you miss tomorrow too.'

'I'm glad the show went well, can't wait to see it.'

He finished his drink, pulled me up and led me to the bedroom. Which he'd done before, of course, but that felt like a long time ago.

'Get into bed. I want to see you there.' He pointed to the bedside table. 'Ah, look at this, no water.'

He went off to the kitchen. I took off my dressing gown and got in, pulled up the covers.

He came back with two glasses. *Two* glasses?

'Drink. One now, one when you wake.'

'Oh – good idea.'

He knelt down and kissed my head again. 'Sleep well, Yoli.'

I let him in. He was shifting from one leg to another, tapping his feet occasionally, twisting his wrists; perhaps he was always this twitchy before a performance. I'd been studying the programme he'd brought me the night before.

'I love the idea of this flamenco-Venezuelan duel.'

'*Duelo?* Yoli. Why you make everything a *batalla?* Is a *diálogo*, a celebration of the connection and contrast. Where...' He picked up the ticket on the table. 'No, too near.'

'It's okay, I'm not going to start waving at you or anything.'

'Is better to see the dancing from a little more far.'

'Jeremy always gets front seats.'

'So when he comes on Friday...'

'Yup. Centre front.'

'*Por Dios.*' He gave back the ticket. 'So, after the show, you will come to the stage door and meet Paco, yes?'

'Mm.'

'Yes, or no.'

'Yes.'

My heart beating away, rather like when I sat – finger on the TV record button – waiting for Jeremy to come on to that book programme. But this was live – anything could happen, and if it did I'd somehow feel it was my partly my fault. We'd joked at lunchtime about Nureyev's complaint to Margot after a meal with her mother – '*chicken dinner, chicken performance*'; sitting there in front of the semicircle of wooden chairs waiting for the performers to come on, it just didn't feel funny anymore.

On crept the unassuming figure of Paco Peña, sitting down in the centre chair, smiling gently at the applause then bending his silver head over his guitar. Silence. A languid solo. Oblivious of us, even when the gloom was broken by a spotlight on him. A black-suited male dancer emerged from behind his chair, as if called by the music. Pacing, his arms in tortured gestures, all tightly held passion and precision, then becoming more vehement, spinning and sending bursts of thundering heel rhythms out into the hushed audience. It was Nando.

He didn't need my nerves, didn't need anyone; he was in his natural element. Just occasionally looking to Paco for the maestro's approval.

The sombre black-clad flamencos took their seats on one side; the sunny Venezuelan musicians, in white, on the other. Paco calmly presided between them as they alternated, the darkly contained sensuality of the Spaniards contrasting with the earthy sassiness of the Latin Americans. But both overpoweringly rhythmical and passionate, and inspiring the dancers – Nando and partners Nuñez and Escobar for the flamencos, and a bare-footed and skirt flapping Dayana for the Venezuelans – to emerge alone or together, respond and disappear.

I pondered Nuñez and Escobar over my mango sorbet in the interval; such a beautiful couple, Escobar rather older than her husband, but Nando had told me they had two little girls back home with her *mamá*. Virtuoso flamenco *puros*, continuing the family line – just as Nando's father would probably like him to do.

In the second half there was melding of black and white, as they danced and sang to each other's music, performed showy competitive solos, egged each other on. And then after an exhilarating finale it was over, and the performers came forward to bow, linking arms and chatting as if they were in a bar somewhere sunny rather than a London theatre.

Round the corner at the Stage Door area there was just a young Spanish couple and three balding Englishmen clutching Paco Peña CDs and a marker pen.

Out came the men who'd played the Venezuelan baby guitar things. Then there was the Venezuelan dancer, looking older but no less amiable than she had on stage. The charismatic black Venezuelan singer was putting his arm round her and could have been a lovely partner for her, but they were all so tactile it was impossible to tell.

Then there were arms round me, a chin on my shoulder. He turned me round and kissed me, and I told him how I'd loved the show.

'Ah, pero qué preferiste – Córdoba o Caracas?' he asked, the Venezuelan couple laughing and encouraging me to answer.

'Both. Los dos. La combinación.'

A quiet voice joined in. Paco Peña, smaller than he'd seemed on stage. Nando introduced me and I bent over slightly so that he could kiss me on each cheek.

'You are flautist, I hear. Playing, composing and teaching – this is the best thing, to be a complete musician,' he said, in softly accented English.

'Well... I enjoy it.'

'And you have been looking after Nando well too. Look, my wife and I are going to a restaurant up the road, would you two like to join us?'

'Oh... well, we've got...' The recorded Spain-Portugal match to watch, but that wasn't going to strike the right romantic note. 'Something at home I—'

'She has made me something special, a surprise,' Nando said, his arm round me.

We made our goodbyes and walked back to the flat together. Once there, the boyfriend-arm left my shoulder; my duty was done, I needed to calm down. I busied myself with the microwave.

'Moussaka again?' he asked.

'I'm sorry, you're probably sick of it by now.'

'Of course not. It is perfect, I'm very hungry. But Yoli, the meat is... what?'

'Ah. It's... not. I was rather hoping you wouldn't notice,' I said, smiling despite the blue shawl on my shoulders.

He shrugged. '*No importa*, I like it.' He looked around the room. 'Where's the...' He picked up the TV controller by the phone. 'Look, you have a message.'

I pressed the Play button.

'Yolette, just to say how much we're looking forward to seeing you and your friend here for lunch tomorrow, about one o'clock. Call me if there are any problems.'

I breathed out heavily. 'God, I'm going to be so glad when this is over.'

Nando came behind me with those arms; I ached for the chin on my shoulder and it arrived. 'I come with you.'

'No. I can't do any pretending there, I simply won't have the energy.'

'It's okay, I can be what you like: friend, boyfriend, friend of boyfriend, boyfriend of friend, friend almost boyfriend...'

32.
reunirse *vr* to meet, reunite

Friend almost boyfriend. Meaning *pretend* boyfriend, as in decoy girlfriend. But it had so unsettled me that I'd found myself agreeing to him coming with me to Mitch's.

Friend almost boyfriend. It kept coming back to me. Along with the ludicrous daydream that Sergei comes back and sweeps Jeremy off his feet, leaving Nando to realise that he's... But minutes later he'd given me a sisterly kiss on each cheek and reminded me of the importance of sleep. Short sharp recap: he's gay, he's in love with Jeremy, end of story.

I tightened a buckle, hoped this was a good idea. Nando said a flamenco class would give me strength, take my mind off it. Take my mind off *Mitch*, that was, the lunch in three hours' time.

Braceo and *taconeo*, the flamenco scales and arpeggios. Then the dance – to all that deliciously alien rhythm and discordance – the arms half-forgotten but the feet... Th-WACK! T-ta ta, ta-ta-ta-ta-ta-ta-TA. God it felt good. But Alicia had gone over to switch off the music without a single *eso es* of encouragement.

'What's happened, Yolanda?'

Since I'd last seen her, quite a lot: the near-death of my best friend, heartbreak, proximity to one of the best flamenco dancers in Spain. But despite the emotional intimacy of the lessons, we never discussed our lives.

'You're saying something at last, not just doing the steps. *Continua.*'

I was in the hall when Nando emerged from a room full of energetic piano and spiky trumpets, the irresistible clatter of timbales and cowbells...

'It was good, *no?*'

'I don't know how I've managed without it.'

He grinned and started pulling me through the door.

'No, I'm all sweaty, I need a—'

'Just quickly, come. A little salsa, like *pudín* after meal *flamenca.* I know you have learnt with Jeremy.'

He started twisting around in front of me to the bounce and lilt of the music, his shoulders and elbows probably too precise, but his hips...

I looked away, my hand going to my face but taken from me, together with the other, to go into the *setenta* moves.

'*Relájate,*' he said, shaking my stiff arms.

I let him follow the movement through until we were entwined.

'This isn't fair, my arms are killing me.'

'*Pues relájate, cede.*'

Relax and give in. Well, perhaps for a few minutes... I started to enjoy the flirtatious push and pull of the dance.

'*Olé* Yoli! We must do this again, with Jeremy. I will show you how to dance as three.' He hugged me. 'Okay, bath. You want me to wash your hair?'

'No thank you.'

'Another time. Go now, we have to leave in a half hour.'

I went back to my flat, started filling the bath. Checked my emails: nothing from Javi, but then it was much too soon. But one from Jeremy, late the previous night.

'*I hear you were a delicious little decoy at the stage door – I knew you could do it! And now you're letting him support you at your father's. So glad you two are getting closer, because it's happened – he's talking about me getting a place near him in Sevilla. That means you too, so re-start your Spanish! I've never known such happiness Yol, and I want to share it with you. So does he. I'll be thinking of you tomorrow xxxxx*'

Never known such happiness: after what he'd been through, and was offering me, he so deserved it. Seville. *Sevilla*. Our baby would be born there, with a hopefully adoring rather than horrified Spanish godfather.

And just possibly an English-French-Dutch grandfather, depending on how it went with Mitch. Maybe there was nothing to worry about; it would all be about now, not then. I'd get to know Judy, ask about their cruise; I'd introduce Nando and he'd want to know about the Trio. We'd have lunch. Then it would be time to go.

We arrived early, staring up at a white stucco-fronted pillared palace of a house that reminded me of the Saturday gig's three-tiered wedding cake.

'All of it? For *two*?' Nando asked.

'Well, there's two doorbells.'

'Even *half* of it?'

I shrugged.

'Ah, we can sit in here, wait a little,' he said, pushing at the gate of the square's communal gardens but finding it locked.

I looked back at the wedding cake mansion. 'He's really done it this time.'

'What?'

'Found himself a rich lady. Latest in a long line.'

'But you don't know, maybe he loves her.'

'He only really loves himself.' I looked at my watch: fifteen minutes to go. I took his arm. 'Shall we walk round the square a few times, I'm feeling a bit—'

'Yolande?' I turned and saw a petite brunette in a silk blouse, delicate glasses on her prominent nose. 'Had to be you – gee, just like your Daddy! I'm Judy,' she said, holding out a warm tiny hand. A soft American accent; they were often American, apparently. But usually described as glamorous.

I said hello, introduced Nando.

'*Do* come in, Mitch *so* can't wait to see you!'

We followed her into the hall and up a deeply carpeted staircase; my knees were weak, only the feel of Nando's hand on my back was keeping me going upwards.

'They're he-re!' she was calling up. It came to me that this would have been choreographed, this watching out for us and taking us up to Mitch's Wizard of Oz.

He was waiting for us in the drawing room, coincidentally wearing an Emerald City green polo shirt with his pressed cream trousers. A wide smile on his tanned and unnaturally taut round face, an unlikely amount of blonde in the fine silvery hair.

'Yollette…' He held my shoulders, kissed each cheek.

I smiled but couldn't meet his eyes for long, glanced round the vast white room with its colourful ornaments and paintings.

'Can I...' He tentatively drew me into his arms. Dense after-shave, peanuts.

'This is my friend Nando,' I said, drawing back.

He looked him up and down with interest. 'Nando?'

'Fernando. He's from Seville,' I said, for something to say.

They shook hands, Judy sat us down in a white sofa.

'Just as I imagined your boyfriend would be,' Mitch said.

'He's not—'

'You know,' he said, leaning over from his armchair towards Nando, 'she was such a quiet little thing as a child, but only I knew she was daydreaming about being snatched away by Tarzan or becoming a Red Indian squaw. There was no way she was going to end up with a boring Englishman.'

Nando smiled and nodded.

'But he's—'

'So let me guess. You're an actor?'

'A dancer. Modern flamenco.'

'Of course. What could be better!' Mitch said, patting my knee.

'How wonderful,' Judy said, pouring the champagne. 'We *love* flamenco.'

They'd been to see *Carmen* during the Sadler's Wells' flamenco festival, so I told them if they'd gone one night earlier they would have seen Nando's company.

'Oh! So how did you two meet?' Judy asked.

Nando told her about the profiteroles at the reception. 'Except my mother, no woman cares for me so well,' he said, putting his hand on mine.

I blushed; we appeared to have fallen into default decoy mode. Then Mitch wanted to hear about the Trio, and Nando told him about my compositions.

'I knew it. I knew you'd be a musician.'

'No you didn't,' I said. 'You were forever telling me to stop playing the recorder. And said wind instruments were for people who wanted to sing but didn't have a voice.' Putting an end to me singing to myself in the back of the car.

He laughed. 'No! Did I? But you have to admit, it was a terrible sound.'

'Not to me it wasn't.'

'I was only encouraging you to try something else.'

'You didn't encourage anything, you were almost never there.'

The room fell large with silence. Mitch rubbed his chin.

'He would have liked to be there more, Yolande. It's something he really regrets,' Judy said.

'And maybe that is why we are here,' Nando said quietly.

'No,' I said. No he *hadn't* wanted to be there. He'd been fun when he was, but the fun was rather tinged by knowing that at any moment he could disappear.

'I was trying to get my career together,' Mitch said.

'*Getting it together.* Yes, that's one way of putting it.'

'Yoli, no. You need to talk, but not like this,' Nando said.

'You don't know how—'

'Yoli is fine musician now, it happen anyway,' Nando interrupted. 'It was *genético*, you are musician too, *no?*'

Mitch gave a smoothed over account of his years in the music business, and Judy, looking relieved that we seemed to be back on track, disappeared to the kitchen. I sank back into the sofa, Nando's warm arm round my shoulders. Nowadays, we learnt, Mitch owned a recording studio but employed staff to run it; his days struggling in the music world were over. So was the destructive lifestyle that went with it, he said, as we sat down to lunch and he poured himself some apple-and-elderflower.

An asparagus starter, cannelloni. Their love of all things Italian became clear: the Murano glass wine goblets and ornaments; the modern paintings of Venice; a bookshelf with *The Italian Lakes* and a huge green-and-red dictionary. They'd met in a deli somewhere between Mitch's studio and the adoption agency where Judy worked part-time. And they were in the process of buying an apartment in Venice – as a wedding present to each other.

I swallowed a ludicrous pang on Mum's behalf. 'Congratulations.'

'And we're hoping that your Trio will play at the ceremony.'

'Oh... We're getting very booked up. When is it?'

Mitch and Judy smiled at each other. 'It's whenever you can do it – we'll have to look at our diaries.'

'Yes, of course. So... have you got a big family?'

'Oh no.' Her smile faded. 'And unfortunately some of them won't come.'

'Long way from the States.'

'No, I've two sons in London and one in Cobham. You see, they don't approve, they think it's too soon after losing their father two years ago.'

'Perhaps it would be better to wait?'

'No,' Nando said. 'Don't let the children direct this.'

'Exactly,' Mitch said, 'because anyway, it's not just the wedding, it's us being together at all. We just have to keep reassuring them.'

'At least one of them's okay with it,' Judy said. 'But then we're just too useful as sitters. Where else can they always leave their girls at short notice?'

'The picture, it is of them?' Nando asked, pointing to a frame on the sideboard showing two small girls with bushy brown hair in Alice-bands like their grandmother's.

'Yes. They *adore* Mitch, and I'm sure they remind him of you and Charlotte.'

Mitch, an adored grandpapa. But *should* he be that?

'Ice-cream with strawberries? I made it myself, Mitch told me you always chose strawberry as a little girl,' Judy said.

'Sounds lovely. I just need the...'

'Of course. Up the stairs, on your right.'

Mitch: sober and non-smoking, apparently in love with a woman who was obviously wealthy but pleasantly down-to-earth and not indecently younger than him. Who would have thought. A doting step-grandfather, and perhaps because of that, reminded of the fatherhood he left behind. No, not left behind, *ruined*.

I used the bathroom, its white-and-turquoise elegance marred by a pink plastic box of gaudy bath toys, a Hello Kitty soap dispenser.

Then back on the landing I wondered how I could have missed it: the door with two wooden signs saying *Rachel* and *Rebecca*. Laughter came up from below; I wouldn't be missed for a few more minutes. I pushed it open.

No wonder the girls liked it here: a huge bright room with every imaginable pink accessory, a pile of cuddly animals on each rosy bed, a Victorian doll's house nearly as grand as the one in which they were staying. A keyboard, for God's sake. And... I went over to the bookshelf built into the alcove, ran my finger along the shiny spines of the entire numbered collection of little hardback Noddy books that I'd craved...

'Still like Noddy, eh?' Mitch. Smiling in the doorway, then bending to pick up a tiny Playmobile pram and putting it on a bedside table.

'Of course.' I turned from him and went over to the window, where pink-painted metal bars would keep Rachel and Rebecca safe from falling onto the flowered but concrete balcony below.

'They *do* remind me of you and Charlie, so much.'

I folded my arms; was I supposed to be pleased about that?

'We haven't got the beach, the woods... but we go to the park and climb the trees...'

Lifting them into the trees.

'Look, I know I wasn't there as much as I should have been, but we had some beautiful times together, we were good playmates, you and I.'

'What about Charlotte?'

Outside, the grey sky was finally letting go of its rain. I waited for him to answer.

'Charlie was... her mother's daughter. Confident, capable... She didn't want to play with me.'

'But she did.'

'Well not—'

I turned round. 'She *did* play with you, that's *exactly* what she did, what you *made* her do! And until you can—'

'No Yollette, you don't understand—'

'I've understood since I was six!'

'But understood *what*?'

The laughter below had stopped, our raised voices echoing through all the white-walled space.

'My God, you're still not admitting it! I take it Judy doesn't know, letting you take her grand-daughters to the park, reading to them in bed...' I was trying to see the lock, but he was standing in front of it. 'Is there a key in that door?'

'Is there a...?'

'Oh what's the *point*!' I tried to get past him, but he put his hands on my arms. 'Get off me!'

'Yollette! Listen—'

'Get *off*, you filthy bastard!' I said, pushing him away.

Judy appeared, her eyes wide and shiny, followed by Nando.

'You don't *know*, do you?' I said to her.

'Yoli, this is *not* the way.' Nando took my arm.

'But he's denying it! Watch, next he'll say dreamy Yollette made it all up. I'm sorry Judy, but this isn't going to work.'

'No, he *won't* say that!' She came forward and looked up at me. 'He's told me about what happened with Charlotte, when he was out of his head... He's *told* me. But it's a long time ago, he's a different man, a *wonderful* man... he wouldn't hurt anybody now.'

Mitch was staring at the floor, breathing heavily.

Judy took his arm. 'It's okay Mitch. She's not going to leave, are you, Yolande?'

Nando held me and shook his head. 'No more running from this, or you can never—'

'Start again,' Mitch said. Out of breath, almost a whisper. From this shaken old man. Papa. As in, *we're meeting Papa for lunch*. It came back to me, Mum saying that, and the joyful jumping up and down that went with it that I'd long ago decided to forget.

'I think I might be ready for some of that ice-cream now Judy, if that's okay.'

'Yoli.' Stroking my hair.

I opened my eyes. I was in his arms on the sofa.

'I need to go soon.'

'Sorry, trapped you.'

'Is okay, I talked with Jeremy.'

'What did he say?' I'd completely overridden his step-by-step advice.

'He understands. It was the best, you can't relax, you and your *papá*, until you talk about these things.'

I sat up.

'Listen, you are very tired. You don't have to come to the show. You can rest and I have *chocolate* with you later, *no*? Any-way, you will come with Jeremy tomorrow night.'

Jeremy, linking arms with me and whispering comments into my ear. 'I've missed him,' I found myself saying. I needed the normality of having him here; this girlfriend role-playing and falling asleep in his lover's arms was all too weird.

Nando nodded. 'But not long now. So you sleep, or come to the show?'

'Of course I'm coming. Can I fix you something before you go?'

'No, no. I'll have something small later at the theatre.'

'In the Stage Door cafe?'

'Yes.'

'I thought I'd... Can I join you there?'

'Of course! I already ask you. At six, *vale*?'

I went back to my flat, revived myself with a bath. Tried on the black floral skirt and found that it fitted again; weight loss was always an additional consolation prize for my heartbreaks. But heartbreak, at that moment, was not on my mind. I found a white blouse that I'd bought on a rare shopping trip with Emma and never worn. A bit low cut, with two pieces of fabric that you had to tie in a bow: too barmaidy. But I was dressing for my role, and a flamenco dancer's girlfriend would be proud of her *tetas*, however small. I looked in the mirror and remembered Alicia's '*La postura!*'

Six o'clock. But he wasn't there. I bought an orange juice and sat down where I could see the stage door. Wondering what I was doing there, not the least bit hungry, and feeling rather buzzily unwell. Otherwise known as feeling *nervous*. What? I was having a snack with Nando – now a good friend, and one whose t-shirts and boxers were hanging up to dry over my boiler. And a bunch of amiable and non-English speaking Venezuelans who were hardly likely to tax my acting skills.

Then he was there, wearing the white shirt that made him Indian-dark, tall in his heeled flamenco boots, fidgety, his feet clacking on the stone floor. Chatting in consonant-light Spanish with the hook-nosed *tocaor*, the black Venezuelan singer with the huge grin and the sweet-faced dancer who I'd hoped was the guy's girlfriend.

'Yoli!' A small beckoning hand gesture that his *mujer* would obey; I got up and went over to him. An arm round me. A kiss. An exchange of greetings with his fellow performers, the *tocaor* staring at me with disapproval but eventually giving a nod and a half-smile.

Nando smiled proudly as I translated the ingredients of the two hot dishes for the Venezuelans. Then we took a school-like bench table, Nando and I sitting opposite the others. They were discussing English food, Nando commenting in slowed down Spanish that he'd managed well on mine. I pointed out that I'd mostly given him Greek or Italian dishes, having been worried about him having an English food *intolerancia*, like Camarón.

They laughed, and Nando looked pleased with my Spanish, or perhaps my knowledge of the flamenco hero, and put a warm hand on my lap. A boyfriend gesture that would surely go unnoticed, off-stage under the table. Although not by me, his firm thumb stroking my inner thigh and sending shockwaves up my leg that prevented any further involvement in the conversation. I pushed the hand towards my knee, preparing to lift it off altogether, but it took hold of mine and brought it to his mouth for a kiss. The others had moved on from in-flight meals to what sounded like experiences with various South American airlines. Then Dayana asked whether I'd be with Nando for the Venezuelan part of his South American tour.

My phone rang: perfect timing, thank you Jeremy. 'Hello you,' I said, turning to the side and putting a finger in my ear as the Spanish continued at full volume.

'Thought I'd give you a wake-up call so you don't miss the... Where are you?'

'Stage door cafe.'

'With Nando?'

'Yes.'

'Oh good. Bet you're exhausted – you need looking after.'

'Mm. He told you I flipped.'

'Yes. But that it all ended well, tears all round. Wonderful. You'll have to give me the full story. Will I meet them soon?'

'Of course. How about you, was it okay today?'

'Mm... *apparently*.'

'You don't sound too sure. I'll ring you when I get back.'

'No, no. You concentrate on having a lovely evening. I'll call you when we're on our way home tomorrow, okay?'

'Yes. But on my mob, I might still be at school.'

'Oh yes, hope the girls do you proud in the concert. And Yol... Nando. It's all going to be fine. Sometimes you have to trust your instincts.'

But Nando seemed to be showing some very *un*trustworthy instincts, the hand back on my thigh even as he grabbed the phone and talked softly to Jeremy.

Then he closed it and turned to me. 'He is hard on himself, but the feedback was very good and is miracle he is there. Any-way, he's happy is nearly time to come home, *no*?'

'But I don't think he'd be too happy about *this*,' I said, gently pushing his hand away.

Wouldn't be too happy about this: how pathetically prim. A hand on my leg: he must have seen Jeremy's hand there loads of times. What's wrong with me? But to be fair, I'd really had quite a day, drunk on fermented resentment and forgotten affection so unexpectedly turning into the start of something special with Papa. And over-sensitized to this beautiful friend who'd supported me through it all...

I fixed on Paco's spot-lit silver head and watched for Nando's appearance behind him. He'd be there, waiting in the dark; it reminded me of how he'd disappeared into the night that first evening long ago. But he was no longer leaving me; he was arriving further and further into my life – for as long as his relationship with Jeremy lasted, which, according to each of them, would be forever.

He materialised. To that slow, contemplative music which could have been a *farruca*, but I couldn't have sworn to it. Flamenco, the Spanish language: always just out of my reach. As Nando had been. I watched him click his fingers, arms raised, deep in concentration; dancing to himself, for himself, as he must. But he also took in the feelings of those around him, he'd said, to inform his dance. A tempestuous burst of rhythmic stamping: my outburst at Papa's, perhaps, was in there somewhere.

The show went on: the contrasts between tightly held passion and warm, easy expression, the spiritual and the sensual, the black and the white. But the boundaries finally blurring, the exchanges celebrating similarities rather than differences. It made me smile, this ecstatic ending that suggested that there was no such thing as attraction of opposites, just unexpected links and connections.

I let people squeeze past me as I tapped out a text for Jeremy.

'Are you going to love this show! And N – it's the pure flamenco stuff, but he's sublime. Also great at Papa's, a word

here, an arm there, really helped. Stop worrying about N and me, it's been good, I love him. CU tom. LU xxxxxxx'

Fifteen minutes; he might have showered by now. Back came the buzzily sick feeling, although I couldn't think why. I went outside, folding my arms despite the warmth of the evening. Then searched for my vibrating phone: Jeremy, probably still at dinner with author friends.

But it was Nando. *'I think the text is for Jeremy? I love you too. N"*

How did I do that? This tiredness was hazardous.

'Sorry. See you back home.'

'No, come here.'

He was outside the stage door, chatting to the dancers with the daughters back home. He introduced me but told them I'd had a big day and he needed to take me home.

We linked arms and walked round the corner.

'Is how you walk with Jeremy,' he said.

'Yes.'

'And how *I* would walk with Jeremy, but I can't do this. Nobody will understand. I am completely in love with him, I make love with him, but I am not gay man. Maybe you don't understand this either.'

'I think I do.'

'I don't want you to feel that I... use you.'

'I don't.' Well, I *do*, but hopefully you'll make it up to me.

We were through the door. Then he unlocked mine; I hadn't noticed that Jeremy had given him my key as well as his.

'I will make the *chocolate*. Today you have done bigger show than me.'

I sat on the sofa. 'Well, it's not that difficult, their dodgy English helps.'

'No, no,' he said, turning round. 'I mean at the house of your Papá. You had to present the truth.' He turned back, took the spotty mugs out of the cupboard. 'At the cafe – this was not show at all.'

'What d'you mean?'

No answer.

'Was there a... problem?'

He came over with the mugs and sat down next to me. 'No, Yoli. Why always you think there is problem?'

Maybe he thought they'd seen me pushing his hand away. 'Was there something wrong with the way I...?'

He sighed heavily. 'No! I just say was not show.'

Oh God. He thinks it's not a show because I *want* to be his girlfriend. 'Look, this is silly, and I'm really–'

'Yes, it is.'

I sipped my drink, burnt my tongue. *Why is he spoiling this?* If he knows I'm in love with him - *if* that's what I am - he could at least have the grace to pretend he hasn't noticed. But he's sitting here looking humiliatingly *bothered* about it.

'I don't know what you're talking about,' I said, clacking my mug back down on the table.

Then he took my hand; an irritatingly brotherly gesture. Bit his lip as if thinking of how to console me.

'Look, if you don't mind, I'm really tired, I think I'll–'

'What I'm trying to say, is not show because... Yoli, you know, we *are novios*.'

My heart stopped. 'You're *novios* with Jeremy.'

'Yes. But from the beginning we have talked of how... also I need a woman.'

'What d'you mean, *need* a woman.'

'*Pues...*' He chuckled. 'For all the usual reasons.'

Randy little cake-and-eat-it *sod*. 'But it would hurt him, don't you care about that?'

'I have to be true to Jeremy and myself. He respect this, understand. And now, he *wants* it, for you and for me, you have not seen this?'

'He wants us to be *close*.'

'No Yoli, think of what he has said. He will not tell us direct, wants that we decide, but he does everything he can. Even tonight, I know there is time for him to come back and return for late class tomorrow, but he wanted that we have another evening together.'

I tried my drink again, but could hardly swallow. *I've never known such happiness Yol, and I want to share it with you... It's all going to be fine, sometimes you have to trust your instincts... You're so stubborn Yol, a right donkey...*

He put his arm round me but I continued to stare into my mug. 'He needs you. And wants this for you because he knows I am only man who will accept you two are... married. He wants us to be together.'

Toge'her, he'd said in hospital, pulling my hand towards the one holding Nando's. Another sip of my drink, trying to think straight, my heart racing, a ringing in my ears...

'I know I leave you before, a part of you hates me for that. But is different now, you know this.'

You have to stop hating him for not falling in love with you. Get over your wanting him for yourself, and give in. Jemery: twisted and cruel but incapable of lies.

'*Por qué no puedes mirarme?*'

Because the moment I look at you I'll give in. As Jeremy is hoping I will. Because he would prefer the *novia* to be me, rather than some demanding Violeta-type *bailaora*, and would prefer my boyfriend to be Nando, rather than yet another man who can't understand our relationship and might want to take me away. But what about...

Nando was turning my face towards him.

'But there's something else,' I blurted out.

He moved his hand to my tummy... 'Ah yes. But you have to wait Yoli, because maybe, after a time, *we* will have this.'

'*Un niño?*' I asked quietly, in case I'd misunderstood.

'*Si, un niño.* Or even *niños.* But *mujer! Poco a poco, no?*' He untied my blouse and laid me back against the arm of the sofa. Our lips touched gently, then he kissed my neck and slowly moved down to where his hand still lay on my tummy. '*Ven,*' he said, standing me up and taking my arm.

I was uneasy on my feet. And uneasy about the lack of *poco a poco* with which he seemed to want this bizarre semi-relationship consummated.

'Just big *abrazo* on the bed, don't worry.'

'Yes, because we need to talk to—'

'No Yoli, *I* will tell him, alone. Don't worry about this – is the last evening for us, we are not alone again until Conil.'

'And how will that—?'

'Jeremy will give us some time, you will see.'

Somehow we'd reached the bedroom and he was taking off his shirt, soft black hair landing on his shoulders. Then he was pulling off his jeans and I looked away.

'I thought we were just having a big *abrazo*,' I said, folding my arms.

The lopsided smile. 'I said *like* a big abrazo.'

'No you didn't, you said—'

But he was in front of me, his lips silencing mine, his hands under my blouse and taking it off. Then he bent his head and muttered as he dealt with the hook and button of my skirt, his hair tickling my arm.

'Look I can't...'

He settled me on the bed and wrapped himself around me. I wanted to stay like that, but he lifted me up and undid the catch on my bra.

'D'you remember... before?' I asked, my heart tapping away.

'Very well. *Muy timida*. Little dot under arm.' He moved his hand down my body. 'Small—'

'Okay, that's—'

'Three times, fly easily, but not the last time... too sad.'

'I don't want to be sad again.'

He took my face in his hands. 'Listen to me Yoli, is different now, I was looking for something, *hurting* to find it... not ready to look after anyone.'

'Or any *two*.'

He grinned. '*Claro*, any *two*,' he agreed, and seemed to take this as my acceptance, kissing me more passionately, pushing hard against me. This intoxicating creature, back here again in my bed, as if visiting from another planet.

'I don't even know where you *live*.'

He shook his head and laughed, then lay back down next to me and opened my bedside table drawer. I heard him clicking a temperamental biro into obedience. I propped myself up onto my elbow, trying to recall what else he was going to find in there. Then saw him pick up the strip of pills and study it.

'You take these?'

'Mostly.' A few of the days hadn't been popped out; I considered telling him that I had the beginnings of period pains.

'Ah yes, I remember. Jeremy say he told you to take it or you become witch with the *hormonas*. But he had a plan. You see it? He think of this, the *clínicas* for us, everything.'

He flicked through an old Sadler's Wells brochure but there was no space; picked up a monkey birthday card, but confirming it was from Jeremy, deemed it sacrosanct; reached in further and found Javi's folded letter, holding it in his hand as if divining the content and then pushing it to the back of the drawer. Where he found another, much smaller piece of paper.

'No...'

He turned it over. Our eyes met.

'*Es mío.*'

'No, it's mine,' I said, putting my hand out for it.

He swept it out of my reach with a grin. 'No, you gave it to *me*.'

'Well... finders keepers.'

'*Qué?*'

'If you find something, you keep it. You'll just lose it again.'

'No, no.'

I put my hand in the drawer. 'What about...' I was holding the translated lyrics of Pilar's song.

'*Perfecto.*' He covered the back of it with his Seville, Madrid and Conil addresses, followed by some numbers, in his large loopy handwriting. '*Vale,*' he said, with a final flourish of the biro that conjured a portrait of him looking beaky and intense.

I chuckled.

Then he picked up the credit card slip again and lay back down next to me so that we could both look at it. The shaky labelling of the roads, the steaming mug showing the flat. And Pilar's 'Aquí vive tu esposa'. I took it from him and put it on the bedside table. Lay down facing him and found him looking at me intently. His eyes for once not commanding but searching for a response. Almost vulnerable. That word in the air between us.

I put my hand to his face and kissed him, pushing myself against his body. There was suddenly that urgency that I remembered from before, a brief struggle to overpower my awkward limbs... and then that primitive act, aggressive if not for the sweet Spanish whisperings in my ear, pleasure becoming almost painful, a final stinging ecstasy making me cry out, then his held breath, a shudder of his shoulders, my name. It was done.

33.

mujer *f* woman, wife

Just the once. Because sleep is important, he'd said, especially for new shows and new starts. A bit later there was *Yoli, I want to sleep here, but you have to be still, entiendes?* I understood. But I had to keep having a look at him miraculously lying there on my pillow. Then his eyes opened and met mine. *Yoli, duérmete ahora.* Sleep now. He rolled me over and stuck the lemurs under my arm.

Just the one night. Waking early and turning over to check he hadn't gone. The long black lashes, the pirate-worthy stubble, the little scar on his chin that I hadn't got round to asking him about. A peek under the sheet at his taut olive-skinned body. Then, heavy with reluctance, carefully sliding out of bed and getting ready for the school, knowing that when I came back he'd be Jeremy's boyfriend, not mine. For a while. But that was okay, because Jeremy was half-mine too.

The concert: Emma surprised to find me happily mentioning that Javi and I were working on something new. The afternoon's end of year Staff Party: knowing it was my last. Then quietly getting into my flat, intending to leave Jeremy and Nando alone until it was time to go to the theatre cafe, but finding they'd been watching out for me. *Nando tells me how well you've looked after him.* Sinking into Jeremy's arms, already weary with the burden of secrecy and guilt. Opening Nando's present: a crimson Kipling bag, with the usual zipped and poppered compartments and fluffy monkey keyring. *I know you have small one already, but this is good size for aeroplanes, I was thinking.*

And it was. I slotted my water bottle into the side pocket, my iPod back into the inner pouch. Twiddled the monkey in my fingers, looking out of the window at the parched landscape below. Thirty minutes to Jerez. We were descending, bouncing along on milky-soft clouds. I was excited, but also feeling yawny and weak rather than strong like I needed to be; Jeremy would now *know*, Nando was going to tell him while they were alone together. Okay, he hadn't yet done so when I'd spoken to him that morning, but he promised he would. Without saying how or when, and cross that I was suggesting that he was behaving anything less than honourably. I relented, because in every other respect as a boyfriend – albeit a shared, absent and secret one – he couldn't be faulted: reliable and responsive with texts and calls, not afraid to say he loved me, happy to talk about our future in Seville and even, on one occasion, how musical and *atractivo* our child would be. He wouldn't let me down.

Twenty minutes until landing. Another wave of buzzy nervousness. The plane had started to lurch and buffet against the innocuous blobs of haze; I wished it would stop. I *really* wished it would stop. I sipped from my water bottle. Reminded myself that I'd grown out of airsickness, it was all in my head. Then the Spanish businessman next to me opened a pungent ham sandwich.

I was in the *Señoras*, brushing my teeth, washing my face, *pinching* my face – but still looking like a ghost. How was I going to cope with my Seville-London-Jersey lifestyle? I'd have to start taking those dopey pills again. I brushed my hair and kept it loose, as he liked it – as they *both* liked it.

And there was Nando. *Only* Nando, as Jeremy had said it would be.

'Yoli, *pobrecita*! You not take your pills for aeroplane? Come here.' The *abrazo* I'd been longing for.

We walked out into the crushing heat of the car park, Nando apparently immune and swiftly pulling me and my case towards a dusty Jeep. We got in and started kissing again, our hands underneath each other's t-shirts.

'And how's Jeremy?' I asked into his neck.

'Fine, fine.'

I waited.

He started talking in Spanish, something about how much he'd missed me.

So he still hadn't said anything. A hot wave of worry and irritation. I let go of him and did up my seatbelt. He started up the engine. There was some swerving on and off dual carriageways, but he drove less hispanically than I'd imagined. I was told how we were having a barbecue when Toni and Pilar arrived that evening; not to worry, Maria the cook had made one of her perfect tortillas for me; I should have a siesta; I was in the little room, but would be the first person to use the newly built bathroom attached to it.

The roads became quieter and narrower, passing through gentle hills, fields of black bulls. He opened the sunroof. Played Jeremy's Chambao CD, his fingers tapping along to the rhythm on the steering wheel. Put a hand on my thigh, under my skirt. I put the hand in mine. He pulled it over and onto his thigh, then onto the hard crotch of his shorts. I pulled it away.

'*Vale. Qué pasa.*'

'You haven't told him, have you.'

'No. It has been not the time.'

'You've had *three* days.'

'Yes, but the time did not happen.'

'I'm sorry, that just doesn't make sense.'

'Tt... Is difficult to explain, in English, while I drive.'

'No it isn't. At some point, during *three* days alone together, you could have told him. You had *mucho tiempo*, you just thought you'd leave it, *mañana, mañana, mañ...*'

He veered off onto a track and scrunched to a halt with a cloud of dust. Fixed me with wild eyes.

'You don't talk to me like this, *entiendes?*'

I hadn't quite come down to earth in his country and started to giggle. 'Keep your hair on, I'm just—'

He slammed his hands down on the steering wheel. '*Entiendes?*'

I took what I hoped was a casual sip of my water and mumbled yes.

'*Qué?*'

'Yes.'

He looked away then turned to me again. 'I take care of this, for all of us, it has to be... I *feel* these things, I will know when is right. You are not stupid girl, you can do this.'

I fussed with the window, hoping the hot breeze would dry up the tears starting to sting my eyes.

His hand on my shoulder. 'You will see, it will be beautiful – you, Jeremy and me.' He let go, re-started the engine. But peered ahead and broke into a smile. 'Ah, we are *here*.'

'Here?' A tiny white derelict building the other side of a scrubby field, a rusted car, a small posse of mongrel dogs.

'Perfect place. But there will be... *sacudidas*.'

He carried on down the track, the jeep swaying and jolting along.

'Bumps?'

'Yes, bumps. Hold your tummy!'

'Where does it go, a beach?'

'*Claro*.'

'But won't Jeremy be—?'

'*No* Yoli, in-fact, he said to me you will ask for the sea.'

I reached behind me and pulled a costume out of my bag.

He glanced over. 'What *is* that?' It was a one piece with an attached skirt; Jeremy liked it, saying it reminded him of something his mum used to wear. 'Is too hot for this. You don't have bikini?'

'Yes...' I dragged out the top and shorts-like bottoms. But he looked over again and tutted, shaking his head.

'Pilar will take you shopping.'

It would be nice to spend some time with her, but I was *not* buying some skimpy...

The track was about to turn sharply to the left; we didn't look like we'd make it. But we went straight on into the pine forest, the wheels hissing on the soft sand and needles and stopping at a small dappled clearing. He reached behind him for some towels and was out of the car and round to my side before I could even get my seat belt off. Saying something in Spanish about us needing something.

'*Ven*, before somebody come.'

'Aren't we allowed here?' He took me into his arms and started kissing and pressing himself against me. Letting go to lay a large towel on the ground.

'What are you... oh.' A warm thrill spread down my body. But I didn't want to arrive at the villa, into Jeremy's arms, having just been ravaged by his lover. 'I don't think we—'

My t-shirt was coming off over my head.

'Just a quick swim...' I said, reaching inside the jeep for my bikini, but he'd whipped off his vest and had his warm chest on my back, his arms dragging me back and then down onto the towel.

'Yes, it has to be quick.'

'But...'

His hand had quickly gone up into my skirt and into my knickers. 'Can be *very* quick,' he added with a grin.

I started to take off my skirt with an embarrassed giggle, but he couldn't wait for that, just lay me back, kissed my tummy and thighs, muttering in Spanish... and then was on top of me, very quickly bringing my weeks of longing to an ecstatic release. Followed by his own shudder of pleasure and whispered feelings of relief, even though surely he'd had plenty of this in the last few days.

Then he did up his shorts and sprang to his feet, saying he could hear something, and passed me my bikini. In a daze I took off my skirt and put it on, just before there were Spanish voices and a young couple emerging from the other side of the clearing.

He led me through the bushes along a path and onto a long sandy beach, where a strong wind was bringing in big wobbling waves. The sort that Jeremy liked to surf while I paddled and whooped.

'I er...'

'More bumps. But is okay, stay with me.'

He carried me up and over a particularly monstrous sea mountain, but soon had us floating in the calm deeper water. He lifted my legs to hold me like a baby.

'Jeremy put you like this?'

'Of course.'

He pressed his lips on mine.

'And kiss you.'

'Not quite like that.'

'And sometimes he sleep in your bed.'

He looked into my face as the swell lifted us up and down. Surely he wasn't going to start having a problem with me and Jeremy. He pulled my legs round him as I hung on with my arms round his shoulders. 'Is pity for him he will never enjoy you like I can.'

He *enjoyed* me.

Nando laughed. 'Yoli! Don't be cross... *claro* enjoy, but also need and love as woman... He does not know these feelings. But will understand. *Ven*, we go to him now, no?'

We crunched down a narrow lane and arrived at some gates in a high stone wall. Nando got out and pressed in a code – nineteen ninety six, he told me, the year he and Toni were joint first in a competition and, rather than becoming rivals, became friends and later started their company. The gate slid back and revealed the bougainvillea-covered villa with its arches and grilled windows that he'd shown me on the computer, telling me how they'd bought it a few years ago to celebrate ten years of working together.

We went round the side to the walled garden, where Jeremy was coming towards us.

'Yoli! Okay?' He gave me a hug.

'She was sick on the plane, but I gave her some big waves and she is better now,' Nando said. Then he spotted something on the sun lounger. 'Khe-re-mi! You have been reading more...'

Jeremy let go of me to grab Nando before he reached the book; a laughing scuffle broke out. Entwining bronze and golden limbs. Apparently they were synchronising their reading of Zafón's new novel – Jeremy in English, Nando in Spanish, but occasionally swapping over – and Jeremy had gone on without him. They ended up in the pool.

I joined them, keen to lose my salt and sand. Then Nando got out to answer his phone, telling us to catch up with each other. So we lolled on an airbed, Jeremy telling me how relaxing it was there, perfect for me after my fraught few months. And perfect for him, forcing him to step back from the now finished novel, which, after a first re-draft on his return, would be ready for me to read.

'I can't wait. Come on, surely *now* you can tell me a bit about it.'

'Well it's called The Reader, so... it's about you, really.'

I knew this. But *hearing* it... He pulled me off the airbed. I was his reader and his best friend, in his arms. But still able to feel where his lover had been inside me only an hour or so earlier.

'Yol! Stop crying, you soppy thing.' He pushed me towards a giant alligator.

'Ooh!' I said, trying to distract myself.

'Apparently Toni has a thing about inflatables. Gives you two something to talk about this evening.'

Nando jumped back in. We played piggy-in-the-middle with a foam ball; Jeremy a cunning trickster of a piggy, Nando a swift, physical predator. Then I was in the middle, laughing at first but tiring; my splashy calumphing no match for their fluency and rapport. I went to the side and fussed about water in my eyes, saved a ladybird from the filter.

'Oh come on Yol, you're not *trying*,' Jeremy said, making the ball bounce on my head on its way to Nando.

'I *am*, but I mean, I could be here forever...'

A splash, then Nando at my side, an arm round my waist, holding the ball with the other hand out behind him but slowing down his reactions to let me win it.

'Ay... We need to give her something to eat, *pobrecita*...'

There were plates of bread, cheese, ham, and giant tomatoes. And then, apparently, it was time for *siesta*.

Nando took me through to my room: white and simple, with colourful pictures and beach-themed oddities like everywhere else in the villa. I was shown the new bathroom, as if it had been built for me. Then he brought me back next to the bed, put his arms round me and started kissing me. Even though he was about to sleep, and do whatever else was involved in a siesta, with Jeremy.

Who was suddenly there beside us.

We drew back, but Jeremy either hadn't seen or didn't seem to mind; he just pointed out the monkey-painted vase on the bedside table that they'd spotted driving past a garden centre, told me to rest and disappeared again.

'God's *sake!*' I whispered to Nando.

'Is okay. Sleep now, *no?*'

'I got some sleep on the plane. Think I'll walk down to the beach.'

'No, no. Too much sun on the first day.' He looked at me and put his hands to my face. 'Yoli, you must not feel...'

'No, I'm fine,' I said. I just didn't want to be in the house while it was going on, I'd get used to it but... not yet, and so soon after... 'I won't be long.'

'Put more cream, and take drinks from the kitchen, there is nothing on the beach, okay?'

It was an appealing little path, twisting through dark humps of greenery, teasing with glimpses of the sea before abruptly dropping down steep steps to a small sandy cove. A locals' beach: women and children looking up at the blonde *guiri* in surprise before returning my smile. The sea was much calmer here, I body-surfed in the waves for a while then came out and lay on my towel.

I couldn't help thinking how nice it would have been – after the satisfying but crude event among the pines – to be lying down for a sleepy cuddle with Nando. Perhaps it could happen later in the holiday, when Nando had talked to Jeremy; I just had to be patient.

I listened to the Spanish family's conversation, but couldn't understand it. Perhaps because the wind was blowing little bits of it away. As it blew some of the heat away. Blew the hair from my face. Like a hand. Like Mum's hand pushing my hair back, on Beauport beach...

'Yol. Answer your *phone*, girl. Bet you didn't even bring it.'

I opened hot eyes to a golden-haired arm rummaging around in my beach bag.

'Three missed calls. Look – you've turned the volume down, you idiot.'

'Oh, it just *does* that...'

Now he was tapping through the menu. Surely he wouldn't read my texts... But he was calling Nando, telling him he'd found me sleeping. We climbed back up the hill and met him standing by the gate. Wearing sunglasses, but his mouth in a line, knuckles on hips.

'*Qué haces*, Yoli, sleeping on beach.' He ran a hand over my hot back and pulled out an almost full bottle of water from my bag. '*Qué tonta, mujer! Y por qué...*' His voice was disappearing into the ringing in my ears; I needed to sit down. I was hoping Jeremy would tell him that I didn't usually behave like a mad-dog sun-starved English tourist, but he seemed to be just standing there in admiration.

I took the bottle and went off to my room. Collapsed onto the bed and stared at the monkey vase with its luscious pink flowers, the softly ticking alarm clock... but I needed to get up before I fell asleep and wasn't ready when Toni and Pilar arrived. The water, a long cool shower, a handful of Jelly Babies from my bag; I started to recover.

I took my Spanish book to a deckchair under a fig tree. There were voices in the kitchen; the woman had come round with some of the food. I should probably have gone in and helped, but I wasn't yet feeling up to my *mujer* duties.

Nando and Jeremy came out, apparently discussing the barbecue in between patting each other. Too bossy men apparently achieving a perfect equilibrium, like two little equal-sized planets peacefully orbiting around each other.

Nando spotted me. 'Ah. Better? You have drunk all your water?'

I nodded.

'Lift up...' He pointed a fork at my book. 'Good! And don't forget we want to hear Spanish with Pilar.'

'Yes, yes.' I went back to the dialogue illustrating uses of the subjunctive: lots of negative commands. Hm, didn't need any more examples of those right now. But he washed his hands and came over to me, took my pencil and sketched a man wagging his finger at a long-haired round-faced woman with dark shoulders.

Then I heard a loud, slightly lispy voice saying something about Nando being in *paraíso* with his two beautiful blondes and looked over to see Toni, wearing an orange Hawaiian shirt and enormous sunglasses. Followed by Pilar, complaining about the drive but looking radiant with her ponytailed hair tumbling onto a spotty t-shirt.

A t-shirt, that's what I should have worn instead of my new sundress, because after the introductions and cheek kisses my burnt back became the raucous topic of discussion. *Cava* was opened, there was talk of a hired boat that Toni patiently translated for me, and laughter when Nando promised we'd tow him behind in an inflatable. Then there was a sudden male urgency about food, and Pilar and I went off to the kitchen to prepare salad while they started the barbecue.

Alone with her, I managed Spanish discussions of vegetarianism, our music college experiences and how I coped with *proximidad* to the most *guapo* man on earth. Meaning Jeremy, of course, her own dark prettiness presumably giving her some immunity to the swarthy beauty of her husband and his best friend.

Then Nando came in and asked for something from the fridge. Pilar pulled out a large bag and opened it on the cutting board. Or rather allowed it to flop out and introduce itself into the air: a large pink half-cylinder of fish, *pez espada* – fish-sword. I stared with my usual masochistic fascination, but the smell was bothering me. Although not as much as the squelch when Nando sank a knife into it.

I needed to be in that lovely new bathroom, and fast; it was okay, they would think I was just going to the loo. But a few moments later there was Nando, watching me as I stared in to the toilet bowl taking big you-don't-have-to-do-this breaths.

'When you have your *regla?*'

'I haven't got my period.'

'Yes, I know this.' Of course he did. 'I'm saying, when was the *last?*'

'I'm on the pill, there's nothing to—'

'*When*, Yoli.'

'Er...' I wasn't entirely sure. 'Four, five weeks, I think. But that's normal recently.'

His gaze started darting around the room. 'Where is your *agenda*... diary.'

I pulled it out of the Kipling bag on the chair. A quick tilt of the chin told me to find the date. I flicked to and fro, Nando shifting from one leg to the other. Possible period pain in Javi-misery Brighton, but more definitely on Emma's rooftop couch. One of the Paco Peña concerts... But no, that was only a week later... Shit, I really had no idea. I hadn't written anything down; I hadn't expected it to matter. It *didn't* matter; I was on the pill and, according to Charlotte and Helen, probably perimenopausal anyway.

'Yoli.'

I looked at him. It looked more like six weeks, but there was no point in flustering him with that. 'It's fine, it looks like—'

He disappeared, apparently satisfied by my lack of concern. I could hear Toni calling his name and asking him something. Then Nando talking to Pilar. A car engine starting up, the squeak of the gate; it looked like Pilar had been sent to fetch something for the barbecue.

I sat on the bed, my head gently spinning. I swigged the last bit of water but it was warm and didn't help. Asked myself what *would* help. My brain clacked through the possibilities and came up with *tomato*. Giant Spanish tomato. It was risky, given its location near the squelch cylinder, but worth the gamble. I took off my sandals and padded into the kitchen, opened the fridge. Picked off a luscious red circle from the salad. And another. Mm. Carried the bowl back to my room and removed the lot. I heard Pilar come back, but was surprised to hear her sandals clapping towards my door.

She knocked and came in. A wide-eyed stare as I owned up to my salad theft, telling her I just *had* to, dehydration after the sunburn perhaps, I'd quickly make another. I repeated this in Spanish but she still didn't look amused; maybe she was irritated by the errand after her long drive. Then she quietly informed me, in slow Spanish, that Nando thought I was embarrassed but I mustn't worry.

Embarrassed? About being a vegetarian at a barbecue? Getting some stupid English sunburn? Yes, that was it, because she was holding out a bag from a *farmácia*. God he was making a big deal of this. And so was she, smiling awkwardly and looking me up and down.

Then, just as she got the packet out of the bag, it came to me. *Embarazada*: a false friend, as my Spanish book called it. Not embarrassed, but *pregnant*.

'Oh... it's okay, I don't need that.'

'He ask me help do it.' Bloody hell. She was opening the box, removing the foil wrapping from a plastic stick. 'You understand?'

'Yes, but...' Perhaps I just needed to get it over with so I could go and make another salad, which – oddly – I was suddenly looking forward to enjoying with that tortilla.

She sat down next to me, an arm round my shoulder. 'Is okay, he say *no te preocupes*.'

'I'm *not* worried, this is a complete waste of...'

She was reading the instructions even though it was all very obvious from the pictures. I stood up and she handed me the stick and the white clock to take to the bathroom.

I called out that I couldn't *orinar*. She fetched me a bottle of water and came in to the bathroom smiling, patting me on the shoulder like she'd done at Sadler's Wells when I first met her. She turned on the taps...

I looked at the second hand on the clock tick round. This was stupid. Bloody man, why can't he listen? I'm on the... *There it was.* Bold and blue. Almost immediately. What? No, no, too soon, it was supposed to take... *Much* too soon, in every way; our half-relationship just started and... bumpy. Jeremy. How was I...?

'Oh God.'

'*Qué pasa?*' She took the stick from my trembling hand. Hugged me and got me to finish and come through to the bedroom. Just as Nando came in. All I could manage was a nod. There was some rapid breathless Spanish with

Pilar, then he suddenly smiled broadly, gave me a tight squeeze, and disappeared again.

Pilar was saying something but I'd gone to the window; Nando had his arms round Jeremy, but I couldn't hear what he was saying. Then I saw Jeremy's face. Crying.

I had to go. Anywhere. Just for a while. I was out of the door, tapping in the code, walking along the now long-shadowed stony road giving up the day's heat to me. For some reason clutching the almost empty Kipling bag.

A baby. A child. A *miracle*. But not for Jeremy; I'd just look like a sperm-bandit as well as a cheat... I heaved with tears, had to stop walking. I'd run from facing Jeremy, but all I wanted to do was run *to* him, as I always did, as I couldn't cope with not being able to do. But we'd had an accident from which, this time, we might never fully recover. Then I found myself holding the crimson monkey. That smile... Nando wanted the baby. And he claimed he could *feel* how to make things right...

A car was coming up behind me. Pilar, no doubt, accepting yet another errand to do with the silly English woman. It stopped. A door opened. A red-eyed Jeremy, somehow managing to grin. Patting the seat next to him.

'I didn't mean to! I don't know how—'

'I know, I know. Nando says it's *un milagro*. Now get in, you stupid girl – it's all going to be perfect, don't worry.'

34.
embarazada *adj* pregnant

In front of us, a huge sparkling turquoise ball slipper against grey London Blitz rubble. Jeremy was reading out the Matthew Bourne interview in the programme: the inspiration of the classic wartime love stories, the darkness of Prokofiev's score, the dedication to his father. He pulled out his phone to switch it off – and grinned.

'"*How are my Cinderellas.*" Are we going to let him talk to us like that?'

'Probably.' I pulled the programme over and studied the pictures.

'And what are you doing gawping at that RAF pilot dancer now you've got your own Prince Charming?'

'I'm looking at *her*. Cinderella looks older than *me* – Matthew Bourne, I love you.'

A buzz: my phone this time.

'*JM dancing much today? And where is my 24 week foto? Te amo monita. xxxx*'

Jeremy watched me replying; he still hadn't quite got out of the habit of guiding our relationship along.

'JM? So he *does* have a name.'

'Yes, but I don't like using it, doesn't seem right.'

'Juan Manuel. No, it'll be José. Oh – and his father, so... José Miguel.'

'Yup. The two ugliest names in Spain, *together*. José's fair enough, but why Nando wants to honour a father who refused to come to his own son's wedding...'

'He's thinking long term – he's told you, they'll get over it. Probably the minute their grandson arrives.'

Maybe, but his parents were going to have to start communicating with more than gruff consonant-free mumble I could never understand. It had been almost a relief when I was admitted to hospital, even if some of the staff – like most of Nando's family – looked like they thought I was just too *guiri*, pale and vegetarian to be carrying a dark gypsy foetus.

'Hey come on, only two more weeks. Nando'll sort them out, don't worry.'

At the mention of his papa's name JM started squirming and kicking.

We laughed. 'Every time!' Jeremy put his hand on my round tummy. 'Or maybe he picks up on your raised heart rate when we mention his name...'

I shifted myself in the seat to ease my hip-ache. 'I'm not sure I've got the room or energy for a raised heart rate.'

'Well that's another thing Nando will have to sort out.' More kicking. 'You dance away, Josemi, we'll have some music for you in a—'

'Ho-se-mi?'

'That's what some José Miguels get called.'

'I like that. Josemi. Sweet. Sounds a bit like Jeremy.'

Then we linked arms as the Blitz bombs, sirens and music started, and were soon caught up in the plight of frumpy-cardiganed Cinderella, her love for an injured pilot, the dream and nightmare at the Cafe de Paris, their eventual reunion in a hospital and their romantic station departure. All directed by a Cary Grant-like – Jeremy-like – guardian angel.

'This is worrying – I'm getting as soppy as you these days,' Jeremy said, wiping a tear. 'Wonderful. But come on, up you get.'

'Emma's going to love it. Why didn't we book *three* evenings of it?'

'*As well as* the Royal Ballet's with Mitch and Judy on Thursday?'

'Tuesday. Thursday we're here with Emma.'

'I could have sworn...' He pulled out the tiny filo from his pocket, despite the crowd surging past us. 'But you're quite right. As usual. *God.*' He frowned.

'Jeremy, even people without holes in their head get dates mixed up.' We reached the entrance. 'Bloody hell, it's dark already. And uh – *freezing.* How did we put up with this?'

'No idea. But come on, we need to get back.'

'Why are we doing this, we hate parties.'

'Oh don't start up again. It's just a way of catching up with everyone. And you don't have to do anything, everyone knows you've been unwell.'

We turned onto our old road.

'Just look at all the miserable hunkered people and crappy Christmas decs.'

He chuckled. 'You've got to stop this. England's going to be part of Josemi's heritage too, you know.'

'True. We'll have to bring him over for regular doses of the better things it has to offer. The theatres. Cream teas in the country...'

'Fish and chips on Brighton pier.'

'Foyles, the gallery... We *are* going to do some of these, aren't we?'

'We'll see what we can fit in without wearing you out. But I've got all these meetings and things to do, Yol.'

'I know, and I want to help. But... couldn't we change our flights and stay a little bit longer?'

'Don't you think you should be home for a week and making some progress with the family before Nando gets back?'

Home? Home was a few *calles* away in Jeremy's spacious apartment with its sunny roof terrace, not far from the Maria Luisa Park; I went there whenever I could. Nando's house shared a patio garden with the rambling family home and was prone to bombardment by unintelligible questions and commands. Only his sketches, and a couple of flute lessons for his sister Carmelita – the last one drawing an unexpected brief *abrazo* from her mother – gave any feeling to it.

Jeremy was concerned that I'd be too busy chatting to eat enough at the party, so he'd asked Ginny to give me a pre-party high tea. She was waiting for us, radiant in her usual flowing purple and dangle of beads. 'How was it? Come in, it's almost ready. Make yourself comfy.'

The same sofa, but now with a multicoloured Indian throw daringly matching my old patterned rug on the floor. Pavlova looked up at us with disdain from a luxurious fuchsia bed on the armchair.

I stroked her head. 'Look at *you*! Remember me, Pav?'

Jeremy knelt down and put his face near hers, scrunched her neck. 'Have you forgiven me yet, gorgeous?'

Ginny laughed. 'Only since Paddy's been around. Think he reminds her of you.'

Jeremy and I exchanged a smile. We'd met him when we'd arrived the previous evening: one of Andrew's new authors, an apparently gifted but unassuming chap from Bolton, boyishly appealing, pushing forty but looking about fifteen – perhaps fortuitously for an author of teen fiction. On hearing his name he briefly emerged from the second bedroom to say hello – with that mid-scene blank stare that I easily recognised – and retreated.

Jeremy went to get things ready next door.

'Honestly, getting caterers in for *thirteen*,' I said.

'I think he wanted to make sure you wouldn't start trying to help. Here you go.' She put a tray on my lap and sat down with hers. 'How are you doing today?'

'Honestly, I'm fine now. Just fed up I'm going to look so scrawny and un-blooming for Nando. It's weird, I've tried for years to lose this much weight, and now I've seen how bloody awful it makes me look!'

'You look amazing, considering what you've been through. And anyway, you've still got a fortnight – including a week of all your favourite English food...'

'Mm, this is divine. So... Paddy likes your cooking?'

She grinned and lowered her voice. 'He's a very appreciative man. Such a sweetheart. And so talented, but I sometimes wonder how he's survived until now – he's in his own world. After we saw you last night he said to me, "Is that the girl who gave Jeremy a writer's block when she left him to search Spain for the ex-boyfriend who'd said he'd give her a baby?" He can't seem to believe it's fiction!'

'I know how he feels. Some of the dialogue... I have to remind *myself* it didn't happen.'

'It's an incredible work. And even though it's written from the author chap's point of view, the understanding of the female mind... This is from you, Yol.'

'And you! Who d'you think the sister's based on?'

'Well, I did wonder! Anyway, with *After Lorca*'s film rights being haggled over, there's a fair chance *The Reader* will attract interest too and we might get to watch ourselves on screen in a few years' time!'

'Oh God. But don't say anything like that to Jeremy, the publisher's excitement – all this stuff about next summer's bestseller – it's making him nervous. He's funny, obviously he wants it to be successful, but he can't stand all the *talk*. In fact I remember this from last time, he was desperate to finish but then goes into a sort of post book-partum blues and isn't really happy until he's started a new one.'

'And has he?'

'Well he says he's mulling something...'

'And what about your composing? I heard you and Javi were working together again.'

'Haven't been for a while, what with... well, neither of us being up to it.'

I told her about Javi's emailed inquisition about Nando. When did it start, he wanted to know, and had I always been in love with him and desperate for his baby – questions I found difficult to answer, and that he had no right to ask. But I'd said, *you know how much I loved you and wanted us to be together, if you just think about it.* And that's what he'd done, for so long that I started to wonder if he'd ever be in contact again.

'But yes, we're back on track. Everything by email of course, but it's great. I think it'll help keep me sane.'

Jeremy tapped on the door and opened it with his key.

'Sorry Ginny, it's going to take a while to get out of the habit.'

'Well don't bother, I'm sure Paddy and I can remember to keep ourselves decent in the living room when you're over.'

'Mitch and Judy are here, Yol.'

'Good God, Papa breaking the habit of a lifetime and turning up *early*?'

'That's exactly what *he* said!'

They wanted to know that all was well with me and the baby now, asked after Nando. They gave me a Christmas present – the cookery book I'd suggested – to give to Charlotte when she came over later in the week; we hoped that by the following Christmas they would be exchanging gifts in Jersey. Then I heard about the wedding preparations and Papa and I commiserated about the non-attendance of our in-laws. It seemed particularly unfair for him after – ever the chameleon – he'd converted to Judaism. 'A-ha. Are we going to have a preview of some of our wedding music?' Papa asked when he saw Helen and Kirsty arrive with flute cases.

'Looks like it.'

More strokes of my bump. But then I'd got used to that – accompanied by grinning but often untranslatable or bizarre advice – whenever I went out in Seville.

'David sends his love,' Helen said. 'Oh, and says another friend wants to use one of your pieces with his college pupils. And the chap's got a sister who works for Music Sales, so you never know...'

Kirsty nudged her. 'And don't forget Sophie's...'

'Oh yes.' Helen opened her bag and pulled out a ribboned Aero bar and a glitter-shedding card showing a woman with a massive tummy playing the flute to a donkey.

'That's gorgeous! I'm going to go and put it somewhere safe right now.'

I pushed myself up from the sofa and went to the bedroom. Helen followed me, saying she wanted to lose her bag and scarf.

Jeremy came in to take off his sweater. 'You see? You *are* enjoying it. But *drink* Yol, the whole bottle of that apple and elderflower Mitch brought you, by the end of the evening.'

'Okay.'

He kissed my cheek and left.

Even the small amount I had drunk had quickly gone through me; I tried to get past Helen but she caught my arm.

'He's such a beautiful man. And...' A little chuckle as she pointed to a wedding photo of the three of us that we'd put on the mantelpiece. 'You are one lucky lady. But go on, I've always wondered... Does a threesome actually work?'

'What?'

'What's it like, I mean, is it lady's first, a sandwich or...'

'No! I'm *married*, Jeremy and I are old friends—'

'That sleep together,' she said, wagging a finger at our two pillows.

'Yes, *sleep*, but not... And anyway it's none of your business. In fact why don't you take your business fucking right out of here?'

'Well I—'

'Hey what's the matter here?' Jeremy had come in to the room with a drink for me.

'She thinks the three of us—'

'Yolly, you really should learn to take a joke,' Helen said, leaving the room.

'She was *not* joking,' I said, dashing in to the toilet and slamming the door.

'Course she was, now calm down. Yol? Come out of there.'

'I'm peeing, for God's sake. It's alright, I'll get over it. But where's Emma?'

'I told you, she's going to be late, Lawrie – or was it the girl – got locked out of their flat or something. At least I think I...'

'No, you didn't tell me,' I said, coming out of the bathroom.

'But it doesn't matter, I'm here now,' Emma said, coming in and taking off her coat. 'Come here you,' she said, giving me a hug. 'You'll get over what?'

'Helen asking what it's like to have a threesome.'

She put a hand to her mouth and snorted.

'It's not funny.'

'Sorry. But she's probably had a few, and let's face it, it's a pretty unique set-up. Come on, let's go and sit down with a bit of that carrot cake.'

'No Jason?'

'Yes, he's here,' she said, tilting her head to where he was enthralling Andrew.

'So how are you now? You look so much better.'

'I am. But God, what would I have done without you and Jeremy?'

'You'd have had to make that scary sister-in-law of yours help a bit more. Any progress there?'

'Not much. But I hardly see her, she's always at the school or out performing.'

'Just make sure you have this flamenco baby after I break up for the Easter holidays, okay?'

Flamenco baby. It had been a while since I'd heard those two words together. But it was different now: this child wouldn't be born of the misery of rejection but with the love and support of the three of us.

'I mean it. He's your baby too.'

Jeremy got into bed beside me. 'It's okay Yol, I've told you – I'm fine with the change of plan.'

'No but really, you'll have a huge influence on his life, don't you see that?'

He smiled. 'That'll be good, sounds like I'm going to have all the best bits of parenting without the tedium.'

'Just a shame we can't all live together. D'you think it'll ever happen?'

'Not while he's dancing and his parents are alive, no. And actually, I'm not sure he'd be prepared to share you to that extent.'

'Me? Share *you*, you mean.'

'Well both of us maybe. And I think he's right, we need two places, just a bit nearer and freer flow between them.'

'Exactly. He and I need to get out of the Morales mansion. *Casa* Manderley. I feel like that drippy second wife in *Rebecca*.'

'Well that all ended well didn't it? Just remember you're there to build relationships, not set fire to the place.'

I looked over at him: I knew he didn't think I tried hard enough, that my complaints irritated him because he would so gladly take my place, but I didn't want to waste time arguing when I could snuggle down and put my head on his chest instead.

'Listen to Nando. He understands, he knows what he's doing.'

'That reminds me of how he kept telling me he'd be able to *feel* when it was the time to tell you about us. It made me so cross.'

'But he was right. Of course I wondered – but I also needed that time to be more sure of my relationship with him.'

'It's such a relief not to have secrets anymore.'

'I'll never understand why you didn't tell me about you and Nando in February.'

'I was too ashamed.'

'It certainly wasn't your finest hour, but I hate thinking of you suffering alone with it. But you know, if your banditry had been successful, it could well be that things would have worked out much the same anyway.'

'Really?'

'On the other hand, if I'd given you the consolation prize baby you wanted after David, then that would have changed the course dramatically.'

I lifted my head. Looked into those smiling dark blue eyes, ran my fingers through his soft waves of hair and felt the little scars of the wounds that had nearly taken him away from me forever. Of course, if he hadn't been gay, that would have changed the course even more.

He prodded my nose. 'Why do I always get the feeling that, somehow, it's always my fault?'

'Well... I'm not complaining. Hotch down and get comfy, Nando said about half eleven.' More kicks. 'Josemi – down boy!'

Then Jeremy's phone sang out its new ring tone: an *alegría*, *bulería* or on-the-fast-side *soleá*, who knows. But we smiled at each other and put our hands on it together.

*****

Acknowledgements

Many thanks to my editor, Linda Lloyd, and all at Indepenpress for their help and belief.

I'd like to give a huge gracias to maestro Paco Peña and his family for allowing me to include him in the story, and to my flamenco teachers in Sussex (Ana Dueñas León) and Granada (Escuela Carmen de las Cuevas) for their inspiration.

I'm also very grateful to Phil Radford, Helen Peacock, Tara Gladden and Maria Alicia Ferrera-Peña for bravely poring over early drafts, and to my family for generally putting up with it all. *Olé* us!

Men Dancing
Cherry Radford
£7.99
978-1-78003-202-3

A chance meeting with a performer you admire – an exciting story to tell your family and friends. But not if that excitement turns into the chronic ache of obsession...

Dr Rosie Buchanan – weary hospital scientist, frustrated musician, cheated wife and struggling mother – finds herself sitting next to charismatic Royal Ballet star Alejandro Cortés on a London train. Half an hour later, she starts to feel she's misheard her true calling – and is soon doing research of a very different kind.

Rosie arranges a bogus research visit at Alejandro's home, and is thrilled when he and his girlfriend ask her to teach them the piano. And she tries to overcome the pain of her failing marriage to Jez, and the obsession with Alejandro, by accepting comfort from consultant Ricardo Pereira. But so begins a complex dance of passion, betrayal, loss and redemption...

Sensual, witty, and at times deeply moving, Cherry Radford's first novel is a sweeping tour-de-force..

'A great read for Strictly fans'
Sir Bruce Forsyth CBE